Haunted Hardy

Also by Tim Armstrong

AMERICAN BODIES (*editor*)

BEYOND THE PLEASURE DOME: Writing and Addiction from the Romantics (*co-editor with Sue Vice and Matthew Campbell*)

MODERNISM, TECHNOLOGY AND THE BODY

THOMAS HARDY: Selected Poems (*editor*)

Haunted Hardy
Poetry, History, Memory

Tim Armstrong
Reader in Modern English and American Literature
Royal Holloway
University of London

palgrave

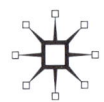

© Tim Armstrong 2000

All rights reserved. No reproduction, copy or transmission of this publication may be made without written permission.

No paragraph of this publication may be reproduced, copied or transmitted save with written permission or in accordance with the provisions of the Copyright, Designs and Patents Act 1988, or under the terms of any licence permitting limited copying issued by the Copyright Licensing Agency, 90 Tottenham Court Road, London W1P 0LP.

Any person who does any unauthorised act in relation to this publication may be liable to criminal prosecution and civil claims for damages.

The author has asserted his right to be identified as the author of this work in accordance with the Copyright, Designs and Patents Act 1988.

First published 2000 by
PALGRAVE
Houndmills, Basingstoke, Hampshire RG21 6XS and
175 Fifth Avenue, New York, N.Y. 10010
Companies and representatives throughout the world

PALGRAVE is the new global academic imprint of
St. Martin's Press LLC Scholarly and Reference Division and
Palgrave Publishers Ltd (formerly Macmillan Press Ltd).

ISBN 0–333–59791–5

This book is printed on paper suitable for recycling and made from fully managed and sustained forest sources.

A catalogue record for this book is available from the British Library.

Library of Congress Cataloging-in-Publication Data
Armstrong, Tim, 1956–
    Haunted Hardy : poetry, history, memory / Tim Armstrong.
        p. cm.
    Includes bibliographical references (p.) and index.
    ISBN 0–333–59791–5
    1. Hardy, Thomas, 1840–1928—Poetic works. 2. Literature and history–
–England—History—20th century. 3. Autobiographical memory in
literature. 4. History in literature. 5. Ghosts in literature. 6. Memory in
literature. 7. Death in literature. I. Title.
PR4757.P58 A76 2000
821'.8—dc21
                                                                  00–033323

10 9 8 7 6 5 4 3 2 1
09 08 07 06 05 04 03 02 01 00

Printed and bound in Great Britain by
Antony Rowe Ltd, Chippenham, Wiltshire

Contents

Acknowledgements vii
List of Abbreviations viii

Introduction 1

1 **Supplementarity** 8
   Poetry as afterlife 10
   Typology and syntax 16
   Latency 23

2 **The Ghosts of Thought** 30
   Haunted materialism 31
   Series and selfhood in 'The Pedigree' 38
   'Ghost theory' versus fetishism 43
   Language and psychical research 51
   Coda: 'The Photograph' 58

3 **The Child in Time** 62
   'Family Portraits': haunting pain 65
   Randy's hand, or the lost son 72
   'A deed back in time' 79

4 **The Politics of the Dead** 89
   'Hurt, misrepresented names' 90
   Mute witnesses 99
   The history of the same 104

5 **History, Catastrophe, Typology** 111
   'The Convergence of the Twain': history as coincidence 112
   Two solutions to the problem of agency 117
   The construction of history 121
   Zionism and typology 127

6	**Mourning and Intertextuality**	134
	Cinders	134
	Dantean purples	148
	Crossed voices: dialogues with the dead	156

Notes 173

Index 192

Acknowledgements

For various forms of help I would like to thank Matthew Campbell, Simon Curtis, Paula Krebs, Alan Lloyd-Smith, John Schad and Trevor Stevens, as well as the late F. B. Pinion. I am indebted to Dennis Taylor for generously answering my own queries at various points, and for providing a standard of scholarly excellence which all contemporary writers on Hardy's poetry must struggle to match. I would like to thank Margaret Bartley and Charmian Hearne at the publishers for their patience.

My thanks also to the British Academy, which funded a research visit to the collections of Hardy material at the Beineke Library, Yale University, and at Colby College, Maine, and also visits to the Dorset County Museum. I am grateful to the curators of each of those collections for their help and for permission to cite from annotated and marked copies of books originally in Hardy's library. This book incorporates parts of earlier drafts which appeared in *Victorian Poetry*, in *Criticism* and in the *Thomas Hardy Journal*. I would like to thank the editors of these journals for permission to reprint material.

Finally, and as always, I have to thank Sue Wiseman for being the first and most honest reader of all my work: this book is dedicated to her.

List of Abbreviations

Quotations from Hardy's poems are from *The Variorum Edition of the Complete Poems of Thomas Hardy*, ed. James Gibson (London: Macmillan, 1979) or from *The Dynasts*, ed. Harold Orel (London: Macmillan, 1978). Where relevant, corrected texts from the *Complete Poetical Works of Thomas Hardy*, 5 vols (Oxford: Clarendon Press, 1982–95) have been incorporated. Quotations from the novels are taken from the New Wessex Edition. I have used the original two-volume version of Hardy's disguised autobiography (*EL* and *LY* below) as the authentically haunted and collaborative text, referring to it as the *Life*; readers may also wish to consult the 'restored' text in *The Life and Work of Thomas Hardy*, ed. Michael Millgate (1985). The following abbreviations are used:

CL	*The Collected Letters of Thomas Hardy*, ed. Richard Little Purdy and Michael Millgate, 7 vols (Oxford: Clarendon Press,1978–88).
EL	*The Early Life of Thomas Hardy, 1840–1891*, by Florence Emily Hardy (London: Macmillan, 1928).
LN	*The Literary Notebooks of Thomas Hardy*, ed. Lennart A. Björk, 2 vols (London: Macmillan, 1985). Referred to by entry number rather than page.
LY	*The Later Years of Thomas Hardy, 1892–1928*, by Florence Emily Hardy (London: Macmillan, 1930).
PN	*The Personal Notebooks of Thomas Hardy*, ed. Richard H. Taylor (London: Macmillan, 1978).
PW	*Thomas Hardy's Personal Writings*, ed. Harold Orel (London: Macmillan, 1967).
Colby	Copies of Hardy's books held in the Thomas Hardy collection at Colby College, Waterville, Maine.
DCM	Copies of Hardy's books and other material held at the Dorset County Museum.
Yale	Copies of Hardy's books held in the Richard L. Purdy Collection, Beineke Library, Yale University.

Introduction

If Hardy were to come back as a ghost, it is interesting to speculate just *where* he would come back. To Max Gate, where he lived for over forty years and died? To Stinsford Churchyard, where he wished to be buried beside Emma Hardy and where his heart was buried; or Westminster Abbey, where, supposedly at the nation's insistence, the ashes of the rest of him lie? To Cornwall, the scene of his most passionate feelings, where he sought Emma's ghost? To his birthplace, now a museum? Might he, in a more gothic mode, haunt one of the actresses who have played his leading ladies, as he seemed to be haunted by Gertrude Bugler in the 1920s, declaring that she 'was' Tess? Or, more whimsically, he could walk abroad in Dorchester to attend the annual conference of the Thomas Hardy Society, where he might, like one of the posthumous characters in his poetry, shake his head at the words expended on his work; or upbraid the scholars who have exposed aspects of his life which his disguised autobiography was intended to bury. Perhaps he might even be seen across the Atlantic in the stacks of the Beineke Library, looking up some forgotten item in one of the books from his library collected by Richard L. Purdy and donated to Yale.

Each of these locations reflects an aspect of Hardy's makeup, allegiances and inheritance; they also reflect the fact that *he* haunts *us*, and in so doing passes on his own shadows. In exploring one of the most ghost-ridden of authors, this study attempts to describe Hardy's hauntedness as a biographical and historical phenomenon, bound up both with his individual self-conception and with nineteenth-century debates about the self and its relation to the material world, ideology, and such issues as religion, biological inheritance, language and literary influence. In the opening two chapters we see a poet who likes to see himself as posthumous and invisible; who struggles with philosophical and historical spectres, worrying, like many other Victorian thinkers, that in a mechanical universe the whole realm of thought might be phantasmal. We also see, in later chapters, a poet whose family stories are replete with haunting secrets (including the allegation that Hardy had a child with his cousin Tryphena); and who is constantly describing and (after the death of Emma Hardy) pursuing ghosts of different kinds in his poetry.

The focus of this study is, however, broader than that suggested by the idea of personal haunting, since it is also an investigation of the construction of history as a discourse (often a haunted discourse) in Hardy's poetry. At the core of the book, expounded in Chapters 3, 4 and 5, is a consideration of Hardy and history, less in terms of 'how does his work reflect historical trends and events' – the shifts in the rural economy in the late nineteenth century produced by mechanization and new working practices, for example – than in terms of the relationship between the self and the world into which it is thrown, and in terms of the way in which the self is constituted by and writes itself into history. Hardy teaches us above all about the entry into history, the trauma of *becoming-historical* which is central to nineteenth-century conceptions of the human. This trauma is particularly associated with two figures which are seen by Giorgio Agamben as representing the limits of human being: the infant or child, discussed in chapter 3; and the ghost. Chapter 4 links the historical and the spectral by considering the spirits of the dead as they are gathered up into and subordinated to official history at 'each year's brink' by the annalist, or as they confront in the figure of Time the terrors of the twentieth century.[1] Hardy also explores, as I go on to argue in Chapter 5, the becoming-historical of poetry itself: the way in which a poem which does not set out to be 'topical' might become so when it is published at a particular moment; the way in which an occasional poem tackling an event that seems starkly singular (like the *Titanic* disaster) is nevertheless forced to become a general meditation on historical representation and the role of the writer; to see the event as troubled by different explanatory paradigms, by a *déjà vu* which renders the instance an echo, and time dis-jointed.

What is a ghost? Hardy's work provides different answers to that question. One answer is that a ghost is the product of modernity and the modes of historicity which the modern gives birth to. Hardy copied into his notebook and underlined the famous passage from Matthew Arnold's essay on Heine in which Arnold writes that:

Modern times find themselves with an immense system of institutions[,] established facts, accredited dogmas, customs, rules which have come down to them from times not modern. In this system their life has to be carried forward; yet they have a sense that this system is not of their own creation, that it by no means corresponds exactly with the wants of their actual life, that, for them it is customary, not rational. The awakening of this sense is the awakening of the modern spirit. (*LN* 1017)

What Europe now experiences, Arnold adds, is a want of correspondence between inherited 'forms' and modern 'spirit'. That which haunts, here, is the systematic form of intellectual and social life rather than the modern 'spirit'. Ghosts, in this account, are not live presences from the past; they are just the opposite, and it is the hollow shell of the past which is a burdening inheritance, or at least the synchronic 'system' from which the modern spirit must extricate itself in order to live authentically, if it is not to live the life of a ghost (of 'The Conformers', in Hardy's poem of that title; or of a 'mere continuator', as he wrote in the early versions of 'The Pedigree'). As Anthony Giddens comments, writing on Comte and Marx as representative thinkers of their period, modernity means that 'the knowledge generated by the social sciences is to rescue humanity from a past in which the most decisive events which affected social development were beyond human mastery, projecting us into a future in which we control our own destiny'.[2]

Yet there is also a pathos attached to the forms of the past subjected to the harsh dissolvents of modernity. Hardy himself marked, in one of his two volumes of translations from Heine, the following passage from 'The Gods of Greece', a poem he echoes in a number of his own meditations on displaced ideals:[3]

> Gods of old time, I have never loved ye!
> For the Greeks did never chime with my spirit,
> And even the Romans I hate at heart;
> But holy compassion and shuddering pity
> Stream through my soul
> As I now gaze upon ye, yonder
> Gods long neglected,
> Death-like, night-wandering shadows,
> Weak and fading, scattered by the wind;
> And when I remember how weak and windy

The gods now are who o'er you triumphed, –
The new and sorrowful gods now ruling...

Here Heine, for all that he is Arnold's representative of modernity, suggests a different mode of haunting in which the past is not the inheritance that must be shrugged off, but rather that which must be attended to precisely because it is subject to supercession. It is a particular kind of historicity which is opened up here, painful and elegiac even as it is inevitable and progressive. 'When ghosts cease to haunt us, their history begins,' is a dictum from a volume called *The History of Ghosts* (1805) which Ernst Bloch cites in a 1935 essay; Bloch adds that 'the boundary between the earlier, "haunted" period and the later "historicizing" one may be found ... at the moment that the eighteenth turned into the nineteenth century'.[4] Modernity generates the history of ghosts, as Heine's poem intimates, but that which it also leaves in its wake is the ghosts of history – those of whom history, in the Hegelian senses of a dialectical development attached to a nation-state, leaves no account; whom it cannot accommodate. Derrida, in *Spectres of Marx*, refers to the process of 'the essential contamination of spirit (*Geist*) by spectre (*Gespenst*)', intimating that the Marxian wish to abandon the past, to forget, to no longer inherit, is itself contaminated – not least by Marx's desire that his own inheritance should not cease to haunt Europe, but also because the idea of a revolutionary content without existing forms falls into paradox: as soon as the revolution is identified and stabilized, it becomes its own parody, its own spectre.[5] Hardy inhabits the middle ground here, seeking truth in and guardianship over a more personal version of the past even as he wishes to free himself from a determining inheritance; projecting himself into the future as a ghost but also seeking to limit that process, to mask or guard his own posterity.

The personal dead considered in relation to literary tradition are the subject of the book's final chapter, which explores Hardy's elegiac mode and the textual ghosts through whom he traces Emma Hardy after her death in 1912. Its focus is more specific, concentrating on the Virgilian and Dantean contexts invoked by the epigraph to the 'Poems of 1912–13', but here too we face the question of the way in which a personal history is constructed and interpreted, and of the extent to which the dead can be allowed a voice. What does it mean to recover the past, to breathe life into its dying embers? How do the words of the dead endure and continue to carry energy? There are two obvious models for the persistence of words in Hardy. In one, the Victorian philological model explored by Dennis Taylor, words are deposited as sedimentary traces, as in the fossil record, and may be re-excavated entire and even re-used like coal, yielding a stored energy. The model here is explicitly textual and visual. But in the rather different scientific model explored by Gillian Beer and others, words are conceived as sound waves, radiating outward from a point of origin in weaker and weaker traces, but also at times resonating within particular objects or spaces (as in the figure of Echo).[6] The voice of the dead as a literary echo contains both these possibilities: a layering of texts and their rekindling; or an attention to faint cries and echoes. Taylor suggests that 'Hardy is generally not an allusive poet in the style of that echoing tradition explored by John Hollander'; but allusion does nevertheless matter at certain crucial points, as does the idea of an interchange of words with others, for example via the rhetorical figure of crossing, *chiasmus*.[7]

Any examination of history inevitably also raises the question of politics and the political, albeit in an extrapolated sense. Hardy was notoriously cagey about political commitment, claiming that writers should steer clear of the subject. But it is obvious that he had strong feelings on issues which are in a broad sense political: on the treatment of the poor and of children; on war and those seen as dispensable in war; on the value of inherited modes of thinking; even on the treatment of animals. He meditated on current affairs with particular intensity in the middle 1880s – a period of economic and political crisis, which many saw as characterized by a fossilization of the party system, by corruption and the threat of populism in the wake of the Third Reform Bill (1884). It is a period which has come to represent for later historians the end of the high Victorian consensus, involving debates on gender and sexuality, on Empire (including Irish Home Rule), on democratic culture (in such areas as education and local government as well as in relation to the franchise), and on the nature of the state. The *Life* has a series of diary entries from the 1880s recording political soirées, meetings with political figures, the excitement of news of events like General Gordon's death at Khartoum. In May 1886 there is a long entry, unique in the *Life*, describing Hardy's observation of parliamentary debates on Home Rule; it follows an entry a month earlier marking 'a critical time, politically' (*EL* 232–3). The entries are interspersed with meditations on history which Hardy himself links to recent events. Hardy's contemporary reading reflects this political involvement: he copied out long passages from a piece on Socialism, from Auberon Herbert's *A Politician in Trouble about his Soul*, serialized in the *Fortnightly Review* in 1883–4, and from other sources on the philosophy of history. Since it was in this period that Hardy solidified his plans for *The Dynasts*, it is unsurprising that the political salons and intense factionalism in the epic have the flavour of the 1880s. Hardy's most radical essay 'The Dorsetshire Labourer', with its meditation on the forms of social life as they interact with modernity, also dates from early in this period.[8]

To note such a formative period in Hardy's mature life, or later flickers of public activity which might be labelled 'political', like his war poetry with its acerbic line on imperial ambition, or his support for Zionism (explored in Chapter 5), is not to say that Hardy's political stance can be clearly identified, or that particular poems can be 'historicized' in any definitive way. One weakness of recent literary historicisms has sometimes been a tendency to see the literary work as *prematurely* political, that is as politicized by any textual context which can be readily placed alongside it rather than by the pressure of an intention to intervene or avoid intervention in a discursive field, which must be more carefully gauged. Hardy's work is valuable precisely because it registers the difficult, often traumatic, relation between the individual voice and the collective discourses of history; because it refuses to simply lay one voice or image from the past down beside another in the manner of the séance. And if recent ideological critique has too often depicted the writer as bound into ideology in ways which offer, at best, symbolic forms of resistance (and more often suggesting a secret complicity with 'power'), then Hardy shows a writer for whom issues of social construction are keenly debated in his poems. The questions which typify recent historical studies – how literary discourses relate to those of state power, colonialism, or economics, for example – are less applicable to Hardy's poetry than questions about agency, the self, the event; about memory, pain and the dead.

A final general comment on the aims of this study. It seeks to offer a reading of Hardy which supplements the work of critics like Peter Widdowson and George Wooton, who depict a writer who cannot readily be described as the embodiment of a 'timeless' English rural tradition. Instead, as suggested above, I portray Hardy as a poet struggling with the pressures of modernity and history. A second aim is to provide an account of Hardy's poetry which acknowledges the depth of his philosophical sophistication, and the way in which his poems often read as if they had already theorized themselves; as if they were as close to the poetic world of Mallarmé and even Celan or Prynne as to that of Crabbe and Clare, despite a tendency for critics to place him within an English tradition running from the ballads to the Movement poets of the 1950s. Accordingly, I often provide a reading of Hardy, and of Hardy's ghostliness, inflected by the work of modern theorists of the spectral, of mourning and of related topics: Derrida, Abraham and Torok, Benjamin and others. My aim is to see Hardy in this way as a more central poet – to move beyond his always too-liminal status as the last Victorian or proto-modern or novelist turned poet or eccentric autodidact or regional writer (all of these views have some truth, of course), and to see him as a poet whose legacy is various precisely because he haunts so many important contexts. Haunting, Derrida suggests, is never unitary, it multiplies into heterogeneous legacies which can never be united; into a slippery coinage (speculation) which demands exchange, rather than remaining, like Timon's gold, buried in the earth. Hardy's legacy has always been contested, but if it were not so, he would have ceased to matter to us at all.

1
Supplementarity

> *I wish to conjure up the figure of a ghostly writer who imagines himself posthumous so as to mediate between his past and future and to judge the present.*
> Jean-Michel Rabaté, *The Ghosts of Modernity*[1]

Hardy's career as a novelist effectively ended in 1895, when he was fifty-five, with the publication of *Jude the Obscure* and the supervision of the uniform edition of his works (the volume publication of *The Well-Beloved* was to wait until 1897). Though his financial security had been guaranteed, this was a period of crisis for him, in his personal life and in his work. He suffered from the criticism that the last two books had brought upon him, and offered this as his reason for abandoning prose. At the same time, he suggested deeper motives in that crisis-poem of December 1896, 'Wessex Heights', with its hints of a withdrawal from the 'great grey Plain' to the solitary heights.[2] Critics have offered a plethora of explanations for the end of his prose-writing: the physical burden of research and writing; the increasingly self-revelatory and obsessional nature of his novels; the pressure of acting as a spokesman for radical views and the cost of those views within his marriage; Edward Said's speculation that with *Jude the Obscure* the familial structures and linear plotting on which the classical novel is based had irretrievably broken down; even a move towards a kind of marginalized modernism.[3]

Whatever the reason – or reasons; they are not mutually exclusive – that he ceased to write prose, Hardy described himself as pessimistic and withdrawn in this period. In his disguised autobiography he wrote: 'His personal ambition in a worldly sense, which had always been weak, dwindled to nothing, and for some years after 1895 or 1896 he requested that no record of his life should be made. His verses he kept on writing from pleasure in them' (*LY* 84). While the claim that his ambitions had died and that he wished no memorial to be made is ingenuous in the context of the *Life*, the purpose of which is to memorialize himself in the voice of another, this claim does reflect his mood in the period as conveyed in his letters and poetry. This passage points, however, to an important problem with Hardy's career as a poet, suggesting as it does that poetry is personal, different from the 'worldly' ambitions of the novelist.

In his autobiography, Hardy portrays his early poetry, written in the 1860s, as part of his 'aloofness', a reaction to the hurly-burly of London literary life (*EL* 62–5). His later withdrawal from the lowlands of prose to the heights of poetry can thus be depicted as a return to an original impulse, something he undertook without ambition and purely 'from pleasure' in verse. Clearly, this is a distortion of the reality of Hardy's career; as Paul Zietlow says, 'a myth of retrospective self-justification'.[4] Hardy had invested a good deal of his emotional self in his novels, and in this they share characteristics with his poetry. Conversely, though he had always written some poetry, particularly in the period 1865–7 but also throughout his career as a novelist, he had had little success in having it published. Instead he had, as Michael Millgate shows, taken up prose-writing as the best way into a literary career.[5] In publishing poetry he was attempting, on the back of an established position as a novelist, to succeed in a second field, a more prestigious one for an author with a firm sense of the classical hierarchy. In so doing, he would be subject to the same pressures as he had been as a novelist – something apparent in his hurt at the mixed reviews of his first volume of poetry.[6] In 1918 he was still complaining to Gosse that his poetry remained a 'bye-product' [*sic*] in the eyes of many critics, for all that he calculated that his career as a poet was now marginally the longer one (*CL* 5: 253). But despite such moments, the protective myth that poetry was a more 'private' undertaking remained important to Hardy, and the interplay between these two opposed ideas largely determined his self-presentation (and often influenced the subject-matter of his poetry) for the rest of his life: on the one hand the return to an original 'aloofness' in the wake of the dying of ambition; and on the other hand the search for prestige in a second career in print. The body of his poetry comprises a corpus different from that of the novelist, who can be said to have died: a more subjective and fragmentary art in which he avoids problems of biographical reference, since poetry is supposed to be a lyric essence, all its emotions cleansed of clear reference.

It is because of this uncertainty over the *status* of Hardy's poems, I would argue, that they can be seen as a ghostly supplement to his life as a novelist, freed from its problems of self-presentation. The supplement is Jacques Derrida's figure for that which, in language, is at once a *surplus*, beyond equivalence and self-presence, and that which *replaces* the 'real' ('the sign is always the supplement of the thing itself').[7] The supplement is both an 'exterior addition' and indicative of a lack of a real presence. The sense in which the supplement is constructed by a lack is suggested by a very late entry in Hardy's notebook, dated July 1926:

> It appears that The Theory exhibited in 'The Well-Beloved' in 1892 – has been since developed by Proust still further: – 'Peu de personnes comprennent le caractère purement subjective du phénomène qu'est l'amour, et la sorte de création que c'est d'une personne supplémentaire, distincte de celle qui porte le même nom dans le monde, et dont la plupart des éléments sont tirés de nous-même.' (*PN* 92)

This 'supplementary person' created by the lover is a product of a replacement: the 'real' love-object is effaced in favour of that which is 'extracted' from the self (Hardy's own word for this process is, as we will see, 'sublimation'). We should also remember that in *Grammatology* Derrida began his original discussion of the supplement with an analysis of the figure of masturbation and sexual self-investment generally in Rousseau: 'The supplement has not only the power of *procuring* an absent presence through its image; procuring it for us through the proxy [*procuration*] of the sign, it holds it at a distance and masters it.' This sense of self-protection and mastery is important in Hardy, as we will see, since it applies to the self as well as to the objects of one's desire. To imagine oneself as supplementary is to extract oneself from the self; to watch oneself as a puppet or 'fantocine' as Hardy does in 'He Wonders about Himself'; to say, as he does in 'He Revisits His First School', that 'I should not have shown in the flesh, / I ought to have gone as a ghost'; or even 'I rose and went as a ghost goes', in 'Apostrophe to an Old Psalm Tune'. Compare Rousseau as cited by Derrida: 'I can certainly say that I never began to live, until I looked upon myself as a dead man.'[8] Or as Hardy wrote, 'I travel as a phantom now....'

Poetry as afterlife

The idea of being 'already dead' is an important part of Hardy's self-conception, particularly after the death of Emma Hardy in 1912: the poet is a leftover, a remnant, and his poetry exists in a peculiarly skewed relationship to his life.[9] In a more defensive sense, being a ghost entered Hardy's work at an early stage as part of the 'sure game' of pessimism (*LY* 91). In a well-known diary entry of 1888, it is linked to his 'detachment':

> For my part, if there is any way of getting a melancholy satisfaction out of life it lies in dying, so to speak, before one is out of the flesh, by which I mean putting on the manners of ghosts, wandering in their haunts, and taking their views of surrounding things. To think of life as passing away is a sadness; to think of it as past is at least tolerable. (*EL* 275)

Couched in this way, being 'already dead' relates not to death itself, but to the way in which Hardy responds to life. It both protects him from the sadness of life and provides a metaphor for the eye of the novelist/poet: he is disembodied, detached, able to register his 'seemings' with uncanny objectivity. Another well-known passage from the *Life* expands on this:

> This unassertive air, unconsciously worn, served him as an invisible coat almost to uncanniness. At houses and clubs where he encountered other writers and critics and world-practised readers of character, whose bearing towards him was often as towards one who did not reach their altitudes, he was seeing through them as though they were glass. (*LY* 179)

Like Hamlet's father, the ghost itself is disguised by the 'invisible coat', disguising the spirit or spectre beneath, rendering its power questionable.[10] How dangerous is this spectre? Hardy goes on to say that he composed satirical notes on those he observed, 'but destroyed all of them, not wishing to leave behind him anything which could be deemed a gratuitous belittling of others'. His 'unassertive air' is thus both an enabling and a bridling of his powers.

Hardy, relatively early in his career as a poet, also linked being dead – or dying – to the experience of grief, and to the self-displacement involved in grief. In the troubled period of 1895–6 he wrote 'In Tenebris I':

> Wintertime nighs;
> But my bereavement-pain
> It cannot bring again:
> Twice no one dies.

But there was, of course, more bereavement to come. Emma Hardy's death had a literary importance for Hardy which transcended any immediate feelings or even the elegiac impulse in the 'Poems of 1912–13', causing him to re-write the plot of his life. It was, as a number of critics have suggested, as if he had woken from a long dream and at last seen the meaning of the way things 'shape' (one of his favourite words, one which can refer both to life and art). It was also as if a part of himself had died. As he wrote in 'The Going', 'I seem but a dead man held on end.' He returned often to the idea of being a ghost-like remnant or already dead in the poems that followed.[11] The two poems that end the main grouping of *Satires of Circumstance* (1914) are good examples. The first, 'Exeunt Omnes', is dated 2 June 1913; it is Hardy's seventy-third birthday, but the party is over and the author seems ready to join the ghosts of his own poem 'After the Fair': 'Everybody else, then, going, / And I still left where the fair was?' The final poem, 'A Poet', is in a sense the epitaph of Hardy's human self. It bypasses the public figure ('Attentive eyes, fantastic heed, / Assessing minds, he does not need') in order to focus on the man who lived, loved, and died:

> Come to his graveside, pause and say:
>
> 'Whatever his message – glad or grim –
> Two bright-souled women clave to him;'
> Stand and say that while day decays;
> It will be word enough of praise.

The eloquence of this elegy for himself necessarily undermines the distinction it attempts to enforce (we might, of course, praise Hardy the poet more readily than the man). But as in a number of other endpieces, Hardy suggests that the man is waiting for the poet to die. The emphasis on his ghostliness shifts from defence (since life has delivered its blows) to supplementarity: the portrayal of the poet as a survivor, the whitened bones of spent passion his own sustenance; a ghost among ghosts. Abandoning an original self, writing under the sign of the supplement, one enters the realm of repetition and displacement.

As a ghost, Hardy became his own documentor, drawing on the passions of a lifetime and writing what are, in effect, a series of supplements to that life. Each volume after 1912 retraverses old terrain and finds both the memory of past feeling and the peculiar absence suggested by the poems in which he fails to find Emma's ghost. In addition, each volume completes his career and finds an image for his death so that the volumes are also supplementary to each other. This helps explain

Hardy's increasing tendency not to bother to fill in the details of what he documents in his own life. He confronts his reappearance in a number of poems, typically needing to explain not his death but his continued existence. In the first poem of his final volume, 'The New Dawn's Business', he explains his survival as the result of being willing to die, where other men resist. If the face of the dawn is 'deedily gray', then so too is Hardy's poetry characterized by 'neutral tones', as he calls them. The association of the dawn with this attitude is worth remarking, reversing as it does the traditional Romantic association of the dawn with new hope. The dawn is, from Hardy's early writings, the symbol of a peculiar brand of vigilance. In a typically prophetic diary entry of 1871 he had associated a dawn consciousness with having already failed:

> Dawn. Lying just after waking The sad possibilities of the future are more vivid then than at any other time...the laughing child may have now a foretaste of his manhood's glooms; the man, of the neglect and contumely which may wait upon his old age...the man who abides by what he thought at dawn is he who is found afterwards in the safe groove of respectable mediocrity. (PN 7)

The 'safe groove of respectable mediocrity' is the pattern of life into which the late Hardy, like Jocelyn Pierston in *The Well-Beloved*, falls, allowing him to survive and guard his energies. In another late poem, 'I Looked Up from My Writing', Hardy is condemned to a deathlessness both crippling and compelling as the moon searches out its victims and overlooks him; and this is only one of a number of poems in which Hardy depicts himself as reading or writing in his study at night or early morning, often disturbed by the light of moon or dawn. Writing is an activity that is linked to death.

If Hardy had anticipated the use of the dawn in his late poetry, he had also done so for the metaphor of 'Life's Winter' – including a variant of the title of *Winter Words* in a list of possible titles he wrote in 1875.[12] Winter is the season of stillness and death, of the frozen survival of that which dies in the autumn. Often for Hardy it is not so much a season as the time after seasons have ceased to have any impression. A number of poems that touch upon the seasons illustrate the democracy of death and the sense of being in a final period. In 'June Leaves and Autumn' Hardy remarks that the leaves which survive summer will soon join the ones that fell early, 'no less embrowned and curst / Than if they had fallen with the first, / Nor known a morning more'. In 'The Later Autumn',

>   Spinning leaves join the remains shrunk and brown
>   Of last year's display
>   That lie wasting away,
>   On whose corpses they earlier as scorners gazed down...

In 'The Master and the Leaves' the leaves cry to an indifferent master as they take their successive colours. He 'mark[s]' their 'early going' but remains curiously indifferent. The secret of the poem is, of course, that the speaker has died, and once again an analogy with Hardy is implicit. Thus, for the man with the 'watching eye', the self-acknowledged 'pessimist' in the Sophoclean sense, all seasons are flattened into an anticipation of winter. Even if his character is turned inside out, so to speak, into the alter ego of 'A Self-Glamourer' (in the poem of that title), the result is the same, since human expectations if accurately tailored to life's promises will produce a life which contains its own pattern within, rather than outside of, the perturbations of Fate:

>   My years in trusting spent
>   Make to shape towardly,
>   And fate and accident
>   Behave not perversely or forwardly.
>   Shall, then, Life's winter snow
>   To me be so?

'A Self-Glamourer' recalls 'In Tenebris I' and other poems on winter. In many, as for example 'Before and after Summer', Hardy links the topic to the figure of 'blankness' which we can, perhaps, see as having its origins in the 'neutral tones' of his early poem of that title. In 'Before and after Summer' Hardy produces a parody of the traditional association of birds with the seasonal cycle. This bird represents the absence of any seasonal fulfilment:

>   Mutely perched he bills no word;
>   Blank as I am even is he.
>   For those happy suns are past,
>   Fore-discerned in winter last.
>   When went by their pleasure, then?
>   I, alas, perceived not when.

The bird is a ghostly presence – 'shadowed' on Hardy's wall, 'blank' – and is part of a complex pattern of disappointments. The same word 'blank', with its Miltonic, Wordsworthian, and Coleridgian associations, is used in 'Exeunt Omnes', the penultimate poem of the main run of poems in *Satires of Circumstance*:

> There is an air of blankness
> In the street and the littered spaces;
> Thoroughfare, steeple, bridge and highway
> Wizen themselves to lankness;
> Kennels dribble dankness.

The 'blank' represents an erasure in which nothing more catastrophic can happen, as in Hardy's poem on the death of a cat: 'Better blankness day by day / Than companion torn away' ('Last Words to a Dumb Friend'). Often, as in 'The Voice of Things', it represents a mood of desolation. Elsewhere, it is a clear space for the mind's etching, as in 'blank lack of any charm / Of landscape did no harm' ('After a Romantic Day'), a *tabula rasa* on which the mind inscribes its fantasies. The reduction of life to a total bleakness thus effected is often itself an anticipation of death, allowing the 'Signs and Tokens' (another poem title) of mortality to be avoided. In that poem, the death of a husband allows his widow to cry:

> For what, what can touch
> One whom, riven of all
> That makes life gay,
> No hints can appal
> Of more takings away!

– and this she says in the face of ominous threats of further doom.

But for Hardy the problem of hope and disappointment was not so easily solved: there were 'throbbings of noontide', as he put it, throughout his later life. Minimalism acts as a cover from which the poet can make raids on the imaginative territory of Romanticism; or, to shift the metaphor, his 'death' provides a basis for moments of revivification supplementing the story of experience. In poems like 'For Life I Had Never Cared Greatly' he insists that life demanded poetry from him, even after he had lowered his expectations to a minimum:

> With symphonies soft and sweet colour
> It courted me then

Till evasions seemed wrong.
Till evasions gave in to its song...

In a free imitation of the chorus from *Oedipus at Colonus*, Hardy in another poem had characterized old age as clouded, a place 'Where sunshine bird and bloom frequent no more, / And cowls of cloud wrap the stars' radiancy' ('Thoughts from Sophocles'). Here, Life calls him to song, and his eventual vision of 'a star, / Uncloaked...burning from pole to horizon' is protected from failure by the fact that the poet has already determinedly willed his own failure, only to be 're-illumed' later. A similar supposition is the basis of the important late poem 'He Never Expected Much', where 'hints' of greater things (Hardy's equivalent of Wordsworth's 'gleams') become the 'neutral-tinted haps and such' which the world had always promised to the child. As in an earlier poem, the 'mysterious voice' of the world inspires the poet. Voice, as we will see throughout this study, usually indicates moments of unusual imaginative influx for Hardy, and almost always, the revivification of a world, a memory, or even a grave which has previously rested inert and dead. The world must be lost before it can be obliquely re-examined.

One macabre metaphor for the relationship with his own life which Hardy establishes within such an aesthetic of 'revivification' is that of parasitism. Hardy often referred to thought as 'parasitic' on biological existence; and he copied a remarkable passage on parasitism from J. G. Wood's *Insects at Home* (1872) into his notebook – particularly interesting if one recalls his 1888 diary note on the writer's interest in the progress of his or her career: 'A naturalist's interest in the hatching of a queer egg or germ is the utmost introspective consideration you should allow yourself' (*EL* 267). Wood writes of the ichneumon fly, which lays its eggs inside the body of a live caterpillar: 'Just in proportion as the fat [of the caterpillar] decreases, the Ichneumon larvae increase, so that to the eye the caterpillar looks quite plump and healthy, when it is in reality absolutely emaciated'.[13] The paradox of the dependence of memory on a vanished life, the death of one 'self' and the life of another, is suggested, as well as the nourishment on hidden sources which characterized Hardy's existence after he retired behind the Max Gate hedges. The career of the writer is founded on death.

Typology and syntax

If Hardy's late life is a supplement, a survival beyond catastrophe, then his understanding of his life is also in a sense 'supplementary'; it comes at a point after the text of his life has been written and is a commentary on that text. In Hardy's case this awareness is informed by a parallel with the biblical pattern of text and its fulfilment, though modified by his loss of faith and consequent despairing distance from the full presence of God in the Bible. A number of poems deal with what could be called the typology of self-understanding. Typically, memory discovers in the past a pattern of repetitions that only become meaningful when it is too late. The pattern is constituted by memory, the moment of belated understanding inevitably linked to a history of misunderstanding.[14] A perfect example of this is 'Quid Hic Agis?', published in 1916, a poem in which Hardy meditates on his repeated hearing of his favourite lesson from I Kings 19 – the most heavily annotated passage in all his Bibles.[15] The passage deals with what I have called supplementarity. Elijah mopes in the wilderness, and the Lord passes by, though curiously, the Lord is not where one might have thought Him to be: 'and a great and strong wind rent the mountains...but the Lord was not in the wind;...And after the earthquake a fire; but the Lord was not in the fire: and after the fire a still small voice.' The 'still small voice' was one which Hardy seems to have associated throughout his life with the aftermath of passionate events; we can link it to the epigraph of the 'Poems of 1912–13' or to the voice from the fire in 'Surview'.

In 'Quid Hic Agis?' the narrator's life is divided into three phases. In his youth he is too busy wooing to see

> That this tale of a seer
> Which came once a year
> Might, when sands were heaping,
> Be like a sweat creeping,
> Or in any degree
> Bear on her or on me!

In his maturity, he reads the lesson aloud from the lectern but still does not understand. In a final period his understanding and identification with the prophet in his despair is complete. He neither listens nor reads but feels 'the shake / Of wind and earthquake, / And consuming fire'. Understanding has been achieved through a tremendous loss – that of his wife – leaving him 'spiritless / In the wilderness' (a wilderness partly linked, the endnote 'During the War' suggests, to the historical moment). Like Elijah, the old poet desiring death is condemned to live on, himself 'a still small voice' like that which asks the question that is the title of the poem. His understanding is a part of that process which the biblical passage describes: the emergence of voice from the fire. The message has always been with him, its unfolding becoming the dynamic of his life in a way that parallels the biblical pattern of typological anticipation and fulfilment – though in Hardy's case the 'fulfilment' is an awareness of failure.[16]

Retroactive meaning is used similarly as a measure for, and re-enactment of, the poet's loss in a later poem, 'The Prophetess'. It describes an episode in which the narrator's mistress sings him a song called 'The Mocking-Bird': a song that, though he did not realize it, prophesied the course of their lives together. Nothing in the original circumstances told him that 'the words bore / A meaning more / Than that they were a ditty of the time'. Only in 'time', however, is their significance apparent:

> But after years
> Of hopes and fears,
> And all they bring, and all they take away,
> I found I had heard
> The Mocking-bird
> In person singing there to me that day.

What was previously just a song has become a 'type', fulfilled in the life of the narrator. He finds that he has unwittingly been acting out a prearranged drama – a fact once again only discoverable as a supplementary awareness that is imposed on the 'story'. The 'late' work for Hardy thus involves the writer in a retrospective vision in which the meaning of a pattern can surface, but only when it is too late. He achieves understanding only at the cost of the death of an earlier innocent self, or of the beloved.

The poems that Hardy wrote after 1912 dwell on the idea of an 'ending' in this peculiar sense. 'Self-Unconscious' (to borrow one of the titles), he suddenly awakes to conclusions like 'My right mind woke, and I stood dumb: / Forty years' frost and flower / Had fleeted' ('The Man Who Forgot'); or 'In the Small Hours':

> It seemed a thing for weeping
> To find, at slumber's wane
> And morning's sly increeping,
> That Now, not Then, held reign.

Dennis Taylor attempts to locate such poems in the period from 1913 to about 1922, but the presence of such poems in Hardy's last volume, as well as a sense that such 'plotting' is present throughout Hardy's career, contradict such precision. One indicator of this repetition is the quotation from Hebrews 12: 27 often used in Victorian defences of reformism in religion and which Hardy places in the mouth of Angel Clare in his argument with his father in chapter 18 of *Tess of the D'Urbervilles*: 'My whole instinct in matters of religion is towards reconstruction; to quote your favourite Epistle to the Hebrews, *"the removing of those things that are shaken, as of things that are made, that those things which cannot be shaken may remain"*. 'The emphasis of the original text – itself a quotation from an Old Testament text – is, however, slightly different. It begins 'And this word, Yet once more, signifieth the removing of those things that are shaken, as of things that are made.' It emphasizes, that is, God's continual shaking of his creation rather than any final state of equilibrium. Unsurprisingly, Hardy used it again. In 1915 when he was asked to contribute to a symposium on 'The War and Literature', he replied to his questioner that the results of the war would be 'Ultimately for good; by "removing (from literature) those things that are shaken, as things that are made, that those things which cannot be shaken may remain"' (*PW* 247). The war, that is, represented a further blow to his faith in mankind, or even, as he said, in an Immanent Will of the kind he had pictured in *The Dynasts*. And he used the same passage once again in his 'Apology' to *Late Lyrics and Earlier*, seeking evidence of a progressive movement to the Church, though even this did not produce the demythologized services he hoped for, and he added a footnote to the later Wessex Edition printing, pointing out that he had been 'too sanguine'. The 'earthquake and fire' of 'Quid Hic Agis?' like the 'throbbings of noontide' of an earlier poem thus signifies a crisis that constantly shakes his literature, 'yet once more' producing the still small voice of understanding.

Finally, we can see the 'supplementary' or after-written, more tentatively, as an element of Hardy's late style. The subtitle as supplement is often used as a defence, as in the poems to which he assigns a secondary status, affixing 'Song' or 'From an Old Draft', or 'To an old air', as if the words of the titles cannot fully describe them. In the same way, the poems are second thoughts on their subjects, qualifications of the real Emma or Mary, and are at best traces of their presence. In other poems, Hardy picks up traces of earlier thought, suggesting that any poem is necessarily incomplete as a container for consciousness. One poem is even entitled 'So, Time', subtitled 'The same thought resumed', reproducing the idea of Hardy's own 'time' as a constant supplementarity, a meditation that exceeds its own forms as the poet writes on. Notice the shift in tense of 'The Dead Quire':

> Beside the Mead of Memories,
> Where Church-way mounts to Moaning Hill,
> The sad man sighed his phantasies:
>   He seems to sigh them still.

This is also the voice of the 'continuator', the word Hardy uses of himself in 'Wessex Heights' and in the first version of 'The Pedigree', before changing the word to 'mimicker' (a continuator is thus a repeater).

We might even apply a similar analysis to the syntax of Hardy's poetry. A typical stanza-form more common in the late verse has a description followed by a late comment or action. Two examples are 'Snow in the Suburbs' and (even more graphic in terms of its punctuation, ending, and comment) 'Tragedian to Tragedienne':

> The steps are a blanched slope,
> Up which, with feeble hope,
> A black cat comes, wide-eyed and thin:
>   And we take him in.
>
> Last, you will flag, and finish
>   Your masquings too:
> Yes: end them: I not there to succour you.

The action (or inaction) which completes each stanza in the subordinate clause comes after the event, and disturbs any sense of a seamless description or evocation of a mood; often we are referred outside the poem to an unavailable world in which the writer lives. The cat disappears, the action ceases. In a pattern that is particularly common in Hardy's verse, a final comment, line of verse, or intruding event disturbs an apparent closure – particularly where the poet has been reciting or narrating – requiring the reader to turn and reflect on what has come before, once again questioning the ability of the poem to 'contain' the experience of life.

Sometimes Hardy achieves the effect by refusing to sum up a theme or point a moral. In 'The Contretemps', a man and a woman who are mistaken for lovers by the husband and actual lover of the woman decide (in a use of chance typical of Hardy) to pair up anyway. The final stanza offers no conclusion. Instead it first reveals the speaker as the sole survivor of these events (the tale is itself a supplement) and then withdraws even his opinion of the events by a series of questions and comments fenced off by colons and semicolons:

> – Of the four involved there walks but one
>   On earth at this late day.
>   And what of the chapter so begun?
>   In that odd complex what was done?
>   Well; happiness comes in full to none:
> Let peace lie on lulled lips: I will not say.

Here, as often elsewhere in Hardy's late poems, the first-person voice comes only after the action, suggesting that the past can never be recovered. The use of the word 'chapter' reinforces the sense of a main action (considered in terms of the novel) that the ending of the poem comments on. The harsh final phrase, 'I will not say,' even manages to separate itself from the alliterative lushness of the first half of the line.

The poems that Hardy wrote looking back over his own life have similar stylistic features: the late arrival of the personal pronoun, terminal questions, the splitting of action from comment. 'So Various', from *Winter Words*, describes various men with opposed characteristics – young/old, fickle/trustworthy, dunce/seer, sad/happy, and so on. But in the final stanza, a perfect example of the self as supplement, Hardy ties all these selves together. They are aspects of himself, but only in a *post hoc* sense, in the moment signalled by the word 'now' and the spaced periods that separate the coda from the rest of the poem:

> Now... All these specimens of man,
> So various in their pith and plan,
>   Curious to say
>   Were *one* man. Yea,
>   I was all they.

Another indicator of supplementarity in style is Hardy's use of the repetition of a line or a refrain, a favourite device. In 'Waiting Both', with which he jocularly opens *Human Shows*, Hardy portrays himself as engaged in a dialogue with a star, which asks him 'What do you mean to do, – / Mean to do?' Hardy replies:

> I say: 'For all I know,
> Wait, and let Time go by,

> Till my change come.' – 'Just so',
> The star says: 'So mean I: –
> So mean I.'

Here, the operations of 'Time' are visible in the final line, a mechanical echoing of the previous line, but also a supplement, in the sense that the writing is carried on (as Hardy's writing is) by the echo that moves the reader beyond the point of apparent closure. Time is invoked similarly in the couplets that form the stanza-endings of 'During Wind and Rain', acting, despite the variations Hardy introduced as he revised, as a refrain. The two formulae 'Ah, no: the years O!' and 'Ah, no; the years, the years' not only introduce the violent images of decay and change in the final lines ('And the rotten rose is ript from the wall'), but also suggest, in their variation, the powerful effects of time as the poem moves from early life to death. In each case, the four spaced periods introduce the refrain, separating it from the body of the stanza; the comment in the refrain follows the open-ended description of life in a way analogous to Hardy following or tracing his own self: at the end of the ellipses are the ghostly comments, written by someone who survives all experience.

'On the Esplanade' is another typical example of the poem which balances a scene with its supplement – an extensively described scene with the 'rest' or 'thing', signalling the passage of time itself, described in half a phrase:

> The broad bald moon edged up where the sea was wide,
>   Mild, mellowed-faced;
> Beneath, a tumbling twinkle of shines, like dyed,
>   A trackway traced
> To the shore, as of petals fallen from a rose to waste,
>   In its overblow,
> And fluttering afloat on inward heaves of the tide: –
> All this, so plain; yet the rest I did not know.

Here the plenitude of the world of sense, described in such metaphorical effusion, is overbalanced – in the third and final stanza the supplementary phrase (the rest of a life) is expanded to a dragging line-and-a-half: 'That, behind, / My Fate's masked face crept near me I did not know!'

A final example of the use of an echoing supplementarity is 'He Never Expected Much', the poem he wrote to celebrate his eighty-sixth birthday. Here, the circle of prophecy and eventual fulfilment is closed, as is fitting in a poem that seeks to sum up Hardy's minimalism. The repeated half-line acts as an echo, a confirmation of the presence of nature as a trace, a secret voice across the poet's whole life. Life, in this poem, is itself a ghostly echo: "'Twas then you said, and since have said, / Times since have said...'. The full title of the poem as we have it, incorporating what seems to be Hardy's unclarified intentions, is 'He Never Expected Much / [or] / A Consideration / [A reflection] on My Eighty-Sixth Birthday' – an extended supplementing of something already in the third person, a meditation of the life of 'him', Thomas Hardy, a 'reflection' of that life, which is finally 'my' life, understood as a pattern at last fulfilled.

Within this pattern, the self is always for Hardy a supplement, the marker of an absence in life which is replaced by his writing. The self, as Derrida says in his discussion of the supplement, 'can accomplish itself, only by allowing itself to be filled through sign and proxy'.[17] There is always, for Hardy, an awareness of the absence of the 'true' self within the body of his poetic writing. The child recalled in 'He Never Expected Much', is like that which Derrida sees in Rousseau's *Confessions*; Nature makes him aware of its alienating deficiency and schools him in negativity. The natural life in Hardy's late works is irrecoverable, always already denied (as it is for Little Father Time in *Jude the Obscure*, with his deathly text). We can trace the gains and losses of this awareness both in the poem and in Hardy's late career as a whole: on the one hand a self-protective freedom from the necessity to *be* anything and an understanding of his predicament; but on the other hand a writing that is always predicated on, or even parasitic on, the death of a fully human self, a state in which writing is always an echo of a remembered life, and the tracing of a text that seems already written.

Latency

There is one related element concerning Hardy's second career that can be explored here, which is the way in which he conceived his late creativity. Some writers spend a good deal of time wondering what it will be like to be old. Yeats is one example, meditating on the theme from his earliest years. Simone de Beauvoir, in *Old Age*, argues that writers who are successful in late life are those who have already forged a picture of old age which they can use in creating an identity as they age: Swift and his Struldbrugs, Hugo and his patriarchs. Other theorists have developed more catastrophic models for this process, suggesting that crisis and a reforging of the self are the preludes to a successful old age as an artist.[18] In this context, Hardy is an interesting case, since he was, in his own words, 'late to ripen' (*LY* 178). He often struck others as being youthful for his age, and thought of himself as someone whose development had been retarded, claiming in 1917, 'I was a young man till I was 16; a youth till I was 25; a young man till I was 40 or 50' (*LY* 179). He was also late in developing any theories about the creativity (or nature) of old age that would explain his own continued productivity. A typical expression of the limited possibilities here is the last section of *The Return of the Native*, where it is suggested that it is better that the book end than that life continue after the deluge of early passion: 'Misfortune had struck them gracefully, cutting off their erratic histories with a catastrophic dash, instead of, as with many, attenuating each life to an uninteresting meagreness, through long years of wrinkles, neglect, and decay.'

In the portrait of old age in the novel which focuses most sharply on the subject, two possibilities are presented. The 1892 serial publication of *The Well-Beloved* has a protagonist, Jocelyn Pearston, who grows old while remaining trapped within his fantasies, marrying the third incarnation of his desire, the grand-daughter of his original passion. He also attempts to commit suicide, since there is no 'solution' to the problem of reconciling desire with reality. In the revised, 1897, volume publication of the novel, Pierston (as he is now called) remains self-deluded, refusing to 'ossify with the rest of his generation' and 'subject to gigantic fantasies'. But at the novel's end he is won over to an acceptance of reality, marrying the aged Marcia who is his obvious partner but for whom he feels no passion, gives up his art, and ages rapidly in appearance. Submission brings a measure of wisdom, but a diminution of passion. What the novel tells us, then, is that two possibilities in aging: a supplementing of the original self which renders it increasingly ghostly, but which maintains its energies; or a realism which gives a life a conventional 'shape', though at a cost. Michael Millgate argues that the second version of the novel represented for Hardy 'the route not to be taken', but it is perhaps more accurate to say that at this stage for Hardy they remain unreconcilable.[19] Where they are resolved is in Hardy's development of a theory of late creativity as latency and repetition.

In the 1900s, there are signs that Hardy was beginning to wonder how his continuing to write (and by extension his second career) could be justified. He copied references to extending the human life-span into his notebooks: one, from 1904, concerns the possibility that 'the age of maturity may be considerably prolonged, and that the life of natural decay may be considerably postponed' (*LN* 2540). He found parallels in the animal world for the apparently unusual continuation of life: he refers, for example, to the 'strange prolongation of life by misfortune' in certain insects which are kept in captivity (*LN* 328) – a comment prophetic of his own life after the death of Emma. More importantly, Hardy began to copy into his literary notebooks references from reviews and articles to the late works of writers, artists, and musicians. He noted the opinion that Ibsen's last plays were an expression of guilt that life had been sacrificed to art; and the statement that Rembrandt's late art 'imperiously demanded absolute submission and fidelity to the inward vision' (*LN* 2159, 2347, 2401). That 'amazing old man – Verdi' was of particular interest, since he had modulated from one style to another in old age, and 'phoenix-like' had two separate careers as a composer (*LN* 2309–10).

Equally importantly, Hardy began to shape these observations toward an understanding of the possible reasons for the appeal of the aged artist. An illuminating comment here is one from 1906, reproduced in his autobiography:

> I prefer late Wagner, as I prefer late Turner, to early... the idiosyncrasies of each master being more strongly shown in these strains. When a man not contented with the grounds of his success goes on and on, and tries to achieve the impossible, then he gets profoundly interesting to me. To-day it was early Wagner for the most part: fine music, but not so particularly his – no spectacle of the inside of a brain at work like the inside of a hive.   (*LY* 117)

This goes further than simply suggesting (as he did in another context in 1904) that old age brings 'performances of larger scope and schooled feeling'.[20] Hardy is arguing that old authors are fascinating for the way in which the dynamics of their thought are rendered more visible, in an almost skeletal fashion. The reader is referred to seemingly subjective criteria: 'What does this reveal about the artist?' is the suggested question, as in Hardy's 1919 assertion that 'there is more autobiography in a hundred lines of Mr. Hardy's poetry than in all the novels' (*LY* 196); poetry is the mode of old age because it reveals more of the mind's working. But crucially, it is a version of the self as supplement: an extension and exteriorization of the mind and its ghostly dream-play. Since the supplement is equated by Derrida with the linguistic sign itself, it offers us the intriguing possibility that Hardy sees himself or at least his life as close to writing itself; that the self is taken up into the sign. This suggestion helps, I think, explain Hardy's project of writing a disguised autobiography: the man who saw himself as an invisible ghost in his lifetime also wished to stabilize his corpus, to provide a textual mask which would protect the ghost set free to wander across the future in the forms of *envoi* which end his last four volumes.[21]

The reference to the workings of 'the inside of a brain at work' above also points the reader towards the work on which Hardy was engaged as he commented on Wagner, *The Dynasts*. There is a principle of latency, of extension, here too. One of the poem's guiding metaphors, as Susan Dean shows, is that of a giant brain which is the Will, dreaming as yet but gradually coming to consciousness. The suggestion that the Will is in a sense akin to Hardy in its (narrative) omniscience and creative unconsciousness is tempting; the old author is identified with the Will and holds, in all his oddity, a similar large fascination.[22] A number of the entries which Hardy copied into his literary notebooks testify to an interest in subjectivity in this period. One, taken from *The Nation* in late 1908, is headed 'An artist's *self*', and implies that the achievement of true individuality comes late in the life-cycle:

> 'An artist's *self*. – ' The most difficult thing in the world for any artist to achieve... is to express himself, to strike out a style of writing which shall be as natural to him as the character of handwriting is to ordinary men. It is a truism to say that individuality is the last quality to be developed in a man.   (*LN* 2348)

There are many such passages, including one directly related to the brain metaphor, copied in 1910, in which the writer whom Hardy reproduces refers to the work of Henry James: 'He asks us to think of our brains as thin & transparent places in [the] material veil, permitting the Infinite Thought to pierce them, as white light pierces glass' – the glass of each mind providing its own 'strange imperfections' and distortions (*LN* 2462). In 1903 he had copied a note arguing that Victor Hugo's 'supreme enjoyment was the exercise of his own brain'; and he reproduced a similar opinion of Browning's 'processes of thought' (*LN* 2252, 2251).

We can, I think, see in these extracts and comments a theory of aged creativity which has the idea of a belated subjectivity as a key term. But instead of that subjectivity being the product of the creative flame of the Romantic tradition, it is more closely bound to the idea of a corpus; it is the product of *having written*. In 1909 he could confidently write to Henry Newbolt: 'Happily one can afford to dismiss the fear of writing one's self out, which we used to hear so much of. No man ever writes himself out if he goes on living as he lived when he began to write' (*CL* 4: 5–6). He dismisses the Romantic (and Pearstonic) stereotype of the artist who burns to the socket, in favour of an extension of what one has achieved. The 'place where one lives' here is less Max Gate than the imaginative real of Wessex. Though the process had begun in the mid-1890s with Bertram Windle's efforts to codify its topography, it is significant that it was in the 1900s that Hardy regularly began to talk of Wessex as a kind of personal property – a well-mapped area with himself as its resident genius.[23] The 'General Preface' of 1912 is both an important indicator of his expanded ambitions of producing a 'comprehensive cycle' in verse, and also a work in which Hardy reviews his career and justifies his procedures. He provides a classificatory system for his novels, dividing them into three groups with similar categories for the poems: 'lyric' and those in 'dramatic, ballad, and narrative form' (*PW* 44–50). This self-anatomization may be less exhaustive than that of Wordsworth in 1815, but it shows a similar attention to the poet's corpus, and a desire to order the works for the benefit of posterity.

If this self-mapping helps us to explain why Hardy saw old age as more of a 'spectacle', then what about the other half of the passage on Wagner quoted above: the writer who is *not* content with the grounds of his success, and goes on and on? Hardy's late creativity is also based, I would suggest, on the idea of a certain lack of self-awareness, so far as the *source* of his poetry goes. The period after 1912 saw a catastrophic change in Hardy's life, effected by the coming of war and the death of his wife. In the poems that follow, the idea of what we could (following one of Hardy's later pronouncements) call 'latency' is a central topic: the disclosure of what had been hidden. *Satires of Circumstance* (1914) and *Moments of Vision* (1917) are both fed by a sense of loss; a preoccupation with his failure to realize feelings until it was too late. Hardy, as we have seen, began to write a poetry in which he set his earlier life off from his 'after-life' as a poet. Like matter itself in the theories that Hardy found attractive in Bergson's *Creative Evolution*, he had belatedly come to awareness of the meaning of his life and love.

In the disguised autobiography which Hardy began to write after 1916, he rationalizes this new stance. The beginnings of this process can be seen in the notes relating to this period which are assembled in and just before chapter XV, 'Reflections on Poetry'. Both the title and the position of the chapter at the beginning of the final section, 'Life's Decline', are significant (Hardy wrote this heading, though the later headings in the final section are his wife's). An entry for October 1917 sees comment on the 'error' of the late Tennyson and Wordsworth, and the suggestion that unlike them he has not fossilized into 'conviction'. He adds 'I was quick to bloom; late to ripen' (*LY* 178). He comments in the main text of the *Life*, 'Hardy's mind seems to have been running on himself at this time to a degree quite unusual with him, who often said – and his actions showed it – that he took no interest in himself as a personage.' He also comments, in this period, on his faculty for 'burying an emotion in my heart or brain for forty years, and exhuming it at the end of that time as fresh as when interred' – an acute metaphor for his late creativity, and an extension of the idea of latency or parasitism into Hardy's explanation of his continued existence as a poet.

In 1918 these considerations of his fecundity continue. He criticizes the idea that the curtailed and tragic careers of Shelley or Marlowe constitute the norm for the life of the poet, contrasting these poets with the writers of antiquity: 'Homer sung as a blind old man... Aeschylus wrote his best up to his death at nearly seventy... the best of Sophocles appeared between his fifty-fifth and ninetieth years' (*LY* 184). He concludes with the classic statement of 'latency': 'Among those who accomplished late, the poetic spark must always have been latent; but its out springing may have been frozen and delayed for half a lifetime.' And Hardy continued to comment in this vein. The value of old age, he wrote in 1920, is that for those who are 'late to develop, it just enables them to complete their job' (*LY* 212). We can place this workmanlike version of the idea alongside the private rebuttal which Hardy made in 1918 to an American periodical which had raised the old objection of his being 'a realistic novelist who... has a grim determination to go down to posterity wearing the laurels of a poet.' Hardy replies: 'Of course there was no "grim determination", no thought of "laurels." Thomas Hardy was always a person with an unconscious, or rather unreasoning *tendency*, and the poetic tendency had been his from the earliest' (*LY* 185). He adds later: 'A sense of the truth of poetry, of its supreme place in literature, had awakened itself in me. At the risk of ruining all my worldly prospects I dabbled in it... was forced out of it.... It came back upon me.... All was in the nature of being led by a mood, without foresight, or regard to whither it led' (Hardy's ellipses). Poetry has now become the secret plot of his life, discovered only in old age and incorporated into the pattern of belated recognition which we see in the poems he wrote after Emma's death. Hardy's late career thus operates, even at the level of his theorization of his own creativity, under the sign of paradox. The late writer simply continues what he has done (that is why he is interesting; he has achieved), parasitically exteriorizing himself, rendering the self a sign. But that sign is not stable; it too operates within the logic of the supplement in which there can be no equivalence, since late work involves a belated recognition of a self, a digging up of what has earlier been buried and not known for what it was, rather than a fossilizing repetition. To age is to realize what one has always been – a poet.

2
The Ghosts of Thought

Of all Victorian writers, Hardy is arguably the one who provides the best sense of an encounter with the demystification of religion and humanism offered by contemporary philosophy and the sciences – both the 'hard' sciences and the 'sciences of man'. The reason is partly that in his various and voluminous notebooks and in his surviving annotated books we have one of the most comprehensive accounts available of what it was like to be a Victorian reader with interests in a variety of fields. But there are also special qualities which Hardy brought to his reading: a freedom from modes of thinking established by the academy; a fascination with debate; a reluctance to commit himself to any final position, despite his knowledge of Mill, Darwin, Comte, Spencer, Huxley, Schopenhauer and other thinkers of the period.

To be sure, Hardy's engagement with nineteenth-century debates on monism, dualism, positivism, materialism and idealism is less than systematic.[1] There is little evidence that he read much Hegel or Kant, for example, though he does refer to their expositors. But he does pay consistent attention to these complex issues as they are translated into the serious journals, particularly in the 1880s, a troubled decade which saw intense debates on materialism, agnosticism, history and politics, and during which Hardy moved within a group of London clubmen including some of the most prominent thinkers of his age, and attended scientific lectures at the Royal Society. If our own sense of the history of philosophy is too often traced along the highways of canonical thought, to follow Hardy into these issues is to deal with all the contingency of forgotten debates as they are mediated by local contexts. In what follows, Hardy's thinking is traced across a sometimes maddening tangle of different subjects: philosophy, psychology, Darwinian biology, anthropology, psychic research, language, and finally, in a tentative coda, photography.

In particular, this chapter considers the way in which nineteenth-century positivist or materialist thinking is implicated in what seems its own opposite, in notions of ghostliness. How is materialism spectral? José B. Monleón notes the confluence, in 1848, of the conjuring of *The Communist Manifesto* and the first modern séances at Fox Farm in New York, describing this moment as one at which the spectres 'haunting' the European bourgeoisie become more material than gothic, more intimate than clearly 'other', as part of an increasing pervasiveness of the fantastic, of unreason, within capitalist ideology itself.[2] This movement between the material and the spectral also applies to conceptions of mind. As Terry Castle has argued, in the nineteenth century the material is imbued with the shapes of the mind, ghosts becoming psychological projections rather than entities in the world, while the mind itself becomes haunted, described in terms of phantasmagoria and atavism.[3] Expounded in the sciences of man, the abstract or hidden forces underlying appearance take on a new materiality, just as the material comes to seem immaterial, permeated by ideology. 'All that is solid melts into air', Marx famously declared in *The Communist Manifesto*, before adding what seems at first sight an opposite conclusion, 'and man is at last compelled to face with sober senses his real conditions of life'. Here, as so often in the period which gave birth to the 'hermeneutics of suspicion', the 'real' is a highly abstract construct, the very opposite to that which presents itself as grounded in common sense and everyday perception.

Haunted materialism

Again, why does positivism generate ghostliness? One route into this question lies in the way in which nineteenth-century positivist philosophy fractures being, consigning thought, and by implication language and aesthetics, to the status of shadowy 'epiphenomena'; as-yet indescribable accompaniments of brain events which might ultimately be reduced to those events by science, but which seem, in the interim, uncertain in status, exiled into the pure specificity implied by Kant's analysis of sensation. Hardy's friend and mentor Leslie Stephen, in his South Place Lecture *What is Materialism?* (1886), demonstrates neatly the trajectory of Victorian thought here. He considers the question of 'whether we shall be cheated out of our belief that reason and emotion exercise some influence, and be driven to hold that our consciousness is a mere phantom, looking on at the mechanical operations of an automaton'. Noting that thought becomes an elusive, ghostly entity in materialist philosophies, he touches on a debate which will be returned to below: 'Men of science have lately occupied themselves with tracing the savage doctrine of animism. Animism is belief in a soul which differs from the body, not in being immaterial, but at most in being composed of a finer matter.' Stephen sees a residue of animism in the séance in which 'so-called spirits can untie knots or write with slate pencils', adding that this is evidence of the fact that we cannot conceive of abstract thought free from 'material embodiment', concluding 'I regard abstract matter and abstract spirit as equally unthinkable.'[4] This eminently Kantian conclusion does nevertheless mean that the relation between the material and thought remains problematic; each is involved in the construction of the other, without a clearly delineated monism or dualism emerging.

If thought can seem ghostly in a material universe, from the point of view of mind, the material can, in reciprocal fashion, also seem distant, particularly as nineteenth-century science pursued objects beyond the range of human senses: atoms, electromagnetism, statistical entities. As one commentator put it in an article Hardy excerpted in 1905, 'there is something ghost-like' in theories of 'knots' in the ether and other hypothetical entities.[5] In Frederick Lange's three-volume *History of Materialism* (published in English translation in 1877–81 – Hardy noted reviews, even if he did not read the book), section titles are summarized in ways that suggest the problems which Stephen confronted: 'Materialism makes theory into reality and the immediately given into appearances'; 'The sense organs are an abstraction apparatus'. The 'real' – that is, atoms – involves abstract entities; the contingent data of sense-experience are universal. Lange's conclusion after a survey of current thinking is that: '1. The sense-world is a product of our organization. 2. Our visible (bodily) organs are like all other parts of the phenomenal world, only pictures of an unknown object. 3. The transcendental basis of our organization remains therefore just as unknown to us as the things which act upon it. We have always before us merely the product of both.'[6] This 'physiologically oriented Kantianism' (as Maurice Mandelbaum labels it) represented a common position in the middle of the century, influenced by Helmholtz, DuBois-Reymond and others; Hardy seems to subscribe to it in 1892 when he writes in his diary: 'We don't always remember as we should that in getting at the truth, we get only at the true nature of the impression that an object, etc., produces on us, the true thing in itself being still, as Kant shows, beyond our knowledge' (*LY* 9). At one limit, such views could point towards the radical scepticism of positivist thinkers like Ernst Mach, who insisted that, strictly speaking, scientific theories can only tell us of the world we perceive and construct for ourselves – a position which, as Mandelbaum argues, reopens the door for the metaphysics of Schopenhauer, Hartmann and others.[7]

This trajectory is illustrated by a third example of phantomization, an article which Hardy excerpted from the *Fortnightly Review* in December 1886 under the heading 'Huxley on Materialism'. Huxley accepts, in part, the Idealist contention that our primary knowledge is of our own sensations and consciousness rather than the 'real'. Consequently the material again seems ghost-haunted, inhabited by the frail spectres of thought, produced by the fact that the mind cannot gain a direct access to the real:

> What would become of things if they lost their qualities? As the qualities had no objective existence, & the thing without qualities was nothing, the solid world seemed whittled away...The question revived as I grew older. On the one hand the notion of matter without force seemed to resolve the world into a set of geometrical ghosts, too dead even to jabber. On the other hand Boscovich's hypothesis, by which matter was resolved into centres of force, was attractive... But...one might as well accept Idealism & have done with it.
> (*LN* 1399, Hardy's ellipses)

Lennart Björk notes that this article is recalled in a diary entry Hardy made a few months later. Meditating how any 'throng' of people might be resolved into 'souls and machines', the sensitive and the dull, Hardy adds: 'I was thinking a night or two ago that people are somnambulists – that the material is not the real – only the visible, the real being invisible optically. That it is because we are in a somnambulistic hallucination that we think the real to be what we see as real' (*EL* 243).

In such thinking, what is at stake is less any traditionally conceived dualism – though the recuperation of ideas of spirit is indeed a hidden aim of books like Lange's – than a dialogue between forms of monism. Hardy could also have encountered an overview of these debates in Arthington Worsley's *Concepts of Monism*, which he read soon after it appeared in 1907. Worsley deals with two kinds of monism: the materialist, which sees physical causes for all phenomena including mind; and the transcendental, which sees all matter as imbued with spirit (a doctrine Hardy flirted with via the thought of W. K. Clifford). As in the examples above, Worsley implies that the effect of relegating the transcendental to the material is to phantomize it, commenting that 'From the general tenor of [Ernst] Haeckel's criticisms it seems that his wish is to sweep aside the whole realm of transcendentalism as a dream, a mere phantasm created by aberration of the mind', before citing Haeckel himself: 'This hypothetical "spirit world" which is supposed to be entirely independent of the material universe, and on the assumption of which the whole artificial structure of the dualistic system is based, is purely a product of poetic imagination.'[8] The poetic imagination is reduced, in Haekel's monism, to being almost a by-product of the material.

Was there any way out of this impasse in which to think of mind or of matter as primary tended to spectralize the other term? The term 'somnambulistic' which Hardy used in the passage cited above is suggestive. Jean-Michel Rabaté argues that the only fully-dialectical nineteenth-century response to the Kantian split, reconciling materialist and spiritualist views and going beyond Kant's distrustful exclusion of the visionary from knowledge, is Schopenhauer's 'Essay on Spirit Seeing and Everything Connected Therewith'.[9] Schopenhauer depicts ghosts and spirits as a manifestation of an order of knowledge which relates to the brain's ability to function separately from reality, in dream-states for example, at a level where 'the body can become totally identical with the will at an unconscious level of perception'. Related ideas are found in a number of nineteenth-century studies of dreaming – for example in G. H. Lewes's attack on sensationalist psychology in *The Physiology of Common Life* (1860), where he stresses the 'action of the brain' in constructing perception, using such examples as the phantom limb.[10]

Schopenhauer focuses in particular on states in which there can be said to be a 'dreaming of reality' (*Wahrträumen*), that is dreams in which a direct perception of the world is effected without the (apparent) use of the senses, via the 'dream-organ' – for example in cases of somnambulism in which the walker with eyes closed seems perfectly aware of obstacles and where to place her feet. In the case of ghosts, there is no 'supernatural' entity present, only a trace of the past given reality by the dream-organ – a perception which points us towards the 'vision' of Emma carried 'In his brain – day, night, / As if on the air / It were drawn rose bright' in Hardy's 'The Phantom Horsewoman'; a vision, that is, which knows its own status as a dreaming. Or as he puts it in an earlier poem with a title itself suggesting the dream-organ, 'In the Mind's Eye':

> Now, as then, I see her
> Moving at the pane;
> Ah; 'tis but her phantom
> Borne within my brain! –

This is a phantom, it should be said, which Hardy does not wish to exorcise: at once presence and projection, she represents a deliberate loosening of the antinomies of matter and spirit, of past and present. Hardy was also capable of imagining the ghost of the *future*, as he does a few poems later in *Time's Laughingstocks*, in 'In the Night She Came', which describes a lover haunted by the 'shade' of his beloved as she will be in old age, confounding his intention to accept Time's depredations. The consciousness that threatened, in Leslie Stephen's formula, to be a 'mere phantom' looking on at the mechanical operations of the world becomes, in such dreaming, a more subtle instrument for the exploration of embodiment and temporality.

If materialist theories of the consciousness destabilize both matter and consciousness, an important third term is the past. It is a truism to say that in the nineteenth century historicity is written into human experience: in the work of the legions of historians against whom Nietzsche protests in *On the Advantage and Disadvantage of History for Life*; in the doctrine of organic memory developed by Ewald Hering, Ernst Haeckel and others, generalized via a series of analogies into a range of other fields; in the analysis of the self offered by psychologists like Lewes, for whom the Kantian *a priori* of sensation is '*historical, not transcendental*'; in the histories of societies and languages offered by anthropology and philology which saw them as passing through successive stages, carrying with them the 'vestiges' of earlier forms; in Herbert Spencer's generalization of the idea of unconscious inheritance into the whole realm of social life, rendering consciousness an entity determined by a hidden historicity. In her discussion of ideas of organic memory, Laura Otis argues that one driving force for this paradigm was its Lamarkian teleology: the sense that human effort *should* result in habits and capacities which could be progressively and concretely transferred to subsequent generations, rather than inheritance being (as it was for Darwin) simply a matter of random variation and differential survival.[11] In this view, organic memory is an attempt to deal with – to embody – the ghost of the social and cultural.

But different possibilities are also present in this paradigm: not just the fear of degeneration, but a sense of the inheritance of the past as haunting imposition. Nietzsche speaks of the importance of those who fight *against history*, and notes that 'since we happen to be the results of earlier generations we are also the results of their aberrations, passions and errors, even crimes'.[12] In the radical tradition, in particular, inheritance is experienced as haunting. Shelley repeatedly refers to the spectres of oppression; though he also imagines a counter-phantom in 'England in 1819'. Or consider the famous meditation on the ghosts of history at the beginning of Marx's *The Eighteenth Brumaire of Louis Napoleon*: 'Men make their own history, but they do not make it just as they please; they do not make it under circumstances chosen by themselves, but under circumstances directly encountered, given and transmitted from the past. The tradition of all the dead generations weighs like a nightmare on the brains of the living.'[13]

Hardy shares Marx's sense of ideology as illusion, as an inheritance which must be replaced by an understanding of the hidden 'real'. Consider his diary entry for 4 March 1886: 'Novel-writing as an art cannot go backward. Having reached the analytic stage it must transcend it by going still further in the same direction. Why not by rendering as visible essences, spectres, etc. the abstract thoughts of the analytic school?' (*EL* 232). He adds that in *The Dynasts* he would have 'Abstract realisms to be in the form of Spirits, Spectral figures, etc. The Realities to be the true realities of life, hitherto called abstractions. The old material realities to be placed behind the former, as shadowy accessories.'[14] This is reminiscent both of Spencer's vision of a history based on underlying causes rather than visible events, and of Schopenhauer's formulation of the Will as at one remove from phenomenal experience. The depiction of characters in *The Dynasts* as sleepwalking through the dream of reality, with the 'real' forces driving history invisible to them, expresses this sense of 'reality' as illusion, and the 'real' as hidden. Reality and the ideal are inverted, or rather are subject to a series of unstable reversals of the kind we saw in Huxley's formulae, rendering the poem itself a projection of internal realities even as it presents a spirit-drama. He later commented to a visitor in a manner which evokes the séance: '*The Dynasts* was crying for materialization, crying to be born, for many years. I wrote it because I had to, because of orders from within.'[15]

One example of Hardy's understanding of ideology as haunting inheritance is provided by his attentive reading of Auberon Herbert, MP and social theorist – a political connection which few writers on Hardy have noted.[16] Herbert was a fascinating figure: the third son of the Earl of Carnarvon, early in his life he was a dare-devil visiting battlefronts in the American Civil War and Paris, and a Tory candidate; later he became a radical, vegetarian, Darwinian, and ardent Spencerian (one of the three executors of Spencer's will in 1903) who was compared to Tolstoy. He entered Parliament as a Liberal in 1870 and declared himself a secularist and republican, supporting such radical figures as Dilkes,

Bradlaugh, and later the agrarian leader Joseph Arch (whom Hardy also approved of). He left Parliament but remained active in public life, organizing the 1878 'anti-Jingo' demonstration in Hyde Park, and moving in such groups as the Dominicans, the dining club founded by Mill. The *Life* tells us that Hardy got to know him in the turbulent period leading up to Gladstone's resignation in 1886, enjoying his company at political salons. Hardy certainly knew of him earlier, since when Herbert's political conversations *A Politician in Trouble about his Soul* were serialized in the *Fortnightly Review* in 1883–4 he had copied long passages into his notebook, later distilling the main points in further entries (*LN* 1316, 1419–25).

In the passages on which Hardy focuses, the meditation on the unreal posturings of party politics placed in the mouth of Angus, the sceptical Liberal MP, broadens into an analysis of what we would call 'false consciousness', a subordination to ideology which gives up the self to 'the half-life of old ghosts left in possession'.[17] In Hardy's later summary, Angus describes '*People who have never spoken the truth to themselves*, & who never will...a vast number. They live believing their own lies, & they have ceased to know what is a lie and what is not' (*LN* 1419). In a form of ventriloquism, public space is inhabited by the 'unreality' of 'voices which have no real owners', and produces an invasion of the self by others: 'Why do we believe what we only half believe...what is only in the air round us, & is in no true sense a real part of ourselves?' Spencer's essay on 'Political Fetishism' broadens this analysis into social symbolism in general: 'even the policeman puts on along with his uniform a certain indefinable power – nay, the mere dead symbols of authority excite reverence in spite of better knowledge'.[18] The result is a social fabric which is radically contingent, woven from the accretions of history and passed on as a challenge to the next generation – a vision we see explored in Hardy's novels and poetry. Herbert's metaphor borrows its evolutionary rhetoric from Spencer: 'In all that seething multitude of men & women...was there a thought or feeling, a habit or a ceremony that, like the tracings on the chestnut leaf, had not been formed in its smallest detail by the infinite succession of touchings & retouchings too many & too delicate to be imagined...' (*LN* 1316). There is a paradox here, too, which Hardy explores: the leaf is patterned by the collective past, but it is also entirely individual, unique.[19]

The psychology implicit in this image is reinforced in Henry Maudsley's *Natural Causes*, which Hardy read a few years later. Like so many nineteenth-century thinkers, Maudsley is systematically inconsistent in his sense of the mind both as the product of the past and as something which might break free from its inheritance. On the one hand he argues that 'The force of originality needed to break through traditional routine of thought, feeling, & conduct & to give freedom of expansion to impulses of variation, is not so great... most of the resistance... being convention' (*LN* 1514). On the other hand,

> The individual brain is virtually the consolidate embodiment of a long series of memories; wherefore everybody, in the main lines of his thoughts, feelings & conduct, really recalls the experiences of his forefathers. Consciousness tells him indeed that he is a self-sufficing individual with infinite potentialities of freewill; it tells him also that the sun goes round the earth. (*LN* 1519)

Here freedom is an illusion, like the Ptolemaic cosmos, and the freight of the past anything but thin convention. Hardy's phantasmagoric mode is above all a means of addressing the issue of mind in a world haunted by the ghosts of thought. The crisis of historicity as it is confronted by a materialist thinker – the tendency of consciousness to exist in a series determined by pre-existing forms, as mocking repetition rather than development – is the subject of Hardy's most visionary poem, 'The Pedigree'.

Series and selfhood in 'The Pedigree'

In the opposition between various forms of idealism and positivism which dominated nineteenth-century thought, an important third term was evolutionary thinking. The challenge repeatedly made by materialist thinkers like Haeckel was that those who believed in 'spirit' should identify at exactly *what point in the developmental chain* this quality evolved in humans or animals – an impossible demand, of course, given the relative continuity implied by evolutionary thinking. It is this problem of 'material discontinuity' (as Matthew Campbell calls it) which is implicit in 'The Pedigree', as well as the issue which flows from it: where is human will to be located within this chain of reproduction? As various scholars have pointed out, one solution was offered by the monism of W. K. Clifford, in which 'mind-stuff' is part of all matter, implicit in all life but more fully organized in the brain – though this is an idea which Hardy, as Campbell notes, found more appealing than believable.[20] Hardy's real solution is more dialectical, as we will see.

'The Pedigree' is Hardy's most complex poem in its perspectivism and intertwined figures; it is perhaps best approached by a schematic paraphrase. Late in the night a half-dressed poet contemplates his family tree, or at least that which 'the chronicler gave / As mine' – an origin, that is, supplied by an external authority. An extraordinary set of similies and metaphors follows, describing the external scene:

> The uncurtained panes of my window-square let in the watery light
>   Of the moon in its old age:
> And the green-rheumed clouds were hurrying past when mute
>   and cold it globed
> Like a drifting dolphin's eye seen through a lapping wave.

The 'sire-sown tree' and its 'hieroglyphs' tangles before his eyes and its lines twist into 'a seared and cynic face / Which winked and tokened towards the window like a Mage' – an image which recalls the earlier 'moon in its old age'. But when he does look, he sees not the moon and external scene, but that the window has become a mirror in which he sees a file of his ancestors and in an internal perspective, that 'every heave and coil and move I made / Within my brain' is anticipated (Hardy's word is in fact harsher, 'forestalled') in the mirroring of the past, which fades from 'surmise and reason's reach'. This is the notion of organic memory rendered as a destabilized haunting.[21] Finally, faced with a spectral existence, Hardy asserts himself in an act of forgetting, creating a dissonance between thinking and the speaking which, here, frames thought:

>   Said I then, sunk in tone,
>   'I am merest mimicker and counterfeit! –
>   Though thinking, *I am I*,
>   And what I do I do *myself alone*.'
>   – The cynic twist of the page thereat unknit
> Back to its normal figure, having wrought its purport wry,
>   The Mage's mirror left the window-square,
>   And the stained moon and drift retook their places there.

As Dennis Taylor points out, it is important here that Hardy voices what he thinks (since the quote marks end only after 'alone', the spoken words *include* what he is thinking). As a result the weight of 'though' here is difficult to judge: does Hardy mean 'I am merest mimicker and counterfeit / But for all that I am still willing to think *I am I* etc.', as he would more clearly mean if the quotation marks came after 'counterfeit'; or does he mean, as the grammar seems to more logically suggest, 'I am merest mimicker and counterfeit / Despite the fact that I may like to think *I am I*'? In the latter case, the poem allows no real freewill; in the former it leaves a small internal space in which the self might assert its freedom. And the difficulties of the stanza do not finish there, since the object of the crucial 'thereat' in the final stanza, quoted above, is not as clear as it should be: the words which are said, or those which Hardy says he is thinking, or both together? Does the fact that the pedigree has 'wrought its purport wry' mean that it has convinced the speaker of his belatedness? And finally, why does this declaration (or pair of opposed declarations) seem to unknit the regressive vision in the window, and restore some kind of dualism of self and world?

To begin to answer these questions, one needs to first of all notice that the poem is remarkable for its language, and is in a sense *about* language; or rather, language as writing, as inscription. To the latter question above, one reply is that the dualism was there in the simile of the first stanza – the cloud and moon are 'Like a drifting dolphin's eye seen through a lapping wave' – and collapses into the direct assertion of metaphor in the third stanza: 'It [the window] *was* a mirror now.' If the metaphor involves the sense that selfhood is an illusion which we saw in Maudsley (a version of language which leads to the infinite regress of a chain of metaphor, paralleling the chain of ghostly ancestors), the earlier simile suggests language which knows its own status and has the ability to 'break through traditional routine of thought' (Maudsley). This suggestion, which to some extent shares the poststructuralist tendency to value simile and allegory more highly than metaphor, seems to be reinforced by the startling originality of the image of the dolphin's eye (for which there seems no obvious antecedent in English poetic tradition[22]), in contrast to the dead metaphor implicit in the merely poetic use of 'glass' for mirror. The final stanza suggests an end to the twistings of rhetoric which write the self – 'normal figure' versus 'purport wry' – just as it returns the poem to the external world. Linguistically the poem moves from a bravura originality, representing the ideal of poetic power, to inherited metaphor, representing the pre-inscribed status of language. It ends, in the final stanza, with a heightened dualism: on the one hand the solipsistic near-tautology of 'I am I'; on the other, things in their places.

The poet's crisis is, then, partly a crisis of language, and particularly of the Darwinian metaphor which makes the brain the 'consolidate embodiment' (Maudsley) of the past, ontogenesis recapitulating phylogenesis, and the move or coil within the brain the tracing of a genealogy, inscribing the past of a language. It is this which generates the paradox that the assertion of selfhood, '*I am I*', is itself dressed in the clothes of tradition, recalling Exodus 3: 14 and a range of subsequent texts (perhaps the most resonant for Hardy is Tennyson's 'Ulysses': 'that which we are, we are'); it is itself a mimicking or continuation. 'Mimicker and counterfeit' and 'sunken tone' together suggests the figure of Echo, of sonic dispersal; Hardy is an echo of his ancestors.

That suggestion returns us to the original question: what is the status of what the speaker tells us he *thinks*? The central issue of the central section of the poem is that of selfhood *as series* – an issue which is implied by the topic of genetic inheritance. Two philosophical texts might help us here. The first is Spencer's discussion of 'ultimate ideas' in *First Principles*. Spencer resolves consciousness into a series of states, for which we can conceive no original or final state; he also attacks the *cogito* as logically inconsistent, since if we declare that the subject–object relation is fundamental to thought, then we cannot be both object and subject of thinking. On the other hand, Spencer also rejects those who assert that mind does not exist as substance, that it is simply a bundle of succeeding perceptions. The thinker is faced with an 'insoluble enigma' in relation to these fundamental categories, and is left with the *assertion* rather than the certainty of selfhood.[23] Though it seems to be severely qualified, Hardy's '*I am I*' rests (or rather it wishes to rest) on a version of this Spencerian self-realization.

A second text which might elucidate this issue is R. B. Haldane's Hegelian *The Pathway to Reality*, the Gifford Lectures in Natural Religion for 1903–4. There is no evidence that Hardy owned this book, but he copied sections from a number of reviews and it seems likely enough that he subsequently read it. Some of Haldane's images may even enter the poem, and his meditation on the grounding of the self helps us, in particular, to unlock that troubling final stanza and its 'thereat'. Investigating the way in which the self is defined, Haldane writes of the discrediting of the 'window' theory of mind, in which it is 'a thing which looks out from windows of sense at other things in the outside world'.[24] This involves a rejection of any absolute status attributable to mind. As his summary puts it, 'with the rejection of the conception of mind as substance, solipsism becomes meaningless, for it is apparent that to try to think of a finite self as the ultimate form of reality is to try to think what is self-contradictory'. Mind is bound up reciprocally with the conceptualization of the external world: to examine the self is necessarily to examine its origins and perception.[25]

Haldane then develops the work of his predecessor in the Gifford Lectures three years earlier, the American Idealist Josiah Royce (who in turn had used the work of the German mathematician Richard Dedekind), examining 'self-conscious mind' in terms of 'the law of the series' in mathematics.[26] The point of Royce's heuristic argument was to partly describe how mind might understand the infinite: using the mathematical idea of the limit, Royce notes that series like $1 + 1/2 + 1/4 \cdots + 1/2^n$ can be understood both in terms of the general term $(1/2^n)$ and in terms of the asymptote (here the number 2). As Haldane puts it:

> He finds that the number series is a purely abstract image of the relational system that must characterize an ideally completed self; that is to say, a self that does not merely pass from expression to expression, but comprehends the relation to each other of these expressions. The system of thought, so far from consisting in the bare conjunctions which are characteristic of appearance, is self-representative in that it is present as a whole in every thought in the series.[27]

The example that Haldane adduces is an infinite series of reflections: 'Today is Thursday'; 'I just reflected on the fact that today is Thursday'; 'I just reflected on my reflection that today is Thursday' etc. Thought can thus comprehend the infinite because each member of the series invokes its totality.

We can apply these reflections to the successive stages of 'The Pedigree'. Initially, the poet is pictured as meditating at a window and looking out, in a version of the isolate self and the representational theory of perception which Haldane rejects. He looks at his genealogy and then at the window again, only to find that it has become a mirror in which he sees an infinite series of 'my begetters, dwindling backward each past each', a version of the self that parallels the recursive function which Haldane derives from Royce. The painful crisis of identity which results – a retreat of causality into the infinite, 'past surmise and reason's reach', seeks a dialectical resolution in which two positions can be held, if somewhat uneasily, together. The self-reflective declaration '*I am I*' illustrates the way in which, as Haldane put it, 'the self in its entirety is the whole of a self- representative system, and not the mere last moment or stage, if such there could be, of the process'.[28] The fact of self-consciousness, that is, necessarily co-exists with the perception of the self's place in a series (whether a Darwinian series or a series of moments of reflection), since self-awareness involves the knowing summation of the series; at the limit, the seemingly fragmentary existence of the self in time is reconciled with identity. This is the ultimate task of Hardy's poem: to negotiate between series and selfhood at the level of identity, just as it negotiates between the weight of a spectralizing inheritance and the assertion of individuality at the level of ideology, and between an inherited language and a language which it makes its own. As he put it in his diary at the end of 1901: 'I have come to this: *Let every man make a philosophy for himself out of his own experience*' (*LY* 91) – the 'coming' here is perhaps the point; the process whereby one arrives at self-assertion. This conclusion is close to that in the discussion of Hardy's self-perception in the previous chapter: he is both a ghostly supplement, and the achieved limit of what Haldane calls 'a self-representative system' – the 'system' which is *all* of 'Thomas Hardy' as he knows and represents himself, including that self's pre-history.

Similar concerns are explored in other examples of the poem of the ghost-seer, which could be said to be a distinctive sub-genre for Hardy, including the two great phantasmagoria 'The Pedigree' and 'Family Portraits', but also a number of other major poems such as 'During Wind and Rain', 'The Five Students', 'The Wind's Prophecy', 'The Flirt's Tragedy', 'The Place on the Map', 'I Looked Up from My Writing', and the final two poems of *Winter Words*. 'A Procession of Dead Days' is another example, with its visionary series of phantoms of the past, many bearing their symbolic regalia – a rainbow, an iron rod – and each providing a version of the past which might permeate a lifetime:

> The next stands forth in his morning clothes,
> And yet, despite their misty blue,
> They mark no sombre custom-growths
>   That joyous living loathes,
> But a meteor act, that left in its queue
> A train of sparks my lifetime through.

'To-day has length, breadth, thickness, colour, smell, voice. As soon as it becomes *yesterday* it is a thin layer among many layers, without substance, colour or articulate sound' (*LY* 58). The self is haunted by its pasts, but in this poem once again Hardy turns what might be a catastrophic series into a version of the self which is summative, unique, self-aware and at the same time defined by its historicity.

'Ghost theory' versus fetishism

If the issues of inheritance and ideology are central to Hardy's sense of what haunts human existence, a more specific debate which Hardy traces in his notebooks also offers an insight into the issue: that between Auguste Comte and his followers and Herbert Spencer on the origins of religion and abstract thought. The two poles of this argument are Comte's 'fetishism', the worship of material objects endowed with supernatural powers, and Spencer's 'ghost-theory' – the idea that the origins of religion lie in the apprehension of the separation of spirit and body in ghosts and in ancestor-worship.[29] Hardy knew both Spencer's and Comte's views well, and alludes to the debate when he has Jude pass through Comtean stages (polytheism, agnosticism) and makes Christminster 'a place full of fetichists and ghost-seers'.[30]

For Comte, fetishism is the first stage of human social existence and thought; it is present at 'the birth of every civilization' (a fact documented in an exhaustive analysis of anthropological reports) and is 'the necessary starting-point of all intellect'. It provides a located form of thinking in which the subject responds directly to the physical world, even if erroneously attributing intentions to objects. Fetishism thus anticipates Positivism's attention to the facts of nature, and is for Comte more closely aligned with the truth of the world than the distant and non-specific absolutes of the Theological and Metaphysical traditions which follow it.[31] Fetishism is also – this point will become more important later – related to Comte's thinking in the chapter on the 'Theory of Language' in the *System of Positive Polity*. For Comte, human communication is founded on a clear historical progression from the body to writing: the progression for Comte runs gesture $\Rightarrow$ music $\Rightarrow$ poetry $\Rightarrow$ prose – gesture suggesting the winking and 'tokening' of the face in 'The Pedigree', a primal meaning.[32] And despite the fact that language is 'the most social of all the institutions', for Comte the signs of language are also founded on the real, and can potentially be traced back to gesture and spontaneous expression: 'All artificial signs are originally derived, even in man, from mere voluntary imitation of different natural signs, which are involuntary and are produced by the physical conditions of life.'[33]

For Spencer, on the other hand, fetishism is simply a historical mistake, based on a literalization of totemic but essentially metaphorical identifications made between people and animals or objects (a man is *like* a wolf and is given the nick-name; his descendants come to think that they are literally descended from wolves).[34] This is a claim which echoes the sense of ideology as a falsifying inheritance expounded in the first section of this chapter: for Spencer the general past is that earlier stage of social evolution which must be stripped away by modern thought. Despite his evolutionism and stress on what he called 'the serial genesis of phenomena', Spencer is in this respect a conventualist: his interest in language, for example, is in its existence as a system which is transmitted and must be modified, rather than being a key to origins – remarking, for example, in his essay 'Specialized Administration', that 'No language is a cunningly-devised scheme of a ruler or body of legislators. There was no council of savages to invent the parts of speech.'[35]

Spencer also objected to Positivism for its over-confidence in the empirical sciences, stressing the persistence of an area of the 'Unknown' beyond the scope of science.[36] In Part I of *First Principles*, he famously argued that the Absolute is not just a negation; rather it designates an area of consciousness outside referential language, only symbolized by arbitrary signs such as X^n. In a similar paradox, Hardy's version of the Unthought or Unknown in the rather ironic 'A Philosophical Fantasy' speaks as a respondent to the poet, insisting that it is *not* the projection of man, a humanized god, as Comtean deities are:

> – Another such a vanity
> In witless weak humanity
> Is thinking that of those all
> Through space at my disposal,
> Man's shape must needs resemble
> Mine, that makes zodiacs tremble!

A place must, that is, be preserved for belief beyond the merely personal assertion posited by H. L. Mansel, whose position Spencer began with. As W. David Shaw puts it, 'Spencer's God is present to the human mind, not as a mere negation but as a kind of nebula out of which the solid nucleus of all later thought is formed.'[37] The 'ghost theory' elaborated in Spencer's later sociology is important here because it locates this 'nebula' in 'primitive' society: the possibility of conceptual thought is founded on a sense of the transcendent and in a respect for the dead. As an explanation for the origins of religion, the 'ghost theory' is largely a version of the anthropologist E. B. Tylor's 'animism', which we have already seen Leslie Stephen allude to. Tylor saw belief in an animating 'ghost-soul' as originating in two factors: the apprehension of the difference between a living and a dead body; and the appearance of people (including the dead) in dreams and visions.[38]

The outlines of this debate can be traced in a number of texts from the late 1870s on, which Hardy read, including J. H. Bridges's 'Evolution and Positivism', published in the *Fortnightly Review* in 1877; George Romanes's 1886 essay 'The World as an Eject', in which Romanes attempts to theorize a responsive universe in terms of the 'eject', the inferred subjectivities of other minds; and Grant Allen's Spencerian *The Evolution of the Idea of God: An Inquiry into the Origins of Religions* (1897).[39] Hardy attended in particular to a debate which erupted in 1884 between Spencer and the English Positivist Frederic Harrison in a series of essays in *The Nineteenth Century* beginning with Spencer's 'Religion: A Retrospect and Prospect'. In a reply entitled 'The Ghost of Religion', published in the March issue, Harrison attacked the residues of idealism in Spencer in terms which portray the Unknowable as a metaphysical ghost: 'Better bury religion at once than let its ghost work uneasy in our dreams.'[40] A more specific target was Spencer's 'ghost theory', which for Harrison opens the path to irrationalism and the occult: 'To many persons it will sound rather whimsical, and possibly almost a sneer, to trace the germs of religion to the ghost-theory. Our friends of the Psychical Research will prick up their ears, and expect to be taken *au grand sérieux*.' The piece climaxes in a sarcastic paean to the 'schools, academies, temples of the Unknowable' which might be built.

Spencer – in an article which Hardy again noted – replied that his Unknown was never intended as a theological entity. He also returned to the debate between fetishism and 'ghost theory'. Garnering his arguments from Tylor and others, he reiterates that the idea of ghosts *precedes* fetishism in primitive religion; the spirits he evokes are active beings rather than ideas contained within the static container of the fetish: crowding around the Karen Islander; rubbing the dress of the Rabbi in the Synagogue; living both inside and outside physical objects in Africa. The presence of ghosts in primitive thought suggests the apprehension of 'a formless consciousness of the inscrutable'.[41] The fetish seems to represent, for Spencer, a collapse of thought into matter.

To the modern reader, this debate can appear obscure, and, as subsequent commentators have been quick to point out, there is less separating Comte and Spencer than they believed. In the climactic chapter of *The Principles of Psychology*, 'Transfigured Realism' (a favourite of Hardy's), Spencer argues that most Anti-Realistic beliefs are 'but ghosts of beliefs, haunting those mazes of verbal propositions in which metaphysicians habitually lose themselves'. 'Metaphysics', he adds, 'in all its anti-realistic developments, is a disease of language' – a sentiment with which Comte would have heartily agreed.[42] Nevertheless, one issue here is important: for Comte the origins of abstract thought lie in a direct, sensuous and incipiently Positivist apprehension of the object, though an object imbued with hidden forces demanding analysis; for Spencer those origins are in loss; in the hauntings of disembodied ideas of the departed; in an apprehension of spirit which is already ghostly or metaphorical, mourning its object, and which is thus already on the road to the Absolute. Comte offers the hope of a world mastered, simplified, and purged of its ghosts; Spencer implies that the human is always haunted by its past.[43]

Why is this debate of interest in relation to Hardy? One answer to that question will be supplied by Chapter 5, in which opposing theological and fetishistic views of disaster are at issue. In relation to Hardy's ghosts, one issue is their status: are they coverings for natural phenomena, or are they intimations of spirit? Do they relate concretely to the past, or to an unknown realm? The answer is that among Hardy's scores of ghosts-poems *both* these possibilities are realized – in different kinds of ghost; and in different kinds of haunting. Hardy does depict Comtean ghosts: entities, that is, which are fetishistic embodiments or abstractions, either explanations for the forces in the world or later personifications of those forces like those which Comte claims develop in the Theological era. As in Comte, these conceptualizations are always likely to be superseded by a new realism, as happens with the ghosts of the Greek, Roman and even Christian gods in 'Aquae Sulis', 'The Graveyard of Dead Creeds' and 'Christmas in the Elgin Room'; or the rather careless spirit of Nature in 'The Mother Mourns'.[44] The personified ideas of *The Dynasts* and of such poems as 'The Well-Beloved' and 'The Ghost of the Past' come into the same category. These ghosts debate the meaning of history and the obscure doings of God or the Immanent Will, but they are in fact part of the mechanism of the world.

But Hardy also depicts more personal ghosts which are typically tied to memory traces and to particular places or objects in the commemorative mode of Spencer – the ghosts which haunt the poet in 'Wessex Heights' and other poems; the ghosts of Emma in various elegies; the ghosts of specific individuals who range from a recently-dead king (Edward VII) to the protagonists of stories told in poems like 'At the Piano' and 'The Church and the Wedding'. Spencer argues that such personal apprehensions broaden into notions of Spirit, and we can see that illustrated in the purely exemplary phantoms of poems like 'A Christmas Ghost Story' and 'The Souls of the Slain', who indicate a general concern for the fate of the recent dead; and in the ghosts of the poetic persona's own self, operating as a figure for posthumous vision in a number of poems.

The competing positions represented by Comte and Spencer can be seen throughout Hardy's poetry. One nice example is a pair of adjacent poems in *Satires of Circumstance*, seemingly related to *Jude the Obscure*, 'The Recalcitrants' and 'Starlings on the Roof'. The first declares a wish for an escape to a place of refuge where the lovers can live 'natural lives', comparing this to the rejection of a 'brazen god' and pious morality; these might be representatives of Comte's Religion of Humanity. The second poem has the birds comment on the empty house, whose occupants have gone to 'look for a new life, rich and strange'. The cynical conclusion is that 'They will find that as they were they are, / That every hearth has a ghost, alack.' As Spencer would teach, a haunting familiarity with death is written into every family scene, so that 'natural life' offers no clear answers.

In fact, these alternatives cannot be considered in terms of an 'either/ or' logic: poems may contain both 'located' spirits and embodied ideas in an unstable mix. A good illustration is 'Channel Firing', which describes the dead woken by 'great guns'. The poem was published in the *Fortnightly Review* in May 1914, months before the start of the war, so that though the immediate occasion was probably naval guns off Portland, Hardy would later call it 'prophetic' of the heavy German guns that would soon be heard across the Channel (*LY* 161). The poem's dead waken to ask whether it is the 'Judgement-day' and God replies: 'No; / It's gunnery practice out at sea / Just as before you went below; / The world is as it used to be ... ' The god-guaranteed plot of history seems an irrelevance here; God even wonders whether he will ever sound the Last Trump. This poem thus offers the trace of a God who is given a voice but nevertheless seems non-transcendent, uncertain about the unfolding of Spirit; it includes a prophecy attributed not to God but to poetic irony; and describes the dead who protest at history's direction, but who include Parson Thirdly, a character from one of Hardy's novels rather than a historical person.

Equally typically, Hardy produces poems which actually debate the status of phantoms in terms akin to those set out by Comte and Spencer. An example is provided by 'In a Whispering Gallery', which recalls Spencer's rubbing, familiar spirits, but in the context of entirely explicable phenomena:

> That whisper takes the voice
> Of a Spirit's compassionings,
> Close, but invisible,
> And throws me under a spell

> At the kindling vision it brings;
> And for a moment I rejoice,
> And believe in transcendent things...

This is, the poet knows, no 'soul's voice', though the gloom in St Paul's dome allows him to think it may be. Here as elsewhere it is *voice* rather than vision that lures Hardy into a subjunctive mood which might momentarily express transcendent longings: the mood of the 'That I could think...' which describes the birdsong in 'The Darkling Thrush'. One reason for this stress on sound has been elucidated by Gillian Beer: in the tradition of psychophysics descending from Helmholtz, it is in the dispersal of sound waves that the energiac trace of the self is figured, as in such poems as 'In the British Museum', where a humble workingman reflects that 'that stone has echoed / The voice of Paul'.[45] The visual image, on the other hand, is more readily associated with over-painting, deception, and fading: in the 'hazed lacune' of the dome of St Pauls in 'In a Whispering Gallery', 'transcendent things' are ultimately illusion; in 'The Shadow on the Stone' Hardy can sustain an imagined vision of Emma in the garden at Max Gate, but the fact that he hears 'no sound but the fall of a leaf / As a sad response' means that he knows this to be a 'dream'. As we will see in a later chapter, the story of the 'Poems of 1912–13' is partly the gradual abandonment of the hope of hearing the voice of the dead.

The other issue raised by the Comte–Spencer debate concerns the powers invested in objects. In a number of poems, Hardy describes the way in which material objects carry the traces of the dead, though here again there is a characteristic ambivalence. In his diary in 1878 he comments that 'the beauty of associations is entirely superior to the beauty of aspect, and a beloved relative's old battered tankard to the finest Greek vase' (*EL* 158); here it is the objects which recall the dead. However in his 1910 speech when he was given the freedom of Dorchester, he insisted that his final loyalty was ultimately not to the transient buildings but to those who lie in the churchyard, to the spirit of the dead (*LY* 146). His most poignant poem concerning ancestral objects is 'Old Furniture', with its evocation of 'relics of householdry / That date from the days of their mothers' mothers':

> I see the hands of the generations
>   That owned each shiny familiar thing
> In play on its knobs and indentations,
>   And with its ancient fashioning
>   Still dallying:

> Hands behind hands, growing paler and paler,
>   As in a mirror a candle-flame
> Shows images of itself, each frailer
>   As it recedes, though the eye may frame
>   Its shape the same.

This seems akin to fetishism in as much as it is objects which carry traces of the departed (these are, as Harrison put it, 'ancestors treated objectively'), rather than their being free-floating ghosts present. The *mise en abîme* here (like that of 'The Pedigree') comes to rest in the subjectivity of the poet and his haunted consciousness: it is the *eye* of the poet which frames; which attends to that which creeps before it; which 'eyes'. The dominant images are again those of sight: flickering candle-flame, the vision of a finger on a clock-face which 'creeps to my sight', the 'face by that box for tinder, / Glowing forth in fits from the dark, / And fading again'. The stanza containing the latter example is not in the manuscript; instead there is a cancelled stanza which seems as though it should belong in another poem, 'To My Father's Violin':

> From each curled eff-hole the ghosts of ditties
>   Incanted there by his skill in his prime
> Quaver in whispers the pangs and pities
>   They once could language, and in their time
>   Would daily chime.

Hardy removes the stanza that might take the reader away from the eye towards sound's persistence, and its location in the immediacy of a bodily response. In 'To My Father's Violin', a poem of tremendous pessimism which largely fails to evoke Thomas Hardy senior's presence, it is, unexpectedly, *sight* which dominates or at least qualifies descriptions of sound: the 'blind / Still profound / Of the night-time'; the theme 'Elusive as a jack-o'-lanthorn's gleam'; the poem ends with the poet 'conning' the 'present dumbness' of the decaying violin.[46]

In such poems, Hardy's stress is again ultimately on something like the Schopenhauerian dream-organ: the function of the mind which embodies the past, creating a world from a few props, rather than finally allowing any separate existence to 'transcendent things' except in the heuristic mode of the personification or as a product of the poet's 'posthumous' eye. In 'Her Haunting-Ground' Hardy insists that Emma's ghost is to be found where she was happiest, in Cornwall, rather than where she is buried:

> – 'Nay, but her dust is far away,
> And where her dust is, shapes her shade,
> If spirit clings to flesh,' they say:
> Yet here her life-parts most were played!

The poem's framing question is whether 'visions have not ceased to be / In this the chiefest sanctuary / Of her whose form we used to know' – a question once again located in the mind of a spectator who might re-imagine the dead. In psychologizing her ghost and assigning Emma to a specific place and to a specified material world ('this turf... this slope and mound ... blossoms here'), Hardy seems to abandon hope of giving his own dead a status beyond the world of things and their associations. One might say that in this view, the poem itself is a fetish: the place of an encounter, always attached to the real and never able to give full reign to the disembodied spirit. As Hardy suggests in 'The House of Silence', the poet is he who conjures up a scene of ghosts. A child asks about a house rather like Max Gate and is told:

> Mid those funereal shades that seem
> The uncanny scenery of a dream,
> Figures dance to a mind with sight...

This is 'the visioning powers of souls who dare / To pierce the material screen'. But the poet himself, in this poem, is the 'phantom', a 'brain [that] spins there till dawn'; there remains for the child 'nobody there', and the piercing of the material screen leads not to a world beyond, to the Unknowable, but to a vision of what has been.

Language and psychical research

A test of this conclusion, and a rather more literal approach to the problem of ghostly materialism, is provided by one mode of explanation of ghosts available to Hardy which is conspicuous in its absence: psychical research. The modern reader needs to recall just how mainstream spiritualism was in the late nineteenth century, and how diverse the range of writers interested in it, from George Eliot to Henry James, Yeats and Radcliffe Hall – not to mention influential thinkers like Freud, William James, and Bergson, for whom parapsychology seemed to hold many of the keys to unknown areas of the mind. A number of his acquaintances had an interest in the subject, so it is an intriguing question why Hardy, who *wished* to believe in ghosts and who constantly registers the voices and traces of the dead, showed little interest in the subject; never even attended a séance, so far as we know. He was certainly aware of the work of the Society for Psychical Research (SPR), and had an interest in the theories of 'secondary' personality closely associated with it. His notebooks include excerpts from Frederick Myers, Eduaard von Hartmann, Henry Maudsley and others on the splitting of the self and 'hierarchy or commonwealth of psychical units that at death dissolves and sinks below the threshold of consciousness'; he took notes from Myers on 'Automatic Writing', and discussed hypnotism and related subjects; and he owned William James's *Human Immortality*, which argued for psychic survival.[47] His poem 'The Noble Lady's Tale', with its guarded suggestion that a 'wraith' may be 'projected' over a distance by a living person, suggests any number of stories involving doubles. But in his 1901 conversations with William Archer, Hardy systematically resists Archer's rather orthodox SPR line, which portrays paranormal phenomena as the result of undiscovered telepathic potential, located in the penumbra of known faculties. He stresses the poverty of the evidence gathered by the SPR, referring Archer to Hume's critique of supernatural explanations in 'Of Miracles'.[48] If for Myers psychic research was ultimately designed to move beyond materialism and prove the existence of the soul separate from the body, that was a step which Hardy could never take. He could not enter what Frederic Harrison called, in his attack on Spencer, the 'schools, academies, temples of the Unknowable'.

One reason for this unwillingness is Hardy's intellectual history, with its typically hard Victorian fall from belief to agnosticism. We can reconstruct a sceptical milieu from his clubland contacts in the 1880s and 1890s, including scientists like Edwin Ray Lankester, the Professor of Zoology at University College, London, who exposed the fashionable medium Slade in 1876, and the eminent psychiatrist and social theorist Sir James Crichton-Browne. In his preface to Hugh Elliot's 1912 attack on Bergson, *Modern Science and the Illusions of Professor Bergson*, Lankester stresses that 'modern science...has arrived at a systematic interpretation of the phenomena which we call "Nature" as a vast and orderly mechanism'.[49] Crichton-Browne was less of a thoroughgoing materialist, stressing the role of Will in mental life, and even participated in SPR-sponsored thought transference experiments in 1883, but he nevertheless regarded mediums as charlatans and sought physiological explanations of 'borderline' mental phenomena.[50] In his 1895 Cavendish Lecture *On Dreamy Mental States* he cites Hardy's *A Pair of Blue Eyes* on what Hardy calls 'those strange sensations we sometimes have, that our life for the moment exists in duplicate, that we have lived through the moment before or shall again'. Such states, Crichton-Browne argues, 'are not themselves part of the evolutionary process, but one of the accidents by which it is attended'; they are 'abnormal', involve 'disorder of the mind' – inattention, crossed wires; even pre-epileptic symptoms – but also allow 'new cerebral combinations' and 'flights of genius'. Dreaminess may even be passed on, like the ancestral dreams which Hardy describes in *Tess* and in various poems: Crichton-Browne tells of a family in which the 'dreamy state' is inherited across 'four generations'.[51]

In focusing on this area of 'disorders' and 'limits' of the mind, the rationalist critique of spiritualism shared an important common ground with psychical research of the more sceptical kind represented by the SPR. Both worked to sharpen the issues, to raise the odds, as it were, in relation to the phantoms which haunt the space beyond science, at once producing and policing their spectral status. Hugh Elliot declares that 'Materializing abstractions is a vice of thought', with Bergson a prime offender. But he also argues that 'The problem of metaphysics is a shadowy spectre which must for ever continue to haunt the mind of man'[52] – an argument that once again specularizes the 'outside-knowledge' which Lankester, like Herbert Spencer, holds in place algebraically by christening it 'X' (the forerunner of our own X-Files, one might say). The regulation of these shadowlands is an impulse visible in Henry Maudsley's polemically anti-spiritualist *Natural Causes and Supernatural Seemings* (1886), which Hardy read carefully soon after it appeared. For Maudsley, supernatural beliefs are firmly attributed, at best, to the natural limits of the mind, and more typically to mania and organic defects:

> The intermediate region or border-land of thought and feeling between soundness and unsoundness of mind is a penumbral region which has been very fruitful of supernatural products. It is less fruitful now than once it was, because, like other enchanted regions, it has been surveyed in part, and taken possession of by positive knowledge, but is yet not barren of wonders. Ghost-seers and ghost-seekers are still to be met with, and in such numbers and of such zeal at the present time as to have organized in England a society for the systematic prosecution of their researches...[53]

Maudsley's terms – spatial, imperial – evoke that extension of power which Foucault describes in nineteenth-century psychiatry, portraying even the opposition in terms of the apparatus of control: the SPR was known for its stringency, its careful tests infuriating more enthusiastic believers.

Hardy's response to Archer cannot, however, be accounted for simply in terms of the rhetoric of scientific scepticism. For a start, he borrows Maudsley's pejorative term 'ghost-seer' in describing *himself* to William Archer:

> W.A.   And have you ever seen one?
>
> Mr Hardy.   Never the ghost of a ghost. Yet I am cut out by nature for a ghost-seer. My nerves vibrate very readily: people say I am most morbidly imaginative; my will to believe is perfect. If ever ghost wanted to manifest himself, I am the very man he should apply to. But no – the spirits don't seem to see it!

'Ghost-seer' suggests a dubious susceptibility, like Jude calling himself 'spectre-seeing' in *Jude the Obscure*. The ultimate derivations of the term are Kant's sceptical (though ghost-ensnared) *Dreams of a Ghost-Seer* (1766) and Schiller's gothic novel *The Ghost Seer* [*Der Geisterseher*, 1787–9], in which the 'supernatural' is produced by elaborate machinery to deceive a credulous Prince. The former is a satire on Swedenborg and others which influenced later equations of metaphysics and necromancy, and influenced Schopenhauer.[54] Hardy's inability to see a ghost has some of Kant's satirical thrust, but also its ambivalence: if ghosts are a matter of imagination or will-to-believe, then he *should* be able to see one; if on the other hand they cannot be produced at will, the possibility remains of their obstinate reality.

Hardy's gentle kidding of Archer provides important hints as to what he *did* seek in a ghost. He implies that the bureaucratic SPR techniques, which might make ghosts 'apply' for a visitation, were absurd, leaving only the hope of 'the ghost of a ghost'. We can say what the 'ghost of a ghost' is quite precisely, if we turn to an exchange with Caleb Saleeby in 1915:

> Half my time (particularly when I write verse) I believe – in the modern use of the word – not only in things that Bergson does, but in spectres, mysterious voices, intuitions, omens, dreams, haunted places, etc., etc.
>
> But then, I do not believe in these in the old sense of belief any more for that...   (LY 271–2)

In an extraordinary series of hedgings-about, Hardy *wishes* to see ghosts; but what he is left with after his half-belief (expressible only in poetry) is the ghost as a psychological figment, perhaps even as a metaphor – the mental presence which Terry Castle portrays ghosts as becoming in the course of the nineteenth century, increasingly interiorized and accompanied by a parallel spectralization of the mind.[55] The 'Idealism of Fancy' which Hardy proposed to a correspondent in 1901 was an 'imaginative solace' rather than something that would 'masquerade as belief' (*LY* 90).

Hardy differed from the SPR in that when he hoped to see ghosts and wrote of ghosts they were naturalistically conceived spirits of a particular place and time, bound to a history, rather than vague presences and voices floating in the ether, evidences of Spirit as an abstract realm. He explained in a letter to Rider Haggard in 1902, that before the breakdown of local traditions in the later nineteenth century, 'ghosts tales were attached to particular sites, and nooks wherein wild herbs grew for the cure of divers maladies were pointed out readily' (*LY* 94). Like the phantoms of 'Wessex Heights', 'They hang about at places' which one might seek or avoid. And indeed, when much later he did see a ghost (on Christmas Eve, 1919), it was that of his grandfather, on whose grave in Stinsford Churchyard he had just placed some holly for the first time.[56] Hardy's personal ghosts, then, are the phantoms of historicity, of a lost tradition; they mark the *place* of mourning. His poem 'The Sailor's Mother' is exemplary here: a son's ghost does not know that his mother has changed house: 'he only knows of *this* house I lived in before'.

These ghosts, specific and historical, are also bound to individual recollection: they are never the mysterious spirits of uncertain provenance of the séance. A number of poems insist that the dead are dependent on the living or on memorials to give them life: in 'His Immortality' the dead man shrinks to 'a thin / And spectral mannikin' as his memory fades; in the paired poem 'The To-Be-Forgotten' the dead lament their 'second death' as they pass from memory; in 'The Obliterate Tomb' even the final traces of monumental inscription are effaced as tombstones are used to pave a churchyard. This sense of supersession or supplanting also works (as the discussion earlier would suggest) at the level of ideology, for Hardy's more Spencerian ghosts: in 'The Superseded' those who 'drop behind'; in poems like 'Aquae Sulis' and 'Christmas in the Elgin Room' the spirits of the Roman and Christian gods who 'fail like a song men yesterday sung'.

If the spooks of the psychic researchers and their fragmentary messages were not the consolation Hardy wished for, then a more general form of haunting is suggested by Dennis Taylor's distinction between Hardy's attitude to language and that of modernist writers. If the latter move towards the synchronic equivalence of linguistic surfaces suggested by Saussure, Hardy, Taylor argues, retains a sharper sense of the history of language, inflected by the positivism of Victorian philology, in which words have attachments to the past that cannot be over-written like a computer disc.[57] Language is not *simply* a medium. The calling up of ghosts from the past like voices on a radio, as practised at the séance-table, aligns spiritualism with the analytic procedures of Saussurean linguistics, or of modernist texts, stripping language of its history and contexts in order to create startling effects.[58] (The radio was itself closely linked to the supernatural in the minds of many of its inventors: Tesla became obsessed with the psychic; W. B. Yeats investigated a radio-like 'mechanical medium'; Ezra Pound saw radio as a form of telepathic action at a distance.)

Archer's 'Real Conversations' are again revealing. Having discussed Hardy's desire to see a ghost, they move on to Hartmann and the Unconsciousness, and the grounding of Hardy's 'pessimism', the novelist attacking recent optimists: 'I do not see that we are likely to improve the world by asserverating, however loudly, that black is white, or at least that black is but a necessary contrast and foil, without which white would be white no longer. This is mere juggling with a metaphor.' Pursuing a philosophical line in which 'white' (the progressive) is developing, bound to a chronology, Hardy resists any opening towards what we would now tend to identify as the mutually generative binaries of Structuralist thinking. The linguistic fallacies generated by the ascription of a false realism to metaphorical language was a theme in Henry Maudsley's *Natural Causes*, in a passage which Hardy part-copied: 'Much error of thought has arisen from the strong propensity to believe that opposite names must mean opposite things in nature'; 'Divisions of knowledge distinguished by their proper names have over and over again been assumed to denote distinct divisions in nature, discontinuities being thus made where continuity prevails everywhere.'[59] Hardy was acutely aware of such 'error' as it attached itself to religious and other dogma; to the way in which the self could be frozen into rigid linguistic structures. He wrote, for example, two poems in which people are locked into intentions they cannot fulfil by inscribing their names alongside that of a dead spouse, as if they wished never to re-marry: 'The Memorial Brass: 186–' and 'The Inscription (A Tale)', in which the living woman is reduced to the status of a 'wraith' haunting the site of her own 'apostrophe'.

The conversation with Archer moves on to language, on which ground Hardy re-states the argument, defending his use of supposedly 'obsolete' Wessex words. He adds: 'I have no sympathy with the criticism which would treat English as a dead language – a thing crystallized at an arbitrarily selected stage of its existence, and bidden to forget that it has a past and deny that it has a future.... Language was made before grammar.' From ghosts to linguistic ghosts: Hardy's desire to believe in the past encompasses a refusal of mere synchronicity. Language is attached to lived experience and its inheritance rather than an analytic grammar which rejects historical analysis.

At the same time, the tendency for language to construct an autonomous world, suggested by Maudsley, could make it seem spectral to those critics in the tradition of Bunsen, who saw language in terms of a falling-away from origins.[60] In his second series of *Lectures on the Science of Language* (1863), the philologist Max Müller – whose work Hardy was at least indirectly exposed to[61] – derives the belief in ghosts from the spectre of language itself; from its abstraction and *différance*, and its power over thought. Analysing the concept of 'nothing', he points out that the term moves from a literal negativity (*ne-filum* or *nifilum*, 'not a shred') to acquiring frightening associations of presence:

> Now, what does not fall within the cognizance of our senses, and what contradicts every principle of our reasoning faculties, has no right to be expressed in language. We may use the names of material objects to express immaterial objects, if they can be rationally conceived. We can conceive, for instance, powers not within the ken of our senses, yet endowed with a material reality. We can call them *spirits*, literally breezes, though we understand perfectly well that by spirits we mean nothing else than mere breezes. We can call them *shadows* or *shades*, though we mean something very different from a mere negation of light. But a Nothing, an absolute Nothing, that is neither visible nor conceivable, nor imaginable, ought never to have found expression, ought never to have been admitted into the dictionary of rational beings.[62]

For Müller and the romantic tradition informing his highly idiosyncratic thinking, language becomes progressively more ghostly as it moves away from its material origins; or rather it carries the ghostly traces of an earlier materiality. Müller's obsessive etymologizing is designed to trace words (and myths) to that original descriptive materiality in a way which parallels Comte's insistence on the fetish as a direct response to the world rather than a theological entity. To contemplate 'nothing', *ne-filum*, a word whose origins are themselves in the conceptualization of an absence (like the Spencerian ghost), is to contemplate language as a frightening negativity, as an absolute and ungrounded system, haunting the human rather than expressing human history.

It is perhaps because of this need for a grounding or historical location of language that for Hardy language is at its most relaxedly ghostly in the discussion of dialect in his introduction to the *Select Poems of William Barnes*. As Taylor shows, the death of dialect is something Hardy often describes in Darwinian fashion; here old words are being 'obliterated' every year by education and metropolitan influences: 'The process is always the same: the word is ridiculed by the newly taught; it gets into disgrace; it is heard in holes and corners only; it dies; and, worst of all, it leaves no synonym.'[63] If the synonym here is what a death *might* leave, then the translated versions of the word, the 'glosses and paraphrases', become a ghostly afterlife, a 'sorry substitute for the full significance the original words bear'. Barnes himself is, says Hardy citing Browning, 'A ghostly cricket, creaking where a house was burned'. The final sentence of the introduction includes the hope that the poems will charm those for whom 'the dying words [are] those of an unlamented language that need leave behind it no grammar of its secrets and no key to its tomb'. Reading Barnes is a form of cryptonomy, opening the tomb, or penetrating the 'veil' which 'partly hides' the material of a dead language. Here, in the field of language, the inheritance of the past becomes a dialogue with ghosts in their places; ghosts which are historical and located, like meeting one's grandfather in a churchyard.

Coda: 'The Photograph'

This chapter has considered the way in which forms of materialism and positivism seem haunted; and how ghosts come to seem mental entities projected onto a specific material location. In one poem in *Moments of Vision*, 'The Head above the Fog', the 'ghostly head' which travels 'with spectre-speed' seems almost cinematically projected by the poet, raising the issue of technologies of reproduction. If we ask what, in the late nineteenth century, is the mode of representation that stands for positivism, the answer is obvious enough: photography, which supposedly represents a mechanical reproduction of the 'real'; which is used to index, catalogue, preserve the world described by science. The photograph represents the known, in a version which has a direct causal link with its origin. But consider this example. A man burns a photograph. It may be of a cousin he once loved; it is in any case of a woman who has randomly returned to him, as suggested by the metaphor he uses, saying she was 'long hid amid packs of years', implying the past may be laid out on a table. So in 'a casual clearance of life's arrears' he burns the image, only to find himself stung by the act, and overtaken by what can only be described as a fascinated voyeurism as the flame attacks 'the delicate bosom's defenceless round':

> Then I vented a cry of hurt, and averted my eyes;
> The spectacle was one that I could not bear,
>   To my deep and sad surprise;
> But, compelled to heed, I again looked furtivewise
> Till the flame had eaten her breasts, and mouth, and hair.
>
> 'The Photograph'

The picture has become a sharp weapon ('unsheathed from the past'), and he only has relief when it is reduced to 'the ashen ghost of the card it had figured on', to the traces of a former flame.

This is, of course, Hardy's meditation on photography and its ghostliness – a subject that has fascinated a range of twentieth-century theorists, from Kracauer to Barthes. Hardy's maturity coincided with the development of the family photograph album in the period which succeeded the daguerrotype – the so-called 'card portrait era' (1860–1900) before the development of a standardized amateur photography. This was also the era which saw that extension of the family album, the spirit photograph.[64] Spirit photographs were produced in large numbers in the period 1880–1920, in which ghostly figures training ectoplasm appear hovering in the air or behind real subjects. Such work can be seen, at the epistemological level, as a response to the newfound simultaneity enabled by the photographic 'medium': simply because different exposures at different times can produce the appearance of co-presence, spirits can appear to attest to the medium's power. The technology which enables the 'materialization' of doubles and ghosts – the term itself is revealing – is itself, conversely, a form of 'ghostliness'.[65]

It is unsurprising, then, that alongside its status as an index of the real, the photograph itself becomes ghostly; it comes to represent mourning, abstracting and estranging its subject-matter from the event of the photograph. The photograph is a token, a fetish even, which carries the trace of the body as it was; it is a keepsake like the severed lock in

'On a Discovered Curl of Hair' (or the locks of Hardy's hair which his barber later sold). The beloved's hair may have turned gray and 'gone into a caverned ark',

> Yet this one, untouched of time,
> Beams with live brown as in its prime,
> So that it seems I even could now
> Restore it to the living brow...

The sense of the removal of the signified implicit in this memorialization is exacerbated as the photograph becomes the ghost of its occasion; in a sense *its own ghost* – Hardy's 'ashen ghost' – an effect described by Eduardo Cadava:

> As its own grave, the photograph is what exceeds the photograph within the photograph. It is what remains of what passes into history. It turns on itself in order to survive, in order to withdraw into a space in which it might defer its decay, into an interior – the closed-off space of writing itself. In order for a photograph to be a photograph, it must become the tomb that writes, that harbours its own death.[66]

The photograph 'captures' Time only under the sign of 'Farewell' ('The hour itself was a ghost' writes Hardy in 'At the Word "Farewell"'). In 'The Photograph' Hardy's memento is consumed 'line by line' – a phrasing which seems puzzling until one understands that this refers most happily to the poem itself, the poem-as-photograph. 'The photograph is a cemetery', the aptly-named Cadava writes; and the cadaverous Hardy seems to respond in his cemetery-poem 'Lying Awake', figuring the coming of morning light in a churchyard as a process like the development of a photograph in the dark-room:

> You, Meadow, are white with your counterpane cover of dew,
>   I see it as if I were there;
> You, Churchyard, are lightening faint from the shade of the yew,
>   The names creeping our everywhere.

If it is considered explicitly in 'The Photograph', the medium is invoked less directly elsewhere in Hardy's texts, not least in *Moments of Vision*, with its title-poem evoking an occult optics, 'That mirror / Which makes of men a transparency'. Other poems suggest a photographic imagination, with all that implies in terms of an image bound up with life-in-death. 'The Rival' has a woman destroy an image of her early self treasured by her husband because it tells her 'he loved not the me then living, / But that past woman still'. 'The Faded Face' suggests a photograph fading with time. 'At Mayfair Lodgings' has a camera's voyeurism in imagining a house opened up for the gaze like a photographic plate ('Had the the house-front been glass, / My vision unobscuring...') – a technique also used in *The Dynasts*. 'Looking at a Picture on an Anniversary' searches for 'consciousness' and a trace of 'old-time recognition' in the portrait, the narrator fearing that only a photographic deadness may be there.[67] In 'The Son's Portrait' the narrator finds a photograph of his son, killed in the trenches, in a junk-shop after his widow has sold it; he buys it, 'And *buried it* – as 'twere he.'

And the flame which reduces the past to ashes in 'The Photograph'; which he is 'compelled to heed'? If desire is a flame in Hardy, it is a flame which consumes, which produces ashes rather than a stable image; it is associated with phantasmagoria and loss – with the scene re-enacted in the flames in 'The Flirt's Tragedy' and 'Surview'. As in Carlyle's discussion of the transience of human existence in the 'Natural Supernaturalism' section of *Sartor Resartus*, 'Force and Fire' are what mark the traces of a human life, rather than anything more solid. Here again the most material of mediums seems to turn into its opposite: that which is indexical and located lending itself to haunting and dematerialization. But that, in a variety of contexts, is the story which has been told in this chapter.

3
The Child in Time

> *Shall I sing, dance around around around,*
>   *When phantoms call the tune!*
>   Hardy, 'Song to an Old Burden'

> *And where is truth? On tombs? for such to thee*
> *Has been my heart – and thy dead memory*
> *Has lain from childhood, many a changeful year,*
> *Unchangingly preserved and buried there.*
>   Shelley, 'Fragment: The Sepulchre of Memory'

Thomas Hardy's poetry, like his life, is full of secrets: occasions not specified, biographical identifications which cannot readily be made, lacunae left to us as the residue of those bonfires at Max Gate from 1918 on, in which he and then his second wife Florence destroyed early diaries, letters, drafts, stirring the ashes of the fire to ensure that no fragment remained to contradict the picture given in his disguised autobiography. Or perhaps we are dealing with ancestral secrets never committed to paper, dying with the memories of his tight-lipped and childless siblings. That secrecy, or its possibility, is thematized regularly in the poetry; a late poem, 'The Single Witness', even has a protagonist willing to kill to preserve a family secret, and Hardy's final poems in the mode of the *envoi* contain repeated references to what he will take with him to the grave.

The movement between apparent confession and withdrawal of context is typical of Hardy's poetry, and is close in structure to his description of the freedoms offered by the lyric mode – the declaration in the *Life* that 'Generally, speaking, there is more autobiography in a hundred lines of Mr. Hardy's poetry than in all the novels' (*LY* 196) co-existing with repeated warnings in his prefaces that his poems are 'fancies' not to be confused with 'fact', so that biographical inferences are both licensed and obstructed. The result is a sense that the author is at once present and absent, both the source of affect in the poetry and, ostensibly, simply a ventriloquizer of 'seemings'. There is, accordingly, a necessary obscurity, a gap in meaning which is constantly presented to the reader of Hardy's poetry, and which is structural rather than simply involving a poverty of information. Some of his poems are so deeply obscure that they appear to be about nothing, signalling an absence which none the less generates poetry and subsequent interpretation. A good example is the inaptly named 'An Experience', a poem which self-consciously describes anything *but* the nature of the experience which is supposedly its subject; which defines it almost entirely in terms of negatives – it was not 'In anything that was said, / In anything that was done' – and concludes with a declaration that it was something that the speaker 'Was never to forget', still with no obvious objective correlative for the reader.

This chapter offers an account of the notion of the secret in Hardy from a number of perspectives: theoretical, interpretive, and (in a limited sense) biographical. In order to provide a framework for my analysis, I will begin with the work of psychoanalysts Nicholas Abraham and Maria Torok.[1] From the 1960s, Abraham and Torok began to offer a reinterpretation of Freudian practice focused less on childhood sexuality, repression and conversion than on the way in which the expanding self encounters and deals with traumatic events and losses, in terms of either the subject's own experience or that of others. The terms *introjection* and *incorporation* are central to their work, the former designating a 'healthy' encounter with the world, broadening the ego; the latter involving a trauma which is simply absorbed into the self or body as a foreign presence. Focusing on the mechanism of incorporation, they produce a psychic topography which includes the *crypt* – the site of a 'preservative repression'; of an incorporation which, in contrast to the dynamic repression of neurosis, cannot (in theory – this is a contentious proposition[2]) be accessed indirectly or expressed via such mechanisms as projection and denial; which is cloaked in a silence that disrupts the possibility of linguistic expression itself. Typically, the crypt is associated with mourning, with the incorporation of a lost object.

A related, and arguably more useful concept is that of trans-generational haunting, articulated via the notion of the 'phantom'. As Torok defines it, the 'phantom' is a formation in the dynamic unconscious that is found there not because of the subject's own repression but on account *of a direct empathy with the unconscious or the rejected psychic matter of a parental object*. Consequently, the phantom is not at all the product of the subject's self-creation by means of the interplay between repressions and introjections. The phantom is alien to the subject who harbors it. Moreover, the diverse manifestations of the phantom, which we call *haunting*, are not directly related to instinctual life and are not to be confused with the return of the repressed.[3]

These are 'family secrets', relating to parents or other love-objects, or to those in previous generations, and passed down as an area of the psyche which is interdicted. The phantom typically appears not in displaced symptoms, but in imaginings which seem to come from outside the self, which are 'gratuitous' (as in phobias or obsessive behaviour) or 'ventriloquized'. Psychology here moves closer to one of its suppressed origins in spiritualism; in the nineteenth-century psychologizing of the uncanny. As Nicholas Rand comments, Abraham and Torok are 'primarily concerned with converting obstructions into guides to understanding...ways in which signification can be conjectured despite its apparent absence'.[4]

It is also important to note that Abraham and Torok first encounter the phantom as an effect in the *analyst*, that is as something already transferred to another person who listens and interprets.[5] To study the phantom, then, may also be to study its effect as a symptomatic structure in others – potentially on anyone who forms an affectual link with the analysand. It is to read with an attention to slippages involving the incorporation of another: the 'I' of the patient's story, Torok suggests, often conceals another, in a movement like that of the author's into a displaced first-person, an 'I' which is disavowed, ghostly, and which signals a removal of affect in the self – since the affect is another's.

Cryptonomy as practised by Abraham and Torok can seem, to the reader outside a tradition in which analytic practice might provide its own justifications, a rather arbitrary search for linguistic clues.[6] Neither does one wish to retrospectively psychoanalyse Hardy. But the strength of their work is that it allows us to conceptualize material which is unspoken and unspeakable, and to conceive that material as part of a broader family history, with all the economic and even political vicissitudes that involves. As Esther Rankin comments, 'reconstituting an unspoken trauma does not imply inventing a false, fantasized past history for a character but rather understanding that the text calls upon the reader to expand its apparent parameters to include invisible scenarios'. She adds, however, that 'although predating the events of the text, these unelaborated dramas have no reality outside the limits of the text. Such limits, however, have to be construed as extending beyond their readily available borders.'[7] The drive beyond the text, with a fictionality both disavowed and partially admitted within this psychoanalytic tradition, is complicated, as suggested above, by the possibility of incorporation on the part of the reader, involving a carrying of the phantom into yet another psyche – a story of Hardy's readers told in one part of this chapter.

'Family Portraits': haunting pain

There are a number of features of Hardy's poetry which suggest less an analysis in the terms offered by Abraham and Torok than a convergence of terminology: a fascination with intergenerational haunting and areas of psychic resistance, with phantoms and secrets. Hardy offers a startlingly self-conscious version of the crypt in his late poem 'Family Portraits' (published in 1924, and then in a substantially revised version near the end of *Winter Words* in 1928).[8] The last of the great phantasmagoric series including 'The Pedigree' and 'The Chosen', with its description of three 'picture-drawn' people stepping from the frame, provides another version of the love-triangle which Hardy had recently explored in *The Famous Tragedy of the Queen of Cornwall*.[9] The three give their names – though to the poem's speaker ('Full well though I knew') rather than to the readers, then,

> They set about acting some drama, obscure,
>   The women and he,
> With puppet-like movements of mute strange allure;
> Yea, set about acting some drama, obscure,
> Till I saw 'twas their own lifetime's tragic amour,
>   Whose course begot me;
>
> Yea – a mystery, ancestral, long hid from my reach
>   In the perished years past,
> That had mounted to dark doings each against each
> In those ancestors' days, and long hid from my reach;
> Which their restless enghostings, it seemed, were to teach
>   Me in full, at this last.

> But fear fell upon me like frost, of some hurt
>   If they entered anew
> On the orbits they smartly had swept when expert
> In the law-lacking passions of life, – of some hurt
> To their souls – and thus mine – which I fain would avert;
>   So, in sweat cold as dew,
>
> 'Why wake up all this?' I cried out. 'Now, so late!
>   Let old ghosts be laid!'
> And they stiffened, drew back to their frames and numb state,
> Gibbering: 'Thus are your own ways to shape, know too late!'
> Then I grieved that I'd not had the courage to wait
>   And see the play played.
>
> I have grieved ever since: to have balked future pain,
>   My blood's tendance foreknown,
> Had been triumph. Nights long stretched awake I have lain
> Perplexed in endeavours to balk future pain
> By uncovering the drift of their drama. In vain,
>   Though therein lay my own.

The 'mystery' here is encoded both as organic inheritance ('blood's tendance') and as an original 'drama'; both as hurting the speaker via a direct transference ('some hurt / To their souls – and thus mine') and as producing a mirroring repetition in his actions. Causation is uncertain; indeed, in the earlier version of the poem the stanza beginning 'Why wake up all this' *precedes* the third stanza above, referring to the 'orbits' of the actors, and the later phrase 'which I fain would avert' replaces an earlier 'but I found them inert', shifting the question of causality radically from the past to the present of the speaker. Moreover, while in the 1924 version the poet is reactive, asking 'Could it have hurt [to have watched?]', in the 1928 version he is fearful and pre-emptive, as if slowly admitting that the blame was in fact his, and that the hurt is bound up with a willed failure to watch and see the truth. This is close to the mechanism of disavowal or repudiation as described by Freud and Lacan: the narrator seems *both* to already know the story ('full well though I knew') and to refuse to know it ('Why wake up all this?').[10] He seems to see that the story *has* tragically predicted his life ('therein lay my own'), but also suggests that the mystery remains intact, unopened, as does the question of the future.

The unstated and deeply compulsive material of this 'drama' is bounded, then, by what is, formally, a refusal to remember. The poem exists in the space of what Abraham and Torok call incorporation, expressed in the ventriloquism, puppet-drama, and phobic avoidance which they see as characteristic of the phantom, the 'mute' and 'numb' state of both the actors and speaker suggesting – but never fully expressing – trauma. The phantom is incorporated as a rigid and frozen foreign object in the psyche, the marker-stone of a secret (becoming-stone is a state traced in Hardy's reading and his poetry, from his marking of lines in Byron's 'The Prisoner of Chillon', 'Among the stones I stood a stone / And was scarce conscious of what I wist', to the late poem 'A Wish for Unconsciousness': 'If I could but abide / As a tablet on a wall').[11] Something strikes the speaker dumb, stiffening and freezing, obscuring the story or origins; in both 'The Pedigree' and 'Family Portraits' the word 'drift' punningly suggests a cloud-hidden primal scene, a drift which we cannot quite *get*.[12] For Abraham and Torok the material of the crypt or phantom cannot be represented directly, but can appear as an 'undecipherable fetish'. The interdicted 'silent word' is, they comment, or can appear as, such an image as Hardy's poem presents: their phrase is 'love disguised and dressed up in a "painting"'.[13]

I am not suggesting that 'Family Portraits' can be directly applied to Hardy's life (what is there to apply?), but rather that it offers an account of what it is like to read Hardy, or to have to read *into* Hardy's poetry. We are presented with various repeated traumatic scenes which invite interpretation, which offer to solve the mystery, but we also face a form of psychic censorship which exiles reading to a deferred and subjunctive mood (the 'had been triumph' which signals an unachieved meaning). Meaning is both present and absent, both figured and declared to reside in an undeclarable literalness. This is a structure we find throughout Hardy's verse, nicely defined by the two mirrored quatrains of 'The Wound':

> I climbed to the crest,
>   And, fog-festooned,
> The sun lay west
>   Like a crimson wound:
>
> Like that wound of mine
>   Of which none knew,
> For I'd given no sign
>   That it pierced me through.

Here the 'sign' is both everywhere and nowhere to be seen; the 'wound' is first bodily, and deployed (to signal redness) in a simile in which its visibility is the point; but then becomes a vehicle in a strangely unrelated simile in which the invisibility of a psychic wound is signalled. It is gestured at in the demonstrative pronoun ('*that* wound'), but only specified in a doubly displaced form: a sunset *like* a wound, a (physical) wound like 'that' (psychic) wound. Trauma is both revealed and hidden in this language. Many of Hardy's poems are encoded in this way, so that, to take an example almost at random, anyone who has read deeply in Hardy can immediately recognize in his cryptic poem 'Where Three Roads Joined' a vocabulary of terms shared with other poems – life laughing onwards; a scene of blankness; muteness in its witnesses; a 'spectre-beridden' place; the void of a 'plumbless well' down which hopes and happiness roll; a dwelling on memory and loss – so that the poem is perfectly readable; even though the details of what it refers to are absent, the reader understands the structure of that absence.

At this point, however, I want to move away from the metapsychology of the phantom (though the subject will remain implicit) to a more specific set of concerns raised by 'Family Portraits', relating to the issues of wounding and pain, and ultimately the notion – not fully articulated in this poem, but circulating throughout Hardy's work – of childhood trauma. For all that 'Family Portraits' describes the impossibility of fully representing its own subject-matter, it is possible to follow threads and clues which extend into Hardy's other texts. One such clue is the repeated phrase in the final stanza, 'balk future pain' – a phrase Hardy added as he re-wrote the poem, replacing 'heal my own pain'. *Pain* is an interesting issue, not only because of the metaphorical link to the idea of psychic wounding or trauma which we have already seen in 'The Wound', but more generally because in the nineteenth century physical pain become an increasingly problematic issue for progressive and Darwinian traditions.[14] In what follows, we will move rather circuitously from a general consideration of the topic back to the issue of childhood pain.

With the waning of religious interpretations of pain (pain as punishment, as Fall), and the possibility of its elimination in many situations as a result of advances in medicine and humanitarian action, a debate on its meaning ensued; a debate which broadened to take in issues such as vivisection, the subject of a Royal Commission in 1875–6 (cruelty to animals is of course a recurrent concern in Hardy's writings).[15] Darwin was a witness in the hearings of the Royal Commission. His interest in the treatment of animals, as one commentator notes, 'effected a powerful conjunction between the assault on pain and the accomplishment of [his] life-work'.[16] But from the evolutionary point of view, the model in which pain was simply the stimulus for action, as in putting the hand in a fire, seemed to fail to account for persistent forms of pain (particularly those with no apparent trauma). In *The Expression of Emotion in Man and the Animals*, Darwin includes pain in his discussion of the stronger emotions, borrowing Herbert Spencer's economic argument that pain produces an 'overflow of nerve-force' which '*must* expend itself in some direction', taking over successive systems of muscles, beginning with those closest to the seat of pain and continuing with the most-used (facial muscles, speech). This argument explains the expression of pain in terms of discharge. But Darwin has trouble uniting this view with that of the *utility* of pain, and indeed the reference to 'nerve-force' suggests the way in which the intensity of pain in humans is a special consideration. For T. H. Huxley, that intensity of human pain was an effect of evolutionary advances which placed consciousness increasingly in tension with the rest of nature. Its excessive nature, the sense that in evolutionary terms its intensity hardly seems necessary (even if it can sometimes be interpreted as a signal of bodily disruption or danger), meant that it seemed like a reminder of a kind of thought which inheres in the body – the complement, Elaine Scarry has recently argued, of imaginative activity which projects the self outwards into other objects.[17] Thinking on the evolutionary redundancy of pain was to culminate in the 1930s in Gerald Stanley Heard's *Pain, Sex and Time*. His book begins with a simple question: is human evolution continuing, and are there untapped human potentials we have not exploited? His answer is a qualified 'yes': the potential is there, but such energies are at the moment wasted. The proof is in the pain: for Heard – as for the early Freud of the *Project for a Scientific Psychology* – pain is waste psychic energy which has not been tapped (thus, the mind can exclude pain if it is concentrating hard on other things). The aim of existence is 'to be conscious in a way which uses up the energy which was leaking and discharging in pain'.[18]

Hardy attacked philosophical attempts to explain away pain in a note on Hegel, in 1886, noting that the argument that 'real pain is compatible with formal pleasure – that the ideal is all, etc.' does not offer much consolation to those in pain (*EL* 234). Schopenhauer, in his powerful essay on 'The Vanity and Suffering of Life', had attacked the Hegelian subordination of individual pain to human destiny in a similar way. For

Schopenhauer pain is a 'positive' force in the neutral sense that its presence outweighs all other factors, while well-being is only strongly defined when it is succeeded by other states: 'We feel pain, but not painlessness; we feel care, not the absence of care; fear, but not security... for only pain and want can be felt positively, and therefore announce themselves; well-being, on the other hand, is merely negative.'[19] Pain binds the individual intensely to a particular moment (in contrast to the Hegelian dialectic, which lifts us towards transcendence), representing the predicament of consciousness in the world, a state of 'debt'.

Hardy was also undoubtedly influenced by John Stuart Mill's famous indictment of the indifference and malevolence of Nature in the first of the *Three Essays on Religion*; it is echoed in his response to a 1902 review of Maeterlinck's *Apology for Nature*:

> Pain has been, and pain is: no new sort of morals in Nature can remove pain from the past and make it pleasure for those who are its infallible estimators, the bearers thereof. And no injustice, however slight, can be atoned for by her future generosity, however ample, so long as we consider Nature to be, or to stand for, unlimited power. (*LY* 97)

The same harsh doctrine is expounded in a letter attacking Henri Bergson in 1915. Writing to Caleb Saleeby, who had sent him a copy of *Creative Evolution*, Hardy denounces Bergson's mixture of Vitalism and materialism:

> the most fatal objection to his view of creation *plus* propulsion seems to me to lie in the existence of pain. If nature were creative she would have created painlessness, or be in process of creating it – pain being the first thing we instinctively fly from. If on the other hand we cannot introduce into life what is not already there, and are bound to mere recombination of old materials, the persistence of pain is intelligible. (*LY* 273)

Pain, here, is the mark of 'mechanism', of animal responses which cannot be eradicated by an act of will, and ultimately, of a view of the world which sees it determined by germ-plasm rather than *élan vital*. In both the passages above it is the residue of the past which is linked to pain – an observation which makes 'balk[ing] future pain' an impossibility. Having denounced Bergson for his Dualism, Hardy continues, in a passage examined in the previous chapter: 'You must not think me a hard-hearted rationalist for all this. Half my time (particularly when I write verse) I believe – in the modern use of the word – not only in things that Bergson does, but in spectres, mysterious voices, intuitions, omens, dreams, haunted places, etc., etc.' (*LY* 271–2). Belief in some provisional 'modern sense' would ultimately involve a refusal to confront the difficulty of positions which cannot be reconciled. If we put these passages together, then it is apparent that pain and the spectral are close together in Hardy's mind – not as cognate, since pain must be believed in whereas spectres are simply assented to, and any notion of the life-force as having an immaterial existence is ruled out. Rather, pain and the spectral are connected in that both represent evolutionary traces of an earlier existence; they act as the human residue of a past which must, strictly, be interpreted in *material* terms, but which nevertheless represents an ineradicable haunting. Pain is ghostly, a haunting persistence of 'old materials'; or of the material itself in its historicity.

Correspondingly, any rationalist attempts to eradicate pain are dubious – as in the comic episode in Hardy's *The Hand of Ethelberta* in which the heroine attempts to decide her course of action using Mill's *Utilitarianism*, reading there that 'The ultimate end...is an existence exempt as far as possible from pain, and as rich as possible in enjoyments, both in point of quantity and quality.'[20] Interestingly, Mill adds that the standard here is 'not the agent's own happiness but that of all concerned', and Ethelberta notes carefully that 'all concerned' normally refers to a small family circle – initiating her self-sacrifice in the name of her siblings. The self may be sacrificed to the family, just as in Hardy's genealogical poems the 'line' may render the individual subject ghostly. Tess O'Toole notes (and she is thinking of *Tess of the D'Urbervilles*) the way in which for Hardy 'the genetic product appears not as an example of rejuvenation but as a crypt inhabited by the relics of those long dead', producing 'the genetic legatee as a kind of ghost or specter'[21] – a ghost inhabiting the site of an ancient passion.

If pain is a register of the spectralized past, the formula 'to balk future pain' which began this discussion is also interesting for the word *balk*. The noun 'balk' is, the *Oxford English Dictionary* suggests, descended from a root meaning 'bar'; its oldest and later dialect meanings refer to ridges or unploughed areas separating different plots. Some of the meanings of the verb are connected, though 'to balk' also has the meaning of shunning a place, hesitating (as with a horse balking at a jump), as well as the common transitive meaning of 'frustrating' or 'placing an obstacle before'. 'Balk' thus has some of the complexity of Freud's antithetical words: it is to mark out ownership by creating a barrier, but also a refusal to cross a barrier. What is enclosed is this a space both shunned and guarded – the space of the *phantom*. Indeed, the word 'balk' is explicitly linked to a sexual secret in 'A Sunday Morning Tragedy', Hardy's controversial poem on abortion: the herb supplied by a shepherd is meant to 'balk ill-motherings' in ewes. Here 'balking' is preventative abortion, the shunning of a life which will prove traumatic. As in Schopenhauer, the issue of pain finds its ultimate focus in the question of being born: Schopenhauer cites Lessing's admiration of his son's understanding, when he refused to be born and 'had to be forcibly brought into [life] with the forceps, but was scarely there when he hurried away from it again'. Hardy's 'To an Unborn Pauper Child', with its stress on the triumph of pain over pleasure, reads like a verse commentary on this essay.[22] The issue of the lost, aborted or mis-placed child leads us to a more developed cryptonomy in Hardy. First, however, an excursis into an interesting episode in critical history, and what we might call the cryptonomy of reception.

Randy's hand, or the lost son

> Free among the dead, like unto them that are wounded, and lie in the grave: who are out of remembrance, and are cut away from thy hand'.
>
> Psalm 88: 5, as marked by Hardy[23]

> *Yet It may wake and understand*
> *Ere Earth unshape, know all things, and*
> *With knowledge use a painless hand,*
>   *A painless hand!*
>
> Chorus of the Pities, conclusion to *The Dynasts*, Part Second

In the late 1960s the world of Hardy studies was disturbed by the claims of Lois Deacon, an 'amateur' scholar from Dorchester, that she had uncovered the greatest mystery of Hardy's life: the existence of a child called 'Randy' (Randolph or Randall), fathered in an affair with his cousin Tryphena Sparks and raised by Tryphena's older sister Rebecca. 'Hardy's marriages were childless', as Deacon rather bathetically notes in the book which she co-authored with Terry Coleman, *Providence and Mr Hardy* (1966), 'but he was probably not altogether without issue.'[24] Her claims were based largely on an identification of a photograph of a boy in a family album, made by Tryphena's daughter, Eleanor Bromell, near death at the age of eighty-six. This, for Deacon, was supported by 'internal' evidence in the form of readings of a number of poems said to deal with the affair and illegitimacy ('To an Orphan Child', 'The Place on the Map' and others), as well as other details like initials in family albums, lacunae in Hardy's autobiography and omissions in the genealogy which he drew up. The aim of *Providence and Mr Hardy* is to rescue Tryphena from her 'suppressed' status, and reveal Randy to the world.

Nothing if not an industrious reader, Deacon also 'discovered' further scandal in the tangled skein of Hardy family history. She suggested that Tryphena was not in fact the daughter of her aging parents (her mother Maria, Hardy's aunt, was a supposedly improbable forty-six when she was born), but was in fact the illegitimate issue of her older sister Rebecca and Rebecca's employer. And – a final twist – Deacon more cautiously suggested that Tryphena and Hardy may have been more than just cousins, and adduces evidence that Rebecca was in fact the early illegitimate offspring of Hardy's mother Jemima (née Hand), subsequently passed off as the child of her elder sister Maria, already married to James Sparks (such transferences were a common rural practice, and are described in Hardy's 'A Hurried Meeting'). This makes Tryphena Hardy's niece – a fact which Hardy was unaware of at the time of their romance, Deacon proposes, but which he subsequently learnt, and which works its way into the Shelleyan theme of near-incest in his late novels. 'Randy' would thus be the issue of a series of tangled illegitimacies and transferences across generations and between sisters.

Deacon's work has been the object of some derision amongst Hardy's subsequent biographers – perhaps understandably, since she can offer no real proof of Randy's existence (there are no written records relating either to his supposed birth in 1868 or death sometime before 1917), and instead engages in highly selective and speculative biographical readings of poems. One Hardy scholar, F. R. Southerington, did support her in 1968, and one or two reviewers thought the story likely enough.[25] Hardy's most recent biographer, Martin Seymour-Smith, is more charitable in describing her book as 'a speculative novel of what, just possibly, might have been'.[26] But the important question here is perhaps less 'Is the story true?' than 'What supports and generates such narratives?' Why is the story so persuasive as a 'speculative novel'? For Deacon is not the only example of a reader who concretizes phantoms in biography: if she obligingly supplies a child to deal with Hardy's childlessness, the sober-minded biographer Michael Millgate suggests that

Hardy might have been impotent – a suggestion vigorously contested by Seymour-Smith, but illustrative of more than simply biological speculation since it attempts once again to identify a defining area of 'deadness' in Hardy, a phantom presence. Deacon's symptomatic reading responds, that is, to a real trauma in Hardy, a trauma which is inevitably reproduced in the stories told by his readers. Deacon's comment in an earlier pamphlet suggests her own involvement in a drama of veiling and unveiling, a play of desire and identification: 'What most Hardy biographers have not perceived is that although Hardy frequently draws a discreet veil over the truth, he invariably leaves gaps and rents in the veil through which he later sheds a powerful and revealing light.'[27] Through these gaps Tryphena emerges as 'the dark lady of the lyrics', the key to Hardy's poetry of non-specification.[28]

One key to Randy – though one which might too easily represent a premature acceptance of a deconstructive line – involves seeing him as a linguistic ghost, a retracing of Hardy's texts and accounts of his life. As Southerington reports, Eleanor Bromell 'described [Randy] as "delicate", "frail", older than herself, fond of birds, reading poetry, and of drawing'; she also claimed that he was an architect. All these were, of course, Hardy's own attributes, suggesting that one unstated case for 'Randy' – unstated because formal, and perhaps also because it suggests a slippage in Mrs Bromell's memory – seems to be a homology between father and proposed son, another intergenerational mapping. A similar sense of assimilation is present in Deacon's stress on the *singularity* of Tryphena. If Hardy's biographers note that he may have had liaisons with many women in the period around 1868 (including Tryphena) and that he identified many women as the model of Tess, Deacon wishes to make Tryphena the great Ur-romance of his life, incorporating even Emma Hardy's body: 'Poor Emma Lavinia! She lent her very eyes and hair, her riding-habit and her Cornish home of St. Juniot's for the effective disguising of the dark-haired Dorset Tryphena in *A Pair of Blue Eyes*.' Tryphena multiplies within his texts. When Tess is described as younger than she looks, Deacon notes that Tryphena had been similarly accused when she applied for the job of headmistress in Plymouth. But a footnote adds that a parallel phrase ('looked more womanly than she really was') is applied to Geraldine in *An Indiscretion*.[29] Here, the very conventionality of the phrase is evidence of its application to a specific 'real' context. In a similar way, Hardy's texts multiply evidence in the world: a footnote remarks that 'it is curious that' a church in Brixton, only one and a quarter miles from where Tryphena taught, 'should be called St. Jude', and that a house in Topsham, 100 yards from where she lived, 'should be called "St. Jude's Cottage"'. The 'should' here signals a textual agency; 'a pattern emerges', Deacon and Coleman note, even as they weave it.[30]

Such 'textual' readings co-exist with a desire to find a 'real' Randy, a body behind the text (Abraham and Torok comment that 'the analyst-judge also acts as a morphologist: they have to reconstruct the event from a few scattered bodily fragments').[31] For Deacon the reality of the body is supplied above all by the two photographs which she identifies as being Randy. But one interesting detail in the story of 'Randy' concerns a missing part of the body, what we could call a 'phantom' limb. Mrs Bromell made repeated reference to an injury to his right hand, attributed to two different causes (a cycling accident, a dog). This is a detail both Deacon and Southerington fuss over without attempting to do more than link it indexically to the boy in the photograph – the latter eliciting opinions from a medical expert that the boy in the photograph might conceivably be missing fingers. It is as if in providing another detail of identity – there was a boy, his hand was hurt – it acts as a symbol of a larger absence.[32] But we might also see that loss as inscribed within the story itself: 'Hand' is Jemima Hardy's 'maiden' name – the name she had when, Deacon suggests, she bore the illegitimate Rebecca, Randy's alleged grandmother (an earlier name in what Hardy called his 'beclouded' maternal line, incidentally, was Childs or Childses, *EL* 7). The wounded hand thus acts as stigmata, marking the ancestral mystery rather than 'proof' of it; it points to the wronged woman, and perhaps also the absent father, the man who makes his living by his pen. Like Oedipus's swollen-footedness (*oideo-pous*), a wound signals incest, a maiming and a secret naming (Oedipus is also etymologically *oi-dipous*, Simon Goldhill points out: 'alas, two-footed', as if he were himself the answer to his own riddle[33]). Randy as riddle; Randy as handy; Randy as the name for desire; 'Randy' as only a stroke away from being an anagram for 'Hardy' – Deacon's story of incest and endogamy itself seems to generate tricks and embodied clues.

Here we might pick up a clue that Deacon misses, and continue with her supplementary story using a poem which features both a bastard child and a missing hand, 'Panthera'. Panthera is a veteran Centurion who still feels twinges in 'the hand he had lost, shorn by barbarian steel'. This is the 'phantom limb' which emerged as a focus in nineteenth-century neurological work, particularly in Weir Mitchell's writings on American Civil War victims – an entity which suggests the virtuality of the body, its being coordinated by an image of phantasmic unity, a body-image. The tale is told by an old soldier, who himself doubts the story Panthera told him years earlier, 'His mind at last being stressed by ails and age: – / Yet his good faith thereon I well could wage.' The speaker had wished for offspring, even if illegitimate, to continue his line, and Panthera had warned him off it with an account of his own Palestinian love-child, fathered during an idyllic stop-over in Nazareth over thirty years earlier, and only re-encountered at the point where the son is being crucified for sedition at Golgotha. Panthera recognizes the weeping mother, but does not care to 'close the silence of so wide a time'. The narrator casts doubt on the story, which Panthera seems to *want* to believe, despite acknowledging 'vagueness of identity' in this case.

This is the shockingly apocryphal Ur-tale of Christ, the child of mysterious origin (for volume publication Hardy was careful to supply a headnote detailing a number of sources for the legend, as if wishing to disclaim it as his 'issue').[34] The relationship to the canonical text is important here: the story is told by a would-be father who can only watch at the point where the son is, like the limb, cut away from him and assigned an afterlife in an entirely separate text with a different story, which both covers and interdicts – balks – the apocryphal account. This might be read, in Deacon's manner, as simply an allegory of the story of Randy. But more obviously, it signals the questions of paternity and narrative which surround the issue of textual authority itself: who authors this account, the Centurion with the missing hand and the secret, or the later teller who doubts the story? How does it relate to the text of the Gospels, ostensibly written by the hand of God? 'Panthera' is a poem on the mysteries of identity within an order which is double-coded: the centurion recognizes the 'ardent blood' of Christ as his own only through the mother and his memories of a sexual idyll, but she is none the less decked in the symbolic insignia of the Virgin (blue cloak) rather than simply being depicted naturalistically. The story supplies a naturalistic account of the paternity of Christ, but none the less depends for its force – and for an explanation of these events – on the Christian world-view.

As in 'Family Portraits' we can attempt to press a little further, to riddle the language of the poem. It is 'cynic Time', the narrator tells us, which maims Panthera and breaks his spirit. 'Cynic' is a word Hardy uses in 'The Pedigree' to mark the twistings of a genealogy, its tendency to go awry: the 'cynic face' and 'cynic twist of the page' suggest the palsy known as a cynic spasm, a deformation of the self created in its antecedents, rather than cynicism in the philosophical sense. Panthera suggests that the lesson of the story is 'That when you talk of offspring as sheer joy / So trustingly, you blink contingencies,' adding that 'He who goes fathering / Gives frightful hostages to hazardry!' 'Blink' is used in its older meaning of flinching from something, shutting one's eyes to it: that is, balking [at] future pain. We can also ask what the Centurion hopes of his child – and it is here that Hardy's pessimism intersects most forcibly with Christianity. If he, the 'ardent soldier', shares his 'ardent blood' with Christ, then he expects nothing of the future, no flame to be kindled. The root of the word 'ardent' is *ardere*, to burn, a root Hardy turns to in 'A Commonplace Day'. There he writes, almost tautologically, of 'that enkindling ardency from whose maturer glows / The world's amendment flows', before noting that it 'has missed its hope to be / Embodied on the earth'. Ardency or enkindling passion is, then, that hope for a meaning to history which is incarnated in Christ (in 'Panthera') but also frustrated, 'benumbed at birth' ('A Commonplace Day'); it is what dies with the day which 'is turning ghost', and which is figured forth in the embers of the fire which Hardy rakes. Compare the following exchange recorded by Ernest Brennecke in his 1925 biography. Visiting Max Gate, he had suggested that Hardy was an 'ardent meliorist'. Hardy replied: 'I am not.... And really, you must never call me "ardent" about anything. I am not. I am as indifferent as I find it possible to be. I wish you success, however. Good-day.' Here, 'ardency' is reduced to a suppressed trace; the word is cancelled.[35] The disruption of Judeo-Christian history described in 'Panthera' is thus the reducing of a flame (perhaps even the Pentecostal flame) to ashes, reducing history to a succession of dead days, to a denatured genealogy carried in Hardy's story of the lost child and the wounded hand.

Interestingly, the hypothetical existence of a 'hidden' story of Christ has been linked to Abraham and Torok's thinking by Nicholas Royle in a recent review article taking in the startling combination of translations of Derrida's *Spectres of Marx* and *The Nag Hammadi Library* of Coptic Gnostic texts.[36] Royle argues that these early Gnostic texts 'phantomize' our reading of the Gospels, and playfully proposes his own phantom text, a non-existent and at best fragmentary story he describes as 'ashes in the wind'. In this phantom text, Jesus speaks to Mary Magdalene after his crucifixion, explaining that he was not the one who was crucified; he had been replaced by a 'stranger' – initiating, for Royle, a dissolution of Christianity's haunted onto-theology into a theology of the lost other. This kind of experiment in deconstructive Christianity (including the figure of the 'real' Christ who survives the crucifixion, perplexed by his cult) was common enough in the late nineteenth century, and seems to find echoes in late twentieth-century theory.

Hardy's fiction contains a striking example of haunting akin to that which we have seen in 'Panthera' and in the Deacon case – one of many examples of lost or displaced children in his prose, most famously the self-cancelling children of *Jude the Obscure*. In her description of the 'cancelled words' in *Far from the Madding Crowd*, Rosemarie Morgan describes the material which Hardy revised or removed under pressure from his cautious editor Leslie Stephen as the book was serialized in the *Cornhill Magazine*. Morgan tells a story of suppression and designification. In the original drafts, Fanny dies with Troy's illegitimate and stillborn baby in her arms, and Bathsheba, now secretly married to Troy, sadly and compassionately inspects mother and baby in their coffin. Leslie Stephen was keen to omit the baby, but Hardy left it in – only, however, as a trace, present as the two words on Fanny's coffin which Gabriel Oak erases, 'and child'. The 'massive cancellations' Hardy did agree to make, Morgan shows, 'have the effect of rendering the stillborn infant entirely invisible' – even, seemingly, to Bathsheba; and further revisions (and one spectacular reversal) shift Bathsheba from a position of empathy with Fanny to something closer to rivalry.[37] The result is to produce a version of Bathsheba who is herself truncated and haunted by the phantom of the child, reduced to a barely-comprehensible passivity and pitifulness. Her motivations have, in the *Cornhill*, to be understood *without* the child, whose trace is nevertheless there (and which was only very partially restored when Hardy revised the book again for volume publication).

Two of Morgan's comments are of further interest here: first, that Bathsheba was 'in his original conception of things, as vivid, as immediate, and as palpably real as his own flesh and blood', but is here reduced to being an 'echo' of that reality; and secondly, that Hardy spoke of censorship as 'paralysing'. Here we have a model for transgression, censorship, and the effect of that censorship on the subject, enacted both in the novel and in Hardy's encounter with social constraint. 'Cancelled words' signal the presence of the crypt (Morgan's title is taken from the volume of verse the secretive heroine publishes in *The Hand of Ethelberta* – their publication under a pseudonym again concealing origins). The crypt in turn opens into the space of reading – the space of Deacon's reading, but that, too, of the reader of *Far from the Madding Crowd*, and of all our reading.

What Deacon's excavations and extrapolations suggest is both the intensity with which Hardy's texts *do* generate readings in terms of phantasmic structures, absences and blockages, and at the same time the hazards of such interpretation. Perhaps the most puzzling aspect of her case is that amidst the welter of 'evidence' which she extracts from various poems in elucidating Hardy's allegedly tangled genealogy, she never cites the two poems which most directly and self-consciously address the issue of the 'dark doings' of genealogy: 'The Pedigree' and 'Family Portraits'. Where poems like 'The Place on the Map' can be mined for displaced clues, these poems meditate on the space of the secret itself.

'A deed back in time'

Where else might we pursue Hardy's ghosts? His family's 'authentic' ghost story, recounted to William Archer, also concerns a lost child. His mother dreamed that a sick friend came to her in the night, just at the time that, some distance away, the friend was dying. The woman appeared with her young child in her arms, 'but the odd thing was that, while she was sinking, she continually expressed a wish that my mother should take charge of the child'.[38] Like the child attributed to Jemima Hardy in Deacon's account, it is offered to another, but its final location is uncertain – no mention is made of its subsequent fate. Phantom presence, orphan, supplement; in the story it never moves beyond spectral status.

This family story gestures towards the *general* instablity of the child in Hardy's texts, an instability which Deacon's account presents in a manageable way, making Little Father Time and other 'lost' children versions of Randy. Hardy often marked poems about dead or bereft children in his reading.[39] The list of possible disruptions of childhood in his own poetry is immense, including illegitimacy; regret at lost children ('The Dead Bastard'); children disowned by their fathers ('The Supplanter'); a woman killed defending a child not her own ('By the Barrows'); a dead child being christened ('Royal Sponsors'); a woman 'giving' her husband to a woman with whom he has a child ('A Wife and Another') or wishing to die so that another woman can have her husband-to-be and child ('The Wedding Morning'); a woman seeking a more vigorous father for her child; and a poem whose speaker wishes that a child whose mother has died might reincarnate her ('To a Motherless Child'). Children may haunt: 'The Bird-Catcher's Boy' describes a child who leaves a 'cruel' home and only returns as a ghost when the sea gives up his body. There are a number of poems including abortions ('the child – *that should have been, / But was not*, born alive' of 'The Ballad of Love's Skeleton'; 'A Sunday Morning Tragedy') and other poems recommending that children not be born ('To an Unborn Pauper Child'; 'The Unborn'; 'Epitaph on a Pessimist').

A cluster of these poems is situated in *Time's Laughingstocks*, the volume in which ballad-memory is most dominant, but also the first volume to appear after the death of Hardy's mother – a fact which might indeed suggest a posthumous release of memory, and even of interdicted material ('The Christening', for example, is a tale of a bastard child dated 1904, the year of Jemima's death; 'Panthera' is in the same volume, and other examples include 'A Trampwoman's Tragedy'; 'Unrealized' with its children whose mother is dead; and one of Deacon's favourites, 'The Dawn after the Dance', with its hinted illegitimacy). It is interesting to meditate on Hardy's dry report in the *Life* that 'By reason of her parent's bereavement and consequent poverty under the burden of a young family, Jemima saw during girlhood and young womanhood some very stressful experiences of which she could never speak in her maturer years without pain, though she appears to have mollified her troubles by reading every book she could lay hands on' (*EL* 9) – a clue, perhaps, to the way in which his own investment in the literary imagination of childhood pain might indeed have centred on his mother.

One repeated topic is that of the child fathered by the rival, with violent results: the 'cuckoo-child' placed in another's house (described in 'At a Pause in a Country Dance', 'A Conversation at Dawn', 'In the Restaurant' and many other poems; even Little Father Time). In 'The Flirt's Tragedy' a man hires a gigolo to seduce the woman who spurned him, then kills the gigolo after she becomes pregnant, raising the child as his, only to have him flee his 'false father... [who] murdered my true!' Arguably the most important such poems, offering a key to Hardy's metapoetics, are those in which the issue is the *plotting* of such a story rather than its actuality. In 'A Trampwoman's Tragedy' a woman pretends that her child is not her lover's, at which point he kills the imagined rival. In such poems, it is the story itself which generates violent acts. 'Her Death and After' also meditates on the status of the story of infidelity. The protagonist is called to the deathbed of a woman he loves who married another; she suspects her unloving husband will not care for their lame newborn child:

> such my unease
> That, could I insert a deed back in Time,
> I'd make her yours, to secure your care;
> And the scandal bear,
> And the penalty for the crime!

The lover haunts her grave, and when he is challenged by the dead woman's husband (who has remarried and does, as predicted, neglect his first child) he concocts the story suggested by the dying wish, telling the husband that the child was indeed his; it is handed over to him to raise. This is the story of a fiction which activates a buried truth. A 'deed' in the sense of a legal intention becomes a deed in the sense of an action validating that intention (as in typology), but there is a residue of guilt attached because the process involves the overwriting of history ('but compunctions loomed; for I'd harmed the dead / By what I said / For the good of the living one'). The 'deed back in time' is not a guilty secret, but rather the *secret of a guilt*: there is no original act of sin. This is perhaps the most cogent comment on the lost child in Hardy: as a device, it concerns itself with the failure of love to find its 'proper' locus; or a love which only finds expression outside its official channels, via an act of imaginative surrogacy which is, here, predicated on mourning. This sense both of the need to recapture the past and of the violence of that process is also, as we will see, a feature of Hardy's relation to history generally.

We can add a final, late, example of this notion of the encrypted (fictional) child. 'Aristodemus the Messenian', published in *Winter Words*, seems the grotesque product of a seriously decayed imagination, to the point where it is almost unreadable (understandably, it has received almost no critical discussion). When King Aristodemus (circa 735 BC) decides that he must sacrifice his virgin daughter to save his people in battle, her lover attempts to prevent the act by claiming that she is pregnant, invalidating the sacrifice – the fictionalizing but recuperative gambit of 'Her Death and After'. The king refutes the story by ripping his daughter's womb open with his sword, an anatomical investigation and violation in which a vortex of issues – paternity, rape, birth, murder – devolve on the question of a sexual secret; a secret whose essence inheres, in fact, in being a fiction which generates rupture and uncertainty. What is in the womb? the poem asks, and the answer might be 'Nothing, just a story'. Could we say that this is the final displacement of the structured absence which constitutes Hardy's crypt?

It is not, I would suggest, easy to press further in discussing Hardy's family secrets; the point is less the need for a definitive account of 'what happened' – a need which in 'Aristodemus the Messenian' is shown to itself be violent – than an acknowledgement of the existence of a topic which is repeatedly raised and evaded, claimed and disclaimed, balked about and balked at; which is resolved into the story of another, or into silence. Some poems might suggest abortion or infanticide as one trauma; other poems the fostering of children. Both topics refer to the displacement of the child from its rightful position in the family, for reasons which are to do with the 'law' of morality, death, economics, or desire itself. For this reason, we might see Hardy as offering both a general account of the vulnerability of the child in rural society and an account of the effect of that vulnerability as it is transmitted through the family; the terror and displacement of childhood as both existential plight and psychic legacy. We might also see that plight as a historical residue, as in a passage from Mahaffy's *Social Life in Greece* (1874) which Hardy summarized: '*Not to be forgotten* in our admiration for Greek culture – conflict between rich and poor: when the demos was victorious the children of the vanquished were trampled to death by oxen: when the rich got the upper hand they burnt in pitch all whom they got into their power' (*LN* 555, Hardy's emphasis).

How is this related to the complex shift in attitudes which, recent historians of childhood have suggested, characterized the nineteenth century? The early part of the century saw the continuation of earlier regimes in which the child was harshly disciplined, imprisoned, transported (up to 1870), or made to work at an early age. In the West Country, Hugh Cunningham reports, the children of the poor were bound out as rural apprentices as early as eight years old.[40] At the same time, in the mid-century (the period in which Hardy was growing up), there emerged a heightened sense of the child as abused by these practices – as a being radically separate from adults, who should be freed from work, protected, educated and nutured. This 'story of outrage' (as Cunningham calls it) was reflected in a variety of philanthropic institutions and legislation: the Ten Hours Act (1847), the Gangs Act (1867), the Agricultural Children's Act (1873); in the work of Barnardo and Booth in London in the 1860s; in the establishment of the National Society for the Prevention of Cruelty to Children in 1884.[41] Scandals like the baby-farming and infanticide cases of the 1870s and Stead's exposure of child prostitution in 'The Maiden Tribute of Modern Babylon' (1885) focused attention on specific abuses.[42]

There is also, some historians of sexuality have suggested, a progressive eroticization of abuse, and one might say a fictionalization of the subject. The most extreme claim here is that of C. J. Somerville, one of a number of revisionist historians attempting to modify earlier studies by Ariès, Stone and others which had stressed the harshness of childhood up to the twentieth century. Somerville argues that stories of abuse by Dickens and others 'do not seem to have much to do with the actual suffering of contemporary children.... Child characters were dying in record numbers in fiction even as actual child mortality was declining.'[43] His conclusion that these figures represent 'the author's self-pity' is unnecessarily crude – one might, for example, argue that a decline in mortality is a necessary precondition of certain investments in children; and the figures suggest that it was only in the twentieth century that child mortality figures fell sharply. But Hardy shows himself conscious of the child-victim as a device in his work – in particular Little Father Time, who appears in *Jude the Obscure* as a figure for the foreclosure of hope, for a folding of the child back into death, of the kind depicted in Elizabeth Barrett Browning's radical 'The Cry of the Children' and Robert Browning's 'The Pied Piper of Hamelin'.[44] Little Father Time could, by an extravagant but not inconceivable leap, be a version of the child who hangs himself with cord and nail in 'Rope', one of the famous prose-poems which Baudelaire published under the heading *The Spleen of Paris* in *Le Figaro* in 1864. Baudelaire's child is full of 'precocious sadness' (compare Hardy's 'Age masquerading as Juvenility'), and with 'an immoderate taste for sugar and liqueurs'. He is adopted by a painter who has used him as a model; when he is threatened with return to his indifferent parents, he kills himself (the story was based on that of a child who hung himself in Manet's studio).[45] Baudelaire describes the death in terms that are both tender and sadistic; both 'the cheeky companion of my life' whom he mourns, and 'the little monster had used a very thin cord which had bitten deeply into the neck and I now had to use a pair of small scissors to find the thread between the two rolls of swollen flesh'. The story climaxes in the child's mother seeing the nail and cord, and asking for it after the painter is about to hurl it out of the window; it is only later that he realizes that she plans to sell sections of it, since a rope from a hanging is considered a lucky charm. This commoditization has, however, already been prefigured in the painter's own activities, which both sexualize the child and associate him with fantasies of death. In painting him, the narrator reports, 'I made him carry the vagabond's violin, the Crown of Thorns and the Nails of the Passion, and the Torch of Eros.'

A similar undoing of the Victorian figure of the dying child as de-eroticized angel (Dickens's Little Nell, Stowe's Eva) is central to the stories of Hardy's children, who flee from their violent parents ('The Flirt's Tragedy', 'The Bird-Catcher's Boy'), often dying in the process. The beaten or whipped child is, as James Kincaid points out, a fixture of Hardy's novels, even if a problematic one in terms of the kinds of identifications which the reader might make and the kinds of pleasures associated with it. Kincaid ultimately sees the child as a figure for 'an erotics of loss'; like the electronic pet, it is the toy that dies. It is 'this emptiness called a child'; it 'could be erased, was in fact in the process of being erased even as we packed the meaning in'.[46] More radically, U. C. Knopfelmacher points out the way in which Hardy's poetry can suggest a child-like return to a lost maternal body; a return involving the reversal of a harsh 'masculine' poetics which might impose discipline.[47] Both these narratives, that of abuse and that of healing regression, confront the problem of pain, of what we have come to call 'trauma' – which is also, since Freud, the problem of consciousness and its obscured origins. What happens to childhood pain? Into the twentieth century it was relatively common practice, in France at least, to operate on newborn babies without anaesthetic, because they, like animals, were thought to have, undeveloped nervous systems and little consciousness.[48] Hardy was certainly aware of some of these issues: he was on friendly terms with Sir James Crichton-Browne, the leading Victorian child psychiatrist, who stressed the vulnerability of children and the necessity to avoid over-taxing their nervous systems (his emphasis on their susceptibility to mental disease points towards Little Father Time).[49]

Hardy's work constantly returns to the issue of childhood pain and its persistence. His 'Lines' – really an epilogue – written for a performance on behalf Lady Jeune's Holiday Fund for City Children in 1890 are perhaps just the kind of awkward occasional verse that one skips over in the *Collected Poems*:

> Most tragical of shapes from Pole to Line,
> O wondering child, unwitting Time's design,
> Why should Man add to Nature's quandary,
> And worsen ill by thus immuring thee?
> – That races do despite unto their own,
> That Might supernal do indeed condone
> Wrongs individual for the general ease,
> Instance the proof in victims such as these.

The poem then wonders whether disadvantaged children would rather not have been born. These lines suggest a response both to the eugenic discourse of 'races' and to Utilitarian calculus of 'general ease' and 'individual wrongs'. With Darwin the relations of resemblance between child and parent are re-coded, with issues of inheritance, variation and, in particular, the development of latent 'faculties' becoming part of a broader social calculus rather than simply an issue of patriarchal succession. This concern is expressed in Herbert Spencer's essay on 'The Rights of Children' in *Social Statics*, in which he asserts that children have the same rights as adults, draws parallels with the emancipation of women, and attacks the 'coercive system' which employs force on children rather than developing self-control.[50] Spencer stresses the duty of the parent to create an environment in which the child's faculties might develop, rather than imposing a disciplinary framework. Hardy similarly focuses on the issue of environment, but registers the place of the individual consciousness within these larger social calculations. The 'wondering Child, unwitting Time's design' and the 'deed back in Time' are both formulae which register the plight of that maimed consciousness, and the paradoxical recovery of pain as part of what this poem (speaking of Lady Jeune's efforts) calls 'Some palliative for ill they cannot cure'.

This conclusion has all the pessimism of Freud's admission of the impossibility of ever resolving the traumas of childhood – though notably we have seen Hardy imply a more socialized account of childhood pain than Freud's patriarchical model. Hardy's account suggests disruptions which may be external to the family as much as internal. Maria Torok has hinted at similar possibilities in her 1984 paper 'Unpublished by Freud to Fliess: Restoring an Oscillation'. Recalling Freud's abandonment of the thesis of actual trauma or abuse in childhood in favour of the notion of universal endopsychic fantasy, she discusses a letter of 1897 to Fliess, partly suppressed, presumably in the interests of theoretical consistency, by the editors of *The Origins of Psychoanalysis* (1954), and only published entire in Jeffrey Masson's *The Assault on Truth* (1984). The letter describes in detail the sexual abuse of a patient and her mother, and concludes with Freud's proposal of 'A new motto; "What has been done to you, you poor child?"'[51]

Was hat man, Dir, Du armes Kind getan? – the words are from the famous song of Goethe's illegitimate, abused and ultimately effaced child Mignon in *Wilhelm Meister*, set to music and re-written throughout the nineteenth century.[52] As Carolyn Steedman argues in her brilliant study of the Mignon legend, *Strange Dislocations: Childhood and the Idea of Human Interiority*, the story's fragmentary meanings, which never achieve a total shape, represent the plight of the child itself as historical rebus, as a necessary obscurity. Torok notes that Freud's letter to Fliess contains its own comments on deletion. Freud writes:

> Have you ever seen a foreign newspaper which has been censored by the Russians at the border? Words, whole clauses and sentences are blacked out so that what is left becomes unintelligible. A *Russian*

censorship of this kind comes about in psychoses and produces the apparently meaningless *deliria*.

This, in Torok's commentary, is the mark of an uncertainty within psychoanalysis which is not simply local – was there abuse *here*? – but fundamental:

> Circulating Freud's letters with fragments happening to pass 'Russian' censorship is enough to throw the reader and psychoanalysis into a kind of *historical neurosis* in which deletions impede us from attempting to read the fact of an oscillation as a symptom-symbol. Once this road is open, it will be easier to read the deletion itself, rendering it intelligible.[53]

A similar question could be applied to the Hardy texts we have examined here: with their cancellations, burnings, and reticences, they are, as we have seen, systematically uncertain about the status of the child and of the trauma attached to the child; to childhood pain. The suppressed motto might be Hardy's, as applicable to the figure of Randy as to Lady Jeune's children, but suggesting a wounded self whose location is problematized by Hardy's own deletions and erasures.

Perhaps it is also the trace of the 'real' of history itself which is erased from Freud's text. One of Steedman's comments on Mignon is useful here: 'child-figures, and more generally the idea of childhood, came to be commonly used to express the depths of historicity within individuals, the history that was "linked to them, essentially"'.[54] The final phrase is a citation from the passage in which Foucault, in *The Order of Things*, describes 'The Age of History', the period in which, for Foucault, the self erupts from the continuum of the classical order, and history becomes, painfully, 'the mode of being of all that is given us in experience'.[55] That sense of the intensity of human pain as out of step with a biological or even cosmic order we saw earlier, is one symptom of the pressure on the notion of origins, of originary trauma, within the new characterization of childhood that was growing up as Hardy did; as Steedman writes, 'a particular form of time came into being in the child's body'.[56] Giorgio Agamben has also argued that the infant is the place where 'the space of history' is opened; and where the discourse of the self-constituting subject erupts from the synchronicity of language. For Agamben, infants are liminal figures, representing the transition from death or non-being to life, and in this way they resemble, and may even come to be entangled with, ghosts rather than adults (since ghosts represent the transition from life to death, and from discourse to language).[57] The 'wondering child, unwitting Time's design' is, then, a trope for the historicity of the self: 'I had glanced down unborn time' is Hardy's figure for prophecy in 'I Said and Sang Her Excellence'. This is one conclusion: that Hardy's sense of the originary trauma of the self's historicity is what underwrites his sense of a haunting pain as written into the construction of the self.

But perhaps a more suitable point of closure is the healing offered by 'He Never Expected Much', Hardy's 'reflection' on his eighty-sixth birthday – surely one of the most astonishing poems in the English canon in its audacious claims for the continuity of the poetic self across eight decades, and in its redemptive minimalism. The poet addresses the World and says that it has 'kept faith' since childhood (note the conjuring of the year's brink as the mark of the self's entry into history: a topic taken up in the next chapter):

>   'Twas then you said, and since have said,
>   Times since have said,
>   In that mysterious voice you shed
>   From clouds and hills around:
>   'Many have loved me desperately,
>   Many with smooth serenity,
>   While some have shown contempt of me
>   Till they dropped underground.
>
>   'I do not promise overmuch,
>   Child; overmuch;
>   Just neutral-tinted haps and such',
>   You said to minds like mine.
>   Wise warning for your credit's sake!
>   Which I for one failed not to take,
>   And hence could stem such strain and ache
>   As each year might assign.

This appears less as a final confirmation of 'pessimism' than as a fantasized utopian warning on the part of Time (or 'World', here), registering a healing contract which Hardy's poetry teaches us *could never have happened*; a constantly-renewed contract in which, impossibly, consciousness is always with the child and carried forward as intention, forever balking future pain. A similar pastoral resolution is offered by another poem in *Winter Words*, 'The Boy's Dream', a poem which picks up on the tradition of Hardy's many bird-poems – in particular 'The Blinded Bird', in which he had marvelled that the bird could sing, 'Thy grievous pain forgot, / Eternal dark thy lot' (the Miltonic echo reinforcing the sense of the persistence of pain). 'The Boy's Dream' describes natural song as recompense for the lameness and deprivation of a 'provincial town-boy' who dreams of owning a green linnet. The poem begins with external circumstances, the courtyard he lives in, 'Where noontide shed no warmth or light', and the corresponding paleness of his face; it ends with his mood radiating outward as he dreams of birdsong: 'His face was beautified by the theme, / And wore the radiance of the morn.' An internalized nature, pastoral – the tropes of mourning return here as a final cure for the ineradicable memory of pain, closing the book on one of Hardy's enduring subjects.

4
The Politics of the Dead

> *I don't care for history. Prophecy is the only thing can do poor men any good.*
>
> Hardy, *The Hand of Ethelberta*
>
> *The Historian is a prophet facing backwards.*
>
> Schlegel, *Athenaeum Fragments*

In his edition of Shelley's poems edited by Stopford Brooke, Hardy wrote a question mark – seemingly indicating a disagreement – beside Brooke's introductory comments about *The Revolt of Islam* being ruined by a 'revolutionary creed'.[1] A similar question mark hangs over Hardy and politics, a subject on which he was famously reticent, often repeating his determination that the writer must remain sceptical and detached from 'political action'. Lance St John Butler has recently attempted to tease out his politics, and concludes that Hardy could appear, on different subjects, either liberal or conservative: relatively conservative about church and tradition; liberal and even radical about the rights of rural working men and the double standards applied to women.[2] Peter Widdowson perceptively traces the distant, liberal stance and the 'passive alternativism' which Hardy often adopted to his class position, stranded between his origins among rural tradesmen and his achieved position as a novelist moving among the metropolitan elite; suspicious both of that elite and of any easy association with the working classes. Widdowson comments that 'Hardy, then is left occupying an apolitical space as a "writer", bolstered by an eclectic and facticious myth of "History".'[3] In what follows, I will test that assertion, especially with respect to Hardy's sense of history, exploring the political stance implicit within Hardy's relations to historical experience, and in particular his concern with what I will call the politics of the dead, a topic which emerges as an issue in a range of historical thinking.

'Hurt, misrepresented names'

Hardy was fascinated by the biblical and classical *topos* of the forgotten dead, the perennial lament marked in his Psalter: 'For in death no man remembereth thee'. He twice used and then deleted Ecclesiastes 10: 5, 'Neither have they any more a reward, for the memory of them is forgotten', as the epigraph for poems, 'The To-Be-Forgotten' and 'Sapphic Fragment'. As the epigraph for the latter he substituted examples of the *topos* from Omar Khayyám and Shakespeare. In Marcus Aurelius he marked 'How quickly all things disappear, in the universe the bodies themselves, but in time the remembrance of them'; he marked as well the Horatian counter-boast *Exegi monumentum aere perennius*.[4]

Hardy also repeatedly describes the dead as wronged, misreported or unreported by the texts of history – those whom a chorus of *The Dynasts*, Part Third, calls the 'Souls passed to where History pens no page' (p. 484). In 'Spectres that Grieve' the dead cry out:

> 'We are among the few death sets not free,
> The hurt, misrepresented names, who come
> At each year's brink, and cry to History
> To do them justice, or go past them dumb.
>
> 'We are stript of rights; our shames lie unredressed,
> Our deeds in full autonomy are not shown,
> Our words in morsels merely are expressed
> On the scriptured page, our motives blurred, unknown.'

What would it be to think of a politics of the dead? In order to answer that question, I will turn to a historical thematics located in Burke and Carlyle, but finding a radical twentieth-century response in the work of Walter Benjamin. Burke was important to Hardy for a number of reasons: as one source of his mixture of liberalism and adherence to tradition; for the scope and sublime spectacle of his writings on the French Revolution, an influence on *The Dynasts*; but also – and this is an element of Burke's influence less commented on – for his sense of the possibilities and dangers of a history which seeks to intervene in the continuum of events in the name of the Idea. An interesting facet of Hardy's response to Burke, suggested by extensive markings in his copy, is his attentive reading of Burke's *Political Letters*, particularly his *Letter to a Noble Lord* (1796). With its mixture of detached hauteur and self-justification, Burke's reply to the Duke of Bedford's attacks on the generous pension awarded to him by the Whig government addresses itself to the individual's role in history, written from the position of one who has ostensibly left public life and has fallen out of history. Remembering the crisis of 1780–2, in a passage marked and partially underlined by Hardy in his edition, Burke describes a revolutionary animus which returns history's counter to zero, and seeks even to raise the dead: '[Revolutionaries] have so determined a hatred to all privileged orders, that they deny even to the departed the sad immunities of the grave. They are not wholly without an object. Their turpitude purveys to their malice, and they unplumb the dead for bullets to assassinate the living.'[5] Necromancy in classical texts, he adds, tends to result in the dead cursing the living, in their crying 'Leave me, oh leave me, to repose' (such responses are typified by the Hades episodes of the *Aeneid*, so important to Hardy's elegies, and themselves often moments in which the cost of an Imperial *telos* is measured). This plea for the dead, conservative in Burke, seeks to reverse the revolutionary conditions which would re-write history, declaring that ghosts must not be raised. Or, in a related but inverted version of the trope of necromancy in 'Thoughts on the Causes of the Present Discontents', those conspirators in government who are not convinced by defences of the constitution 'would not receive conviction *though one arose from the dead*'.[6] Doubting Thomases, they would not listen, he implies, to Christ himself, the ultimate judge of historical action.

The moment in which Burke most famously confronts history as necromancy is in the *Reflections on the Revolution in France*. Meditating on the moral lessons to be drawn from history, and on the National Assembly's pursuit of the crimes committed by the Church in the past, he comments that history may be 'ransacked' and misused as a 'magazine, furnishing offensive and defensive weapons for parties in church and state'.[7] It is futile, he adds, to seek to revenge the evils of the past. The lesson which Burke draws from history is that the 'same' underlying vices continually re-present themselves beneath the 'pretexts' of 'religion, morals, laws, prerogatives, liberties, rights or men'. That does not mean that religion, morals, laws and liberties are to be abandoned, but that in contemplating history the wise man must distinguish the symptom from the cause, the transitory from the enduring. The failure to do this is depicted in terms of haunting and revivification:

Whilst you are discussing fashion, the fashion is gone by. The very same vice assumes a new body. The spirit transmigrates; and, far from losing its principle of life by the change of its appearance, it is renovated in its new organs with the fresh vigour of a juvenile activity. It walks abroad; it continues its ravages; whilst you are gibbeting the carcass, or demolishing the tomb. You are terrifying yourself with ghosts and apparitions, whilst your house is the haunt of robbers. It is thus with all those, who, attending only to the shell and husk of history, think they are waging war with intolerance, pride, and cruelty, whilst, under colour of abhorring the ill principles of antiquated parties, they are authorizing and feeding the same odious vices in different factions, and perhaps in worse.

This seems to speak, proleptically, to Marx's equally ironic evocation of spirits in *The Eighteenth Brumaire*, in which the Burkean ghosts are put to work as the coverings of new organs. Marx notes that it is 'precisely in such periods of revolutionary crisis they anxiously conjure up the spirits of the past to their service and borrow from them names, battle-cries and costumes in order to present the new scene of world history in this time-honoured disguise and this borrowed language'. Despite their opposed senses of what the ghost *is*, for Marx as for Burke the material body of the ghost itself, as well as its phantomal clothing, must be conjured away.[8]

To more radical thinkers, Burke's stance could seem deathly. In *The Rights of Man*, Tom Paine was to cast Burke, as Steven Blakemore puts it, 'in the role of the knight of the dead traducing the rights of the living', binding humanity to 'mummy words', to dusty manuscripts and the intentions of the past. In his stress on first principles and the calculus of rights rather than the re-negotiation of origins, Paine, like so many Enlightenment thinkers, refuses to negotiate with the dead.[9] Burke's position, finally, is underpinned by the vision of history as turbulent and chaotic which he presents in the *Reflections*, a text which raises the dead (Rousseau, for example) to register their shock at the way in which history has caricatured them.[10] Rejecting the possibility of re-ordering history, he is left, in the *Political Letters*, with the pragmatics of rational government based on a study of a range of existing institutions. The view of the state which was to emerge in Germany in the nineteenth century with Fichte and Hegel, which sees it both as the absolute embodiment of a progressive history and as the vehicle for the expression of individual being, is alien to Burke – not because he would have disapproved of evolutionism (though the later Burke is gloomy enough), but more because of its stress on modernity as the triumph of the transcendent Idea rather than the pragmatic modification of a range of inherited institutions.

Burke's plea for the dead finds a twentieth-century reply in Walter Benjamin's 'Theses on the Philosophy of History', when he meditates on the historian's obligation to move beyond any global notion of dialectical progress and redeem the past in all its fragmentation, since 'nothing that has ever happened should be regarded as lost to history'. The 'lost' includes the dead: 'Only that historian will have the gift of fanning the spark of hope in the past who is firmly convinced that *even the dead* will not be safe from the enemy if he wins.' There is, as ever, a sting in Benjamin's tail when he adds: 'And the enemy has not ceased to be victorious.' Sharing with Burke a sense that the dead must be protected, Benjamin's aims are radically different: he insists on the Messianic possibility of blasting open the 'continuum of history' and permeating it with the revolutionary 'now'; rescuing the forgotten dead rather than allowing them to lie defeated.[11] History must be directed towards a revolutionary *telos*, not in the absolute and dialectical sense of Hegel, but in relation to that to-be-achieved future which Benjamin self-consciously allegorizes as 'that sun which is rising in the sky of history'.[12] Historicism – a procedure which restores a historical horizon, which pretends not to know the future of the past – is the object of Benjamin's scorn, as involving 'a process of empathy whose origin is the indolence of the heart', in a sense that the past is not alive in the present. Friedrich Schlegel's aphorism in the *Athenaeum Fragments*, which surely informs Benjamin's famous image of the Angel of History, suggests a sense of the past which Hardy shares: 'The Historian is a prophet facing backwards'.[13] Or, as Sol (whose name itself might suggest a kind of heliocentrism) puts it in Hardy's *The Hand of Ethelberta*, chapter 46, expressing his doubts about any official history, 'I don't care for history. Prophecy is the only thing can do poor men any good'. The future of the past must be part of its writing.

For Benjamin, a redemptive history must be captured in flashes of illumination, in sudden *images* (or moments of vision – the visual basis of this critique is important) which burst through the continuities of established stories, like the Surrealist *hasard objectif*. As Helga Geyer-Ryan puts it, 'authentic experience is always the salvaging of something in danger of being forgotten or repressed: the ever-vanishing traces of the historically defeated who do not write history, or the engrams of the unconscious described by Freud in *Beyond the Pleasure Principle* and by Proust as the context of *mémoire involontaire*'.[14] That salvage may involve a revivification: as Benjamin writes in his essay on Eduard Fuchs, 'Historical materialism conceives historical understanding as an after-life of that which is understood, whose pulse can still be felt in the present' [15] – that is as a negotiation with the unfulfilled and possibly even unselfconscious intentions of the dead. This sense of an open (or 'weak', as Benjamin calls it) messianism, working under the sign of mourning and recovery, is taken up by Derrida in *Spectres of Marx*, where his acknowledgement that the dead cannot (be allowed to) watch over the dead means that a narrow historicism is once again the object of attack:

> To exorcise not in order to chase away the ghosts, but this time to grant them the right, if it means making them come back alive, as *revenants* who would no longer be *revenants*, but as other *arrivants* to whom a hospitable memory or promise must offer welcome.... Not in order to grant them the right in this sense but out of a concern for *justice*. Present existence or essence has never been the condition, object, or the *thing* [*chose*] of justice.[16]

Derrida's notion of justice extends also to the ghosts of the future, to those who are not yet present and who are not contained within our own historical horizon. He insists, that is, on an expanded historicity which both cares for the dead as the objects of justice, and registers the presence of the unborn in whom a hope for future justice might be invested.

One could invoke as an example here the complex negotiations of Hardy's 'At the Entering of the New Year' (published in the *Athenaeum* on 31 December 1920, but with the endnote 'During the War' and a manuscript dating of '1917 or 1918'). The first section ('Old Style') has the Melstock Quire welcoming the New Year within a fixed historical order (the shepherds and poachers going about their 'rounds') in which an allegorical 'Time unrobed the Youth of Promise.' The second section ('New Style') has a different, catastrophic mode of historicity in which the flow of time has been broken:

> But our truest heed is for words that steal
> From the mantled ghost that looms in the gray,
> And seems, so far as our sense can see,
> To feature bereaved Humanity,
> As it sighs to the imminent year its say: –

> 'O stay without, O stay without,
> Calm comely Youth, untasked, untired;
> Though stars irradiate thee about
> Thy entrance here is undesired.'

The allegory which stabilizes Time has grown obscure and spectral; its continuity and transparency are challenged in the name of both the dead and those who will be dead in the battles to come. This ghost of Humanity might also be the ghost of Human*ism*. It also recalls Stan Smith's remarks on Hardy's ghosts, which allude in turn to Benjamin: '[The supernatural] consistently occurs at that point where the mind struggles with a recalcitrant material world bodied over against it, and struggles to re-appropriate that world. The supernatural, that is, is a sign and a site of a desperate attempt to "brush history against the grain".'[17] There are, surely, less desperate ghosts in Hardy, but Smith's comment works very well for those who repeatedly appear 'at each year's brink', as 'Spectres that Grieve' puts it; who intersect, that is, with the becoming-historical, the time of the annalist or the Spirit of the Years, and demand that it do them justice.

The ghost thus signals what Derrida calls the 'non- contemporaneity with itself of the living present', the fact that the time is *always* out of joint.[18] A sense of ghosts as fragments of displaced time is present in poems by Hardy in which the speaker feels he should return as a ghost (for example the paired poems 'Jubilate' and 'He Revisits His First School'); poems in which ghosts return uneasily to former haunts ('His Visitor'); and poems such as 'In St Paul's a While Ago', in which he imagines a 'strange Jew, Damascus-bound', the Christ who returns to find himself untimely. St Paul's is an imperial edifice,

> Whose haunters, had they seen him stand
> On his own steps here, lift his hand
> In stress of eager, stammering speech,
> And his meaning, chanced to reach,
> Would have proclaimed him as they passed
> An epilept enthusiast.

The fact that the building's present occupants are themselves its 'haunters' suggests a temporal instability: if as Emerson said, a religion is the shadow of a great man, these 'haunters' have been led astray by a corrupted vision, themselves becoming ghostly in relation to the original 'vision'.

What a history which sought guardianship of the dead might involve for Hardy is suggested, though not I think realized, by another historian whom he read attentively, Carlyle – for whom 'of our History the more important part is lost without recovery'; the history, that is, of the texture of individual lives.[19] In Carlyle's essay on 'Biography' he singles out the story of the peasant feeding Charles II in Clarendon's *History of the Rebellion* as involving a visionary – though also, crucially, real – moment in which this 'genuine flesh-and-blood rustic of the year 1651' enters history: 'for one moment, the blanket of the Night is rent asunder, so that we behold and see, and then closes over him – forever'.[20] This is an aspect of Carlyle described by J. A. Froude, in one of a number of passages from his biography which Hardy copied out in 1885: 'And this was Carlyle's special gift – to bring dead things & dead people actually back to life.' The result is a 'spectral' history: 'Spectral, for the actors appear in it without their earthly clothes: men & women in their natural characters, but as in some vast phantasmagoria with the supernatural shining through them, working in fancy their own wills or their own imagination; in reality, the mere instruments of a superior power' (*LN* 1337, 1345).[21]

If the sense of a 'superior power' here has often been seen as supporting the phantasmagoric machinery of *The Dynasts* (with its origins in von Hartmann and the Hegelian tradition), for Carlyle it is also the specificity and irrevocably lost status of what is described by the historian which is poignant, particularly where the humble step briefly onto the stage of history. Boswell's description of a prostitute who approaches Dr Johnson leads Carlyle to the following meditation:

> Do but consider that it is *true*; that it did in very deed occur! That unhappy Outcast, with all her sins and woes, her lawless desires, too complex mischances, her wailings and her riotings, has departed utterly; alas! her siren finery has got all besmutched, ground, generations since, into dust and smoke.... Johnson said, 'No, no, my girl; it won't do'; and then, 'we talked'; – and herewith the wretched one, seen but for the twinkling of an eye, passes on into the utter Darkness.[22]

This remains in the mode of the phantasmagoria: the dead are conjured up as a spectacle by the historian or biographer, flitting before the eye, and are banished again. But compare Hardy, offering a metaphor for the emergence, indeed eruption, of a prophetic *voice* from the silence of obscurity, a voice which cannot fully be aware of its own status but which is nevertheless *historical*:

Also in that village near Yeovil about 100 years ago, there lived a dumb woman, well known to my informant's mother. One day the woman suddenly spoke and said:

> 'A cold winter, a forward spring,
> A bloody summer, a dead King';

She then dropped dead. The French Revolution followed immediately after. (*EL* 165)

The importance of the chain of individual memories here – 'known to my informant's mother' – finds an echo in the comment of Carlyle's which Hardy included in his prefatory note to Joshua James Foster's *Wessex Worthies* (1920):

> In all of my poor historical investigations it has been and always is, one of the most primary wants to procure a bodily likeness of the personage enquired after – a good portrait if such exists; failing that, even an indifferent if sincere one. In short, any representation made by a faithful creature of that face and figure which he saw with his eyes, and which I can never see with mine, is now valuable to me, and much better than none at all. (*PW* 88)

The point is both a visual or eidetic image, a Lockean connection in which the action of sense-impressions can be traced, and something close to an ethical demand attached to the 'bodily likeness'.[23] Compare Hardy's remarks on the vanishing Dorset dialect in his introduction to his selection from Barnes: 'gesture and facial expression figure so largely in the speech of husbandmen as to be speech itself; hence in the mind's eye of those who know it in its original setting each word of theirs is accompanied by the qualifying face-play which no construing can express'.[24] Textual history must be supplemented by a trace of the body itself, by the gesture which, Comte argued, represents the origins of language, before even speech. And as the memory of the woman who prophesies the French Revolution suggests, Hardy stresses, even more than Carlyle, and in contrast to Benjamin, the need to rescue a *voice* from history: not only the image of those talked about, but their own self-constructions. If Carlyle's peasants step onto the stage of a theatrically-conceived history, in minor walk-on parts in which they might feed a king, Hardy implies that their stories may not only be worth telling in themselves, but may be an important part of historical process.

As both Burke and Benjamin indicate, the stakes in that recollection are high: it is because the dead may be re-written or unwritten in history's texts that they must be recognized as living voices; rescued from the 'voiceless, crippled, corpselike state' described in Hardy's 'Haunting Fingers'. A literal model for the historical 'freezing out' of the insignificant is provided by one of the most striking scenes in *The Dynasts*, part of the description of the retreat from Moscow in Part Third. Napoleon has just fled, saying, as one soldier puts it, that he must go 'To quiet France, and raise another army / That shall replace our bones'. The news of the main actor's departure throws the straggling soldiers into despair; one goes mad. They have fallen out of history, and as the night falls they huddle round a fire:

> With the progress of the night the stars come out in unusual brilliancy, Sirius and those in Orion flashing like stilettos; and the frost stiffens.
> The fire sinks and goes out; but the Frenchmen do not move. The day dawns, and still they sit on.

The pursuing Russians approach and prepare to kill them, only to find that they are already dead, though 'They all sit / As they were living still', burnt at the front and ice-cold at the back. Seared by events and frozen into a tableau beneath the stars – we might remember that 'constellated' is Benjamin's term for the relation between historical elements and the fragmented context within which they are re-positioned by a later historian – these are the kind of historical 'extras' whom Hardy attempts to recall in *The Dynasts*, writing a more determinedly marginal history rather than that offered in Carlyle's anecdote. Thus the cast of dozens of obscure characters, named, individuated, and even at times footnoted, in *The Dynasts*. In Part Second, the forgotten English army dying of marsh-borne diseases at Walcheren is lamented by the Chorus of Pities in terms which recall 'Spectres that Grieve':

> *'We might have fought, and had we died, died well,*
> *Even if in dynasts' discords not our own;*
> *Our death-spot some sad haunter might have shown,*
> *Some tongue have asked our sires or sons to tell*
>   *The tale of how we fell;*

> '*But such bechanced not. Like the mist we fade,*
> *No lustrous lines engrave in story we,*
> *Our country's chiefs, for their own fames afraid,*
> *Will leave our names and fates by this pale sea*
>   *To perish silently!'*
>
>   (*The Dynasts*, Part Second, IV, viii)

In these lines – one of the few evocations of the title in the text of the poem – telling, memorializing, and official history come together in a protest dismissed by the Spirit of the Years as a 'frail tune upon this withering sedge / That holds its papery blades against the gale', a writing in the storm of history which returns us to Benjamin's Angelus Novus.

Such marginal characters as those described above have a programmatic place in Hardy's poem, alongside the 'main' actors, and (as Hardy asserted in his General Introduction) make the provincial and local as important imaginatively as the metropolitan. Hardy's fantasy in his early Waterloo poem 'The Peasant's Confession' – that the fate of Napoleon might have been determined by one peasant misleading and killing a messenger in order to protect his land – implies that all actions may become historical; that the desire of a smallholder to save his crops and 'capple cow' may be as important an element as the motivations of the lists of dead officers in the official necrology ('Gordon, Canning, Blackman, Ompteda, / L'Estrange, Delancey, Packe'). The awkward use of dialect ('capple') alongside the language of the chronicle and poetic locutions like 'as lated tongues bespoke' suggests a complex negotiation between different historical and geographical registers. Indeed, Hardy showed that he was sensitive to such issues in responding to William Archer's criticism that his peasant spoke in too sophisticated a fashion, explaining that 'Concluding that the tale must be regarded as a translation of the original utterance of the [Belgian] peasant I thought an impersonal wording admissible' (*CL* 2: 207). The role as the transmitter of a tradition which might recall a dumb woman who predicted the French Revolution, or imagine that byword for the inconsequential, a peasant's confession, is registered in its tension with the ostensibly impersonal and unaccented chronicle of history.

Mute witnesses

In the process of recollection central to Hardy's poetry, the specifics of the personal past are important, since it binds the narrator to the pasts of others. 'In a Former Resort after Many Years' is a key poem in terms of Hardy's sense of the dead. In two short stanzas it describes a protagonist who returns to the 'slack-shaped and wan' acquaintances of his youth, asking

> Do they know me, whose former mind
> Was like an open plain where no foot falls,
> But now is a gallery portrait-lined,
>   And scored with necrologic scrawls,
> Where feeble voices rise, once full-defined,
>   From underground in curious calls?

Nothing could differentiate Hardy's sense of inarticulate, to-be-realized voices more clearly from Carlyle's phantasmagoria. If Arnold, in 'The Buried Life', had portrayed the voice of the self as 'floating echoes' from 'the soul's subterranean depth upborn', Hardy's voices are at once texts and echoes; the voices of the dead are written into the self (Hardy deleted 'autographic' before substituting 'necrologic'; a necrology is a list of the dead). Hardy's 'open plain' suggests, of course, the Lockean *tabula rasa*; its inscriptions are, as elsewhere in his work, the products of 'time's etching' on the self.[25] But they are also the markings of the place of the dead, like the epitaph itself, preserving the trace of a voice. Such voices require care; a fact hinted at, perhaps, in the roots of the word 'curious'.

What threatens the dead is *mutism*: the silence suggested by lines from 'Alastor', marked and underlined in one of Hardy's copies of Shelley:[26]

> Among the ruined temples there,
> Stupendous columns, and wild images
> Of more than man, where marble demons watch
> The Zodiac's brazen mystery, and dead men
> Hang their mute thoughts on the mute walls around...

The danger, in Hardy's poem as in Shelley's, is of a meaning given up to death (the word 'mute' can also signify a funeral attendant or hired mourner). Hardy's 'Mute Opinion' echoes Shelley's phrase, ascribing truth not to the 'spokesmen [who] spake out strong / Their purpose and opinion / Through pulpit, press, and song', but to those marginal figures whom the narrator at first barely notices, the 'mute' whom he sees best when as a Shade he re-traverses 'That land in lifetime trode':

>   I saw, in web unbroken,
>   Its history outwrought
>   Not as the loud had spoken
>   But as the mute had thought.

In 'A Wet Night' the poet similarly casts his lot with the mute dead, wishing to 'calendar' his toils as he trudges for miles in the rain before remembering the hardier ancestors who 'Times numberless have trudged across this spot / In sturdy muteness on their strenuous lot'.

The story which 'Mute Opinion' tells, of an official history assigned a voice and a mute collective experience, is told again in 'The Souls of the Slain', the first of Hardy's great meditations on the cost of war (here the Boer War), though with a more subversive conclusion. The narrator sits on Portland Bill watching the souls of the dead return from South Africa. It is the dead soldiers themselves who at first numbly support an official history of 'deeds' and 'glory', leaving the narrator to tell them that they are remembered in more humble ways, for the texture of their lives, for 'dearer' things, 'homely acts' and 'commonplace facts' – for a historical significance outside that of the annals. His revelations produce a new version of the Last Judgement as depicted in John Martin's swirling picture in the Tate Gallery. The host splits in two: 'Those whose record was homely and true' return to England; the martial remnant of 'bitter traditions' depart for 'the fathomless regions / Of myriads forgot' – of those swallowed by history. But if Hardy seems to place himself in the position of the Archangel, dividing the throng, it is to assert that the choice belongs to the dead rather than to the poet, and that it is a choice of spectral *voice*: the 'homing' spirits are only half-ironically likened to 'the Pentecost Wind', as if they will carry their message to others; the martial spirits vanish into the background of 'sea-mutterings'.

The word 'mute' often signals a moment or place at which a historical apprehension might erupt, for example in the mimes and dumb-shows of *The Dynasts*. Hardy's travel-poem 'In the Old Theatre, Fiesole' has a young girl who shows the speaker a Roman coin she has dug up, and he remembers the same coin dug up in Dorset, so that 'her act flashed home / In that mute moment to my opened mind / The power, the pride, the reach of perished Rome'. In 'The Moth-Signal' a husband continues 'his mute and museful reading / In the annals of long ago' while his wife meets her lover outside, and the spirit of the 'Ancient Briton' in the nearby tumulus grins at the continuation of crossed destinies 'In these days as in mine'. In two of the great phantasmagoria in which Hardy confronts his own past, 'The Pedigree' and 'Family

Portraits', it is from a 'mute' witness or historical actor that the hidden story flows. In 1920 Hardy's Armistice-poem '"And There Was a Great Calm"' it is the 'mute bird on the spray' which signals the interruption of history's continuum, the uncanny silence into which meaning might be poured.

The word 'spectre' (recall Froude's 'spectral history' and Hardy's 'Spectres that Grieve', cited at the beginning of this essay) is also interesting, often linked to the personal past in Hardy – in 'His Immortality' the 'thin / And spectral mannikin' is the memory of the dead held within the living; in 'The Ghost of the Past' the poet and the past perform a 'spectral housekeeping'. In 'The Two Houses' the 'spectral guests' of the old house are 'printed' presences which 'inbe', and dead children 'obsess' the house – a return of 'obsession' to its root meaning of a ghostly occupation. Of particular interest is Hardy's use of 'spectral' where he is dealing with a *sequence* of ghosts. He is 'the last one / Outcome of each spectral past one / Of that file' in 'Sine Prole'; and in 'The Flirt's Tragedy' there is another phantasmagoria carried in memory, 'spent flames limning ghosts on the wainscots':

> My drama and hers begins weirdly
>   Its dumb re-enactment,
> Each scene, sigh, and circumstance passing
>   In spectral review.

Again the spectral sequence is an (im)printing of the 'dumb' or mute; of the child who vanishes in this story, Hardy writes 'nevermore sighted was even / A print of his shoe'.

What saves the dead from history, then, is carried within the phrase 'mute thought' and its cognates: in the recollection of ghosts; in the evocation of the muttering and vanishing of the souls of the slain; in close attention to the curious calls of the dead. This is a historiography of the spectral, of the lost and disenfranchised, but in Hardy, as in Benjamin, such mute thoughts mark the place of a negotiation between past and present, between forgotten but nevertheless prophetic intentions and a living care which renders the inarticulate particularity of the past real. Among Hardy's strongest statements of a disjunction between the time of historical experience and the time of judgement is 'Fragment' (an important but little-discussed poem, with a self-referential title strikingly atypical of Hardy). The narrator enters 'a long dark gallery, / Catacomb-lined' and sees 'the bodies of men from far and wide / Who, motion past, were nevertheless not dead'. This is clearly the space of the 'gallery portrait-lined' of 'In a Former Resort after Many Years' – a space of a crisis of response which recurs in Hardy's poetry, and climaxes in the portrait-gallery of 'Family Portraits'. Why is the place of the dead so often a *gallery*? The answer is, surely, that the dead exist in the realm of representation rather than voice; the restoration of a voice is what is demanded of their frozen and suspended status: in 'Family Portraits' their 'puppet-like movements of mute strange allure'. In the conflagration in the picture-gallery whose burning ends *A Laodicean*, it is the jerking to life of the portraits which signals the fulfilment of a prophecy. In 'Fragment' the speaker asks the dead:

> 'The sense of waiting here strikes strong;
> 'Everyone's waiting, waiting, it seems to me;
>   What are you waiting for so long? –
> What is to happen?' I said.

The answer, he is told, is that the undead are waiting for the arrival of the God who is *demanded* by human consciousness and suffering:

> 'O we are waiting for one called God', said they,
>   '(Though by some the Will, or Force, or Laws;
>   And, vaguely, by some, the Ultimate Cause);
> Waiting for him to see us before we are clay.
>   Yes: waiting, waiting, for God *to know it.*' ...
>   'To know what?' questioned I.
> 'To know how things have been going on earth and below it:
>   It is clear he must know some day.'

This God has yet to achieve the self-consciousness of 'us humble pioneers / Of himself in consciousness of Life's tears', but (in a phrase whose depth of irony is hard to measure) 'he will overtake us anon, / If the world goes on'. Judgement, that is, is in a skewed relationship to experience; the totality represented by 'God ... the Will, or Force, of Laws' represents a *telos* always outside human history, but nevertheless implicit within and utterly dependent on it – to the point that human consciousness is prior to it.

It is this poem which brings into focus an implicit historiography which works in contrast to Hegel's description of an unfolding *Geist* utilizing the 'cunning of reason' to realize its aims. For Hegel the world is an emanation of *Geist*, and while it must be limited in its realization of the world, it remains in a sense latent, like Providence in the Christian world-view. Those world-historic individuals who perform the work of Spirit are often out of step with their own time, but will *necessarily* be recognized and recuperated by later generations. For Hardy, that is precisely the point of uncertainty. The word 'waiting', which tolls like a bell through the poem, tells of the death of a hope for historical redemption rather than its realization.

The history of the same

Finally, we can reflect, more tentatively, on a related aspect of Hardy's historical understanding. One name for the history which resists dialectics is the history of the *same*. That is, a strategy which enables one to connect the past and present and to assert the presence of the former in the latter (as in haunting) is the assertion that in certain important features *they are in fact the same*, rather than part of a progress in which the past is always subsumed to the Idea. In most thinking about history, the *same* is not worth notice: Hardy himself marked the observation in Burke's 'Thoughts on the Causes of the Present Discontents' that 'true political sagacity manifests itself in distinguishing that complaint which only characterizes the general infirmity of human nature, from those which are symptoms of the particular distemper of our own air and season'.[27] The 'only' here is dismissive, but Burke himself, as we have seem, was interested in what returns and haunts; and in the twentieth century the study of that which endures – the history of the *longue durée* – has offered intriguing possibilities. It was Schopenhauer, an influence on Hardy that critics often underestimate by restricting it to his pessimism, who, with the Nietzsche of *On the Advantage and Disadvantage of History for Life*, protested most vociferously against Hegelian dialectics at the end of the nineteenth century, and indeed against any notion of history which did not recognize a constancy based on the possibility of repetition rather than development and fruition:

> We sit together, talk and excite one another; eyes gleam and voices grow louder. Thousands of years ago, *others* sat in just the same way; it was the same and they were the *same*. It will be the same a thousand years hence. The contrivance that prevents us from becoming aware of this is *time*.[28]

In 'After the Fair' (one of the 'Set of Country Songs'), Hardy invokes the ghosts which at midnight haunt the High Street, 'From the latest far back to those old Roman hosts', all those 'Who loved, laughed, and fought, hailed their friends, drank their toasts / At their meeting-times here, just as these!' Here too Time creates the illusion of difference: Hardy describes how 'the Cross, lately thronged, is a dim naked space / That but echoes the stammering chimes', before adding a footnote stating that 'The chimes' have been 'abolished some years ago' – Time itself becoming a ghostly presence, differing, as it were, internally (as in 'At the Entering of the New Year'), a supplement rather than a stable progression fixed in the name of the Ideal. The same effect is apparent in 'The Ghost of the Past', in which the Past as the everyday is set against the passing of chronological time itself. The poet and an embodied Past share a 'spectral housekeeping':

> As daily I went up the stair
>   And down the stair,
> I did not mind the Bygone there –
>   The Present once to me;
> Its moving meek companionship
>   I wished might ever be,
> There was in that companionship
>   Something of ecstasy.
>
> It dwelt with me just as it was,
>   Just as it was
> When first its prospects gave me pause
>   In wayward wanderings,
> Before the years had torn old troths,
>   As they tear all sweet things,
> Before gaunt griefs had torn old troths
>   And dulled old rapturings.

The personal past takes on a strangely contradictory role here, both as the quotidian, a progressive fraying ('no jarring tone'), and as an 'ecstasy'; prospective as well as retrospective; implicated in the tearing of the 'years' but also, as an allegorical figure, quite separate from them. In the final stanzas the Past itself becomes subject to time, fading and skeletal, seemingly as memory fades. This is Bergsonian time, a time which cannot be separated from human experience; in which the past may be present.

Time for Schopenhauer is what opens the way to Will and ego, and hence to the illusion that one's moment is an absolute, part of a teleology. We might compare Michel Serres, in many ways Schopenhauer's twentieth-century inheritor, launching a deliberately extreme polemic against any stance which implies that 'The first to arrive, the winner of the battle, obtains as his prize the right to reinvent history to his own advantage':

> Instead of condemning or excluding, one consigns a certain thing to antiquity, to archaism. One no longer says 'false' but, rather, 'out-of-date', or 'obsolete'. In earlier times people dreamed, now we think. Once people sang poetry; today we experiment efficiently. History is thus the projection of this very real exclusion into an imaginary, even imperialistic time. The temporal rupture is the equivalent of a dogmatic expulsion.[29]

For a sense of what might be involved here we can turn to Hardy's 'In Time of "The Breaking of Nations"', which seems to adhere in its title to a typographical (and thus teleological) notion of history (*this* time, the Great War, may be the fulfilment of the biblical text, Jeremiah 51: 21). But in its text there is a time which is both specific and continuing, a repetition of the cherished same rather than a development towards a goal:

> Yonder a maid and her wight
> Come whispering by:
> War's annals will cloud into night
> Ere their story die

Here as elsewhere, the 'annal' (the official account written at the end or 'brink' of a year, described both in 'Spectres that Grieve' and in 'At the Entering of the New Year', akin to the 'calendaring' of 'A Wet Night') is dubious, something close to a catastrophe occluding the ordinary stories of men and women. Hardy is almost certainly recalling a passage from Charles Reade which he copied into his notebooks around 1882, commenting that 'The chronic history of Waterloo field is to be ploughed & sowed & reaped & mowed: yet once in a way these acts of husbandry were diversified with a great battle, where hosts decided the fate of Empires. After that agriculture resumed its sullen sway' (*LN* 1283). He is also, perhaps, echoing Carlyle's essay on history: 'Battles and war-tumults, which for a time din every ear and with joy or terror intoxicate every heart, pass away, like tavern brawls.'[30] Or as Serres suggests, rather than being dialectical, war 'gives birth only to nothingness and, identically, to itself. So, destruction repeats itself....

History fairly regularly vindicates those who don't believe in such Hegelian schemas.'

That is also the import of Hardy's postwar meditation 'A Night of Questionings', in which a series of questions are asked by the dead as to whether the world has changed (questions set on 'the eve of All-Soul's Day'; 'the same eve'; 'the self-same eve'). The answer supplied by the wind is that life goes on 'just as in your time', 'with little difference'; men do things 'as you did'; despite efforts to snuff out evil 'Men have not shown... More lovely deeds or true.' 'A Night of Questionings' anticipates the final two poems of *Winter Words* in its vision of history as phantasmagoric, as a ghost-ridden and cyclic delusion, closer to Nietzsche's tragic view than to Comte's progressivism. The 'troubled skulls that heave / And fust in the flats of France' ask how the world fares, and are answered:

> 'As when
> You mauled these fields, do men
> Set them with dark-drawn breaths
> To knave their neighbour's deaths
> In periodic spasms!
> Yea, fooled by foul phantasms,
> In a strange cyclic throe
> Backward to type they go...'

Here the discourse of typology and evolution coalesce and clog: this is more than the temporary backwards loop described by Comte and referred to by Hardy in the 'Apology' to *Late Lyrics and Earlier*, it is a failure of historical recollection. History repeats itself as phantasm because its ghosts cannot be laid to rest; because of the illusion that Time is Progress, that the New Year brings development.

That does not mean that Hardy could not also represent Time as an abstract entity which gathers up all history within it; but he usually does so in satiric mode. His most extreme, if uneven, philosophical expression of this position is his postwar poem 'The Absolute Explains'; with its sense of the flat continuum of 'Being' and the hopelessness of influencing the future. Here history is said to be laid out to view 'down the Void, / Live, unalloyed', with all moments existing at once in the view of the Absolute. But even here there are cyclic returns of the 'same'; as elsewhere in Hardy's corpus, it is song, 'a score times sung, / With all their tripping tunes', which mediates between the transient (the entropic pulse of the sound-wave) and the repeated forms of things. This is particularly the case with bird-song, which is 'self-same' despite different singers in so many poems by Hardy and by his tradition.[31] A human example is 'Music in a Snowy Street', with its

> bygone whirls, heys,
> Crotchets, quavers, the same
> That were danced in the days
> Of grim Bonaparte's fame,
> Or even by the toes
> Of the fair Antoinette, –
> Yea, old notes like those
> Here are living on yet! –

The reference to the French Revolution suggests what has been hinted throughout this chapter – the Revolution and Napoleonic Wars as the Ur-trauma which for Hardy can stand for History itself, for the irruption of European events into the lives of ordinary people. He had, of course, heard stories of the wars handed down by his grandmother, and visitors to Max Gate after the Great War commented that the time of Waterloo seemed more real to him than the twentieth century. The song heard by Marie Antoinette serves as an image of continuity, or the customary, even if tenuous and (elsewhere) threatened, which counters the nineteenth-century history of progress and supersession, and perhaps even the catastrophe of history itself. Mourning and the persistence of song are often linked in Hardy's poetry, for example in 'Haunting Fingers', subtitled 'A Phantasy in a Museum of Musical Instruments'. These instruments are mute: as a contra-basso says, they are 'Doomed to this voiceless, crippled, corpselike state'. Nevertheless they *do* speak in order to recall the dead fingers which haunt them with remembered music:

> 'My keys' white shine,
> Now sallow, met a hand
> Even whiter... Tones of hers fell forth with mine
> In sowings of sound so sweet no lover could withstand!'

The poem evokes the curious status of musical instruments as both made objects – 'all of our glossy gluey make' – and tools involved in the construction of an inanimate entity. Music signals the flow of life seen in its passing, recaptured as memory and a history of the ephemeral.

The return of the 'same' indicates, then, a non-dialectical history. It might be tempting to say that this history is outside even the Darwinian dispensation which is elsewhere so important for Hardy; but Hardy's version of Darwin, unlike that of Spencer, is non-progressive, constantly alive to the tendency of evolution to drift, repeat, over-develop or isolate. This non-dialectical time is to an extent reflected in *The Dynasts* itself. As Isobel Armstrong notes, the various Spirits remain locked into fixed and mutually exclusive positions – the Spirit of the Pities remains compassionate and learns nothing; the Spirit of the Years knows all within its 'bounded prophecy' but learns no compassion.[32] The minimal extent of their development is suggested by an exchange late in the epic, when the Spirit of the Pities observes that many of the participants at the Waterloo ball are accompanied by phantom footmen:

SPIRIT OF THE YEARS

Multiplied shimmerings of my Protean friend,
Who means to couch them shortly. Thou wilt eye
Many fantastic moulds of him ere long,
Such as, bethink thee, thou hast eyed before.

SPIRIT OF THE PITIES

I have – too often!

This is exactly the kind of thing that the Spirits have been saying to each other throughout the epic. The fixity of position here is interesting because it is against the background of an Immanent Will which is, in theory, slowly growing conscious, moving towards the recuperation hinted at in 'Fragment'. If the Immanent Will suggests a dialectical conception of history with its roots in von Hartmann and Hegel, the 'hollowness' of the various Spirits suggests their fixed positions as responses to a history in which catastrophe is a recurrent feature.

If history is a phantom, what is its status, and what the status of historical hope? Shelley, in 'England in 1819' (a sonnet which Hardy marked), listed the corruptions of the four Estates before declaring them 'graves, from which a glorious Phantom may / Burst, to illumine our tempestuous day'. But Hardy was all too aware of the failures of Shelley's hopes. Between Burke and Benjamin lies the Hegelian dream of a history in which all suffering is ultimately recuperated, in which a dialectical process ensures a predetermined *telos*; the very history which Burke protested against in the name of the dead; the history which Nietzsche dismissed for its pretense at science and its burial of any sense of the need to intervene in the present moment. For Benjamin the Hegelian and Marxist teleology has collapsed: historical recuperation must again, as it did for Burke, work as mourning, in a fragmentary mode in which the pattern of the past is re-energized by the present. For Hardy, whose 'Fragment' represents, perhaps, a final hope of historical recuperation of all the dead, the mute voices of the forgotten dead must be attended to alongside any narration of world-historical events. Beyond both Hardy and Benjamin lies our own world, marked by a partial recognition of different and excluded histories, but also by Derrida's mourning for Marx himself; for the memory of history, for the inheritance of the past. Hardy, working in the tradition of Burke and Carlyle, was one of the last writers for whom a historical resistance enacted in the name of individual experience, memory and the dead was possible; in contrast to the disconnection, dominance of rationalizing capital, and inescapable technology of the postmodern world, the *de facto* triumph of state power – but that, too, is a story with its own ghosts.

A final comment. We began with Peter Widdowson's assertion that his *déraciné* position means 'Hardy... is left occupying an apolitical space as a "writer", bolstered by an eclectic and facticious myth of "History".' As we have seen, Hardy was acutely aware of the problems implicit in the 'myth of History'. Indeed, it can be argued that the outsider position that Widdowson describes informs his sense of the dangers of a history which neglects those whom it ploughs under. If Hardy were to forget that, he would be forgetting his own past, and the ancestors of 'A Wet Night' who 'trudged across this spot / In sturdy muteness', and instead casting his lot with the culture which wished to make *The Dynasts* an unequivocally national epic during the Great War. In writing of a history of the 'same', one might add, he attempted to make peace with his ghosts, to assert a continuity which may have been denied by his own experience of a painful modernity, but which nevertheless wished to recognize a fidelity to the past that would allow it to be encountered and understood.

5
History, Catastrophe, Typology

> *For though the whole meaning [of the Past] lies far beyond our ken; yet in that complex Manuscript covered over with formless inextricably-entangled unknown characters, – nay, which is a* Palimpsest, *and had once prophetic writing, still dimly legible there – some letters, some words, may be deciphered; and if no complete Philosophy, here and there an intelligible precept, available in practice, be gathered: well understanding, in the mean while, that it is only a little portion we have deciphered; that much still remains to be interpreted; that History is a real Prophetic Manuscript, and can be fully interpreted by no man.*
>
> Carlyle, 'On History'

Hardy's sense of history has received a great deal of critical attention, usually seen in relation to his novels and *The Dynasts*, with a particular focus on his depiction of changes in rural life and economies in the novels, and the sweep of European history and the forces behind history exemplified by the Will and the various Spirits in *The Dynasts*.[1] What has been less explicitly discussed is his historiography, that is his sense of how history is constructed as a discursive field. In this chapter, I will examine what could be thought of as two extremes on the scale of historical understanding: the catastrophe or seemingly random event as exemplified in the *Titanic* disaster; and the 'plot' of history as understood within a rigid typological scheme and applied in the project of Zionism, which seeks to realize the promises made by God in Genesis. What is at issue throughout is the relationship between history and texuality, between writing, time, and historical understanding. In his 1850 edition of Aristotle's *Poetics* the famous claim that 'poetry speaks more of universals, but history of particulars' is underscored – an argument he would have found confirmed in Schopenhauer's essay on history, included in *The World as Will and Idea*, with its attack on all claims for general historical knowledge.[2] Such scepticism, which portrays history as a chaos of detail, co-exists in the nineteenth century with the systematic and progressive historiographies of Hegel (the particular object of Schopenhauer's attack), Comte, Spencer, and others, in which Hardy was equally well read. We will see, in his poetry, a debate on these positions enacted; a debate which sometimes bears on the individual word as much as the creaking apparatus of Immanent Will and Spirit of the Years.

'The Convergence of the Twain': history as coincidence

When the *Titanic* went down in April 1912, the catastrophe was almost immediately seen as the end of the 'gilded age', a fulcrum around which history might turn. It quickly became one of the most heavily predicted events ever recorded: people found that there were portents of the disaster in dreams, in literature, and even in the name of the ship, with its reference to a mythical race of over-ambitious giants. The Sunday after the disaster the Bishop of Winchester sermonized that 'the *Titanic*, name and thing, will stand for a monument and warning to human presumption'.[3] the editor of The *Irish News* focused on the mythological source of the name, and pointed out that the story of the Titans 'symbolized the vain efforts of mere strength to resist the ordinances of the more "civilized" order established by Zeus'.[4] Some of the portents or anticipations were obvious, the most shocking being Morgan Robertson's 1898 novel *Futility*, which had told the story of a massive ship full of the richest men and women in the world wrecking itself on an iceberg. Robertson called his ship the *Titan*, and even got the tonnage more or less right. Some were more private. The social historian Wynn Craig Wade, in his book on the aftermath of the sinking, describes how William Alden Smith, the American Senator who was to lead the Senate Committee investigating the disaster, pulled these verses out of his wallet, where he had apparently tucked them in 1902.[5] They described a shipwreck:

> Then she, the stricken hull,
> The doomed, the beautiful
> Proudly to fate abased
> Her brow, Titanic.

Even some of the passengers seemed to have anticipated the disaster: the journalist W. T. Stead (whom Hardy knew) was last seen smoking a cigar in the ship's lounge. As a psychic researcher his position on the ship suggests a remarkable lack of prescience, one might say – but he had in fact written a story in 1892 about the shipwreck of a great liner, and another about a ship which collided with an iceberg, the sole survivor being picked up by another vessel called the *Majestic*.[6] Strangely, there was a real ship called the *Majestic* at the time, under the command of – this seems almost demanded by the logic of the myth – Edward Smith, later captain of the *Titanic*. There are other, more fugitive, anticipations of the disaster: Dennis Taylor notices a particularly striking one, Carlyle's description of the death of Mirabeau in *The French Revolution*: 'His death is Titanic, as his life has been! Lit up, for the last time, in the glare of coming dissolution, the mind of the man is glowing and burning. . . . He is as a ship suddenly shivered on sunk rocks.'[7] As well as such literary anticipations, a very large body of literature exists about people who had dreams of the disaster before it happened, or cancelled their passages because of sudden premonitions. Part of the historical resonance of the wreck of the *Titanic* seems to be its omen-ridden nature, its ability to attract predictions as a gravitational mass attracts matter and (in Einstein's theories) rearranges the universe about itself.

In 'The Convergence of the Twain', Hardy describes the sinking of the *Titanic* as 'one august event'. Given the amount of literature surrounding the 'prediction' of the *Titanic* disaster, it is tempting to think that Hardy, one of the most etymologically informed of English poets, meant 'august' in its root sense of 'prepared by augury' and 'brought to fruition'. Indeed, as I will show, his poem seems to partake of the *Titanic* myth both in the popular sense in echoing a 'prediction' of the disaster, and in the more profound sense in suggesting that the potential for disaster was carried within the words that might be used to characterize such a ship, and within its particular impelling force or 'bent'. Hardy's poem, in part, questions the meaning of history and its apparent accidents.

After the sinking of the *Titanic*, the press was flooded with moralizing literature (Joseph Conrad, for example, wrote two pieces criticizing the 'monster ships' and the commercial values which produced them). Hardy's poem, first published as a part of the souvenir programme for a charity event in aid of a disaster fund, was part of that literature. But it was not without its own antecedents, perhaps even a model.[8] In the issue for the week ending 20 April 1912, the *Spectator* published a letter by B. Paul Newman containing a poem called 'A Tryst', which described a ship and an iceberg with a 'dread appointment':

Sir, – I do not know whether you care to print the enclosed poem by Celia Thaxter, an American poetess, who is, I am afraid, little known on this side of the Atlantic. It was published more than thirty years ago in the *Atlantic Monthly*.... It tells of a disaster less terrible, though more complete; than that which has befallen the 'Titanic'.[9]

Indeed this poem by a New England maritime poet, the daughter of a lighthouse keeper, did seem oddly prophetic, and it sparked off what threatened to turn into a literary competition in the *Spectator* as rival anticipations of the wreck were found in De Quincey, Kipling, and elsewhere.

Hardy's poem could almost be another contribution to the *Spectator* (in which he published poems in the 1910s). The timing is tight: there would have been a little over a week between the *Spectator*'s coming out and Hardy's date of composition, 24 April, but it is entirely likely that the weeklies were read avidly in the weeks following the disaster. The similarity of the scheme of his poem to Thaxter's is striking. Both posit the ship and iceberg as thesis and antithesis and alternate descriptions of them; both picture a version of Fate watching the scene. Thaxter begins with the iceberg rather than the ship (the ellipses below are those in the *Spectator*):

> From out the desolation of the North
> An iceberg took its way,
> From its detaining comrades breaking forth,
> And travelling night and day.
>
> At whose command? Who bade it sail the deep
> With that resistless force?
> Who made the dread appointment it must keep?
> Who traced its awful course?
>
> To the warm airs that stir in the sweet South,
> A good ship spread her sails;
> Stately she passed beyond the harbour's mouth
> Chased by the favouring gales;
>
> And on her ample decks a happy crowd
> Bade the fair land good-bye;
> Clear shone the day with not a single cloud
> In all the peaceful sky.

. . . .

Storms buffeted the iceberg, spray was swept
Across its loftiest height;
Guided alike by storm and calm, it kept
Its fatal path aright.

. . . .

Ever Death rode upon its solemn heights,
Ever his watch he kept;
Cold at its heart through changing days and nights
Its changeless purpose slept.

Syntactical similarities and common words might imply that Hardy's poem is an 'improvement' of Thaxter's poem:

Thaxter   Like some imperial creature, moving slow,
            Meanwhile, with matchless grace,
            The stately ship, unconscious of her foe
            Drew near the trysting place.

Hardy   And as the smart ship grew
            In stature, grace, and hue,
            In shadowy silent distance grew the Iceberg too.

Thaxter   She rushed upon her ruin. Not a flash
            Broke up the waiting dark;
            Dully through wind and sea one awful crash
            Sounded, with none to mark.

Hardy   Till the Spinner of the Years
            Said 'Now!' And each one hears,
            And consummation comes, and jars two hemispheres.

The parallels here are suggestive. But this is not an influence-study, and indeed, the uncertainties surrounding the postulate of a connection between Hardy's poem and Thaxter's are as interesting as the 'facts' of the case. Is that connection causal – was Hardy's poem 'inspired' by Thaxter? Or is the connection coincidental and produced by the eye of the critic – the eye that sees 'The intimate welding of their later history', to adopt Hardy's own phrase? As that borrowing suggests, the juxtaposition of the two poems involves problems of the limits of knowledge and interpretation akin to those raised by the *Titanic*: was the wreck spontaneous, or part of a pre-existing pattern which would bring about the end of any 'Titanic' vessel? In both cases we can ask: is it coincidence or a hidden relationship we are seeing?

In fact, Thaxter's 'anticipation' (call it that) of Hardy's poem fits into a pattern of prophecy and consummation, of type and anti-type, which is (as a number of critics have suggested) common in Hardy's poetry. The two poems form a pair like that of the iceberg and ship: secret sharers, separated by time, drawn together in the mind of an observer by 'paths coincident' – a mind which may be Hardy's (if he read Thaxter's poem), but may also be any Hardy-like reader, a person who notices coincidence and meanings which slowly emerge. 'The Convergence of the Twain' itself involves an interplay of buried meaning and its release. Central to that structure of anticipation is an unconsciousness of the meaning of the words of the original action or utterance. Just as Thaxter or Carlyle or Morgan Robertson cannot have known of the potentially prophetic nature of their words, Hardy often depicts the original speakers or readers or hearers of songs, biblical lessons, and other messages as unconscious of a latent meaning which only unfolds in time.

The person who finally reads such meanings is the saddened historian who observes the spectacle of history. Unlike Thaxter, Hardy begins with the outcome of disaster, and works backwards from it, so as to suggest that the causes of events can only be known in a *post hoc* fashion. He remains at a distance: there is no attempt to break through the barrier between teller and tale, to cry out against what is happening in some apostrophic moment, as Thaxter does: 'O helmsman, turn thy wheel! Will no surmise / Cleave through the midnight drear?' The sublimity of the shipwreck does not interest Hardy – the sunken ship is described in terms that are deliberately grotesque and emphasize the irony of the final position of the boat in comparison with its opulence (non-human agents enforce a distance: the 'moon-eyed fishes' which wonder 'What does this vaingloriousness down here?'). The question of why it happened – which he then goes on to answer – is thus removed from any immediate perspective; it is effected through a reconstruction which begins 'Well: while was fashioning'. However, the poem is not simply the neat (and essentially progressive) thesis/antithesis/synthesis structure which J. O. Bailey describes, but rather something more complex: a belated and self-consciously fictional attempt to explain a catastrophic outcome.[10] For Hardy, writing about the *Titanic* disaster involves an exploration of the possibility of explaining such events, and of his own tendency to resolve 'coincidence' into pattern.[11]

Two solutions to the problem of agency

The most important question raised by 'The Convergence of the Twain' is what, ultimately, caused the *Titanic* disaster? Or perhaps (a more abstract question): what is the status of our explanation of the disaster? How do the human explanations which we call 'history' relate to the flux of events which brings together a ship and an iceberg? Disasters are a particular focus for an understanding of the structure of history because they are points of relief, nodes in the flux of events. But according to a strictly materialist and necessitarian view of the universe they do not exist:

> <u>Order & disorder</u> are abstract terms & can have no existence in a nature, where all is necessary & follows constant laws. Order is nothing more than necessity viewed relatively to the succession of actions. Disorder in any being is nothing more than its passage to a new order.   (*LN* 1066)

Hardy copied into his notebook this passage from an essay by John Morley in the *Fortnightly Review* in 1877. In the source it continues:

> Hence there can never be either monsters or prodigies, either marvels or miracles, in nature. By the same reasoning, we have no right to divide the workings of nature into those of Intelligence and those of Chance. Where all is necessary, Chance can mean nothing save the limitation of man's knowledge.[12]

The same passage from Morley suggests that 'in the most violent tempest that agitates the ocean, not a single molecule... of water finds its place by *chance*'. The seeming 'prodigy' of a ship called the *Titanic* wrecking itself is thus not, in theory, exceptional at all, merely a discontinuity in knowledge – and therefore, implicitly, not to be mythologized or moralized. But this stark positivist view of events was not, I hope to show, one which Hardy supported; his view of history allows for the human need for meanings, patterns, and marvels, and for the struggle between 'intelligence' and seeming 'chance'.

Hardy read a great deal on the philosophy of history in an attempt to form his ideas about its relation to that 'Necessity' which governs the positivist's universe. In the 1870s and 1880s he copied material from a number of writers into his notebooks: Auguste Comte, Leslie Stephen (whose essay 'An Attempted Philosophy of History' he studied carefully), John Stuart Mill, von Hartmann, Macaulay, Froude, and others. Comte, in particular, provided a focus. He attempted to provide the grounding for a systematic and scientific history, and Hardy copied some of his tree-like diagrams into his notes. Comte also made a distinction between two views of the universe: the Fetishistic, which sees things driven individually by their inbuilt pulsions, and the Theistic, which sees a supernatural force behind events (whether God or something like the Hegelian Will). The latter implies a *telos*, a plan to history (even if human beings are therefore powerless), where the former is much more suggestive of a world of confused individual forces, and of sheer accident. In passages which Hardy excerpted into his notebooks, Comte argues (as we saw in Chapter 2) that the Fetishistic is the more materialist and therefore more accurate view, simpler in its assumptions; and at the same time the more poetic view, as it animates both the external world and language. But he also suggests that the hypothesis of 'Directing Wills' controlling events could be useful to the historian as an explanatory and aesthetic device – a hint which, Björk suggests, Hardy may have used to justify his mouthpieces in *The Dynasts*.[13] Indeed, Comte's own Positivism can be seen as Theistic to the extent that it inherits a freight of Hegelian idealism, a tendency to totalize.

Hardy, like other Victorians for whom the 'Death of God' left a palpable absence, was interested in alternatives to the personal God of the Scriptures. In *The Dynasts* he borrows from von Hartmann and others the idea of the Will or First Cause, a moving principle within evolution and history which may be slowly moving towards consciousness. The Immanent Will hovers between Comte's two poles (indeed that seems partly its function): it is immanent within events, and thus can be seen as Fetishistic; but in as much as it is unitary and posited as coming to consciousness it also seems Theistic, a God-replacement. The suggestion of consciousness is, however, hardly allowed in *The Dynasts*: in the Fore Scene the Spirit of the Years insists that the Will is (as we have seen) somnambulistic, weaving its web 'in skilled unmindfulness ... with an absent heed'. Indeed F. B. Pinion suggests that in the period after completing *The Dynasts*, and particularly after the First World War, Hardy moved away from abstract ideas of a Will, towards a greater emphasis on (and sadness at) human agency and folly.[14] Certainly by 1920 he stressed that all names for 'the Power behind the universe' which he had used were heuristic, 'fancies... mere impressions of the moment'

(*LY* 217). 'The Convergence of the Twain' thus offers an interesting test case in terms of its sense of the causes of events: was the wreck the product of a Fate or of human folly?

Hardy's answer to the question of what 'caused' the disaster that is the occasion of the poem at first seems implicitly 'Theistic', linked to the Immanent Will which watches and 'prepares' events. There is a hint of the moralizing typical of *Titanic* literature in his references to 'human vanity' and 'Pride of Life', derived from Ecclesiastes and 1 John 2: 1 6, and the latter allusion suggests that what the Apostle calls the 'lust of the eyes' and the excessively worldly extravagance of the ship produce a chastisement, a moral lesson imposed from without. The ironic rhymes reinforce this bitter conclusion about the fate of a latter-day Ship of Fools: opulent/ indifferent; mind/blind. That the *Titanic* was a piece of Vanity was a lesson universally drawn, by a range of public opinion from the Bishops to Conrad and the popular press. Moreover, as Jeremy Hawthorn points out, Hardy distances himself from more material explanations of the disaster, abstracting it away from the issues of speed, signalling, lifeboat provision which were to occupy the official inquiries, and offering what seems a meditation on 'timeless' absolutes.[15]

But Hardy is also interested in investigating more deeply, in looking at the process through which such a moral lesson might be suggested: the simple contrast between sunken opulence and a 'creature of cleaving wing' is not sufficient. The second half of the poem, couched as it is in ambiguous terms which might be seen to both offer and withdraw a sense of active forces at work, raises more interesting questions about where responsibility is to be placed:

> Well: while was fashioning
> This creature of cleaving wing,
> The Immanent Will that stirs and urges everything
>
> Prepared a sinister mate
> For her – so gaily great –
> A Shape of Ice, for the time far and dissociate.

The unusual participle suggests that what happens merely happens: 'was fashioning' implies an absent subject ('[the Immanent Will] was fashioning'), but then withdraws it; it is not the Immanent Will that fashions the ship, not even mankind or the White Star Line seemingly, but just a process of 'being fashioned'. Nevertheless, the use of the Immanent Will does suggest a force behind history, and the allusions to angel and archangel, type and anti-type, sexual fusion and Platonic halves, place the event within a discernible pattern – even though at this point 'No mortal eye could see', as he puts it, 'the intimate welding of their later history.' 'Welding' is one of Hardy's jokes, referring to the construction of ships, but it also raises the question of whether the ship's fate is welded into it by its makers, or whether the welding is imposed from without by the Immanent Will. The stanza which follows is equally ambiguous with respect to agency. Hardy first wrote:

> And so coincident
> In course as to be meant
> To form anon twin halves of one august event,

where 'meant' seems to be the imposition of Fate. But the poem as revised for the *Fortnightly Review* and in its final version was more ambiguous, saying 'Or sign that they were bent / By paths coincident / On being anon'. 'Bent' can be either active or passive here: it seems at first to suggest an outside force that they were 'bent / By'. But then, in the third line of the stanza, the arrival of the adverbial preposition 'on' seems to alter that, indicating that the ships themselves have an embodied will, being 'bent on' collision – an interpretation which suggests Comte's 'Fetishistic' universe of self-motivated objects. Was the collision willed by or somehow built into the *Titanic* itself? Or was it simply Fate? There is a systematic uncertainty at work within these lines, what we could call a 'bent by/bent on' principle which permeates them. The words used to describe the ship also carry a number of ambiguities. The ship is described as 'smart', that is elegant, neat, and perhaps also brisk, alert. David Perkins suggests that 'smart' here 'may be pejorative', and indeed it is: the word has associations of hurt, and even, as the *Oxford English Dictionary* puts it, of 'suffering of the nature of punishment or retribution' ('smart-money' is the money paid to widows of seamen).[16] The adjective thus carries a hint of the ship's destiny. 'August' in the phrase 'august event' can mean, as I have said, either grand or predicted and ripened, as if one should have known what was going to happen. We might even see a quibble on 'anon': was it, or was it not, an anonymous deed? Once again, are disasters caused or accidental? 'Anon' is curious: it means 'soon' of course, but that would be redundant in this context, except for filling out the metre. Perhaps Hardy is also thinking of the older meaning suggested by the Old English roots *on an* and *on ane*, a unity 'in one body, mind, state, act, way, course, motion, movement, moment', as the *Oxford English*

Dictionary climactically phrases it. In that case, the word itself recapitulates the argument: their being 'anon twin halves' means that they are fated to be coincident. The only question, as in all discussions of fate, is that of the 'moment'; it is a matter of waiting,

> Till the Spinner of the Years
> Said 'Now!' And each one hears,
> And consummation comes, and jars two hemispheres.

The ambiguity about agency is retained by this Pataphysical 'explanation' (an example of Alfred Jarry's 'science of imaginary solutions'). The string of three 'ands' seems more like a Humean constant conjunction than the actions suggested by the verb of command ('then' would imply a different effect). The word 'consummation', with its biblical overtones, again suggests typological thinking, but once more the indirect construction weakens the sense of agency: not 'it is consummated' but 'consummation comes', through the back door as it were. At this point, the perspective of Hardy (and the reader) is curiously like that of the Immanent Will, merely watching what has been set in motion. Agency seems to have been offered, only to be removed, or rather be made an effect of the text, something hidden in the words of the poem rather than embodied in its personified first cause. Even Hardy's revision of the name of that entity suggests a qualification: the term he first wrote, 'Mover', implies implosion, while 'Spinner', while it fits in with a pattern of Shelleyan imagery which permeates Hardy's poetry, also suggests an aesthetic effect more like the work of the writer than that of a 'Mover', an effect only perceptible once the pattern is finished. As language is 'animated' (to borrow Comte's phrase), History becomes art.

The construction of history

What then is the view of the writing of history suggested by this poem, with its tendency to hover between the Theistic and the Fetishistic, and to dwell on the hidden meanings of words? Hardy knew Herbert Spencer's attack on official history in the name of a totalizing social history which focuses on deeper causes, and as his notebooks attest, he studied Comte's systematic history. He was also aware (mainly through secondary works) of Hegel's philosophy of history; in the late 1880s he abridged the following from the Whig historian T. H. Green's introduction to *The Philosophical Works of David Hume* (1874):

How the history of mankind should be studied. – 'There is a view of the hist. of mank.^{d}, by this time familiarized to Englishmen, which detaches from the chaos of events a connected series of ruling actions & beliefs – the achievements of great men & great epochs, & assigns to these in a special sense the term "historical". According to this theory – which indeed, if there is to be a theory of history at all, alone gives the needful simplification – the mass of nations must be regarded as left in swamps & shallows outside the main stream of human development.... They have trodden the old round of war, trade, & faction, adding nothing to the spiritual heritage of man.' (*LN* 1370)

But if Hardy was interested in such concepts as the 'Immanent Will', he tended to reject the tradition of systematic and universal history which descends from Hegel to Marx and Comte (a tradition which attributes to history a logic and a *telos*, an implicit order beneath apparent disorder). Despite copying Comte's comments on the continuity of history (*LN* 718), Hardy remained sceptical. In 1884 he wrote:

Is not the present quasi-scientific system of writing history mere charlatanism? Events and tendencies are traced as if they were rivers of voluntary activity, and courses reasoned out from the circumstances in which natures, religions, or what-not, have found themselves. But are they not in the main the outcome of *passivity* – acted upon by unconscious propensity?   (*EL* 219–20)

Here, it is the suggestion that historical action is 'voluntary' or willed which is the main target, though Hardy admits that there may be an unconscious cause at work. His position here does not in fact seem so different from that which he criticizes (particularly when we remember the 'rivers' of people pouring across Europe in the Fore Scene of *The Dynasts*), but what he finds offensive is the suggestion that causes are accessible to reason, that history can be predicted and diagrammed as well as represented as drama. The anti-Comtean rhetoric is continued in a note written the following year, in 1885, in the context of a reflection on the turbulent politics of the early 1880s. Again he stresses accident and chaotic movement:

History is rather a stream than a tree. There is nothing organic in its shape, nothing systematic in its development. It flows on like a thunderstorm-rill by a road side; now a straw turns it this way, now a tiny barrier of sand that. The offhand decision of some commonplace mind high in office at a critical moment influences the course of events for a hundred years.   (*EL* 225)

This is not to say that history does not have a 'plot'; but rather, that the plot of history is only knowable as a reconstruction. The passage continues:

> Thus, judging by bulk of effect, it becomes impossible to estimate the intrinsic value of ideas, acts, material things: we are forced to appraise them by the curves of their career. There were more beautiful women in Greece than Helen; but what of them?

No science can discover and appraise the precise makeup of any historical situation, in terms of its elements and agents. Only the 'curve of a career' allows us to write history and gives us a sense that in retrospect certain elements were important. Indeed, the phrase 'curve of a career' suggests another response to Comte, via an entry in Hardy's notebook:

> <u>The course of Humanity, an arc</u> – 'Social Dynamics have . . . explained in detail an arc of sufficient length to enable us to foresee what course the arc must take when continued.'   (*LN* 721)

Where Comte's 'arc' is predictive, Hardy's 'curve' is retrospective, the product of a necessary blindness which means understanding is belated.

One possible philosophical move at this point is to suggest that despite human blindness there may still be a power within history, an unconscious Will of the universe which is, as Hardy himself put it in explicating *The Dynasts*, 'growing aware of Itself'. The problem with this entity is that the process of its growth must be very slow, and its putative 'intelligence' remains an epiphenomenon (as consciousness always is for Hardy): a useless excrescence itself exposed to the cruelty of chance, rather than an impelling force central to the Will's essence. Indeed, the postulate of 'intelligence', where that intelligence is limited, necessarily demands that it is opposed to the 'Chance' which represents the area of its ignorance, and of its actual operation (in this, it reflects the human subject). If that is the case, then the 'Immanent Will' which Hardy places in *The Dynasts* and 'The Convergence of the Twain', and which is at times seen as lying behind human actions and history, is perhaps less important for Hardy's poetry (and, ultimately, for his idea of history) than the Spirit of the Pities which comments on the pathos of human affairs. For if the Immanent Will does bend events, and is 'immanent' within them, it is, nevertheless, to just that extent outside history, in so far as 'history' is a human creation, a product of the consciousness with which the Will is not yet properly invested. The 'Will' can only be seen as the force behind events, creating the 'curve' or web of history, at the cost of a recognition of its manifesting itself as 'accident'. Catastrophe – whether the *Titanic* disaster or the outbreak of war – tends to confirm that limitation, and to underscore the Will's essential emptiness as an explanatory device. We see that emptiness in a letter which Hardy wrote to Frederic Harrison in late 1913, explaining his times:

> I agree that the times have a strange & disturbing colour just now. I have always said that if wrong ideas & wrong doings had been withdrawn from the so-called civilized world's mind & actions gradually in the last century, catastrophes might have been avoided in its future history. But these things have been persistently bolstered up – are bolstered up every day that dawns, & they must come down 'with a run' soon. (*CL* 4: 319)

Here, Hardy uses similar ambiguously passive constructions to those which describe the catastrophic course of the *Titanic* in 'The Convergence of the Twain' ('was fashioning'). Who might have withdrawn these ideas? Who bolstered them? How might history have been altered? Outside of human agency there are no answers to these questions from the apocalyptic observer of the 'run' of things.

'The Convergence of the Twain' has two entities usually regarded as being effectively the same: the 'Immanent Will' and the 'Spinner of the Years'. But in one crucial respect they are different. The Immanent Will acts, but like its counterpart in *The Dynasts* it is silent. The 'Spinner of the Years' seems to me to be closer to the Spirit of the Pities (and to Hardy himself) through having a voice which marks, rather than simply impelling, the consummation which 'comes'. Hardy's view of history is similarly divided between the desire for an agent within history, and a recognition of the fact that the idea of agency as an imposed direction (a 'curve' or 'run') is bound up with human hopes, expectations, and recognitions, always belated and subject to accident. His poem suggests that there are two ways of looking at what happened to the *Titanic*. In one, its sinking was a chastisement of mankind prepared by the Immanent Will and inflicted on the ship. In this view of things, which, as we saw, the poem initially seems to support (and moralize), 'history' is an abstract entity like that which the Idealist tradition postulates, 'bending' human fate. In the other way of looking at things, however, the sinking of the *Titanic* was not the action of a Will, but rather was built into it, not so much by the builders, who are unconscious of what they do, but by Hardy himself, in the words which describe it in his own poem and trace its career as he watches and marks like the 'Spinner of the Years'. In this view, history is always the product of the interaction of human efforts and designs, and ultimately of the act of interpretation itself and the tropes used to describe it (a trope being itself a kind of 'bending' or 'welding' of words).

We can relate this realization to another set of quotations in Hardy's notebooks: the comments on the writing of history, and on the need to see it as a kind of 'drama' or literary construct, engendered by the historian's need to impose order on that chaos of human events which goes under the sign of 'fact' or 'necessity'. The historian must create a narrative with 'every part naturally springing from that which precedes', as Trevelyan put it in a passage on Macaulay which Hardy copied and underlined (*LN* 1047); 'All is required [of the historian] which is required of the dramatist', as Froude wrote of Carlyle (*LN* 1345). It is no accident that all four historians involved in these passages are English narrative historians. Carlyle's view of history as a chaotic and sublime drama is in clear opposition to the ordered, 'scientific' history of Comte and others; it demands human ordering, but implicitly mocks such order, making it not so much a testable hypothesis as a structure of words which seeks to assuage our desire for meanings.

That is why there is, as Dennis Taylor puts it, an '"intimate welding" of aesthetic pattern and world pattern' in 'The Convergence of the Twain'.[17] 'Anon', soon or eventually, becomes 'anon', that which is one mind or motion. 'Smart', elegant and quick, becomes a 'smart', a loss, pain, or punishment. Even the shape of the stanzas resembles a ship low in the water. So if we were to ask why the *Titanic* sank, the answer hidden in Hardy's poem would be that conceivably its sinking was built into the process of its creation: to make a 'Titanic' ship is to invite a catastrophe of the kind that one will not predict, but which will become apparent in retrospect. The 'meaning' of the ship is carried as a kind of latency, as submerged material – like the iceberg itself, whose hidden bulk seems to suggest something like a return of the repressed in so much of the literature on the *Titanic*. But that meaning is latent rather than active; indeed it exists only once the poem is created.

'The Convergence of the Twain' allows us, momentarily, to support both the views of agency suggested earlier, to see the ship both as 'bent by' the Will and 'bent on' its own destruction. In so doing, it forces us to examine what we mean by 'history', and to confront, as I have suggested, what it means to write history, establishing it as a pattern of events which lead to each other, or even redouble on each other as Hardy's poem seems to do with Thaxter's. As we saw, in redrafting the poem Hardy replaced 'meant' with 'bent', as if all meaning were itself a process of bending things one way or another until they make contact (as it might be argued that I did in comparing Hardy and Thaxter in the first place). It is pleasing to imagine that when, over a decade later, Hardy wrote of Einstein's theories in 'Drinking Song', he was thinking of his poem on the *Titanic*:

> And now comes Einstein with a notion –
>   Not yet quite clear
>   To many here –
> That there's no time, no space, no motion
>   Nor rathe nor late,
>   Nor square nor straight,
> But just a sort of bending-ocean.[18]

There is a similar relativity about the 'bending-ocean' on which the *Titanic* floats in 'The Convergence of the Twain'. According to the historiographer Hayden White, all forms of historical understanding are 'equally relativistic, equally limited by the language chosen in which to delimit what is possible to say about the subject under study'.[19] Just what causes catastrophe is impossible to say, since the outcome depends on how you construct it, on the terms you use – even the word 'catastrophe' is, in its origin, an aesthetic term. Moreover, events like the sinking of the *Titanic* create a kind of Einsteinian gravitation field and seem to encourage us to bend events around them. Hardy's sense of history allows for catastrophe and indeed expects it, but he sees it under the sign of irony, as a product of an inbuilt blindness in human affairs, in which things can only be seen properly by those who reflect from a distance. If 'The Convergence of the Twain' may, as I have suggested, be linked to Celia Thaxter's poem, that too is another example of the fact that everywhere in Hardy's work 'shapes' are – for a time – 'far and dissociate', before the writing of a personal or public history bends them together in a grotesque consummation. But even if Hardy never saw 'A Tryst', and the similarity between the two poems is merely 'coincidence', that too is part of the ironic process of reconstruction which we call history, and justify to ourselves as we write it, finding the right words.

Zionism and typology

If the account offered above stresses historical relativity and the agency of the historian, I want in the remainder of this chapter to turn to a topic which might seem to return us to the collective history, based on the tribe or nation-state, which is so characteristic of romantic historiography.[20] As we have seen, in poems like 'Quid Hic Agis?' Hardy adheres to a scheme which we could call 'agnostic typology'; that is the patterning of life around the slow revelation of the meaning of a biblical text, but without the sense of fruition and providential closure which would be offered by a belief in God. Such examples are personal, the expression of the individual's search for meaning in a world where the sacred texts have become de-sacralized, but have lost none of their rhetorical power. But what of the more collective mythologies which might inform history?

One example of such a collective vision, offering the possibility of historical action, is early twentieth-century Zionism. Zionism involves a strict version of typological (or Theistic) history, a dream of realizing the ancient promises made to Israel that its lands would be restored (the Zionist slogans of 'Divine Promise' and 'Biblical Fulfilment' were derived from Genesis 13: 15; 15: 18; 28: 13 and elsewhere). Hardy's engagement with the subject has never, so far as I am aware, been explored, though his interest in the Jews as the 'People of the Book' was deep-rooted. His notebooks, for example, contain an 1876 review of J. P. N. Land's *The Principles of Hebrew Grammar*, dealing with word-play in the Old Testament and the relationship between the written script and speech, which provided him with a model of continuity in contrast with the decline of dialect he saw everywhere in Dorset: if the 'Death of a language' was threatened after the Diaspora, its 'Careful conservation...by the grammatical schools' saved it (*LN* 848, 850). Judaism serves as the model for a prophetic and typological history, stabilizing such catastrophes as the Diaspora with a vision which spans the centuries. This is suggested by the way in which the Spirit of the Years takes human form in the final scene of *The Dynasts*, Part Second, to warn of the coming war in Europe, with what Castlereagh sees as the 'manner...of an old prophet' of 'Jewish cast' and 'Hebraic style'.

We know something of Hardy's attitude to Zionism because in the *Life* he includes a letter of support, written in November 1905, to Israel Zangwill (whom Hardy knew, well enough to be invited to his wedding in 1903). This is one of the rare occasions on which Hardy broke his resolution not to be allied to any political cause. Zangwill had recently split from the mainstream English Zionist Federation (EZF) and set up the Jewish Territorial Organization (Ito); what he sent to Hardy was the First Ito Manifesto, dated 18 August 1905.[21] At issue in the EZF/Ito split was the offer which the British government had made in 1903 of land in Uganda for a Jewish homeland. The offer was partly cynical – Chamberlain wished to encourage Jewish immigration as a buffer against German ambitions in Africa – but Zangwill nevertheless saw it as a realistic proposition, considering the aim of the 'Zion Zionists' to achieve a Palestinian homeland to be a dangerous fixation; akin to an overly narrow definition of typology. Instead Zangwill portrayed himself as a pragmatist, interested in the present: the East End; the fate of Jews in Russia. His lobbying of Hardy and other public figures was aimed at gaining support for his new movement, using the idea of Jewish settlers as servants of Empire; he published the resulting letters early in 1906.[22]

Hardy's response in this 'pragmatic' context is interesting. He sees the attractions of the East African scheme as 'a good practical idea, and...possibly all the better for having no retrospective sentiment about it' (*LY* 115–16). But he adds that it is precisely the 'retrospective sentiment' attached to the idea of a return to Palestine which would attract him if he were a Jew, '"like unto them that dream" – as one of you said in a lyric which is among the finest in any tongue'. He adds in an aside that he is at one remove from the source of the psalm ('You, I suppose, read it in the original; I wish I could'). The aside equates the imagined plenitude of Zion with a return to the original text, with an escape from translation. At one remove on the political issue, Hardy proposes his own translation:

> The only plan that seems to me to reconcile the traditional feeling with the practical is that of regarding the proposed Jewish state on virgin soil as a stepping-stone to Palestine. A Jewish colony united and strong and grown wealthy in, say, East Africa, could make a bid for Palestine (as a sort of annexe) – say 100 years hence – with far greater effect than the race as scattered all over the globe can ever do; and who knows if by that time altruism may not have made such progress that the then ruler or rulers of Palestine, whoever they may then be, may even hand it over to the expectant race, and gladly assist them, or part of them, to establish themselves there.   (*LY* 115)

Here, the possible development of consciousness is typological as well as meliorist: the African state will shadow forth the ultimate goal of Israel; it will be carried across (translated) to its point of origin. Typology will be effected not so much through a divine opening of the way as through a series of successive human efforts aimed at the realization of a goal.

It is worth noting that the phrase *like unto them that dream* was to have a more personal meaning for Hardy. The 'lyric' it comes from is Psalm 126, one of the psalms for Evening Service on the 27th day of the month in the Anglican order of service, and therefore the psalm beside which he was, seven years after his letter to Zangwill, to insert a slip in his psalter reading 'ELH died on November 27. 1912'.[23] Its triumphant prophecy of Israel's release from captivity – 'They that sow in tears: shall reap in joy' – must have seemed deeply ironic as Hardy woke from his own dream, an awakening itself chronicled in typological poems like 'Quid Hic Agis?', and seen in terms of the apocalypse of the war as well as his personal loss. The carefully-negotiated meliorism illustrated by the letter to Zangwill is replaced, after 1915, by a harsher sense of a world in turmoil, barely to be structured by human dreaming.

A sense of that chaos is offered by a later set of references to Zionism. In 1917 the British government offered explicit support for Zionism in the Balfour Declaration, partly as a way of indirectly controlling the British Protectorate in Palestine. Suddenly the 'dream' of Israel was more of a possibility than ever before, producing a wave of campaigning and debate. Hardy associates two poems with these events, one directly and one more indirectly. The first, 'Jezreel', is subtitled 'On Its Seizure by the English under Allenby, September 1918' (Hardy placed 'No copyright' under the poem when it was printed in *The Times* on 27 Septemper 1918, as he often did with war-poems). Early printings did not include the subtitle, leaving it to the reader to supply the topical context of Allenby's lightning defeat of the Turkish 4th, 7th and 8th Armies in Palestine. The campaign was widely interpreted in terms of one possible historical precedent: both *The Times* (in an article dedicated to the subject) and the *Spectator* compared Allenby's manoeuvres to those of Richard Coeur de Lyon during the Third Crusade in 1191.[24] But Hardy carefully steers clear of such nationalist typology, preferring to see the battles in terms of what the *Spectator* called 'biblical geography'. The poem maps the General's attack on the town onto that described in 2 Kings 9, positing a series of questions as to whether some 'Vision' of the past struck the modern soldiers 'in that long-ago place'. Did they see the cursed King Joram, or the ghost of 'that proud Tyrian woman', his mother Jezebel?

> Faintly marked they the words 'Throw her down!' from the Night eerily,
> Spectre-spots of the blood of her body on some rotten wall?

And the thin note of pity that came: 'A King's daughter is she',
As they passed where she trodden was once by the chargers' footfall?

Could such be the haunting of men to-day, at the cease
Of pursuit, at the dusk-hour, ere slumber their senses could seal?
Enghosted seers, kings – one on horseback who asked 'Is it peace?'...
Yea, strange things and spectral may men have beheld in Jezreel!

What is central to the poem is less any systematic parallel which might be applied to the events – such as Ahab's usurpation of the vineyard of Naboth, the event lying behind the death of Joram and Jezebel, acting as a type of the Turkish occupation of the Holy Land – than a sense that repetition, in the typological sense, is part of the pathos of history, and the ghostly tendency of stories to haunt particular places at either end of time. Indeed, this is anything but a typology which finds a fulfilment in the British victory, or even in the way in which that victory opened up the Holy Land to Jewish settlement (*The Times* ran a report on the civilizing influences of a Hebrew University in Jerusalem only days after the battle).[25] Hardy assigns an imaginative priority to the soldiers who might hear the ghostly echo of Joram, and the point of the poem's repeated questions is whether they apprehend his presence. He leaves to the reader the implicit negative answer to the question 'Is it peace?': there is more violence to come, exacerbated with 'arms of new might'. At the historical level, typology does not work to stabilize meanings, it merely opens out questions; the 'spectre-spots' which represent a mapping of time and place lead to no sure confirmation. The fact that a more personal impulse lingers behind the biblical text of 2 Kings – Hardy's deep identification with the 'gaunt mournful Shade' of Elijah, the reluctant prophet whom the 'still small voice' of the Lord awakens as he flees from Jezebel and Ahab into the wilderness outside Jezreel – again means that this poem must be read as a meditation on the individual's apprehension of the ironies and terrors of history rather than as the fulfilment of typology.

Two other distracting elements also complicate the picture: the intrusion of the textual ghost of Wordsworth in this Old Testament scene ('A slumber did my spirit steal') reinforces the sense of a restless moiling of words. More importantly, the fact that, as Hardy surely knew from newspaper accounts, the cavalry who 'smote through the ancient Esdraelon Plain' were not 'Englishmen' at all, but Indian Lancers, adds a further layer of irony in an imperial war. In the same page of the *Life* as the report of his support for Zionism, Hardy had wondered whether it might be better to 'let Western "Civilization" perish, and the black and yellow races have a chance' (*LY* 190), a reflection which imagines the end of the Judeo-Christian dispensation. The attenuation of that tradition is conveyed by another typological poem, 'I Met a Man', dated 1916. It begins by imaging a modern-day Moses who relates his vision of the Godhead, now closer to Hardy's ambivalent watching Absolute than to the Old Testament God, pondering on the scene of war in Europe, and on the history of 'swollen All-Empery plans':

> 'With violence the lands are spread
>   Even as in Israel's day,
>   And it repenteth me I bred
>   Chartered armipotents lust-led
> To feuds... Yea, grieves my heart, as then I said,
>   To see their evil way!'

The 'then' of this utterance is the days of Saul, but the recollection here offers no moment of fulfilment, only a weak echo on the part of a God who is barely audible to his reporter and meekly fades from view.

If 'Jezreel' is explicitly related to the postwar debate on Zionism, '"According to the Mighty Working"' is more oblique in its reference. It too answers Joram's question in the negative: peace is an illusion in a world of 'Transmutation' (the poem's earlier title). But its publication raises more general issues about the way in which a text may be applied to history – indeed, may be haunted by history. In 1919 John Middleton Murray wrote asking for something for the *Athenaeum*, and Hardy sent this poem. His comments on the publication in a letter to Arthur McDowall provide what we could see as a general model for the way in which a political relevance might be demanded of a poem, be ostensibly refused, but none the less enter into its context:

> It must have been more of an accident than design I imagine that the lines suited the present date, for I told the editor that I had nothing 'topical'. That is always the difficulty when one is asked for verses for a periodical: it is easy enough to send *something* that one has lying about, possibly on the moon, stars, trees, grass or shadowy kine; but the reader of the paper says on seeing it – 'Why, what I want is the author's last word upon the world's events; not this stuff!'   (*CL* 5: 306–7)

What he has at hand is eternal subjects (moon, stars, trees). Yet even a poem which uses these universals, or draws from the Bible as ' "According to the Mighty Working"'' does, enters the public domain as an *event*. Indeed, in the *Life* Hardy does admit that the poem – written in 1917 – was topical in a prophetic sense, since in marking the end of the war but also suggesting that 'Peace' was an illusion it anticipated yet more troubles, including the Zionist agitation over the British Protectorate in Palestine, a context gathered into the same sentence:

> In February [1919] he signed a declaration of sympathy with the Jews in support of a movement for the 'reconstitution of Palestine as a National Home for the Jewish people', and during the spring he received letters from Quiller-Couch, Crichton-Browne, and other friends on other near and dear relatives they had lost in the war; about the same time there appeared a relevant poem by Hardy in the *Athenaeum* which was much liked, entitled in words from the Burial Service, 'According to the Mighty Working'. (*LY* 190)

Where is the 'relevance'? '"According to the Mighty Working"' evokes the flux of existence, in which there is no point of stability, no achieved consummation like that supposedly embodied in Zionism's messianic expectations:

> Peace, this hid riot, Change,
>   This revel of quick-cued mumming,
>   This never truly being,
>   This evermore becoming,
>   This spinner's wheel onfleeing
> Outside perception's range.

The 'becoming' celebrated here, like that in *The Dynasts* (the unconscious spinner working mindlessly), precludes any notion of arrival; of peace or even, in the context of the war, of resolved mourning. As in that other great war poem with a biblical title, 'In Time of "The Breaking of Nations"', it is the status of the poem as an open text, as unresolvable type, which generates its topicality, its timely-ness. Both poems, that is, need to be seen as theoretical interventions, as meditations on a text which both seems to predict the world's progress and that in fact offers no stable antitype which might resolve history. Indeed, Hardy had also, in the 1870s, seen parallels between Exodus, Milton's Satan, the march of the persecuted Mormons west in America, and the forcing of Native American tribes west to Montana (*LN* 837, 1013) – a set of parallels which breaks the normal boundaries of typology and introduces a general notion of religious and racial persecution and exile. In relation to Zionism, it is as if Hardy suspected the government policy which made support just another imperial intervention, diplomacy (or 'peace') acting as a covert form of war rather than the realization of a prophecy.[26]

The stable forms of typological or of any providential or externally plotted history work, then, only as forms of irony. Whether in the ship and iceberg of 'The Convergence of the Twain' or the repetitions of Biblical history in the Holy Land, it is forms of human intentionality which shape the chaos of history, but ultimately only as what Hardy called, in his letter to Zangwill, a 'retrospective sentiment'. The timeliness of a poem is, for Hardy, a product of interpretation rather than being a product of its immanence within anything like a world-historical sense; it cannot attach itself to history except as a construction of events. The lines from John Morley which we saw Hardy copy into his notebook – 'Disorder in any being is nothing more than its passage to a new order' – apply to poetry, in the sense that it is always transitional, never resolved in its relation to the world.

6
Mourning and Intertextuality

This final chapter concerns itself with ghosts of a literal and textual kind: with Emma Hardy, conjured up fleetingly in the 'Poems of 1912–13' and related poems; and with the ghosts of other texts which also flicker through the poems – both of Hardy's own texts and those of literary tradition. In some cases, these two traces come together, suggesting that mourning may involve an incorporation of the words of others not present, either the lost loved one or a textual surrogate. Emma Hardy's own writings offer one such set of words, and it is well known that Hardy read her early diaries as he mourned.[1] But the later Emma was a more baleful ghost, leaving Hardy to burn the vituperative notebook supposedly labelled 'What I think of my Husband', consigning its words to ashes, to non-knowledge. We need, then, to think of Hardy's mourning as a double process, requiring both textual displacement and textual recovery; as involving the elision of some words, and the recollection or substitution of others. Three linked topics related to that process will be investigated here, the first two suggested by the epigraph to the 'Poems of 1912–13': the metaphorization of the cinders or ashes of romance in Hardy's own corpus; the Virgilian and Dantean context evoked by the epigraph; and finally, the possibility that part of Hardy's response to Emma's death was an attention to the trope of crossed voices evoked by the rhetorical figure of chiasmus, and including a turn to two women poets of the nineteenth century who might offer a dialogue with the poet.

Cinders

In 1895 Hardy was mailed 'a packet of ashes' from Australia; it was his own novel, *Jude the Obscure*, sent back to him. This episode is one of the illustrations of public bigotry in the *Life*, explaining why he might have wished to move from prose to poetry (*LY* 39). But the story also obliquely suggests that the poems *are* the ashes of the novels, or of the novels returned to him as ashes.[2] That is a possibility which is explored in the 'Poems of 1912–13', with their careful retracing of the romance-landscape of *A Pair of Blue Eyes*, and their meditation on the end of romance. The story of other novels – for example the account of marital regret in *The Mayor of Casterbridge* – is also recalled in the sequence. And of course, the topic of ashes is written into the sequence's epigraph, *veteris vestigia flammae*; the phrase spoken by Dido when her capacity for love, which she thought had died with her husband Sychaeus, is rekindled as she listens to Aeneas tell his story – a phrase variously translated as 'traces of the former flame', 'ashes from an old fire' (Hardy's favourite translator, Dryden, has 'sparkles of my former flame'). It is an ambiguous phrase: as Peter Sacks points out, *flammae* can signify both fire and the ruins of a fire; *vestigia* can imply both traces or embers – that which might lead one to something, or be rekindled – and the irrevocably lost. This ambiguity reflects the most obvious incongruity in Hardy's use of the Virgilian epigraph: he refers to a reawakened love not, as Dido does, at the point of a new romance, but rather beside the grave of the old; at the point where he realizes what he has lost, rather than at the point where he has put his losses behind him. The allusion is complicated, of course, by the fact that the story of Dido and Aeneas is itself one of love betrayed and death; Dido's words are a presage of her own funeral pyre. But this itself is part of the way in which Hardy's epigraph offers a potential circularity, a collapse into a foreclosed past (and once again into the logic of the supplement) rather than the Virgilian progression in which life must go on.

What follows is a meditation on Hardy as a poet of ashes, and on the wider meanings of the Virgilian, Dantean and philosophical context conjured up by his epigraph. My starting point is Derrida's mysterious and hermetic 1987 text *Feu la cendre*, published simultaneously as a book with meditations placed alongside self-citations (a layering of texts) and as a cassette (an echoing of voices) in a series entitled 'Bibliothèque des Voix', and translated into English as *Cinders*. *Cinders* is at once a meditation on the Holocaust and a consideration of time, language, tradition, Derrida's own corpus, and the possibilities of mourning. *Il y a là cendre*, Derrida writes, 'there are cinders, there', noting that he has written the phrase often before. In the sporadic left-hand pages of his text, he traces it through his own writings, seeking the trajectory of his own awareness, or rather, a textual account of the later text's re-gathering of the scattered embers of a phrase encrypted in the acknowledgements of *Dissemination* (1972) and elsewhere. Derrida thus also makes the cinder the figure of intertextual reference, and remembers the volcanic passions of earlier writers such as Quevedo – the traces of an ancient flame carried by tradition, alongside which one might place the figure of rekindled ashes, carried, as we will see late in this chapter, from Virgil to Dante in the *translatio* of classical succession (the standard French translation of Aeneid 4: 23, incidentally, has 'je reconnais en moi les traces du feu dont j'ai brûlé').[3]

'Cinder' (*cendre*) is Derrida's name for the indelible trace of an erased presence, and for the losses involved in signification, language falling away from a lost origin, but none the less carrying the freight of being. If the cinder is a name which carries no privilege, no truth nor final signified, or even possibility of metaphorical revelation, it nevertheless is his preferred name for the possibility that a truth may be re-covered in language; that something *is* there which might be mourned. *Feu la cendre* is, as David Farrell Krell comments, a title which carries notions of the smouldering ashes and of the recent dead, as well as that which is extinguished and defunct.[4] It conjures up mourning and fire, with some of the ambiguities of Hardy's epigraph: literally 'burn the cinder' or 'fire, the cinder', but also 'the departed cinder' – *feu*, gone or deceased, so that the phrase suggests that which stands in the place of mourning, the remnants of a fire which remains hidden in the ashes of language, invoked and re-invoked:

> Who would dare run the risk of a poem of the cinder? One might dream that the word 'cinder' was itself a cinder in that sense, 'there', 'over there' in the distant past, a lost memory of what is no longer here. And thereby [*par là*] its phrase would have meant, without holding anything back: the cinder is no longer here. Was [*fut*] it ever?[5]

Or as Hardy put it in 'A Dream or No', remembering his 'dreams of that place in the West' and of Emma, and using the word 'sheen', often used to mark the traces of a life in his work, in 'A Dream or No':

> But nought of that maid from Saint-Juliot I see;
>   Can she ever have been here,
>   And shed her life's sheen here,
> The woman I thought a long housemate with me?

> Does there even a place like Saint-Juliot exist?
> Or a Vallency Valley
> With stream and leafed alley,
> Or Beeny, or Bos with its flounce flinging mist?

As for Hardy, cinders for Derrida signal a feminine ghost – the '*là*' of 'il y a *là* cendre' – 'someone vanished but something preserved her trace and at the same time lost it, the cinder' (pp. 34–5); a cinder-ella. One of the burdens of the Cinderella story is mourning for the mother, for a maternal plenitude restored in the dubious or 'risky' magic of the wish-fulfilment. In the 'Poems of 1912–13' Hardy prepares to follow a ghost through a landscape which is no longer there – 'Through the years; through the dead scenes I have tracked you' – and which even in his own romance-novel had been rendered as the scene of lost love. Above all, the poet must avoid that collapse of meaning into sameness, into the tautologies of loss, implicit in the reiterative phrases of the burial service: 'Earth to earth, ashes to ashes, dust to dust'. Between ashes and ashes, the fire must burn again. Derrida: 'In writing this way, he burns one more time, he burns what he still adores although he has already burned it, he is intent on it.'[6] In 'The Dead Man Walking' (*Time's Laughingstocks*) Hardy had already written of himself as 'A pale past picture, screening / Ashes gone cold'. Now, in 1912, he would have to rekindle those ashes, so that they might burn and be extinguished once more. *Veteris vestigia flammae.*

The first location of these traces, as I have already suggested, is in Hardy's own writings: novels and poems. Like Derrida's phrase in his corpus, *Veteris vestigia flammae* recalls a flickering history within Hardy's work. But it is a history within which suggestions of betrayal are already inscribed, for example in the allusions to fire and passion in *A Pair of Blue Eyes*. In chapter 18, Elfride reads Knight's notebook, with its jotted thoughts on her character, and she comments: 'If they are interesting when enlarged to the size of an article, what must they be in their concentrated form! Pure rectified spirit, above proof; before it is lowered to be fit for human consumption: "words that burn" indeed.' These are meditations which are attached to a particular context, 'secrets' (as Elfride calls them) which are only decoded with care, as the novel's ensuing argument about the status of what Knight has written shows. 'Words that burn' is a phrase from Gray's 'The Progress of Poesy', one of the key intertextual references in the novel; more specifically, it is from

Gray's description of Dryden: 'Bright-eyed Fancy hovering o'er / Scatters from her pictured urn / Thoughts that breath, and words that burn.' Gray in turn echoes Cowley's 'Words, that weep, and tears that speak', invoking a language which is embodied, replete with agency – though also, in the chain of citations here, with the opposite of agency: with memory and mourning.

This hope that words may be enkindled can be opposed to the bitter prediction of the song which Elfride sings in *A Pair of Blue Eyes*, Shelley's 'When the Lamp is Shattered', which reads like a late Romantic decomposition of Gray:

> When the lamp is shatter'd
> The light in the dust lies dead –
> When the cloud is scatter'd,
> The rainbow's glory is shed.
> When the lute is broken,
> Sweet tones are remember'd not;
> When the lips have spoken,
> Loved accents are soon forgot.

This is what in fact almost happens in *A Pair of Blue Eyes*, as the intensity of passion attached to a particular place and time is replaced by repetition and doubt, Elfride returning with Knight to the scenes of her earlier romance with Stephen. The topics of Shelley's poem – irradiation, light, music and voice – echo across the 'Poems of 1912–13', often following Shelley in mocking the possibility of reversing the flow of time. 'Slip back, Time!' begins 'St Launce's Revisited', one of the final three poems added in 1919, only to figure Time itself as slippage, consigning 'thought' to 'nought' (the rhyme is anticipated in the internal rhymes of the stanza of 'A Dream or No' quoted above: another temporal echo). The phrase 'words that burn' also returns in one of the mysterious, anonymous love lyrics of *Time's Laughingstocks*, 'In the Vaulted Way':

> You paused for our parting, – plaintively;
> Though overnight had come words that burned
> My fond, frail happiness out of me.

In such negative recurrences, the word itself becomes an ember, decaying away from a textual occasion whose plenitude can never be recovered.

A number of other poems also show the flickering anticipatory traces of *veteris vestigia flammae*, inscribed within the same pattern of predictive loss. 'The Flirt's Tragedy', published in *Time's Laughingstocks*, initiates a series of poems, culminating in 'Surview', in which phantasmagoria is linked to a ruined fire:

> Here alone by the logs in my chamber,
>   Deserted, decrepit –
> Spent flames limning ghosts on the wainscot
>   Of friends I once knew –
>
> My drama and hers began weirdly
>   Its dumb re-enactment,
> Each scene, sigh, and circumstance passing
>   In spectral review.

In 'The Two Rosalinds' a poster advertising a performance of *As You Like It* reminds the speaker of his earlier entrancement by the character of Rosalind: 'Now the poster stirred an ember / Still remaining from my ardours of some forty years before.' He encounters an aged 'creature' selling 'the words' outside the playhouse, but spurns them as 'the well-known numbers needed not for me a text or teacher / To revive and re-illumine'. It is only after he has entered and found the play lacking its old energy that he finds that the actress he saw so many years ago is the 'hag' outside. Embers here are a textual trace which cannot be revived; 'the words' are what the speaker thinks he knows and what he thinks transcend time, but which were in fact bound to a particular time and place, reappearing only to mock him as the ashes of his desire. This text *is* a teacher, and what it seems to predict, in 1909, is that Hardy would fail in any attempt to rekindle the passion of the past.

An earlier poem on Time's losses, 'The Dance at the Phoenix', has what is arguably Hardy's closest to a translation of Virgil's words: *the fire that lately burnt*. The protagonist Jenny spends a wild youth as a lover of soldiers before marrying a husband who knows nothing of her past. Decades later the regiment returns to town and she creeps off to their ball to recapture her youth, dancing all night. She returns guiltily to her sleeping husband and has a seizure:

> The fire that lately burnt fell slack
>   When lone at last was she;
> Her nine-and-fifty years came back;
>   She sank upon her knee
> Beside the durn, and like a dart

> A something arrowed through her heart
> In shoots of agony.

Here, the phrase signals another doomed attempt to return to the past; it is tied to the waning of domestic affections and guilt at betrayal: 'She felt she would give more than life / To be the single-hearted wife / That she had been erstwhile...'. Hardy's own failure to be single-hearted and his subsequent grief is thus prefigured in a poem on the ironies of feminine inconstancy, in which the recapturing of lost energies is in tension with, rather than consonant with, the persistence of love.

Emma's death would collapse these tensions, imposing on the poet the task of reconciling early romance with late disillusion, but none the less leaving him with the problem of the *status* of the energies so released. This is the question asked by Donald Davie in 'Hardy's Virgilian Purples', and more generally by Derrida in *Cinders*: Can the fire burn again? Does the elegy represent anything like a metaphysical recovery of lost passion, or rather a late and disillusioned passionate occasion in its own right, with a separate and supplementary status, knowing its own (inter)textuality? The latter possibility is suggested by one word involving the application of heat which Hardy uses to describe the creation of a substitute image of the beloved: *sublimation*. In *A Pair of Blue Eyes* Knight's feelings for Elfride are described in this way: 'Not till they were parted, and she had become sublimated in his memory, could he be said to have even attentively regarded her' (ch. 20). In *The Hand of Ethelberta* the same term is used of Christopher: 'a sublimated Ethelberta accompanied him everywhere' (ch. 40). Sublimation is the fire that burns away life, leaving only the supplement.

'Traces of an old flame' thus has a largely negative pre-history within Hardy's corpus, signalling a deluded hope, and consequently it appears, at the head of the elegiac sequence, as a challenge rather than a clear hope. Perhaps a better, if looser, comparison with Derrida's cinder is Hardy's repeated use of the word 'sheen' and related terms (the 'each shiny familiar thing' of 'Old Furniture'). In its modern use 'sheen' is a cognate of 'shine' (particularly in Dorset: William Barnes uses 'sheen' for 'shine' in all his dialect poems). It can be used figuratively for the light of a life, as in Carlyle's *Sartor Resartus*: 'Ever in the dullest existence there is a sheen either of Inspiration or of Madness.' But an older adjectival sense, close to the German *schön*, signifies 'beautiful' (a beautiful place, object, day), and in particularly applies to feminine beauty, as in Spencer: 'Her daintie corse so faire and sheene'; 'a sheen' or 'the sheen' can even mean a beautiful woman. A sheen is thus an irradiated (feminine) trace.

Hardy's use of the word regularly involves a phantasmal or elegiac context: the sheen of 'The Sick Battle-God' is his spirit crossing centuries; the sheen of things in 'At Casterbridge Fair' and 'Overlooking the River Stour' is that which will be forgotten; the sheen of a dress in 'At a Fashionable Dinner' is its appearance as a shroud. The cognate 'shine' also takes on ghostly overtones: 'the piteous shine / That home-things wear when there's aught amiss' in 'Her Death and After'; the soul's shine in 'His Immortality'; the shine associated with phantoms in 'A Singer Asleep', 'The Pair He Saw Pass', 'In the Moonlight' and other poems; the 'sudden shine' which is a death-signal in 'The Last Signal'. The word occurs twice in the 'Poems of 1912–13': in the 'flickering sheen' of lights on Emma's face in 'Your Last Drive'; and in the question asked of Saint-Juliot in 'A Dream or No': 'Can she ever have been here, / And shed her life's sheen here...?' This flickering light tracing the persistence of the self punctuates the sequence: memories of Emma's 'rose-flush coming and going'; her 'bright hair flapping free'; the vision of her 'In his brain – day, night, / As if on the air / It were drawn rose-bright' – though these reclaimed light effects are matched, as we will see, by a blanching and whitening towards death which represents the cinder as dead ash.

At this point we can turn to the 'Poems of 1912–13' for a more extensive discussion of the ashes of passion – a discussion which will place the remembered flames of romance against the black and white of print. The 'Poems of 1912–13' seem initially to avoid signification rather than investigating the traces of memory. The sequence opens with *askesis*, with a self-undoing which threatens to empty language and freeze time. In the opening poem's pun Hardy sees 'morning harden on the wall'; Emma's passing is reduced to the space of a 'breath'; and the possibility of adjustment is denied in 'All's past amend / Unchangeable'; the poet himself is rendered the ashes of her passing, divided from her, 'To sink down soon' (Derrida: 'What a difference between cinder and smoke: the latter apparently gets lost, and better still, without perceptible remainder, for its rises, it takes to the air, it is spirited away, sublimated [*subtilise et sublime*]. The cinder – falls, tires, lets go, more material since it fritters away its word; it is very divisible.'[7]) The early poems present a poet who refuses to even read the signs of death. 'The Going' is structured around what is strictly speaking a euphemism – 'be gone' rather than the word 'die' – and what is 'dead' is displaced into 'those days long dead' (the past) and metaphorically onto the mourning poet himself, 'a dead man held on end'. In 'Your Last Drive' he remembers the lights on Emma's face, 'To be in a week the face of the dead'. But this is an abstract and clumsy phrase, and in the stanza which follows, the awkward rhyme-scheme ('where you lie/heedless eye/everlastingly') seems to see the poet struggle not to use the verb 'die'. Moreover 'Your Last Drive' includes another unsaid word, perhaps one of the unrepeatable accusatory works of Emma's diary: the poem ends 'You are past love, praise, indifference, blame.' If 'indifference' is the middle term between the proverbial praise and blame, then the occluded counterpart of 'love' which would complete the sequence is 'hate'; the word haunts the line beyond the closure offered by the rhyme, recalling the lingering hurt of earlier lines in the poem referring to 'censure' and 'slight'.

It is only with the fifth poem of the sequence, 'I Found Her Out There', that Hardy moves beyond this locked-in and defensive position to begin to engage with memory-traces which might rekindle passion, remembering how 'the dipping blaze / Dyed her face fire-red' at Tintagel – though even here the word 'dyed' carries traces of mortality rather than recovery. The poet must recapture what 'A Dream or No' again calls 'life's sheen'. As we saw, 'sheen' signals an animated irradiation, the presence of the events of a life in memory; it is cognate with the shine of the remembered scene in 'After a Journey', in which 'the mist-bow shone / At the then fair hour in the then fair weather' – another reply to the extinguished rainbow of 'When the Lamp is Shattered', a colouring-in of the traced outline of the past.

It is 'After a Journey' which confronts most directly the monochrome whiteness or grayness of the dead. The poet hears the hollow voice of the cave and compares the image which is 'aglow' in his mind with the Cinder-ella, 'the thin ghost that I now frailly follow!' The whitening of the dawn which banishes this flitting ghost is a double movement: 'For the stars close their shutters and the dawn whitens hazily'. The brilliant contrasts of the night are rendered an ashen uniformity, as if writing itself were bleached. Compare Derrida:

> Where the cinder within a sentence has for consistency only its syntax and for body only its vocabulary? Does this make the words warm or cold? Neither warm nor cold. And the gray form of these letters? Between the black and white, the colour of writing resembles the only 'literality' of the cinder that still inheres in a language. In a cinder of words, in the cinder of a name, the cinder itself, the literal – that which he loves – has disappeared. The name 'cinder' is still a cinder of the cinder itself.

In Hardy's copy of the thoughts of Marcus Aurelius he would have found the following passage: 'Soon, very soon, thou wilt be ashes, or a skeleton, and either a name or not even a name; but name is sound and echo.'[8] Sound and echo is what Hardy confronts in 'After a Journey', described in the hollow voice of the cave and materialized in the unhappy rhymes: 'knowing/going'; 'tracked you/lacked you'; 'lours/sours'. The cave has 'a voice still so hollow / That it seems to call out to me from forty years ago'. Would it be right to detect an echo of the 'voice so hollow' with which Knight asks for confirmation of Elfride's death in *A Pair of Blue Eyes*, an echo which would undo the occasion and return it to the context of mourning?

There is another set of traces we can pursue here in relation to 'After a Journey'. Matthew Campbell points out that line 25 chimes with, and seems to answer, a line from Tennyson's 'Oh! that 'twere possible', the lament for Hallam which was to become the core of *Maud*.[9] Tennyson wishes to raise the dead; Hardy seems to close off that possibility:

A shadow flits before me – / Not thou, but like to thee   (Tennyson)

Ignorant of what there is flitting here to see   (Hardy)

This juxtaposition does some violence to Hardy's grammar (the subject of 'ignorant' is the birds and seals which see no ghost, rather than the ghost itself), but Campbell's echo is striking. It can, moreover, be complicated by (rather fancifully) adding another line which just about chimes with Tennyson's: the penultimate sentence of *A Pair of Blue Eyes*. These words are uttered by Knight as he pulls his fellow-mourner Stephen away from the sight of Lord Luxellian weeping over Elfride's coffin: 'Another stands before us – nearer to her than we!' Luxellian represents the force of a distant past which has seen Elfride's ancestor ejected from his family because of an elopement like the one she attempts with Stephen; he is, himself, a ghostly returner, a shadow haunting the vault and suggesting the presence of ancestral passions which have issued forth in the doublings and redoublings of the Stephen/Knight romance plot; and in the plot of love belatedly recognized, once again inscribed in Hardy's return to Cornwall in the 'Poems of 1912–13'. Knight with his 'voice so hollow'; Luxellian, via Tennyson, as the frustration of mourning – the scene of textual traces here renders the poem an echo-chamber in which Emma's 'voiceless ghost' tends to vanish, leaving the speaker to fall back on his final solipsistic declaration:

> Trust me, I mind not, though Life lours,
>   The bringing me here; nay, bring me here again!
>   I am just the same as when
>   Our days were a joy, and our paths through flowers.

What does it mean to say that one is 'the same' or (as Hardy often wrote) 'self-same'? It is worth recalling that in Maurice Blanchot's *The Writing of the Disaster* (a text close in focus and spirit to *Cinders*), identity is always constructed through an engagement with an Other who is radically weakened; identity (being identical with oneself, self-same) is necessarily catastrophic, gained only by surrendering to the other, to passivity and patience: 'It is through the other that I am the same, through the other that I am myself.'[10] It is in weakness, in the naked dispossession of self, that Blanchot finds transcendence. Hardy's assertion of selfhood has a similar weakness to it, predicated on following a ghost and abandoning knowledge, 'Up the cliff, down, till I'm lonely, lost, / ... Where you will next be there's no knowing'.

A similar story of interweaving and mutually interfering paradigms of metaphysical recovery and textual dissemination can be told via the other traces which thread through the more affirmative middle sections of the 'Poems of 1912–13'. When Hardy declares of his memories of 'Myself and a girlish form benighted' in 'At Castle Boterel', he remembers a time which 'filled but a minute. But was there ever / A time of such quality, since or before, / In that hill's story? To one mind never.' This declaration is bolstered with the sedimentary model in which the 'Primaeval rocks' are impressed, 'in colour and cast', with his memories of courtship. But again an echo is interposed: in *A Pair of Blue Eyes* Hardy had written of the climactic encounter between Knight, Elfride and the returning Stephen, who now realizes he is abandoned:

> Measurement of life should be proportioned rather to the intensity of the experience than to its actual length. Their glance, but a moment chronologically, was a season in their history. To Elfride the intense agony of reproach in Stephen's eye was a nail piercing her heart with a deadliness no words can describe. With a spasmodic effort she withdrew her eyes, urged on the horse, and in the chaos of perturbed memories was oblivious to any presence beside her. (p. 214)

A faint echo ('but a minute'/'but a moment chronologically'), but it comes, I would suggest, as enough of a perturbation of memory to reinforce the subjectivity and contingency of the claim the poem makes as to memory's status. Instead of being written in the rocks as the record of one singular moment, textual memories echo as ironic commentary throughout Hardy's work. Other examples can be generated from within Hardy's texts. In 'At Castle Boterel' it is asserted that:

> to me, though Time's unflinching rigour,
>   In mindless rote, has ruled from sight
> The substance now, one phantom figure
>   Remains on the slope...

This 'to me' is echoed in another poem in *Satires of Circumstance*, 'Beyond the Last Lamp', subtitled 'Near Tooting Common', which is even more insistent on the way in which the possibility of resisting time is held, at best, in the individual will-to-remember, in a version of H. L. Mansel's subjectivist idealism. Hardy recalls the scene of a man and a woman he has seen in a lane; a scene effaced by 'thirty years of blur and blot', and asks where the couple have gone:

> Whither? Who knows, indeed.... And yet
> To me, when nights are weird and wet,
> Without those comrades there at tryst
>   Creeping slowly, creeping sadly,
>   That lone lane does not exist.
> There they seem brooding on their pain,
> And will, while such lane remain.

The metaphysics are the same – it is human presence which writes the landscape into being – but the context here is one of dissipation and of randomness (it seems entirely accidental that *this* scene and lane survive in memory), again providing a contrast to the self-defining memories of 'At Castle Boterel'. The 'moments of vision' which might sustain and concentrate a memory of Emma are thus placed within a frame in which memory plays across the field of Hardy's texts as a whole, in 'the gray form of these letters', as Derrida put it.

According to one logic, the climax of the 'Poems of 1912–13' is the impassioned kindling of the cinders of its epigraph in 'The Phantom Horsewoman' – the final poem of the sequence in its original form. The poem offers a picture of the young Emma, 'Warm, real, and keen', carried 'In his brain – day, night, / As if on the air / It were drawn rose-bright – '. Yet even here the pull of the intertextual trace places the 'real' in brackets. Hardy would have known Donne's 'Presence in Absence' from his much-thumbed copy of Palgrave, with its declaration of the primacy of the image, and brain, over reality:

> By absence this good means I gain,
>   That I can catch her,
>   Where none can match her,
> In some close corner of my brain:
>   There I embrace and kiss her;
> And so I both enjoy and miss her.[11]

Donne declares that the image of his beloved is 'Beyond time, place, and morality'; Hardy that 'Time touches her not.' The tropes of mourning, here almost commonplace, render the sublimated Emma a textual rather than a real presence – as Hardy is ultimately forced to admit.

A progressive distancing follows with the three poems which Hardy added to (or rather moved from elsewhere into) the sequence in 1919. The rose-flush of Emma's face collapses from the simile of 'After a Journey' to the near-allegory of 'The Spell of the Rose' – in which the rose is itself a symbol of a reconciliation never achieved. 'St Launce's Revisited' is dominated by images of grayness, gloom, waste and darkness. The last poem of the sequence in its final shape, 'Where the Picnic Was', offers a determined avoidance of the glowing of ashes suggested by the epigraph, conjuring up the traces of romance only to assert a difference. Here the poet can 'scan and trace / The forsaken place / Quite readily' because he sees only the black and gray of grass and charcoal, signifying the end-point of the trajectory of his mourning:

> Now a cold wind blows,
> And the grass is gray,
> But the spot still shows
> As a burnt circle – aye,
> And stick-ends, charred,
> Still strew the sward
> Whereon I stand,
> Last relic of the band
> Who came that day!

In Hardy's copy of Byron, he had marked with a triple line the last three lines of the following stanza from *Child Harold's Pilgrimage*, Canto III, 75, underlining the third:

> Are not the mountains, waves, and skies, a part
> Of me and of my soul, as I of them?
> Is not the love of these deep in my heart
> With a pure passion? should I not contemn
> All objects, if compared with these? and stem
> A tide of suffering, rather than forgo
> Such feelings for the hard and worldly phlegm
> Of those whose eyes are only turned below,
> Gazing upon the ground, <u>with thoughts which dare not glow?</u>

To refuse to allow one's thoughts to glow is to 'prefer her earthly', as a later title puts it, opposing the sublimated glory of the sunset with its 'chasm of splendor... / Which glows between the ash cloud and the dun' – a possible site for the resurrected dead – to the cold ashes of mourning.

Arguably the strongest intertextual presence in 'Where the Picnic Was' is Shelley, whose depth of despair Hardy could never quite match – here taking in the different moods of Shelley's 'The Recollection' (Palgrave) and 'The Triumph of Life'. In the former, Shelley describes his memory of a walk in Italy, and the 'magic circle' which surrounded the poet and his addressee, Jane Williams, within 'A firmament of purple light':

> And still I felt the centre of
>   The magic circle there
> Was one fair form that filled with love
>   The lifeless atmosphere.

Hardy's burnt circle of stick-ends which 'strew the sward' seems to combine this elegiac memory of the circle of love with the bitter trampling of the ashes of hope in 'The Triumph of Life' ('And all the gazer's mind was strewn beneath / Her feet like embers; and she, thought by thought, / Trampled its sparks into the dust of death'[12]). The embers of the sequence's epigraph are snuffed out and strewn across the sward. A 'sward' is a skin as well as grass; it is as if a funeral pyre has been lit and extinguished, the ashes of the dead body scattered on the body of the earth. This is the end of 'Poems of 1912–13'. The rhyme-scheme of the final stanza enforces closure in its regularity; it also rhymes 'brine' and 'line', but refuses us the 'shine' or sheen of memory. The 'you' repeatedly addressed earlier in the sequence has become 'one', an absence, a subtraction from the original 'four' described in the poem;

the Emma who was successively a face, a child, a prisoner, a ghost and a voice is dissipated in the coldness of arithmetic.

As a coda, one can note that in later poems the terms I have described (the rekindled fire of the Virgilian epigraph; traces; shine or sheen; the pain of love) return in a more relaxed mood. In 'Come Not; Yet Come!' (subtitled 'Song') the speaker wishes her lover away in 'foreign regions' before relenting:

> But the thought withers. Why should I
>   Have fear to earn me
> Fame from your nearness, though thereby
>   Old fires new burn me,
> And lastly, maybe, tear and overturn me!
>
> So I say, Come: deign again shine
>   Upon this place,
> Even if unslackened smart be mine
>   From that sweet face,
> And I faint to a phantom past all trace.

This could be a displaced version of Hardy's earlier evocations of Emma; even, with the reference to fame, an apologia for reviving memory and rendering it artefact.[13] The pain of the poem of ashes has become more distanced, the ember converted into the ritualized altar-fires of a goddess. Hardy's own words no longer burn as he achieves an equality with the dead, himself a phantom left for others to trace, in the texts from which his presence shines forth.

Dantean purples

If ashes suggest that which is rendered colourless and cold, Hardy's elegies also turn to another colour, as we have already seen: the purples of romance. Donald Davie's 1972 article 'Hardy's Virgilian Purples' is a landmark of Hardy studies; John Lucas calls it 'far and away the finest written on Hardy as poet'.[14] It both suggested in a radically new way the hidden depth of Hardy's reading and allusiveness, and set the agenda for subsequent discussions of the 'Poems of 1912–13' with its claim that the addition of three poems in the final sequence represented a swerving away from Hardy's original allegiance to the 'purple light' of Virgilian romance, in favour of a mere realism which allows the fading of grief. This is a magnificently combative claim. Davie implicitly accuses Hardy of metaphysical cowardice in not clinging to the actual presence of Emma's ghost as it is asserted in visionary moments like that in 'At Castle Boterel' (a failing which is strategically crucial for Davie's view of English poetry, since it implies that tradition of realist poetry of diminished returns which Davie laments – and perhaps also celebrates – in *Thomas Hardy and English Poetry*). But I think we can construct a defence for Hardy, not just in terms of the psychology of mourning and the trajectory of elegy (as Peter Sacks does in *The English Elegy*) but in terms of that Virgilian context which Davie so brilliantly suggests.[15] It is, as I hope to show, a more shaded context than Davie allowed.

Davie's argument begins with the motto *Veteris vestigia flammae*, the words which link the pilgrimage to Cornwall described in the 'Poems of 1912–13' to the journey which Aeneas makes to the underworld in Book VI of the *Aeneid*, where he meets the accusing shade of Dido. The 'purples' which 'prinked the main' in 'Beeny Cliff' are related by Davie to the marvellous *purpureus* or purple light of the fields of Hades, a linkage reinforced by Hardy's reference to the same Virgilian passage in *A Pair of Blue Eyes*, chapter 4 – an allusion mediated, to be sure, by Gray's rhapsodic 'The Progress of Poesy', but nevertheless also returning us to the Virgilian context.[16] In Dryden's translation, Aeneas enters

> Where long extended Plains of Pleasure lay,
> The verdant Fields with those of Heav'n may vye;
> With Aether vested, and a Purple Sky:
> The blissful seats of Happy Souls below:
> Stars of their own, and their own Suns they know.
>
> (VI 869–73)

Hardy's remembrance of Emma is thus, for Davie, linked to a visionary world of the imagination in which it can be reasserted that she is present; a world normally denied to the sceptical poets: 'Virgil's purpureus describes a light that is not in any terrestrial light, however preternaturally radiant and keen; it is preternatural through and through, the light of an alternative cosmos.'[17] Davie takes his argument a stage further, suggesting that Hardy knew that his epigraph is also the words quoted by Dante at the climactic moment in *Purgatorio* XXX, in which Beatrice replaces Virgil as his guide – again, the *translatio*. Hardy read the *Inferno* in a parallel Italian–English text and was familiar with Cary's translation of the *Commedia*.[18] Dante's words are *conosco i segni dell'antica fiamma*, translated by Cary, 'The old flame / Throws out clear tokens of reviving fire.' They are spoken at a point where the Virgilian context of loss is replaced by the Christian context of recovery, and the dead are restored to the living.

The chain of allusions we have been looking at is central to Hardy's vision of loss and (for Davie) visionary recovery. But it is not the only such chain one can pick up in *Purgatorio* XXX, and it is here that I would wish to supplement Davie's account in order to look at other 'purples' in the Virgilian and Dantean context. In the same Canto, Virgil is quoted, uniquely in the *Commedia*, in the original Latin – again from *Aeneid* VI. The occasion is the scattering of lilies which signals the arrival of Beatrice: the angels cry *Manibus o date lilia plenis*, rendered by Cary 'from full hands scatter ye / Unwithered lilies' (*Aeneid* VI 883/*Purgatorio* XXX 21). Virgil refers to the lilies of mourning: purple lilies. But in the *Commedia* these are the white lilies of resurrection, used by Dante to convey the supersession of the Pagan world and its doctrine of stoical grief by the Christian covenant. Virgil's words, spoken by Anchises, relate not to Dido but to Marcellus, the lost hope of Imperial Rome. The lines in Dryden's translation read:

> Full Canisters of fragrant Lillies bring,
> Mix't with the Purple Roses of the Spring:
> Let me with Fun'ral Flowers his body Strow;
> This Gift which Parents to their Children owe,
> This unavailing Gift, at least I may bestow!
>
> (VI 1223–7)

In Allen Mandelbaum's modern translation this is rendered:

> With full hands, give me lilies; let me scatter
> These purple flowers, with these gifts, at least,
> Be generous to my descendant's spirit,
> Complete this service, although it be useless.[19]

Here there is a 'purple' which relates not to rhapsody, but rather to irrecoverable loss; to the moment in Virgil's epic where his Imperial purpose is threatened, and where the poet's ability to recall the dead seems 'useless'.

Davie presents Hardy's Virgilian and Dantean allusions as examples of the resonance which the 'Poems of 1912–13' achieve, and asserts that the 'purples' of Beeny Cliff point us to another world; a visionary world beyond the material existence which Hardy's agnosticism usually confined him to. Yet it seems to me that this declaration runs counter to his own evidence. He refers to Hardy's 'personal purgatory', and says that in his sense of topography 'Hardy stands closer to Dante than to Virgil.' Both the passages which I have discussed in *Aeneid* VI and *Purgatorio* XXX involve a turn from the pagan, pessimistic world-view to the Christian one, in which there is the possibility of personal redemption. Dante's cry 'Virgilio, Virgilio, Virgilio' is also, John Frecero points out, a transumption of the Virgilian 'Eurydice, Eurydice, Eurydice' of the Fourth *Georgic*. Frecero comments: 'So the dark eros of Dido is transformed into the retrospective redemption of Beatrice's return... poetry becomes stronger than Death and for the first time in the poem, the Pilgrim is named as Beatrice calls him; Dante!'[20] But we need to ask with which Hardy *does* identify: with the 'dark eros' of Dido, or the redemption of Beatrice? With the purple lilies of mourning, or the white lilies of resurrection? The question is a particularly trying one because Emma, unlike Beatrice, does not speak Hardy's name; indeed her voice remains a shadowy presence which only 'calls' to him in the most equivocal way. There is little in the poem to suggest that Hardy achieves the dialogue which he seeks; Emma's voice fades into wind, her 'thin ghost' vanishes.

So what does Davie's remark about the Virgilian topography mean? Davie's claim is that while Dorset represents the landscape of loss and betrayal, Cornwall represents love and recovery; and it is crucial to distinguish the two. Implicitly, Cornwall is *Purgatorio*, a place of redemption, including a meeting with a ghost who leads the poet back to the visionary world of innocence. Even if it is only in memory that Emma Hardy can be held in place in the poems which Davie so admires, it is vital that that landscape exists in poems like 'At Castle Boterel':

> Primaeval rocks form the road's steep border,
>   And much have they faced there, first and last,
> Of the transitory in Earth's long order;
>   But what they record in colour and cast
>   Is – that we two passed.
>
> And to me, though Time's unflinching rigour,
>   In mindless rote, has ruled from sight
> The substance now, one phantom figure
>   Remains on the slope, as when that night
>   Saw us alight.

Is that enough? For Davie, yes, and the falling away from intensity of the final poems in the sequence represents for him a betrayal. So presumably does the final topography: the return to Dorset and loss in 'Where the Picnic Was'.

Yet this, I believe, does not represent the full story. Part of the reason is that Davie suspends Hardy in his moment of greatest intensity, like an Orpheus who will not turn (Hardy uses the same image in 'The Shadow on the Stone'). It is not as if that stance were ever possible. Even poems like 'At Castle Boterel' ultimately turn away from memory, and use rain, dawn, or other images of fading and blurring to represent Emma as vanishing into obscurity. Hardy seems to me, throughout the sequence, to adhere to the 'dark eros' of Dido rather than to a recoverable Beatrice. Hardy copied a passage on 'Dante's philosophy' from a 1909 review of W. H. V. Reade's *The Moral System of Dante's Inferno*, in which the reviewer stresses Dante's independence from the Christian dispensation in the *Inferno*: all the damned are 'damned on the moral level' (*LN* 2634). Hardy's lack of Christian belief and the purple of the lilies alone might suggest a return to Virgil, but we can also recall that in the first of the three poems added to the sequence in 1919, Hardy links his wife to another flower: to a rose which she planted before her death, paralleling the roses in Dryden's translation of Virgil. Here, he has her ghost conclude that she cannot know what he feels for her now, and for the rose she planted: 'Perhaps now blooms that queen of trees / I set but saw not grow.' These flowers never reach their destination, they are the symbol of a love betrayed, and of a service which Hardy, like Virgil's spokesman Anchises, now admits may be useless. Similarly, in a poem outside the sequence, Hardy very deliberately describes finding a withered flower left by Emma, in contrast to the 'unwithered' flowers of Cary's Dante. If, as Hardy states in 'He Prefers Her Earthly', a memory of a physical presence is better than the thought of a disembodied soul, then the absence of that body must be allowed to enter the poetry, as the withering of flowers, the passing of material things. In 'On a Discovered Curl of Hair', a poem dated February 1913 but only published in *Late Lyrics and Earlier*, Hardy confronts once again a double displacement, a double absence: the fact that Emma's hair was not red any longer when she died, and the fact that she has in any case 'gone into a caverned ark, / Ever unopened, always dark!' Facing this double removal, the poet can assert a continuity in memory, but he cannot remove the context of loss, since Emma Hardy (rather than Emma Gifford) was already lost to him when she died.

In order to explore this sense that Hardy's recovery of the dead is located against a background of absolute loss, we need to consider

Dantean, as well as Virgilian, purples, and to shift from Davie's favoured topography, Purgatory, to the darker terrain of the *Inferno*. We find them when we turn to that section of the Inferno where the shade of Dido is glimpsed (and which thus corresponds topographically to the Hades episode in the *Aeneid*): Canto V, the abode of the unhappy spirits of the lustful, and the location of another famous story of doomed lovers. If Hardy was likely to have paid attention to the recapturing of Beatrice in the *Purgatorio*, he must have been touched, as most readers are, by the story of two lovers locked into a hell of their own creation: the tale of Paolo and Francesca in *Inferno* V. Indeed, Hardy underlined lines 121–3 of this Canto in the John Carlyle translation which he read in the late 1880s, lines which would have a bitter resonance in 1912: 'There is no greater pain than to recall a happy time in wretchedness.'[21] It is in Canto V in Cary's edition that we find another purple; or rather purple mixed with black. When the affected Dante calls to the two tormented shades they respond:

> 'Oh, gracious creature and benign! who go'st
> Visiting, through this element obscure,
> Us, who the world with bloody stain imbrued....'

Cary's note concerns this 'element obscure':

> 'L'aer perso'. Much is said by the commentators concerning the exact sense of the word 'perso'. It cannot be explained in clearer terms than those used by Dante himself in his 'Convito': 'Il perso é un colore misto di purpureo e nero, ma vince il nero', 'it is a colour mixed of purple and black, but the black prevails'. The word recurs several times in the poem.[22]

Purple mixed with black is the colour of hell, and here of a passion which has irrevocably intersected with darkness and death. The love of Paolo and Francesca is romantic, indeed born, famously, from the reading of a romance; though the afterlife of that romance is torment. Hardy's retracing of his own love takes on similar overtones: his own courtship novel *A Pair of Blue Eyes* is mined for memories and even phrases in the 'Poems of 1912–13', but it also signifies a world forever lost, only remembered across a chain of error and betrayal. Hardy's love, like that of Dante's doomed pair, contains death, darkness, and torment within it; it is described with a wistful sense of the impossibility of purging sin and error from memory. In Hardy's short story 'The Fiddler of the Reels', yet another tale of love, separation and lost opportunities, the lost woman and her child vanish at the end of the tale into what the writer calls the 'Dantesque gloom' of the heath, as if to signal Hardy's awareness of this darker context.[23]

The equation of death and darkness is something Hardy often notes in his reading – 'the regions destitute of day' in Dryden's Virgil; the movement 'from sunshine to the sunless land' in Wordsworth's 'Extempore Effusion upon the Death of James Hogg'.[24] Perhaps the most extensive fragment on the *topos* which he marked was Epitaph XXI from the *Greek Anthology*, 'Dearer than Day'. The translation reads:

> 'Farewell', I would say to you; and again I check my voice and rein it backward, and again I stay beside you; for I shrink from the terrible separation from you as from the bitter night of Acheron; for the light of you is like the day. Yet that, I think, is voiceless, but you bring me also the murmuring talk of that voice sweeter than the Sirens, whereon all my soul's hopes are hung.[25]

'After a Journey', with its voiceless ghost, vanishing as the dawn whitens, seems to offer an explicit version of the trope of an encounter with the underworld. Dantesque echoes are detectable elsewhere in the sequence: consider, for example, the opening of 'Rain on a Grave' ('Clouds spout upon her / Their waters amain / In ruthless distain') in relation to Cary's translation of *Inferno* VI, the episode which follows Paolo and Francesca: 'Large hail, discolour'd water, sleety flaw / Through the dun midnight air stream'd down amain.'[26]

The 'Poems of 1912–13' are thus negotiated through a darkness which might well be described by Dante's *aer perso*, a mixture of the purples of romance and the darkness of hell. This is registered at precisely that point in the sequence where Hardy, following Virgil and Dante, enters the equivalent of the fields of Hades in 'After a Journey':

> Yes: I have re-entered your olden haunts at last;
>   Through the years, through the dead scenes I have tracked you;
> What have you now found to say of our past –
>   Scanned across the dark space wherein I have lacked you?
> Summer gave us sweets, but autumn wrought division?
>   Things were not lastly as firstly well
>   With us twain, you tell?
> But all's closed now, despite Time's derision.

The cruel rhyme (tracked you/lacked you) is negotiated across an intervening 'dark space' which is that of a 'division' which existed even before death, which existed in Time. The poem cannot deny – indeed its rhymes suggest – Emma Hardy has vanished into what 'The Going' called a 'darkening dankness' and 'yawning blankness', and that Hardy visits her across a gap of time and difference. Even the colours of 'Beeny Cliff', for Davie Hardy's most ecstatic poem, are mixed with the 'darkened air' of Dante's descent: there is 'the opal and the sapphire of that wandering western sea', and the famous 'purples'; but the background of this is a 'nether sky' in which there is a possible obscurity:

> A little cloud then cloaked us, and there flew an irised rain,
> And the Atlantic dyed its levels with a dull misfeatured stain,
> And then the sun burst out again, and purples prinked the main.

Before the 'purples' is the 'dull misfeatured stain', and the word 'stain' might even recall Dante's lovers, 'who the world with bloody stain imbrued'. The 'chasmal beauty' of Beeny represents, surely, a purple mixed with black, a passion remembered in the dark chasm of loss, in which it is admitted that 'The woman now is – elsewhere – whom the ambling pony bore, / And nor knows nor cares for Beeny, and will laugh here nevermore.' As Peter Sacks suggests, that interpolated '– elsewhere –' is itself chasmal, it points us towards an obscurity through which Hardy must reach for his lost love, and into which she must return after those moments of vision and affirmation in 'Beeny Cliff', 'At Castle Boterel', and 'The Phantom Horsewoman'.[27]

Davie objects to the last three poems in the sequence of 'Poems of 1912–13', as qualifying the Platonism of the earlier poems, distorting the whole shape of the sequence. But the context sketched above, it seems to me, implies that the negative ending is inevitable. Emma's ashes are, finally, cold and black; the poet seems himself to trample them into earth. Hardy is, perhaps, psychologizing his own metaphysical insights, as Davie says he is doing, completing the trajectory of grief. But to suggest that he could do otherwise is mistaken: his visionary moments, in the 'purple light' of remembered passion, are always achieved against the background of an 'element obscure' through which the poet goes visiting, the 'dark space' across which he must scan. The darkness can be penetrated momentarily, but always returns as the mixed shades of mourning. *Perso*: as Dante says, 'a colour mixed of purple and black, but the black prevails'.

Crossed voices: dialogues with the dead

If the *topos* signals the place of allusion and interchange with the dead, Hardy's Virgilian allusions seem to distance passion, enabling it to be rekindled but also controlled. But what would it mean to imagine exchange itself, or to posit an other who is more than just the site of exchange? In the remainder of this chapter, I want to shift focus from the *topos* to the *rhetoric* of interchange, and tentatively consider the possibility of a more dynamic and dangerous use of allusion, in which the texts of others might substitute for the dead.

For the writer of what Rod Edmond calls 'domestic elegy', one of the central issues is exchange or reciprocity – the question of whether the elegiac voice is ultimately solipsistic, or whether some response may be elicited from the beloved, whether that response is seen in terms of a revenant or an imaginative construct. What echo responds to the voice of the elegist? How may a hand be extended to the dead? A picture of the literal impossibility of crossed hands is provided in Hardy's 'A Duettist to Her Pianoforte', subtitled 'Song of Silence (E.L.H.–H.C.H.)'. The initials recall Emma and her sister Helen Holder playing a duet, and the poem both evokes a lost interchange ('I am doomed to counterchord / Her notes no more... / I fain would second her, strike to her stroke... / fellow twain of hands so dear') and sees the collapse of music into the solipsistic repetition suggested by the leaden refrain ending each stanza: 'So it's hushed, hushed, hushed, you are for me!'; 'For dead, dead, dead, you are to me!'; 'And mute, mute, mute, you are for me!' If the tolling and muted sounds of death which haunt all elegies seem to offer a ritual comfort, they can also imply a designification, a fall into the rhythms of the body which Linda Austin has recently characterized in terms of the fixity of depression rather than the 'working-through' of 'successful' mourning.[28] But perhaps it is also the case that to imagine the music or voice of the dead would be excessive: as this speaker has it, 'upping ghosts press achefully', so 'how shall I bear / Such heavily-haunted harmony?'

In writing the 'Poems of 1912–13' Hardy was also engaging with a traditional elegiac discourse, predominantly masculine, which ultimately celebrates the sequentiality of desire, lamenting the passing of old love to make space for new; or which philosophically marks love's impermanence in order to imply mastery of such pains. Some lines which Hardy marked in Heine's poems suggest this mastery:

> Don't think that I deem it my duty
> To shoot myself any the more;

> For all of this, my beauty,
> Has happen'd to me before.[29]

Satires of Circumstance itself included, to Hardy's sharp regret, a set of 'Satires' partly in this mode; *Time's Laughingstocks* had included 'The End of the Episode' and other relatively conventional songs on lost love. We can see a reply to that dismissive masculine voice in Hardy's response to one of Swinburne's characteristically cynical meditations on the ashes of love, 'Félise'. With its stress on forgetting and disengagement, Swinburne's poem – which Hardy knew very well – asserts the hopelessness of raising 'love's ghost'. The speaker declares, in an oppositional chiasmus:

> I that have slept awake, and you
> Sleep, who last year were well awake.
> Though love do all that love can do,
> My heart will never ache or break
> For your heart's sake.[30]

The chiasmus signals a distancing of the male speaker from love. But in 'The Haunter', the poem in which the dead Emma's voice first enters the 'Poems of 1912–13', she declares that despite the appearance of non-conjunction, hearts may still move together, echoing and answering Swinburne:

> Tell him a faithful one is doing
> All that love can do
> Still that his path may be worth pursuing,
> And to bring peace thereto.

All that love can do is a good deal here, and the phrase signals both an acceptance of heartbreak and the possibilities of a dialogue with the past (the poem also seems to echo the climax of *The Prelude*, in which the same phrase signals the feminine complement to imagination[31]). Swinburne's sceptical question – 'What breath shall fill and re-inspire / A dead desire?' – is one which Hardy must confront again and again as he writes. In what follows, we will take two related routes in answering that question, and the broader question of response raised above: one via chiasmus, the rhetorical figure of interchange; and a second through Hardy's response to poetry by women, producing an exchange of voices.

Chiasmus, the figure of crossing (from the Greek *chi* or X), is a useful rubric for the search for reciprocity since it involves both a near-algebraic equivalence and a rhetorical substitution or reversal.[32] The *chiasm* is a mirroring and an exchange; for this reason Jean-François Lyotard (in *Discours, figure*) sees it as a master-sign, implying both a theory of figuration and a model of subjectivity.[33] In Merleau-Ponty's *The Visible and the Invisible*, an expanded notion of chiasmus signals a defining intersubjectivity, determined by the fact that to perceive or touch objects in the world, the subject must itself be already an object of seeing and touching. Here the flesh is the point of crossing; not the union of two substances but an element in itself, the site of the intercorporeal:

> The chiasm is not only a me–other exchange (the messages he receives reach me, the messages I receive reach him), it is also an exchange between me and the world, between the phenomenal body and the 'objective' body, between the perceiving and the perceived: what begins as a thing ends as consciousness of the thing, what begins as a 'state of consciousness' ends as a thing.[34]

To consider chiasmus in this way is to consider that subject and object might be interchanged, that relationships are commutable, as in Swinburne's 'Hertha': 'I am thou...thou art I.' Hardy produces what we could call chiasmic pairings in this mood: poems in which reciprocal situations are applied to a man and a woman and they realize their interimplication ('Her Immortality' and 'His Immortality'; 'His Heart. A Woman's Dream' and 'I Thought, My Heart').

In the Phenomenological allegorization of chiasmus, the trope stands for worldliness; it is what tells us that thought cannot exist outside the world of sense. But it is crucial to note that in elegiac verse this relation is both exploited and inverted: since the object is necessarily present only as sign, the 'body' imputed to the dead is a phantasm which is *called into being* by Merleau-Ponty's chiasm; by the fact that it is impossible to think of the thoughts of another without implying a bodily existence – an existence which none the less can only achieve a virtual and ghostly status. Derrida writes of the spectre as involving 'a supernatural and paradoxical phenomenality, the furtive and ungraspable visibility of the invisible, or an invisibility of a visible X...the tangible intangibility of a proper body without flesh, but still the body of some*one* as some*one other*'.[35] The notion of commutability which is at the heart of chiasmus thus reveals itself, in elegy, as unstable, since the other of discourse is absent, or only present-in-absence. As in all mirroring (for example in Lacan's figuring of the self in language), things which are mirrored are unbalanced; the exchange figured by chiasmus is never fully reciprocal, exposing the lack which constitutes and wounds the self and underlies all desire, as in Hardy's 'In Her Precincts': 'Yes, her gloom within at the lack of me / Seemed matching mine at the lack of her.'

Chiasmus, that is, ultimately signals linguistic exchange rather than Merleau-Ponty's embodiment; it can even, in its extreme rhetoricity, suggest the emptiness of language, reducing it to the status of token. In this purely rhetorical opposition the body is all too readily absent – an absence, one might say, which is indicated by a textual mark, the X which marks the place of its dislocation. Swinburne is a famous source of this hyper-rhetorical emptiness, of a decontextualized language, as Hardy seems to recognize. In his *Studies, Specimens* notebook Hardy marks with an 'X' 'Those eyes, the greenest of things blue / The bluest of things grey' in Swinburne's 'Félise', and diagrams another poem with the chiasmic cross:[36]

        fair   deep
            X
        face   thought

This relationship between thought and its outward expression is reproduced in one of Hardy's 1883 diary entries, predicated on a repressive barrier which estranges all discourse from being: 'Write a list of things which everybody thinks and nobody says; and a list of things everybody says and nobody thinks' (*EL* 211). In this formula, the trope signals the necessary non-confluence of self and language, of history and utterance, even as it suggests the possibility of a restorative crossing to equivalence.

One further general point about chiasmus. As the point of reflection it may also signal a point of see-sawing instability, of oppositions unreconciled or ironies unresolved. This may, as Derrida argues, be the place of the literary itself, of an absolute imbalance between sign and referent, text and history, which allows neither to be stabilized.[37] One might point in Hardy to those rhetorical reversals which signal a troublingly subtle shift in position: in 'A Drizzling Easter Morning' from the opening 'And he is risen?' to the concluding 'though risen is he'; the shift from 'Nothing matters much' in the poem of that title to the concluding 'Nothing much matters' – in both cases the reversal offering a negative closure on the more open first version. Even the word *crossing* seems to carry tremendous weight of dislocation for Hardy, signalling not only death (the 'crossing breeze' of 'Afterwards'; the pet 'crossing at a breath / Into safe and shielded death' in 'Last Words to a Dumb Friend'), but also the crossroads and the cross itself, both included in 'Near Lanivet' as figures for the ironies of his own life. Here the crossing signals destinies at cross-purposes, as in 'A Hurried Meeting', one of Lois Deacon's favourite choices as a poem describing Hardy's secret life. The pregnant woman declares that she and her lover must be separated, geographically and temporally: 'We are crossing South – near about New Year's Day / The event will happen there.' Their farewell is described in another oppositional structure: 'And with one kiss again the couple parted: / Inferior clearly he; she haughty-hearted.'

'Cross-Currents' registers this oppositional plot in its title. The narrator sees a 'pallid, trembling pair' parting and learns from the woman involved that the proposed marriage has been thwarted by her lover's relations. He proposes that 'Love will contrive a course?' but the woman replies that she had in any case been screwing up courage to tell her lover that she did not want to marry him – and has now escaped the necessity of doing so. The final twist is that the woman still grieves 'for his sake, / That I have escaped the sacrifice / I was distressed to make'. The important thing to notice here is that there is no stable 'course' for desire; no resolution of the 'cross' on which it is impaled, despite a parting which seems to settle the issue. This is a situation Hardy's poetry inherits, of course, from his novels: one of the most visual of chiasmic situations is that in *A Pair of Blue Eyes* in which Elfride and Knight on the cliff, look through a telescope at Stephen on a ferry offshore, who is also looking back at them through a telescope, at the moment at which Elfride's affections are finally transferred between the two men. Chiasmus marks, then, the intersections of self, language and world, and the instabilities of the subject constructed by those intersections. That strange allegory of desire 'The Chosen' has the narrator pursuing his chosen woman, having discarded five others with different qualities. Haunted by these partial loves, she flees, and will only stop when he prays at a 'Christ-cross stone' on the moor; at which point he sees that she has become a 'composite form' of all five. The cross is the place of a conundrum which can only achieve stability in the figure of crossing itself.

In relation to the representation of mourning, chiasmus is particularly fraught, as we have already seen, since it calls another into existence where there is no Other present; it carries the possibility of both imagined exchange and the collapse of exchange into rhetoric, or voice into writing. That Other may be clearly a projection – Abraham and Torok describe a state, particularly apparent in melancholy and mourning, in which 'The identification concerns not so much the object who may no longer exist, but essentially the "mourning" that this "object" might allegedly carry out because of having lost the subject; the subject, consequently, appears to be painfully missed by the object.'[38] In poetic terms this potentially reverses priority between the living and dead, and assigns the mourning voice to the latter – as Hardy does repeatedly in picturing mourning and disconsolate ghosts in the 'Poems of 1912–13' and elsewhere.

As a model here, consider the chiasmic structure of Christina Rossetti's 'The Last Look', one of many poems in which she situates herself as the mourned-for object:

> If I remember her, no need
>   Of formal tokens set;
>   Of hollow token lies, indeed
> No need, if I forget.

Rossetti's poems are often structured in this way, most famously her sonnet 'Remember' ('Nor I half turn to go yet turning stay') and, less precisely, the song marked in Hardy's copy of Palgrave's *Golden Treasury*, Second Series, 'When I am dead, my dearest' ('Haply I may remember, / And haply may forget'). The equivalence of remembering and forgetting in Rossetti is an attempt to signal the indifference of the dead, even their status outside language and formal logic, closeted from the world – a riddling status which Angela Leighton has characterized in terms of its tendency to avoid clear oppositions like those of gender or life and death in favour of a secret, dreamlike state.[39] In a comparable sense, in Hardy's 'We Sat at the Window' (subtitled 'Bournemouth, 1875') it is the very *lack* of equivalence and reciprocity which is carried in the double chiasmus and reinforced in the formula which moves 'waste' from quality to substance:

> We were irked by the scene, by our own selves; yes,
> For I did not know, nor did she infer
> How much there was to read and guess
> By her in me, and to see and crown
>   By me in her.
> Wasted were two souls in their prime,
> And great was the waste, that July time
>   When the rain came down.

These are parallel losses, their reciprocity sealed tomb-like in a particular 'time' and 'scene'. Even later, in 'Alike and Unlike (Great-Orme's Head)', he suggest that the shared scene may separate rather than unite, that there is no tracing of experience back to source without a primal scene of division:

> We watched the selfsame scene on that long drive,
> Saw the magnificent purples, as one eye,
> Of those near mountains; saw the storm arrive;
> Laid up the sight in memory, you and I,
> As if for joint recallings by and by.
>
> But our eye-records, like in hue and line,
> Had superimposed on them, that very day,
> Gravings on your side deep, but slight on mine! –
> Tending to sever us thenceforth alway;
> Mine commonplace; yours tragic, gruesome, gray.

This is the Lockean version of time's division, offering the very opposite of Merleau-Ponty's intercorporeality founded on a common engagement with the phenomenal world; the superimposed gravings signal the solipsistic textuality of experience rather than its location in a shared embodiment.

Given this potential for *chiasmus* to revolve around a lack, a mirrored absence, a crucial element in the 'Poems of 1912–13' is the moment of crossing and reversal which seeks to call Emma into being. Such moments signal a desire for reciprocity which occurs in various contexts: Hardy's crossing to Emma's territory in Cornwall ('After a Journey'); crossings between past and present ('Beeny Cliff', subtitled 'March 1870–March 1913'); and most importantly of all, the crossings which seem to signal a potential interchange of voices between living and dead. But as we will see, Hardy's rhetoric offers limited gains here. In 'The Haunter', as we have already seen, the voice of Emma seems to answer Swinburne's cynicism. But the poem also strongly registers the opposition of 'now' and 'then' in a quasi-chiasmic structure:

> How I would like to join in his journeys
>   Seldom he wished to go.
> Now that he goes and wants me with him
>   More than he used to do.

But the distance between the infinitive 'to go' and the definite 'goes', and (in the same order) between the concrete 'I would like' and the indefinite 'used to do', signals a complex double opposition in which temporality and intentionality are inexorably at cross-purposes. In 'His Visitor', where Emma says 'I come across from Mellstock while the moon wastes weaker', the temporal 'contrasts' (Hardy borrows the title of Pugin's famous comparison of medieval and modern) are even stronger, and Emma's ghost, like Rossetti's retiring spirits, returns willingly to the grave and to the past. Both poems fall short of the rhetorical ideal of an even exchange.

One example of such an exchange which Hardy knew well was Tennyson's 'In the Valley of Cauteretz' (included in Palgrave, Second Series, 1897) with its crucial chiasmus:

> The two and thirty years were a mist that rolls away;
> For all along the valley, down thy rocky bed,
> Thy living voice to me was as the voice of the dead,
> And all along the valley, by rock and cave and tree,
> The voice of the dead was a living voice to me.

The equivalent moment for Hardy, in the process of mourning if not rhetorically, is the greatest of all his elegies, 'After a Journey', the poem in which he crosses to Cornwall:

> Hereto I come to interview a ghost
>   Whither, O whither will its whim now draw me?
> Up the cliff, down, till I'm lonely, lost,
>   And the unseen waters' soliloquies awe me.

Or so Hardy wrote in 1914. In later editions he changed the first line to 'Hereto I come to view a voiceless ghost', and the 'soliloquies' of the fourth line to 'ejaculations'. As Melanie Sexton argues, the shift here is from voice to vision, to the successful creation of an ideal memory-image of Emma which is one achievement of the later part of the sequence; even the voice-like soliloquies of the waves lose content in becoming 'ejaculations'.[40] But here, in the original opening, the possibility of dialogue is opened, and held open at least to the second stanza, an interchange of voices implicit in the phrase structure and multiple rhyme. The mirrored phrase 'Summer gave us sweets, but autumn wrought division' carries us across a temporal dislocation, and into the more distanced world of some of the later elegies, in which memory is a playful mapping, a matter of position – here Hardy tracks and scans, just as in 'The Chosen' he 'traces', 'scans', 'tends', while the woman 'swerves', 'turns', 'lies'. The 'dark space' between 'tracked you' and 'lacked you' is something like the space of the chiasm itself, the textual space in which the absence of the body may be marked; it is also the space into which Emma's voice vanishes with the hollow rhetoricity of 'you tell?' This is Emma's impossible voice; the voice of a shade. Where her voice does resurface in the sequence, it is in the highly-distanced allegorical mode of 'The Spell of the Rose', which admits that she cannot hear his voice and gives her a voice which can barely be called lyric (the last two stanzas in particular are halting and grammatically convoluted). When Emma says that 'Perhaps . . . He sees me as I was, though sees / Too late to tell me so', it is, once again, the dislocation of sight and voice which is figured. The possibility of an embodied interchange carried in the crossing to Cornwall, the *inter-view* which suggests a mutual seeing of the other, has been extinguished.

The climax of Hardy's rhetorical journey is the equivalence and reciprocity represented in 'Beeny Cliff', which evokes 'The woman whom I loved so, and who loyally loved me'. But again, it is the crossing of *voices* rather than rhetoric which is problematic: Hardy asks 'And shall she and I not go there once again now March is nigh, / And the sweet things said in that March say anew there by and by?' It is the 'by and by' which signals the difficult nature of this claim, and the final stanza – originally beginning 'Nay. Though' and then amended to the only marginally less dismissive 'What if . . . ?' What if Beeny exists as the place of this imagined meeting, since 'The woman now is – elsewhere'? The temporality of the moment is skewed, edging into the supplementarity and then outright contradiction of 'by and by' and 'Nay. Though/ What if?'

In following Emma's shade, Hardy explores the relationship between seeing and speaking, or viewing and interviewing, as well as the relationship between the recently dead woman (whose voice is employed) and the youthful lover (whose image is evoked).[41] The dead woman's voice is naturalized through the tropes of mourning, in being linked to the pulsating sound of the sea; evoked in a ventriloquized soliloquy in which it addresses the mourner; its status doubted; and finally it dissolves into 'roomy silence' and voicelessness, as Hardy, at the end of the sequence, constructs a stable image of the dead, located firmly in his own 'figuring' rather than in the real. The most poignant stilling of voice in Hardy's corpus is 'The Shadow on the Stone', in which the refusal to turn and confirm that the 'shifting shadows' of the garden are not Emma is figured as the conscious sustaining of a dream. For all that this is Orphic in its scheme, voice here is a merely natural dying fall:

> I thought her behind my back,
> Yea, her I long had learned to lack,
> And I said: 'I am sure you are standing behind me,
> Though how do you get into this old track?'
> And there was no sound but the fall of a leaf
> As a sad response; and to keep down grief
> I would not turn my head to discover
> That there was nothing in my belief.

The 'old track' which shadows 'lack' here is that of Hardy's own work – it is a reversal of the fall into absence of 'After a Journey': 'through the dead scenes I have tracked you; / ...Scanned across the dark space wherein I have lacked you?' The vocabulary suggests the idea of verse itself (standing and *stanza*; the turn; the 'rhythmic swing' of the trees; the 'track' of rhyme); the printed text here is the shadow of a voice which is not present.

The 'Poems of 1912–13' thus present chiasmic structures which can achieve a tenuous rhetorical balance, but not a temporal equivalence. Exchange may be figured; it cannot, finally, be voiced and stabilized by the rhetoric which figures it; the body of the dead may be implied as a ghostly presence, but it cannot be produced. The sense of repose and balance carried by a very late example, 'Epitaph', offers a sharp contrast: 'I never cared for Life: Life cared for me / And hence I owed it some fidelity' – though here, of course, the object of this outrageous exchange is an abstract personification, and in a sense a version of the self, rather than a person.

This conclusion should not surprise us. As Elizabeth Bronfen and others have pointed out, the figure of a dead or absent woman is an important ground for the aesthetic itself. The connection between a woman's absent voice and rhetoric is nicely figured in George Campbell's *The Philosophy of Rhetoric* (1801), a volume Hardy marked extensively. The following example is the climax of Campbell's discussion of catachresis, the trope which has been described as a master-trope: 'Her voice is but the shadow of a sound.' The phrase is from Young's 'Satire V'; Campbell ponderously explains that 'The sentiment is, that the same relation which the shadow bears to the substance of which it is the shadow, the lady's voice bears to an ordinary sound.'[42] Behind this we can also detect Plato's parable of the cave, with its figuration of language as deferred presence, and also, for all the supposedly 'random' nature of the example, the implication of the feminine body in mourning, in deferred presence, in all that the myth of Echo suggests about the translation of bodies into signs. 'The shadow of a sound', a trope repeated in many nineteenth-century poems, reads like a figure for print, and particularly for the metrical pulse itself (compare Swinburne's 'Hesperia': 'Filled as with shadow of sound were the pulse of invisible feet'). It is as if the voice of a (woman's) shadow underpins the symbolic order, as its catachretic limit, marking the place of *différance* itself.

If masculine elegy is founded on the death of a love-object, it can (as we saw in relation to Swinburne) readily subside into solipsism. One answer to the impasse of voice which Hardy faced in 1912 was to turn, or return, to the voice of women in poetry, to seek an *inter*textual crossing of voices in which the desire of the other might be mixed with his own. I would suggest that Hardy could have had recourse to two women poets in particular, Christina Rossetti (already invoked above) and Jean Ingelow.[43] Indeed, at moments in the sequence one can almost glimpse a fleeting compound spirit, an Emma–Ingelow–Rossetti ghost, Ingelow's poems of crossed love and forgiveness and Rossetti's testamentary sonnets and ghost-poems providing models for responsive and unresponsive or perverse mourning respectively. I say 'almost' in order to register a certain tentativeness here: in some of the juxtapositions which follow, we can get a sense of Hardy's response to poems from his notebooks and annotations; elsewhere the intangibility of intertextual tracing testifies to the occult status of such links, their positing as an empathetic telepathy.

Consider, for example, the structured oppositions, often carried by the rhyme, which inform Hardy's 'Poems of 1912–13' – here/near/dear/there; now/then/away/that day – in relation to Ingelow's 'Song of the Old Love', a poem Hardy marked in his copy of Palgrave, Second Series.[44] It describes a man who sails in disappointment to the North:

> Thou didst set thy foot on the ship, and sail
>   To the ice-fields and the snow;
> Thou wert sad, for thy love did nought avail,
>   And the end I could not know;
> How could I tell I should love thee to-day,
>   Whom that day I held not dear?
> How could I know I should love thee away
>   When I did not love thee anear?

As we have already seen, Hardy was to have Emma remind him that his words are too late: 'When I could answer he did not say them: / When I could let him know / How I would like to join in his journeys / Seldom he wished to go.' Ingelow's final stanza concludes: 'We shall part no more in the wind and the rain, / Where thy last farewell was said' – another flickering presence among the many sources of 'During Wind and Rain', here attached to the possibility of reply. In entering a dialogue with such poems, as well as the now well-mapped dialogue with Emma's own diaries, he opens a line on which traffic is two-way.

Another Ingelow poem which Hardy knew is 'Divided' (the opening poem of her *Poems* of 1863 and of subsequent collections). It is built around a simple conceit. Two lovers meet by a beck and walk along it holding hands; the beck widens to a stream and separates them, and neither will cross over to accommodate the other; it broadens into the river of life, flowing to the sea, and they are parted permanently.[45] (There is a parallel scene in *A Pair of Blue Eyes*, chapter 21; and Hardy's 'Before Knowledge' provides something like a reversal of this trope, depicting lovers moving on 'closing lines which... / Will intersect and join some day!', mirrored in the narrowing form of the poem.) Ingelow's poem seems, at first, to signal the failure of exchange, and voices unheeded:

> A little pain when the beck grows wider;
>   'Cross to me now – for her wavelets swell;'
> 'I may not cross' – and the voice beside her
>   Faintly reacheth, though heeded well.
>
> No backward path; ah! no returning;
>   No second crossing that ripple's flow:
> 'Come to me now, for the west is burning;
>   Come ere it darkens;' – 'Ah, no! ah, no!'

The scene of romance which opens Ingelow's poem is 'pranked' with the same purples which 'prink the main' in 'Beeny Cliff' and colour the strand in '"I Found Her Out There"', and which are described in chapter 21 of *A Pair of Blue Eyes*. Prink and prank are cognate, and there is strong evidence that Ingelow's poem is the point of origin for Hardy's usage, since he had copied the word 'prank' from it into his *Studies, Specimens* notebook some 40 years before he wrote 'Beeny Cliff'. This is Ingelow:

> An empty sky, a world of heather,
>   Purple of foxglove, yellow of broom;
> We two among them wading together,
>   Shaking out honey, treading perfume.
>
> ...
>
> We two walk till the purple dieth
>   And short dry grass under foot is brown;
> But one little streak at a distance lieth
>   Green like a ribbon to prank the down.

If Ingelow's poem marks separation, its conclusion offers a voice of reconciliation from the woman, parted from her lover but forgiving:

> And yet I know past all doubting, truly –
>   A knowledge greater than grief can dim –
> I know, as he loved me duly –
>   Yea, better – e'en better than I love him.
>
> And as I walk by the vast calm river,
>   The awful river so dread to see,
> I say, 'Thy breadth and thy depth for ever
>   Are bridged by his thoughts that cross to me.'

This 'crossing' is what we have already seen the 'Poems of 1912–13' straining towards; here is the reciprocal of the anguished non-communication in the first half of Hardy's sequence, admitting the possibility of traffic across a seemingly absolute barrier. Ingelow's poem also points forward to the more measured tones which Hardy gives to Emma in 'The Phantom Horsewoman' and 'The Spell of the Rose'. In a later poem, 'Days to Recollect', Hardy seems to remember his own brook-side walks with Emma, and accept their separation as simply part of a story, with nature as itself a cyclic presence (as he notes in 'This Summer and Last': 'Still the alert brook purls / Though feet that there would tread / Elsewhere have sped').

    Christina Rossetti provides a more negative moment in the elegy, with her tendency to suggest a deeply unstable relationship between living and dead, and to portray the dead as disturbed rather than reconciled. Her connections with Hardy are less clearly documented than Ingelow's: there are fewer annotations, and no copy of Rossetti's poems from Hardy's library. But he certainly knew and marked some of the 15 poems included in his copy of Palgrave's *Golden Treasury*, Second Series (1897), and probably knew work from other anthologies. Rossetti's importance is, like Ingelow, in providing a model of interchange. But she is also unique among women poets in the intensity with which she gives voice to the figure of the dead woman described by Bronfen; like Hardy she adopts a regularly posthumous stance, but in a different manner, portraying herself as the object of mourning in a way that he does only in a few poems, most of them formal *envoi*. In this respect, she offers a complement to his poems of mourning; a vision of the corpse-who-speaks.[46]

One of the poems in Palgrave is 'Come to me' (properly entitled 'Echo'), with its extraordinary call for a reunion of the living and dead in dream. Most readers probably begin the poem assuming that the poem's speaker is the living calling the dead from 'memory'; but no, this is a call *from* the dead that they be reanimated, that the figure of Echo may be given body:

> Yet come to me in dreams, that I may live
>   My very life again tho' cold in death:
> Come back to me in dreams, that I may give
>   Pulse for pulse, breath for breath:
>   Speak low, lean low,
>   As long ago my love, how long ago.

In 'A Dream or No', Hardy enters that dream, if even in a spirit of scepticism. In poems such as 'Circus-Rider to Ringmaster', he goes further, adopting a feminine voice to present a comparable demand: that love be rekindled or guarded for the sake of the dead.

Rossetti is also, as we saw earlier, the source of a sense of the dangerous lack of equivalence in the relation between living and dead, writing poem after poem in which the betrayal of the dead by the living is the issue. Her poem 'After Death' signals that non-equivalence at the point where the chiasmus fails, at which 'no love' is matched by 'pity' rather than the 'love' which the syntax seems to demand: 'He did not love me living; but once dead / He pitied me; and very sweet it is / To know he is still warm tho' I am cold.' Perhaps the most bitter Rossetti poem of non-reciprocated mourning is 'The Hour and the Ghost', in which a bride is haunted and eventually claimed for death by the ghost of a forgotten lover, who tells her that she too will soon be forgotten and supplanted; other poems, like 'The Poor Ghost', enact similar betrayals.[47] But that process of forgetting is, elsewhere, one in which Rossetti declares herself complicit, for example in her famous sonnet 'Remember'. In a variation on the Orphic scheme of Wordsworth's 'Surprised by Joy', Rossetti has the mourned woman insist that forgetting is natural, an insistence which licenses the muted Orphism of Hardy's 'The Shadow on the Stone', in which, as we saw, the mourned object is only present as a natural trace, and in which the mourner may *choose* to remember rather than facing a chilling injunction to do so. 'The Summer is Ended', also in Palgrave, makes a similar plea: 'Weep not for me when I am gone, / Dear tender one, but hope and smile: / Or if you cannot choose but weep / A little while, weep on / Only a little while.'

What Rossetti offers the possibility of, then, is a highly dynamic vision of mourning: a depiction of the love-object at times self-protective and secretive, at times aggressive or masochistic. It is a version of elegiacs which allows expression of the sadistic elements present in mourning: the sadism which sets Hardy to writing on the claustrophobia of the coffin in 'Lament', even describing it being screwed shut in the unpublished poem 'The Sound of Her'; or having her beseech the reader to 'tell him' she is a 'good haunter' (in 'The Haunter'), before imagining the reaction of Emma's ghost to Florence's changes in her house in 'His Visitor'. It also allows him to have the ghost of Emma (or at least a version of her) chastise him in such poems as 'An Upbraiding' and 'The Monument-Maker'. Two poems by Rossetti are marked in Hardy's 1897 copy of Palgrave, Second Series: 'Next of Kin' and 'Song'. The former is one of Rossetti's voices *in extremis*, with a speaker who sees herself as near death and declares her distance from the healthy:

> The shadows gather round me, while you are in the sun;
> My day is almost ended, but yours is just begun:
> The winds are singing to us both and the streams are singing still,
> And they fill your heart with music, but mine they cannot fill.

The latter again celebrates the indifference of the dead and provides, for Hardy, a negative catalogue of terms – rain on a grave, rose-bushes, song itself – which are taken up in the 'Poems of 1912–13', as if they offered a challenge to the poet:

> When I am dead, my dearest,
>   Sing no sad songs for me;
> Plant thou no roses at my head,
>   Nor shady cypress tree:
> Be the green grass above me

>   With showers and dewdrops wet;
>   And if thou wilt, remember,
>   And if thou wilt, forget.

Compare the opening of Hardy's 'An Upbraiding': 'Now I am dead you sing to me / The songs we used to know.' In this poem Emma chides Hardy for an attention in death which is strangely contrasted to his coldness in the later years of their life together, and speculates that when he is dead and they are 'not differenced', he will revert to indifference. Rossetti's song offers a way out of this sharp opposition, softening it into the natural cycle, just as Hardy does in 'Rain on a Grave', placing himself in the grave, 'Exposed to one weather / We both', before withdrawing to note the 'green blades' it sprouts. In 'The Spell of the Rose' it is Emma who remembers planting the rose, and wonders whether Hardy might think of her. Both these examples suggest a distancing of love. By going to the place where Rossetti's voice crosses with hers, Hardy finds a version of Emma which licenses his more distant stance.

In the story told in this chapter, then, mourning works through intertextuality in various ways, producing anything from learned allusion to a self-reference, from effects which might undermine a poetic stance to those which might enable it. If mourning involves the incorporation of others, then we need a model of textual incorporation which includes more than just connections between texts; which extends to a rhetoric of interchange like that suggested by chiasmus, in which questions of stance and the status of the Other are allowed into play. At the same time, we need a model of intertextuality which allows for more than the inter-psychic battles posited by Harold Bloom; which might explore the way in which a text comes to haunt an author, or provide a route to the dead via various forms of substitution – in Hardy's case, substitutions that work alongside the bonfires which destroyed Emma's unspeakable words (including that word 'hate' which, as we saw, haunts the margins of 'Your Last Drive'). Intertextuality as haunting and necromancy: that is a possibility written into turn-of-the-century understandings of the operation of the psyche. Automatic writing and related mediumistic techniques produced scripts, published in the *Proceedings of the Society for Psychical Research* and elsewhere, which were a jumble of fragmentary citations embedded in other materials, and which the extensive annotations attached would often painstakingly source in order to provide a key to the 'message'. Yeats's notion of the Anima Mundi was one way of theorizing such material. Equally important is the way in which such texts also provided a crucial example for the possibilities of reading texts like *The Waste Land* – Eliot himself likened the poem to automatic writing – allowing a mode of intertextuality in which different voices could be layered as traces, ghostly echoes, repetitive fragments drifting across an imputed multiple consciousness. As we have seen, Hardy rejected the SPR's understanding of ghosts in favour of a more painful and located historicity apparent throughout his poetry. We cannot say that his intertextuality is informed by anything like Eliot's colloquy of disparate voices, or Yeats's notion that creativity is itself occult. Nevertheless, reading Hardy's elegies does involve a set of dialogues with the dead, though always with voices which must be rescued and accorded a presence; which must be located both topographically and tropologically.[48] Words that burn, ashes from an old flame, purple air, all that love can do, the prinking or pranking of purples, the light in the dust dead – to read Hardy is to trace these words across the history of his reading, registering their places; measuring their supplementary status, to be sure, but seeking, as well, the fire that lately burnt, the traces of Hardy's ghost in the places it haunted.

Notes

Notes to the Introduction

1. Giorgio Agamben, *Infancy and History: The Destruction of Experience*, trans. Liz Heron (London: Verso, 1993).
2. Anthony Giddens, *The Nation-State and Violence* (London: Polity, 1985), p. 335.
3. *Heine's Book of Songs*, trans. Charles G. Leland (New York: Henry Holt, 1881), p. 232 (Yale). Cf. Hardy's 'Christmas in the Elgin Room', among other poems.
4. Ernst Bloch, 'Technology and Ghostly Apparitions', in *Literary Essays*, trans. Andrew Joron et al. (Stanford, CA: Stanford University Press, 1998), p. 318.
5. Jacques Derrida, *Spectres of Marx: The State of the Debt, the Work of Mourning and the New International*, trans. Peggy Kamuf, intro. Bernd Magnus and Stephen Cullenberg (New York: Routledge, 1994), pp. 113ff. I use the English spelling of 'spectre' for this title throughout.
6. Gillian Beer, 'Hardy and Decadence', *Celebrating Thomas Hardy: Insights and Appreciations*, ed. Charles Pettit (Basingstoke: Macmillan, 1996), pp. 90–102.
7. Dennis Taylor, *Hardy's Literary Language and Victorian Philology* (Oxford: Clarendon Press, 1993), p. 293.
8. On the politics of this, Hardy's most explicit political statement, see Roger Ebbatson, *Hardy: The Margin of the Unexpressed* (Sheffield: Sheffield Academic Press, 1993), and Peter Widdowson, *Hardy in History: A Study in Literary Sociology* (London: Routledge, 1989).

Notes to Chapter 1: Supplementarity

1. Jean-Michel Rabaté, *The Ghosts of Modernity* (Gainesville, FL: University Press of Florida, 1996), p. 3.
2. See Frank R. Giordano, Jr, 'Hardy's Farewell to Fiction: the Structure of "Wessex Heights"', *Thomas Hardy Yearbook*, **5** (1975): 58–66.
3. See *inter alia* Robert Gittings, *The Older Hardy* (London: Heinemann, 1978), p. 85; Edward Said, *Beginnings: Intention and Method* (New York: Basic Books, 1975), pp. 137–9; Neil Covey, 'The Decline of Poetry and Hardy's Empty Hall', *Victorian Poetry*, **31** (1993): 61–78.
4. Paul Zietlow, *Moments of Vision: The Poetry of Thomas Hardy* (Cambridge, MA: Harvard University Press, 1974), p. 42.
5. Michael Millgate, *Thomas Hardy: A Biography* (Oxford: Oxford University Press, 1982), pp. 170–1.
6. See Lloyd Siemens, 'Hardy among the Critics: the Annotated Scrap Books', *Thomas Hardy Annual*, **2** (1984): 188.
7. Jacques Derrida, *Of Grammatology*, trans. Gayatri Chakravorty Spivak (Baltimore, MD: Johns Hopkins University Press, 1976), pp. 144–5.
8. Derrida, *Of Grammatology*, pp. 153, 143.

9 Perhaps the most subtle exploration of this topic is Mary Jacobus's 'Hardy's Magian Retrospect', *Essays in Criticism*, **32** (1982): 258–79.
10 On Hamlet's father and the mask or visor, see Jacques Derrida, *Spectres of Marx: The State of the Debt, the Work of Mourning and the New International*, trans. Peggy Kamuf, intro. Bernd Magnus and Stephen Cullenberg (New York: Routledge, 1994), p. 8.
11 One might note, here, the lines Hardy underscored in his copy of John A. Carlyle's *Dante's Divine Comedy: The Inferno. A Literal Prose Translation*, 2nd edn (London: George Bell & Sons, 1882), Canto 34: 'I did not die, and did not remain alive' (DCM).
12 Millgate, *Thomas Hardy*, pp. 170–1.
13 J. G. Wood, *Insects at Home* (London: Longman, 1872), p. 77 (summarized *LN* 318).
14 See Dennis Taylor, *Hardy's Poetry, 1860–1928* (London: Macmillan, 1981), pp. xi–xiii; and Philip Davis, *Memory and Writing: From Wordsworth to Lawrence* (Liverpool: Liverpool University Press, 1983), pp. 390–9.
15 See Robert Gittings, *Young Thomas Hardy* (London: Heinemann, 1975), p. 50; and the (incomplete) list in Kenneth Phelps, *Annotations by Thomas Hardy in his Bibles and Prayer-book*, Monographs on the Life, Times, and Works of Thomas Hardy, no. 32 (St Peter Port, Guernsey: Toucan Press, 1966), pp. 1–2, 5.
16 Other typological poems, in terms of imagery or scheme, include 'Near Lanivet, 1872', 'An Evening in Galilee', 'The Wood Fire', 'I Met a Man', 'Apostrophe to an Old Psalm Tune', and (in inverted form) 'On the Tune Called the Old-Hundred-and-Fourth'.
17 Derrida, *Of Grammatology*, p. 145.
18 Simone de Beauvoir, *Old Age*, trans. Patrick O'Brian (London: André Deutsch/ Weidenfeld & Nicolson, 1972), p. 296. Cf. Leon Edel, 'A Portrait of the Artist as an Old Man', *Stuff of Sleep and Dreams: Experiments in Literary Psychology* (London: Chatto & Windus, 1982), pp. 138–63.
19 Millgate, *Thomas Hardy*, p. 384.
20 Unpublished preface to the poems of 'Lawrence Hope' (Adela Nicholson), quoted in Taylor, *Hardy's Poetry*, p. xv.
21 On the autobiography as a strategy aimed at controlling Hardy's posterity, see Michael Millgate, *Testamentary Acts: Browning, Tennyson, James, Hardy* (Oxford: Clarendon Press, 1992).
22 Susan Dean, *Hardy's Poetic Vision in 'The Dynasts': The Diorama of a Dream* (Princeton, NJ: Princeton University Press, 1977), pp. 39–40, 295. Cf. J. Hillis Miller, *The Linguistic Moment: From Wordsworth to Stevens* (Princeton, NJ: Princeton University Press, 1985), pp. 309–12.
23 Millgate, *Thomas Hardy*, pp. 361–2, 421–2; cf. *CL* 2: 131–2; 2: 12, 16.

Notes to Chapter 2: The Ghosts of Thought

1 The best guide in distinguishing different currents of thought here is still Maurice Mandelbaum's *History, Man and Reason: A Study in Nineteenth-Century Thought* (Baltimore, MD: Johns Hopkins University Press, 1971). I use the term 'materialism' in its loose sense, however; in Mandelbaum's stricter definition, materialism (of which he finds few English proponents) is separ-

ate from positivism as represented by Comte and Spencer, and also from the scientific version of pragmatic empiricism which was the common currency of Victorian thinking in Huxley and others.
2. José B. Monleón, *A Spectre is Haunting Europe: A Sociohistorical Approach to the Fantastic* (Princeton, NJ: Princeton University Press, 1990), p. 60. These issues are also, of course, implicit throughout Derrida's *Spectres of Marx*.
3. Terry Castle, *The Female Thermometer: Eighteenth-Century Culture and the Invention of the Uncanny* (New York: Oxford University Press, 1995), ch. 9.
4. Leslie Stephen, *What is Materialism?* (London: W. Allen, 1886), pp. 2–3, 8, 10, 12.
5. E. Armitage, 'The Scientist and Common Sense', *Contemporary Review*, **87** (May 1905): 730 (*LN* 2627). Hardy continued to note the more paradoxical formulae of science up to his death, including his well-known engagement with Relativity in the early 1920s, and a discussion of Quantum Physics in 1928 which refers to time reversal, probably influencing 'He Resolves to Say No More' (*LN* 2476).
6. Frederick Albert Lange, *History of Materialism and Criticism of Its Present Importance*, 3 vols, trans. E. C. Thomas (London: Trübner, 1877–81), vol. 2, p. vi; vol. 3, pp. vii, 219. Cf. *LN* 1229.
7. Mandelbaum, *History, Man and Reason*, pp. 17–18. In his copy of G. H. Lewes, *The History of Philosophy from Thales to Comte*, 5th edn, 2 vols (London: Longman, Green, 1880), vol. 1, p. 267 (Yale), Hardy marked the following passage on Plato: 'The wisest word he has uttered on Theology is one rarely quoted, and not likely to be acceptable to theologians, namely that we know nothing about the Gods, "the speculations about the Gods are simply speculations about the opinions men form about the Gods".'
8. Arthington Worsley, *Concepts of Monism* (London: T. Fisher Unwin, 1907), p. 159 (citing Haeckel's *Riddle of the Universe*). For Hardy's notes from Worsley, see *LN* 2441, 2595–7; on Haeckel, *LN* 2628.
9. Arthur Schopenhauer, 'Essay on Spirit Seeing and Everything Connected Therewith', *Parerga and Paralipomena: Shorter Philosophical Essays*, 2 vols, trans. E. F. B. Payne (Oxford: Clarendon Press, 1974), vol. 1, pp. 225–309; Jean-Michel Rabaté, *The Ghosts of Modernity* (Gainesville, FL: University Press of Florida, 1996), pp. xix–xx.
10. G. H. Lewes, *The Physiology of Common Life*, 2 vols (London: William Blackwood & Sons, 1850–60), vol. 2, pp. 366 ff.
11. See Laura Otis, *Organic Memory: History and the Body in the Late Nineteenth and Early Twentieth Centuries* (Lincoln, NE: University of Nebraska Press, 1994).
12. Friedrich Nietzsche, *On the Advantage and Disadvantage of History for Life* (1874), trans. Peter Preuss (Indianapolis: Hackett, 1980), pp. 23, 49.
13. Karl Marx, *The Eighteenth Brumaire of Louis Napoleon* (London: Lawrence & Wishart, 1954), p. 10.
14. Also informing his thinking is the entry on 'Metaphysics' in the *Encyclopedia Britannica*, 9th edn (1885): see *LN* 1372.
15. Ernest Brennecke, *The Life of Thomas Hardy* (New York: Greenberg, 1925), p. 9.
16. An exception, here as elsewhere, is the engaging if uneven political reading of Hardy in G. W. Sherman's *The Pessimism of Thomas Hardy* (London: Associated Universities Press, 1976).

17 The instalment which Hardy excerpted is Auberon Herbert, 'A Politician in Trouble about his Soul', IV, *Fortnightly Review*, 33 (1883): 354–76, esp. the more general material 361–6 (365 is cited here: all other material is taken from Hardy's transcriptions). The series – which focuses on a sceptical politician, Angus – continued as 'A Politician in Sight of Haven' in 1884, in which the off-stage figure of Markham, Herbert's Spencerian alias, offers solutions. The pieces were republished in book form as *A Politician in Trouble about his Soul* (London: Chapham & Hall, 1884).
18 Herbert Spencer, *Essays: Scientific, Political and Speculative*, 3rd edn, 3 vols (London: Williams & Norgate, 1868–74), vol. 3, p. 182. Hardy owned this edition.
19 On this issue in relation to individuation, 'species-being' and the classical *topos* which compares the generations to autumn leaves, see Robert Pogue Harrison, 'The Names of the Dead', *Critical Inquiry*, 24 (1997): 176–90.
20 Matthew Campbell, *Rhythm and Will in Victorian Poetry* (Cambridge: Cambridge University Press, 1999), pp. 233–4; cf. *LN* 1215.
21 Otis discusses Hardy, *Organic Memory*, pp. 158–80, without touching on the poetry. Her conclusion is that in the novels he used the idea, but remained closer to Darwin than to Lamark; and that he ultimately presents organic memory as one of a number of competing paradigms.
22 Given that Hardy originally wrote 'dying fish's eye', perhaps the closest parallel is James Thompson's 'A Real Vision of Sin' (1859), which begins: 'Like a soaking blanket overhead / Spongy and lax the sky was spread / Opaque as the eye of a fish long dead.'
23 Herbert Spencer, *First Principles*, 4th edn (London: Williams & Norgate, 1880), pp. 63–7.
24 R. B. Haldane, *The Pathway to Reality*, 2 vols (London: John Murray, 1903–4), vol. 1, p. 85. For reviews of Haldane in the notebooks, see *LN* 2234, 2259, 2261, 2276–7.
25 Haldane, *Pathway*, vol. 2, p. xviii. This was an implication in the work of a range of thinkers: cf. Mandelbaum, *History, Man and Reason*, ch. 11, on Comte, Spencer, W. K. Clifford and others; and cf. also the work of F. H. Bradley. For an application to Hardy of Hume's critique of identity, see J. Hillis Miller, *The Linguistic Moment: From Wordsworth to Stevens* (Princeton, NJ: Princeton University Press, 1985).
26 Josiah Royce, *The World and the Individual*, 2 vols (New York: Macmillan, 1900–1). The point of Royce's work was partly to retain a space for 'Absolute Mind', that is for a version of God.
27 Haldane, *Pathway*, vol. 2, pp. 78–9.
28 Haldane, *Pathway*, vol. 2, p. 81.
29 When not quoting from primary sources I use the modern spelling 'fetishism' rather than the nineteenth-century 'fetichism'.
30 *Jude the Obscure*, Part 3, ch. 4; see T. R. Wright, *The Religion of Humanity: The Impact of Comtean Positivism on Victorian Britain* (Cambridge: Cambridge University Press, 1986), p. 212. Hardy excerpted heavily from the second chapter ('Fetichism') of Comte's *Social Dynamics, or The General Theory of Human Progress*, vol. 3 of *System of Positive Polity*, 4 vols, trans. J. H. Bridges, Frederic Harrison et al. (London: Longmans, Green, 1875–6); see *LN* 752 ff.

31 This is also, of course, an area of debate into which Marx entered, making the fetish a figure for commodity-relations within Capitalism. As William Pietz points out, for Enlightenment thinkers 'fetishism was a radically novel category: it offered an atheological explanation of the origin of religion, one that accounted equally well for theistic beliefs and nontheistic superstitions; it identified religious superstition with false causal reasoning about physical nature, making people's relation to material objects rather than to God the key question'. William Pietz, 'Fetishism and Materialism: the Limits of Theory in Marx', in *Fetishism as Cultural Discourse*, ed. Emily Apter and William Pietz (Ithaca: Cornell University Press, 1993), p. 138. Pietz points out the convergence between Kant's analysis (in the first half of the *Critique of Judgement*) of the 'purposiveness' inhering in aesthetic objects and 'Comte's theory of the ineluctable, heuristically valuable mode of "fetishistic" pseudocausal thought' (139 n. 57).
32 Hardy notes this progression in Comte, *LN* 763.
33 Comte, *System of Positive Polity*, vol. 2, *Social Statics*, pp. 185, 190.
34 Spencer, 'The Origin of Animal-Worship' [1870], *Essays: Scientific, Political and Speculative*, vol. 3, ch. iv.
35 Spencer, *Essays: Scientific, Political and Speculative*, vol. 3, p. 129.
36 On his defensive attitude to Comte, see J. D. Y. Peel, *Herbert Spencer: The Evolution of a Sociologist* (London: Heinemann, 1971).
37 W. David Shaw, *The Lucid Veil: Poetic Truth in the Victorian Age* (London: Athlone Press, 1987), p. 126.
38 George W. Stocking notes that Tylor and Spencer disputed priority on this issue: see his *Victorian Anthropology* (New York: Free Press, 1987), pp. 196, 192.
39 *LN* 487, 1383, 2535. Allen's book was reviewed under the heading 'From Ghosts to Gods'.
40 Frederic Harrison, 'The Ghost of Religion', *The Nineteenth Century*, **15** (1884): 493–506 (497 cited). The debate continued: Spencer replied in 'Retrogressive Religion', **16** (1884): 3–26; Harrison again in 'Agnostic Metaphysics', **16** (1884): 353–78; and finally Spencer in 'Last Words', **16** (1884): 816–39 (cited below). Hardy also read Harrison on religion in 1880 (*LN* 1213) and later in *The Positive Evolution of Religion* (1913) (Yale).
41 Herbert Spencer, 'Last Words about Agnosticism and the Religion of Humanity', *The Nineteenth Century*, **16** (1884): 812, noted by Hardy, *LN* 1335.
42 Herbert Spencer, *The Principles of Psychology*, 2 vols (London: Williams & Norgate, 1870–2), vol. 2, pp. xix, 500, 502 (on Hardy's reading of this chapter, see *LN* 1375). Spencer's differences from Comte are also tabulated in his 'Reasons for Dissenting from the Philosophy of M. Comte', in *Essays: Scientific, Political and Speculative*.
43 Spencer also argued, in 1881 in an article which Hardy excerpted, that hereditary succession involved both the idea of transferred qualities and a ruler maintaining 'relations with his progenitor's ghost': see *LN* 1221–7.
44 Cf. Heine's 'The Gods of Greece', discussed in the Introduction. In his copy of *The Works of Horace*, trans. C. Smart (London: Bohn, 1859), p. 7, Hardy wrote beside the phrase 'the altered gods' (Odes 1: 5) the original Latin: 'mutatos Deos' (Colby).
45 Gilliam Beer, 'Hardy and Decadence', in *Celebrating Thomas Hardy: Insights and Appreciations*, ed. Charles Pettit (Basingstoke: Macmillan, 1996),

pp. 90–102. On voice and vision in the elegies, see Melanie Sexton, 'Phantoms of His Own Figuring: The Movement toward Recovery in Hardy's "Poems of 1912–13"', *Victorian Poetry*, **29** (1991): 209–26.
46 A counter-example here is 'Haunting Fingers', but in that poem the remembered dead (instrumentalists) are abstract rather than personal. For a fascinating discussion of music, performance and death in Victorian culture, see Richard Leppert, *The Sight of Sound: Music, Representation and the History of the Body* (Berkeley, CA: University of California Press, 1993).
47 See *LN* 1357, 1504, 1474; *LY* 34.
48 *A Conversation between Thomas Hardy and William Archer* (St Peter Port, Guernsey: Toucan Press, 1979), np. Originally published as 'Real Conversations: Conversation 1, – with Mr Thomas Hardy, *The Critic*, (1901).
49 Ray Lankester, preface to Hugh Elliot, *Modern Science and the Illusions of Professor Bergson* (London: Longman, Green, 1912), p. x.
50 See Janet Oppenheim, *'Shattered Nerves': Doctors, Patients, and Depression in Victorian England* (New York: Oxford University Press, 1991), pp. 76–7.
51 Sir James Crichton-Browne, *On Dreamy Mental States* (London: Ballière, Tindall & Cox, 1895), pp. 6, 7, 20.
52 Elliot, *Modern Science*, pp. 130, 166.
53 Henry Maudsley, *Natural Causes and Supernatural Seemings* (London, 1886), p. 159. For Hardy's notes from this text, see *LN* 1495–8, 1501–20.
54 The translation 'Ghost-seer' was used for both titles in the nineteenth century, though 'Spirit-seer' is more accurate. Kant's *Dreams of a Spirit-Seer: Illustrated by Dreams of Metaphysics* was not translated into English until 1900.
55 Castle, *The Female Thermometer*, ch. 9.
56 Florence Hardy to S. C. Cockerell, 27 Dec. 1919, *Letters of Emma and Florence Hardy*, ed. Michael Millgate (New York: Oxford University Press, 1996), p. 165.
57 Dennis Taylor, *Hardy's Literary Language and Victorian Philology* (Oxford: Clarendon Press, 1993), p. 373.
58 Notoriously, when Théodore Flournoy was studying Hélène Smith's automatic writing, later published as *From India to the Planet Mars* (1900), the linguist he walked down the corridor to consult was his colleague Saussure. For an interpretation of these events, see Tzvetan Todorov, 'Saussure's Semiotics', *Theories of the Symbol* (London: Blackwell, 1982).
59 Maudsley, *Natural Causes*, p. 110; *LN* 1495. Maudsley gives examples of false oppositions (life–death; mind–body) before attacking the medical doctrine of signatures.
60 The background to this debate is considered in Hans Aarsleff, *The Study of Language in England, 1780–1860* (London: Athlone, 1983), ch. 6.
61 Taylor, *Hardy's Literary Language*, pp. 100–2 *et passim*.
62 Max Müller, *Lectures on the Science of Language*, 2nd series [1863], rev. edn (London: Longman, Green, 1885), pp. 380–1.
63 *Select Poems of William Barnes*, chosen and edited with a preface and glossorial notes by Thomas Hardy (London: Henry Frowde, 1908), pp. iii–xii.
64 It is important to keep the equivocal status of photography in mind when we note, in Chapter 3 below, that Lois Deacon's case for Hardy's lost 'son' rests heavily on her identification of a *photograph* in which 'Randy' appears magically before us, a historical spectre embodied. Her faith in this image recalls the complex relationship between photography and hoax, and the paradox-

ical malleability of a supposedly indexical medium, in which to re-produce the body is to attest to its reality. Randy's photograph is thus a form of psycho-technological argument in which the photograph becomes a revenant. Ironically, in *Providence and Mr Hardy* the key examples – photographs of 'Randy', Tryphena and others from the family album, which would give 'additional authenticity to the written record' – are not actually present in the book, Mrs Bromell's daughter having decided to withdraw permission to reproduce them after her mother's death (some were later published elsewhere). Nevertheless, Deacon lists the photographs which she had *intended* to reproduce 'in the interest of historical record', so that they hover on the edge of the text as ghostly presences.

65 'Materialization' received definitive treatment in Baron von Schrenck Notzing's *Materialisations Phaenomene*, translated as *Phenomenon of Materialization* (1920–3).
66 Eduardo Cadava, 'Words of Light: Theses on the Philosophy of History', *Diacritics*, 22, 3–4 (1992): 84–114 (90 cited).
67 It is interesting in this respect that Hardy noted the passage in Worsley's *Concepts of Monism* which differentiates the 'instantaneous photograph' and 'our own (momentary) vision', which carries within it the trace of time (*LN* 2595).

Notes to Chapter 3: The Child in Time

1 The principle works of Abraham and Torok translated into English include *The Wolf-Man's Magic Word: A Cryptonomy*, trans. Nicholas Rand, foreword by Jacques Derrida (Minneapolis: University of Minnesota Press, 1986); *The Shell and the Kernel*, vol. 1, ed. and trans. Nicholas Rand (Chicago, IL: University of Chicago Press, 1994); and Maria Torok and Nicholas Rand's continuation, *Questions for Freud: The Secret History of Psychoanalysis* (Cambridge, MA: Harvard University Press, 1997).
2 A forceful criticism of Abraham's and (especially) Torok's metapsychology is made by Christopher Lane, 'The Testament of the Other: Abraham and Torok's Failed Expiation of a Ghost', *Diacritics*, 27, 4 (1997): 3–29. Lane argues that many of the intrapsychic distinctions made by Abraham and Torok are unsustainable, and critiques both their claims to supersede Freud and the optimism about analytic outcomes implicit in their ego psychology. Nevertheless, their allegorization of interdicted psychic spaces, at the level of the story, remains useful in relation to the positing of family histories and transmitted secrets.
3 Abraham and Torok, *The Shell and the Kernel*, p. 181.
4 Nicholas Rand, 'Towards a Cryptonomy of Literature', translator's introduction to Abraham and Torok, *The Wolf-Man's Magic Word* pp. li–lii.
5 Abraham and Torok, *The Shell and the Kernel*, p. 140.
6 The most famous literary case-study is their analysis of *Hamlet* in terms of an encrypted paternal pre-history, in *The Shell and the Kernel*. However, their suggestions as to the content of the crypt are at best suggestive and at worst tendentious.
7 Esther Rashkin, 'Tools for a New Psychoanalytic Literary Criticism: The Work of Abraham and Torok', *Diacritics*, 18, 4 (1988): 31–52 (51 cited).

8 The poem appeared as 'The Portraits' in *Nash's Magazine and Pall Mall*, Dec. 1924, within an illustrated two-page Art Deco frame by Harry Clarke. For the earlier text, see my *Thomas Hardy: Selected Poems* (London: Longman, 1993), pp. 363–4.
9 The 'Epilogue' to *The Famous Tragedy of the Queen of Cornwall* (1923) seems, in particular, to share its ghost-drama with 'Family Portraits'.
10 See the entries on 'Disavowal' and 'Foreclosure' (the latter representing Lacan's development of Freud) in J. Laplanche and J.-B. Pontalis, *The Language of Psychoanalysis*, trans. Donald Nicholson-Smith (London: Karnac, 1988).
11 *Poems* by Lord Byron (London: Routledge, Warne & Routledge, 1864), p. 355 (Yale).
12 One element of Abraham and Torok's work which is less easily detected in the literary text is the evacuation of the signifier which they term – without a clear explanation – 'de-metaphorization'.
13 Abraham and Torok, *The Wolf-Man's Magic Word*, pp. 81–3.
14 On suffering in Hardy's poetry, see Brian Green, *Hardy's Lyrics: Pearls of Pity* (London: Macmillan, 1996).
15 See Richard D. French, *Antivivisection and Medical Science in Victorian Society* (Princeton, NJ: Princeton University Press, 1975); and on the general issue of pain, Roselyne Rey, *The History of Pain*, trans. Louise Elliott Wallace, J. A. Cadden and S. W. Cadden (Cambridge, MA: Harvard University Press, 1995).
16 Donald Fleming, 'Charles Darwin, the Anesthetic Man', *Victorian Studies*, **4** (1961): 219–36 (227 cited). Fleming argues that Darwin's flight from literature in later life was partly a hypersensitivity to the pain it depicted.
17 Elaine Scarry, *The Body in Pain: The Making and Unmaking of the World* (New York: Oxford University Press, 1985), ch. 3. When Scarry writes that 'The more a habitual form of perception is experienced as itself rather than as its external object, the closer it lies to pain; conversely, the more completely a state is experienced as its object, the closer it lies to imaginative self-transformation,' she is working within the parameters set down by William James, but also suggesting (unlike James) a version of the dis-embodied imagination which is highly debatable.
18 Gerald Heard, *Pain, Sex and Time: A New Hypothesis of Evolution* (London: Cassell, 1939), pp. 49–53. Scarry's *The Body in Pain* might be seen as a later entry in this tradition, attempting to unify prosthetic (evolutionary) and Marxist models of artefaction and identification.
19 Arthur Schopenhauer, *The World as Will and Idea*, 3 vols, trans. R. B. Haldane and J. Kemp (London: Kegan Paul, Trench, Trubner, 1883), vol. 3, pp. 384–5.
20 J. S. Mill, *Utilitarianism* (1863) as cited in *The Hand of Ethelberta* (1876; London: Macmillan, 1975), pp. 222–3.
21 Tess O'Toole, *Genealogy and Fiction in Hardy: Family Lineage and Narrative Lines* (Basingstoke: Macmillan, 1997), p. 22.
22 Schopenhauer, *The World as Will and Idea*, vol. 3, p. 391.
23 *The Cathedral Psalter containing the Psalms of David* (London: Novello, n.d. [*c.*1890]), Psalm 88 (Yale).
24 Lois Deacon and Terry Coleman, *Providence and Mr Hardy* (London: Hutchinson, 1966), p. 183, subsequently referred to in the text. Some of the material on Tryphena in the book was presented earlier (see references below).

25 F. R. Southerington, *Hardy's Child: Fact or Fiction?* Monographs on the Life, Times, and Works of Hardy, no. 42 (St Peter's Port, Guernsey: Toucan Press, 1968). William Kean Seymour, in the *Contemporary Review*, **209** (Oct. 1966): 219–21, was probably the most credulous reviewer. Deacon's evidence is eminently disputable: the questions directed at the elderly Mrs Bromell are very leading; Deacon reports that her mind tended to wander; and while identifying the photograph as 'Hardy's boy' on one occasion, Mrs Bromell never suggested that he was her mother's child.

26 Martin Seymour-Smith, *Hardy* (London: Bloomsbury, 1994), p. 428.

27 Lois Deacon, *'The Chosen' by Thomas Hardy: Five Women in Blend – an identification*, Monographs on the Life, Times, and Works of Thomas Hardy, no. 31 (St Peter Port, Guernsey: Toucan Press, 1966), p. 5.

28 Lois Deacon, *Hardy's Sweetest Image: Thomas Hardy's Poetry of his Lost Love, Tryphena* (Chagford, Devon: the Author, 1964).

29 Deacon, *'The Chosen'*, p. 6; *Providence*, p. 179.

30 Deacon, *Providence*, pp. 110, 67.

31 Abraham and Torok, *The Shell and the Kernel*, p. 122.

32 In *The Visible and the Invisible*, Merleau-Ponty stresses the fact that the left hand can always touch the right, that the possibility of one hand touching the other illustrates the nature of the body, simultaneously subject and object. A wounded hand thus implies a wounded subjectivity.

33 Simon Goldhill, *Reading Greek Tragedy* (Cambridge: Cambridge University Press, 1986), p. 217.

34 See letter of 18 Sept. 1909 to Sir Frederick Macmillan, *CL* 4: 48.

35 Ernest Brennecke, *The Life of Thomas Hardy* (New York: Greenberg, 1925), p. 11.

36 Nicholas Royle, 'Phantom Review', *Textual Practice*, **11** (1997): 386–98.

37 Rosemarie Morgan, *Cancelled Words: Rediscovering Thomas Hardy* (New York: Routledge, 1992), pp. 141–50 (141 cited).

38 *A Conversation between Thomas Hardy and William Archer* (St Peter Port, Guernsey: Toucan Press, 1979), np. Originally published as 'Real Conversations: Conversation 1, – with Mr Thomas Hardy', *The Critic* (1901).

39 Examples include Wordsworth's 'Lucy Gray' poems (*Poetical Works*, 1864, DCM); Lamb's 'On an Infant Dying as Soon as Born' (marked in his Palgrave, DCM); the 'Infant crying in the night' section, *In Memoriam*, p. 54 (DCM); various poems on childhood by William Barnes; and Psalm 131, marked both in his *Cathedral Psalter* (Yale) and his earlier *Book of Common Prayer* (1858, DCM): 'But I refrain my soul, and keep it low like as a child that is weaned from his mother: yea, my soul is even as a weaned child.' Perhaps the most intriguing example is the single poem marked in the index of Wordsworth's *Poetical Works*, 8 vols (1864, DCM), 'Vaudracour and Julia' – Wordsworth's tale of illicit, doomed lovers and their tragic child.

40 Hugh Cunningham, *The Children of the Poor: Representations of Childhood since the Seventeenth Century* (Oxford: Blackwell, 1991), p. 30.

41 See also Hugh Cunningham, *Children and Childhood in Western Culture since 1500* (Harlow: Longman, 1995); James Walvin, *A Child's World: A Social History of English Childhood, 1800–1914* (London: Penguin, 1982).

42 Margaret L. Arnot, 'Infant Death, Child Care and the State: The Baby-Farming Scandal and the First Infant Life Protection Legislation of 1872', *Continuity and Change*, **9**, 2 (1994): 271–312.
43 C. John Somerville, *The Rise and Fall of Childhood* (London: Sage, 1982), p. 170. A more careful revisionist approach is provided by Linda A. Pollock, *Forgotten Children: Parent–Child Relations from 1500 to 1900* (Cambridge: Cambridge University Press, 1983).
44 See also Frank R. Giordano, Jnr, *'I'd Have My Life Unbe': Thomas Hardy's Self-destructive Characters* (University, AL: University of Alabama Press, 1984).
45 Charles Baudelaire, *The Prose Poems and La Fanfarlo*, trans. Rosemary Lloyd (Oxford: Oxford University Press, 1991), pp. 77–80, 123–4n. Hardy could have encountered the story in Parisian journals in London (as well as appearing in *Le Figaro*, it was also published in *L'Artiste* in 1864, and in *L'Événement* in 1866), or later when it was collected in the posthumous *Oeuvres complètes*, vol. 4 (1869).
46 James R. Kincaid, 'Girl-Watching, Child-beating and Other Exercises for Readers of *Jude the Obscure*', in *The Sense of Sex: Feminist Perspectives on Hardy*, ed. Margaret R. Higonnet (Urbana, IL: University of Illinois Press, 1993), pp. 132–48 (71, 78 cited). See also his *Child-Loving: The Erotic Child and Victorian Culture* (New York: Routledge, 1992).
47 U. C. Knopfelmacher, 'Hardy's Ruins: Female Spaces and Male Designs', *PMLA*, **105** (1990): 1055–70.
48 Rey, *The History of Pain*, p. 293.
49 See, e.g., James Crichton-Browne, 'Psychical Diseases of Early Life' (1860), in *Embodied Selves: An Anthology of Psychological Texts, 1830–1890*, ed. Jenny Bourne Taylor and Sally Shuttleworth (Oxford: Clarendon Press, 1998), pp. 335–8.
50 Herbert Spencer, *Social Statics; or, The Conditions Essential to Human Happiness Specified, and the First of them Developed* (1851; New York: D. Appleton, 1888), p. 483. On the discourse of the 'faculties' in respect to education, see John Stuart Mill, *On Liberty, Collected Works*, vol. 18, ed. J. M. Robson (Toronto: University of Toronto Press, 1977), p. 262.
51 Abraham and Torok, *The Shell and the Kernel*, p. 229; Freud to Fliess, 22 Dec. 1897, *The Complete Letters of Sigmund Freud to Wilhem Fliess, 1887–1904*, trans. and ed. Jeffrey Moussaieff Masson (Cambridge, MA: Belknap Press, 1985), p. 289. Torok works from the text Masson had first published a year earlier in *The Assault on Truth*.
52 A copy of Goethe's *Novels and Tales* (1875) is listed in Frank Hollings's Sales Catalogue of books from Hardy's library (Cat. no. 212).
53 Abraham and Torok, *The Shell and the Kernel*, p. 233.
54 Carolyn Steedman, *Strange Dislocations: Childhood and the Idea of Human Interiority* (London: Verso, 1995), p. 12.
55 Michel Foucault, *The Order of Things: An Archeology of the Human Sciences* (London: Tavistock, 1970), p. 219.
56 Steedman, *Strange Dislocations*, p. 87.
57 Giorgio Agamben, *Infancy and History: The Destruction of Experience*, trans. Liz Heron (London: Verso, 1993), pp. 52, 83–6. Agamben uses Beneviste's opposition of *language* and *discourse* rather than Saussure's *langue* and *parole*.

Notes to Chapter 4: The Politics of the Dead

1. *Poems of Shelley*, ed. Stopford A. Brooke (London: Macmillan, 1882) (Yale: the volume is inscribed to Florence Dugdale, but the markings seem to be Hardy's).
2. Lance St John Butler, 'Stability and Subversion: Thomas Hardy's Voices', in Charles Pettit (ed.), *Celebrating Thomas Hardy: Insights and Appreciations* (Basingstoke: Macmillan, 1996), pp. 39–53.
3. Introduction, Peter Widdowson (ed.), *Thomas Hardy: Selected Poetry and Non-Fictional Prose* (Basingstoke: Macmillan, 1997), pp. xxvi–xxvii.
4. The examples cited could be supplemented by many others. *The Cathedral Psalter containing the Psalms of David* (London: Novello, n.d. [c.1890]) (Yale); *The Thoughts of the Emperor M. Aurelius Antoninus*, trans. George Long (London: Bell & Daldy, 1862), p. 22 (Yale); *The Works of Horace*, trans. C. Smart (London: Bohn, 1859), p. 93 (Colby). In the latter, Odes 3: 30 is underlined at 'I shall not wholly die' and Hardy has written the Latin in the margin: 'Non omnis moriar'.
5. *The Works of the Right Honorable Edmund Burke*, 5 vols (London: Bell, 1877), vol. 5, p. 112 (Colby). There are other points of identification in this essay: the passages marked in Hardy's copy include ones in which Burke stresses his humble origins.
6. *Thoughts on the Present Discontents*, in *The Writings and Speeches of Edmund Burke*, vol. 2: *Party, Parliament and the American Crisis*, ed. Paul Langford (Oxford: Clarendon Press, 1981), p. 295.
7. *Reflections on the Revolution in France*, in *The Writings and Speeches of Edmund Burke*, vol. 8: *The French Revolution*, ed. L. G. Mitchell (Oxford: Clarendon Press, 1989), pp. 189–90.
8. Karl Marx, *The Eighteenth Brumaire of Louis Napoleon* (London: Lawrence & Wishart, 1954), p. 10. Cf. Derrida's remarks, *Spectres of Marx: The State of the Debt, the Work of Mourning, and the New International*, trans. Peggy Kamuf, intro. Bernd Magnus and Stephen Cullenberg (New York: Routledge, 1994), p. 142. Hardy's version of this regression to the ghosts of the past is contained in his remarks on poetry and history in the 'Apology' to *Late Lyrics and Earlier (1922)*:

    the visible signs of mental and emotional life, must like all other things keep moving, becoming; even though at present, when belief in witches of Endor is displacing the Darwinian theory and 'the truth that shall make you free', men's minds appear, as above noted, to be moving backwards rather than on.

9. Steven Blakemore, *Burke and the Fall of Language: The French Revolution as Linguistic Event* (Hanover, NJ: University Press of New England, 1988), pp. 21 ff.
10. See Burke on the 'pedigree of crimes' attributed to the exhumed, *Reflections*, pp. 189 ff, 219.
11. Walter Benjamin, *Illuminations*, ed. and intro. Hannah Arendt, trans. Harry Zohn (London: Fontana, 1973), pp. 257, 263.
12. This image and the related idea of rescue, Margaret Cohen points out, derives from Nietzsche's discussion of the 'retroactive force' of the individual in the

'Historia abscondita' fragment in *The Gay Science*; and also from Breton's figure of a flower which follows a secret historical sun. See her *Profane Illumination: Walter Benjamin and the Paris of Surrealist Revolution* (Berkeley, CA: University of California Press, 1993), pp. 202–3.

13 Friedrich Schlegel, *Athenaeum Fragments*, 80, in *Philosophical Fragments*, trans. Peter Firchow (Minneapolis, MN: University of Minnesota Press, 1991), p. 27. On Benjamin and Schlegel, see Howard Caygill, *Walter Benjamin: The Colour of Experience* (London: Routledge, 1998), pp. 41 ff.

14 Helga Geyer-Ryan, 'Counterfactual Artefacts: Walter Benjamin's Philosophy of History', in *Visions and Blueprints: Avant-garde Culture and Radical Politics in Early Twentieth Century Europe*, ed. Edward Timms and Peter Collier, intro. Raymond Williams (Manchester: Manchester University Press, 1988), pp. 66–79 (72 cited). Cf. Cohen's remarks on Benjamin's messianic Marxism and Breton's psychoanalytic model, *Profane Illumination*, pp. 204–5.

15 Walter Benjamin, 'Eduard Fuchs, Collector and Historian', *One-Way Street and Other Writings*, intro. Susan Sontag, trans. Edmund Jephcott and Kingsley Shorter (London: New Left Books, 1979), p. 352.

16 Derrida, *Spectres of Marx*, p. 175; cf. his comments on Benjamin's 'weak messianic power', pp. 180–1n.

17 Stan Smith, *Inviolable Voice: History and Twentieth-Century Poetry* (Dublin: Gill & Macmillan, 1982), p. 44. 'To brush history against the grain' is from Benjamin's 'Theses on the Philosophy of History', section vii.

18 Derrida, *Spectres of Marx*, p. xix.

19 Thomas Carlyle, 'On History', *A Carlyle Reader*, ed. G. B. Tennyson (Cambridge: Cambridge University Press, 1984), p. 58. On Carlyle and history, see esp. Peter Allen Dale, *The Victorian Critic and the Idea of History* (Cambridge: Harvard University Press, 1977).

20 Thomas Carlyle, 'Biography', *Critical and Miscellaneous Essays*, 4 vols in 2 (London: Chapman & Hall, 1888), vol. 3, p. 44.

21 In his notes for *The Dynasts* he wrote: 'Poem. A spectral force seen acting in a man (e.g. Nap.) & he acting under it – a pathetic sight, this compulsion' (*PN* 59).

22 Carlyle, 'Biography', *Essays*, vol. 3, p. 45.

23 The figure of the misplaced body runs through Hardy's poetry. 'Sapphic Fragment' places itself firmly in a genre which Hardy's reading in the *Greek Anthology* made him familiar with: the epigraph for the absent body, particularly of those 'died at sea'. Such deaths render impossible the epitaph attached to a locus; they represent the body unhoused, as in Hardy's 'The Three Tall Men', in which a man obsessively makes then remakes his oversized coffin, only to drown. A notebook entry records '*Grave Unknown* – St Patrick's – [& Moses']' (*LN* 165). The body of Drummer Hodge is 'uncoffined – just as found'; other bodies in Hardy's poetry are lost or scattered.

24 *Select Poems of William Barnes*, ed. and intro. Thomas Hardy (London: Henry Frowde, 1908), p. viii.

25 See Tom Paulin's discussion of Locke in *Thomas Hardy: The Poetry of Perception* (London: Macmillan,1975).

26 'Alastor', lines 116–20, *Poems of Shelley* (Yale).

27 Burke, *Works*, vol. 1, p. 307 (Colby).

28 Arthur Schopenhauer, 'On the Doctrine of the Indestructibility of Our True Nature by Death', *Parerga and Paralipomena: Shorter Philosophical Essays*, 2 vols, trans. E. F. B. Payne (Oxford: Clarendon Press, 1974), vol. 2, p. 276.
29 Michel Serres with Bruno Latour, *Conversations on Science, Culture and Time*, trans. Roxanne Lapidus (Ann Arbor, MI: University of Michigan Press, 1995), pp. 49–50.
30 'On History', *Carlyle Reader*, p. 58.
31 The tropes of the 'self-same' bird and the bird which sings 'darkling' echo from Milton to Wordsworth, who wrote of the cuckoo, 'the same whom in my schoolboy days / I listened to'; to Keats, who in the 'Ode to a Nightingale' listens, 'darkling', and writes of 'the selfsame song that found a path / Through the sad heart of Ruth'; to Hardy's 'The Selfsame Song', 'The Darkling Thrush' and other poems.
32 Isobel Armstrong, *Victorian Poetry: Poetry, Poetics and Politics* (London: Routledge, 1993), p. 487.

Notes to Chapter 5: History, Catastrophe, Typology

1 On history in *The Dynasts*, see Walter Wright, *The Shaping of The Dynasts* (Lincoln, NE: University of Nebraska Press, 1967), and G. Glen Wickens, 'Hardy's Inconsistent Spirits and the Philosophic Form of *The Dynasts*', in *The Poetry of Thomas Hardy*, ed. Patricia Clements and Juliet Grindle (London: Vision Press, 1980), pp. 101–18. Wickens supports what is ultimately one conclusion of this chapter: that 'man's subjective response to the universe is never absent in any explanation of it' (p. 116). Cf. also, J. Hillis Miller, 'History as Repetition in Thomas Hardy's Poetry: The Example of "Wessex Heights"', in *Victorian Poetry: Stratford-upon-Avon Studies*, ed. M. Bradbury and D. Palmer (London: Arnold, 1972).
2 *Aristotle's Treatise on Rhetoric and The Poetic of Aristotle*, trans. Thomas Buckley (London: Bohn, 1850), p. 424. In his *Two Essays by Arthur Schopenhauer*, trans. Karl Hillebrand (London: George Bell, 1889), p. 13, Hardy marks the comment on 'so thoroughly pitiable creature as Hegel, whose whole pseudo-philosophy is but a monstrous amplification of the Ontological Proof ...' (both at Colby).
3 Quoted by Geoffrey Marcus, *The Maiden Voyage* (New York: George Allen & Unwin, 1969), p. 298.
4 Quoted by Walter Lord, *The Night Lives On* (New York: Morrow, 1986), p. 26. Lord comments on Morgan Robertson's *The Wreck of the Titan; or, Futility* (1900) in *A Night to Remember* (1956; Harmondsworth: Penguin, 1981), p. 11. See also Rustie Brown, *The Titanic, the Psychic, and the Sea* (Lomita, CA: Blue Harbor Press, 1981).
5 Wynn Craig Wade, *The Titanic: End of a Dream* (London: Macmillan, 1980), p. 145. No source is given for the poem.
6 Brown, *The Titanic*, pp. 61 ff.
7 Quoted by Dennis Taylor, *Hardy's Poetry, 1860–1928* (London: Macmillan, 1981), p. 117. Hardy was certainly aware of the aesthetics of Romantic Titanism which lie behind these anticipations: the opening of *The Return of the Native* describes the 'Titanic form' of the heath silently awaiting the 'final catastrophe'.

8   I am, here, setting aside other possible influences on Hardy's poem, such as R. S. Hawker's 'The Fatal Ship'.
9   *Spectator*, 20 April 1912, p. 620. Thaxter wrote extensively on marine subjects; she ran a hotel on Appledore Island, New Hampshire, frequented by the Transcendentalists.
10 J. O. Bailey, *The Poetry of Thomas Hardy: A Handbook and Commentary* (Chapel Hill, NC: University of North Carolina Press, 1970), p. 266.
11 A tentative aside. There are some curious resonances which connect Hardy's poem to the catastrophic vision of history in Edmund Burke's 'Letter to a Noble Lord', an essay which Hardy read carefully: words like 'coincident' (which Hardy marked in Burke); a certain nautical flavour. Burke describes, in another passage Hardy marked, how 'In Ireland things ran in a still more eccentric course. Government was unnerved.... Indeed, a darkness next to the fog of this awful day, loured over the whole region; for a little time the helm appeared abandoned.' Even the culminating description of Burke's enemy Russell portrays him as a maritime hazard: 'The Duke of Bedford is the leviathan among all the creatures of the Crown.' *The Works of the Right Honorable Edmund Burke*, 5 vols (London: Bell, 1876–7), vol. 5, pp. 129, 123 (Colby).
12 John Morley, *Fortnightly Review*, **22** (1877): 268–9 (cited *LN* 1066n).
13 On Hardy and Comte, see Björk, *LN* 618n. The selections from Comte's *Social Dynamics, or the General Theory of Human Progress*, vol. III of *System of Positive Polity*, trans. and ed. S. Beesley *et al.* (London: Longman, Green, 1876) on 'Fetishism' and on 'Directing Wills' are *LN* 641, 647, 754–62 and 739–40.
14 F. B. Pinion, *Hardy the Writer: Surveys and Assessments* (Basingstoke: Macmillan, 1990), pp. 251–63.
15 Jeremy Hawthorn, *Cunning Passages: New Historicism, Cultural Materialism and Marxism in the Contemporary Literary Debate* (London: Arnold, 1996), pp. 109–24.
16 David Perkins, *A History of Modern Poetry: From the 1890s to the High Modernist Mode* (Cambridge, MA: Belknap Press, 1976), p. 151. While Perkins writes that 'nothing follows from the sinking of the *Titanic*; no moral is drawn', it seems to me that the conventional moral is clearly drawn in the opening section.
17 Taylor, *Hardy's Poetry*, p. 87.
18 Samuel Hynes, in the *Complete Poetical Works of Thomas Hardy*, 5 vols (Oxford: Clarendon, 1982–95), vol. 3, p. 249, corrects an error in the fourth line of this stanza, but chooses 'ether-ocean' over the 'bending-ocean' of *Winter Words* and Gibson's *Variorum*, neither alternative (the former in ink and the latter in pencil) being deleted in the manuscript. Aside from the appositeness of 'bending-ocean' for my purpose here, 'ether-ocean' suggests an outmoded theory in physics in which 'the ether' is the postulated carrier of electromagnetic radiation. As the *Longman Encyclopedia* (London: Longman, 1989) puts it, 'the theory of relativity eliminated the need for such a medium' – and Hardy had already, in 1905, read attacks on the ether-theory (*LN* 2627). Thus 'bending-ocean' is closer to Einstein's actual theories, and we might do Hardy a service by restoring it.
19 Hayden White, *Tropics of Discourse: Essays in Cultural Criticism* (Baltimore, MD: Johns Hopkins University Press, 1978), p. 117. White attacks systematic history (which he associates with the Marxist tradition in particular) in ch. 3

of his *The Content of the Form: Narrative Discourse and Historical Representation* (Baltimore, MD: Johns Hopkins University Press,1987). Gerald Gillespie more urbanely remarks that 'the craving for a super-construct which would overcome real disorder in human affairs has never died', and points out that Erich Voegelin, long before White, pleaded for an abandonment of transcendent history. Gerald Gillespie, *Garden and Labyrinth of Time: Studies in Renaissance and Baroque Literature*, ed. Katharina Mommsen (New York: Verlag, 1988), p. 143.
20 See Martin Thom, *Republics, Nations and Tribes* (London: Verso, 1995).
21 *Speeches, Articles and Letters of Israel Zangwill*, ed. Maurice Simon (London: Soncino Press, 1937), pp. 242–8. See also Stuart A. Cohen, *English Zionists and British Jews: The Communal Politics of Anglo-Jewry, 1895–1920* (Princeton, NJ: Princeton University Press, 1982), ch. 3.
22 Israel Zangwill, 'Letters and the Ito', *Fortnightly Review*, April 1906, pp. 633–47, including replies from J. M. Barrie, Hall Caine, John Davidson, Conan Doyle, W. S. Gilbert, Rider Haggard, Frederic Harrison, H. G. Wells and others. Hardy's letter has an appended comment from Zangwill stating that 'He has expressed in a nutshell my own views on every point of a complex question.' In the wake of her husband's efforts, Emma Hardy offered her own help to Zangwill, though her militant Protestantism meant that she more punitively advocated a return to Palestine for the Jews 'at last when their penance was over'. *Letters of Florence and Emma Hardy*, ed. Michael Millgate (Oxford: Clarendon Press, 1996), p. 33.
23 *The Cathedral Psalter containing the Psalms of David* (London: Novello, n.d. [*c*.1890]) (Yale). Hardy's copy of *The Book of Common Prayer* (1858, DCM) is also much marked at this psalm, and he notes four occasions where he attended 'alone' and heard it in the 1900s.
24 'Historic Ground', *The Times*, 26 Sept. 1918, p. 5; *Spectator*, 28 Sept. 1918, p. 1. The latter adds 'It is piquant to learn from the *Echo de Paris* that the organizer of this desert cavalry, which has inflicted heavy losses on the Turks for many months past, is a young English archeologist of the British Museum staff, Colonel Lawrence' – an early report of T. E. Lawrence ('Lawrence of Arabia'), who was to visit the Hardys regularly in the 1920s.
25 'The University of Jerusalem', *The Times*, 25 Sept. 1918, p. 6.
26 Some anti-Semites also supported Zionism, with the aim of removing Jews from England – a possible element in both Lloyd George's and Balfour's feelings, as their fellow Cabinet-member Edwin Montague recognized. Montague probably influenced the drafting of the third clause of the Declaration, protecting 'the rights and political status enjoyed by Jews in any other country': see Frank Hardie and Irwin Herrman, *Britain and Zion: The Fatal Entanglement* (Belfast: Blackstaff Press, 1980), pp. 80–1.

Notes to Chapter 6: Mourning and Intertextuality

1 Among the best examinations of that process, proposing a model in which 'propinquity' rather than contact is the ultimate aim, is P. Robinson, 'In Another's Words: Thomas Hardy's Poetry', *English*, **31** (1982): 221–46. See also David Gewanter's exploration of Hardy's use of Emma's text in ' "Under-

voicings of Loss" in Hardy's Elegies to his Wife', *Victorian Poetry*, **29** (1991): 193–207.
2. In part, my argument here is anticipated in Phillip Davis's *Memory and Writing: From Wordsworth to Lawrence* (Liverpool: University of Liverpool Press, 1983).
3. Jacques Derrida, *Cinders*, trans., ed. and intro. Ned Lukacher (Lincoln, NE: University of Nebraska Press, 1991); Virgile, *Énéide*, ed. Henri Goelzer, trans. André Bellessort (Paris: Société d'édition les belles-lèttres, 1946), p. 100. The extent of Derrida's familiarity with the classical tradition (outside the history of philosophy and rhetoric) is difficult to discern: there is little evidence of it in his major writings.
4. David Farrell Krell, *Of Memory, Reminiscence and Writing: On the Verge* (Bloomington, IN: Indiana University Press, 1990), p. 310.
5. Derrida, *Cinders*, p. 31.
6. 'En écrivant ainsi, il brûle une fois de plus, il brûle ce qu'il adore encore mais qu'il a déjà brûlé, il s'y acharne', *Cinders*, p. 43.
7. Derrida, *Cinders*, p. 73.
8. Derrida, *Cinders*, 49; *The Thoughts of the Emperor M. Aurelius Antoninus*, trans. George Long (London: Bell & Daldy, 1862), p. 77, para. 33 (Yale). Hardy did mark the following passage: 'How does the ruling faculty make use of itself? for all lies in this. But everything else, whether it is in the power of thy will or not, is only lifeless ashes and smoke' (p. 216).
9. Matthew Campbell, *Rhythm and Will in Victorian Poetry* (Cambridge: Cambridge University Press, 1999), pp. 224–32. A sharp contrast to Hardy's uncertainty is provided by the lines from Psalm 56 which he marked in his *Cathedral Psalter*: 'Thou tellest my flittings; put my tears into thy bottle: are not these things noted in thy book?' (Yale).
10. Maurice Blanchot, *The Writing of the Disaster*, trans. Ann Smock (Lincoln, NE: University of Nebraska Press, 1986), p. 18.
11. Francis Palgrave (ed.), *The Golden Treasury of the Best Songs and Lyrical Poems in the English Language* (London: Macmillan, 1861), pp. 6–7 (DCM). In this, the first edition, the poem was listed as by 'anon'.
12. The text quoted is the uncorrected version from *The Poems of Shelley*, ed. Thomas Hutchinson (1905; London: Oxford University Press, 1943), p. 516 (ll. 385–8). Harold Bloom provides a partial history of this *topos* in his essay on Shelley in *Poetry and Repression* (New Haven, CT: Yale University Press, 1976), pp. 103–9.
13. The latter subject is addressed, pessimistically, in 'The Monument-Maker', a few poems earlier in the volume: memorialization is, the two poems suggest, a revival more fruitful for the subject than the object of mourning.
14. John Lucas, *Modern English Poetry: From Hardy to Hughes* (London: Batsford, 1986), p. 36; Donald Davie, 'Hardy's Virgilian Purples', *Agenda*, **10**, 2–3 (1972): 138–56.
15. Peter Sacks, *The English Elegy* (Baltimore, MD: Johns Hopkins University Press, 1985), pp. 234–59.
16. F. B. Pinion, ' "Beeny Cliff" and Virgilian Purples', *Thomas Hardy Journal*, **8**, 3 (1992): 86–9, argues that Hardy's immediate source is Gray here, and certainly 'The Progress of Poesy' is also alluded to, ironically, in Elfride's phrase 'words that burn'. But Virgil enters the novel elsewhere, via Dryden (e.g. the 'nether sky', ch. 21, repeated in 'Beeny Cliff'), the lines cited are part of Gray's

description of Dryden as the translator of Virgil (another trace leading back to the *Aeneid*), and Gray alludes to Virgil with his 'purples', as Hardy surely knew. Moreover, Hardy's copy of *The Works of Virgil*, trans. John Dryden (London: Thomas Allman, n.d.), is marked at the passage referring to 'purple sky' (DCM). The opposition between Gray and Virgil as competing rather than composite sources which Pinion uses is, therefore, too sharp.

17 Davie, 'Hardy's Virgilian Purples', p. 144.
18 Surviving texts from his library include an annotated copy of John A. Carlyle's bilingual edition, *Dante's Divine Comedy: The Inferno. A Literal Prose Translation*, 2nd edn (London: George Bell & Sons, 1882), in the DCM; and a copy of an 1879 edition of Cary's translation, at the University of Texas. Tom Paulin suggests that Hardy was influenced by Cary's Dante: see 'Words, in all their intimate accents', *Thomas Hardy Annual*, 1 (1982): 84–94. For a summary of other material, see Björk (*LN* 367n).
19 Allen Mandelbaum, *The Aeneid* (Berkeley, CA: University of California Press, 1981), p. 168.
20 John Frecero, letter cited by Harold Bloom, *The Anxiety of Influence* (New York: Oxford University Press, 1973), p. 123.
21 *Dante's Divine Comedy*, p. 57 (DCM). This and related annotations are discussed by Walter F. Wright, *The Shaping of The Dynasts* (Lincoln, NE: University of Nebraska Press, 1967), pp. 12–13.
22 *The Divine Comedy*, trans. Francis Cary (1814; London: Bibliophile Books, 1988), p. 36. There is an annotation to similar effect, quoting the *Convito*, in the Carlyle edition.
23 *Life's Little Ironies and A Changed Man*, ed. F. B. Pinion (London: Macmillan, 1977), p. 137.
24 Marked passages in Hardy's copies of *The Works of Virgil*, trans. John Dryden (London: J. Cuthell, 1819), p. 301; *Poems of Wordsworth*, ed. Matthew Arnold (London: Macmillan, 1886), p. 320 (both Yale); and *Poetical Works of William Wordsworth*, 8 vols (London: Macmillan, 1896), vol.8, p. 28 (DCM).
25 *Select Epigrams from the Greek Anthology*, ed. J. W. Mackail (London: Longmans, Green, 1911), p. 104.
26 Hardy marked descriptions of rain in Canto 6 in Carlyle's translation, *Dante's Divine Comedy*, pp. 60ff (DCM), including underlining 'Thus passed we through the filthy mixture of the shadows and the rain' (p. 67).
27 Sacks, *The English Elegy*, p. 225.
28 Linda M. Austin, 'Reading Depression in Hardy's "Poems of 1912–13"', *Victorian Poetry*, 36, 1 (1998): 1–17.
29 'Pictures of Travel', Poem 57, *The Poems of Heine*, trans. Edgar Alfred Bowring (London: Bell, 1878), p. 217 (Yale).
30 A. C. Swinburne, *Collected Poetical Works* (London: Heinemann, 1935), vol. I, p. 189.
31 'For all that friendship, all that love can do, / All that a darling countenance can look / Or dear voice utter, to complete the man...', Wordsworth, *Prelude* (1850) XIV, lines 221 ff, in *The Prelude 1799, 1805, 1850*, ed. Jonathan Wordsworth, M. H. Abrams, Stephen Gill (New York: Norton, 1979), p. 471.
32 *Chiasmus* (lit. 'placing crosswise') is a term which has no very clear definition, as any survey of recent dictionaries of literary terms shows. It is often used to describe a very general reversal of segments within a syntactically equivalent

structure – J. A. Cuddon's *Dictionary of Literary Terms and Literary Theory*, 3rd edn (London: Penguin, 1991) gives as an example 'His time a moment, and his point a space' (Pope); in such examples the figure risks simply becoming a form of antithesis. Martin Gray in *A Dictionary of Literary Terms*, 2nd rev. edn (Harlow: Longman, 1992) provides a different definition, applying the term more correctly to the inversion of syntactic units. But his example – 'Smooth flow the waves, the zephyrs gently play' (adverb–verb–subject; subject–adverb–verb) – is so general as to apply to almost any set of balanced phrases, and omits any element of lexical repetition. The example in Karl Beckson and Arthur Granz's *Literary Terms: A Dictionary*, 3rd rev. edn (London: André Deutsch, 1990) seems closer to the mainstream of modern usage of the term: 'For his mourners will be outcast men, / And outcasts always mourn' (Wilde), and their definition is succinct: 'a passage consisting of two balanced parts which have their elements reversed'. For a more general description of the figure in terms of an *a b b a* structure at any level (from the phoneme up to the episode or other plot element), that is as 'an "emblem" or icon of reversal or inversion generally', see Max Nänny, 'Chiasmic Structures in Literature: Some Forms and Functions', in *The Structure of* Texts, ed. Udo Fries (Tübingen: Gunter Narr Verlag, 1987), pp. 75–98. Among more literary studies, Patricia Parker's exploration of the trope in *Literary Fat Ladies: Rhetoric, Gender, Property* (London: Methuen, 1987), pp. 77–81, is exemplary.

33 Jean-François Lyotard, *Discours, figure* (Paris: Éditions Klincksieck, 1978), p. 11. Emmanuel Levinas also uses 'chiasmus' for the meeting with the 'other': see Simon Critchley, *The Ethics of Deconstruction: Derrida and Levinas* (Oxford: Blackwell, 1992), p. 52n17, for a summary of usages.

34 Maurice Merleau-Ponty, *The Visible and the Invisible, followed by working notes*, ed. Claude Lefort, trans. Alphonso Lingis (Evanston, NJ: Northwestern University Press, 1968), p. 215.

35 Jacques Derrida, *Spectres of Marx: The State of the Debt, the Work of Mourning and the New International*, trans. Peggy Kamuf, intro. Bernd Magnus and Stephen Cullenberg (New York: Routledge, 1994), p. 7.

36 Pamela Dalziel and Michael Millgate (eds), *Thomas Hardy's 'Studies, Specimens &c.' Notebook* (Oxford: Clarendon Press, 1994), p. 49. The poem appears to be 'The Triumph of Time'.

37 Derrida speaks briefly of the chiasm in *Positions*, ed. and trans. Alan Bass (London: Athlone, 1981), p. 70, referring to it as a sign for his discussion of Mallarmé's 'fold' in *Dissemination*. See also Allen S. Weiss, 'Structures of Exchange, Acts of Transgression', in *Sade and the Narrative of Transgression*, ed. David B. Allison, Mark S. Roberts, Allen S. Weiss (Cambridge: Cambridge University Press, 1995), pp. 199–212.

38 Nicholas Abraham and Maria Torok, *The Shell and the Kernel*, vol. 1, ed. and trans. Nicholas Rand (Chicago, IL: University of Chicago Press, 1994), p. 141.

39 Angela Leighton, '"When I am dead, my dearest": the Secret of Christina Rossetti', *Modern Philology*, **87**, 4 (1990): 373–88.

40 Melanie Sexton, 'Phantoms of His Own Figuring: the Movement Toward Recovery in Hardy's "Poems of 1912–13"', *Victorian Poetry*, **29** (1991): 209–26.

41 Among recent discussions of voice and vision in the sequence, see Sexton, 'Phantoms of His Own Figuring'; Gewanter, '"Undervoicings of Loss"'; Eric Griffiths, *The Printed Voice of Victorian Poetry* (Oxford: Clarendon, 1989).

42 George Campbell, *The Philosophy of Rhetoric*, 2 vols (London: A. Strahan, 1801), vol. 2, p. 195 (Yale).
43 Other candidates ruled out here include Charlotte Mew and Mary Coleridge (whose 1910 poems Hardy marked).
44 Jean Ingelow, 'Song of the Old Love', in Francis Palgrave (ed.), *The Golden Treasury*, Second Series (London: Macmillan, 1897), p. 213 (Yale). This song is excerpted from a longer poem, Ingelow's 'Supper at the Mill'.
45 Jean Ingelow, *Poems* (London: Oxford University Press, 1913), pp. 1–5.
46 One of the few poems which seems written directly in Rossetti's shadow is 'The Woman I Met' (1918), with its interview with a 'soul departed' whose love for the poem's narrator was never reciprocated.
47 *The Complete Poems of Christina Rossetti*, ed. R. W. Crump, 3 vols (Baton Rouge, LO: Lousiana State University Press, 1979–90), vol. 1, pp. 37–8, 40, 120. Other poems by Rossetti are cited from Palgrave, *Golden Treasury*, pp. 207, 227, 72, 229. Rossetti may have also offered a general model for a number of interchanges between lovers (for example Hardy's paired poems 'His Heart. A Woman's Dream' and '"I thought, my Heart"' may be partly modelled on Rossetti's 'Twice', with its vocabulary of scanning the heart and judging).
48 Cf. J. Hillis Miller's 'Topography and Tropography in Thomas Hardy's "In Front of the Landscape"', *Tropes, Parables, Performatives: Essays on Twentieth Century Literature* (Hemel Hempstead: Harvester Wheatsheaf, 1990), pp. 73–90. Miller writes that 'writing functions as a successful "trope of defense" against all those reproaching and beseeching phantoms from his past' (p. 84) – a formula which seems less useful than his later comment that 'writing is the act which raises the ghosts by turning dead signs into beseeching phantoms'.

Index

Abraham, Nicolas, 63–5, 75, 77, 160–1, 179n2
Agamben, Giorgio, 2, 86–7
Allen, Grant, 46
animism, 32, 45
Archer, William, 52–7, 79, 99
Aristotle, 111–12
Armstrong, Isobel, 109
Arnold, Matthew, 3–4, 100
ashes 61, 62, 77
  and mourning, 134–41
  see also Derrida, Cinders
Austin, Linda, 156

Bailey, J. O., 116
Barnes, William, 58, 97, 140
Baudelaire, Charles, 'Rope', 83
Beer, Gillian, 5, 49
belated awareness, 12, 17–23, 116, 135–6
  see also latency
Benjamin, Walter, 93–4, 98, 109–10
  Angelus novus, 93, 99
Bergson, Henri, 27, 69–71, 105
Björk, Lennart, 33, 118
Blakemore, Steven, 92
Blanchot, Maurice, 144
Bloch, Ernst, 4
Bloom, Harold, 171
body, 74, 97, 156
  absent, 75, 152, 159, 165–6, 84n23
  wounded hand, 75–7
Brennecke, Ernest, 77
Bridges, J. H., 45
Bromell, Eleanor, 73, 74, 75
Bronfen, Elizabeth, 165, 169
Brooke, Stopford, 89
Browning, Elizabeth Barrett, 83
Browning, Robert, 26, 58, 83
Burke, Edmund, 90–3, 186n11
Butler, Lance St John, 89

Byron, George Gordon, Lord, 67, 146–7

Cadava, Eduardo, 60
Campbell, George, 165
Campbell, Matthew, 38
Carlyle, Thomas, 61, 106, 111, 113, 125, 140
  'Biography', 96–7
Castle, Terry, 31, 55
catastrophe, see history
censorship, 78
  psychic, 67, 86; see also crypt; phantom
chiasmus, 156–66, 189n32
child
  eroticized, 83
  as fiction, 80–1
  and history, 85–7
  'lost', 78–80, 181n39
  illegitimate, 73, 80
  in nineteenth century, 82–5
  and pain, 72, 80, 84–6
Clifford, W. K., 33, 38
Coleman, Terry, 72
Comte, Auguste, 44–51, 107, 118–23
Conrad, Joseph, 113
Crichton-Browne, Sir James, 52–3, 84
crypt, as psychic structure, 63, 78, 81
  see also Abraham; phantom
Cunningham, Hugh, 82

Dante, 149–55
Darwin, Charles, 68–9, 84
Davie, Donald, 140, 148–55
Deacon, Lois, 72–9, 160, 179n64, 181n25
dead, the, 45
  dead woman, as figure, 165–6, 169

as forgotten, 90, 93
  and history, 94–104
  see also ghosts; haunting
Dean, Susan, 26
de Beauvoir, Simone, 23
Derrida, Jacques, 7, 10, 23, 25, 94–5, 159
  Cinders, 135–7, 141
  Specters of Marx, 4, 77, 94, 158
  on the supplement, 10, 25
Donne, John, 146

echo, 22–3, 143–5
  as figure 5, 41, 166, 169
Edmond, Rod, 156
Einstein, Albert, 126
Eliot, T. S., 172
Emerson, Ralph Waldo, 95
end-of-year poems, 94–5, 106

family secrets, *see* secrets
fetishism, 37, 43–51, 118
Fliess, Wilhelm, 85
Foucault, Michel, 86
Frecero, John, 151
Freud, Sigmund, 66, 69, 85–6, 93
Froude, J. A., 96, 125

Geyer-Ryan, Helga, 93
ghosts, 2–3, 54–5, 91–2, 129–34, 142–4
  of the future, 35, 94
  Hardy as, 1, 10–16
  'ghost theory', 43–51
  and places, 55
  and modernity, 2–4, 86–7
  sequences of, 42–3, 50, 102
  see also the dead; haunting
Giddens, Anthony, 3
Gillespie, Gerald, 187n19
Goethe, Johann Wolfgang von, 85
Goldhill, Simon, 75
Gray, Thomas, 137, 149, 188–9n16
Greek Anthology, 154, 184n23
Green, T. H., 121–2

Haeckel, Ernst, 34
Haldane, R. B., 41–3

Hardy, Emma, 12, 134–6, 140, 156, 162–6, 170–1, 187n22
Hardy, Florence, 62
Hardy, Jemima, 73, 79–80

Hardy, Thomas
  alleged illegitimate son 'Randy', 72–5, 79
  autobiography, 8–9, 26, 27
  on creativity in old age, 23–9
  ghostliness of, 1, 10–16
  and mourning, 134–71, 141–71
  move from prose to poetry, 8–10
  obscurity of, 63, 67–8, 74–5
  and politics, 5–6, 110, 127
  self-protective attitude, 11, 62
  and war, 19, 106–8, 118
  and Wessex, 27

Poems
  'The Absolute Explains', 107
  '"According to the Mighty Working"', 131–2
  'After a Journey', 142–4, 154–5, 162, 163–4, 165
  'After a Romantic Day', 15
  'After the Fair', 104
  'Afterwards', 160
  'Alike and Unlike', 162
  '"And There Was a Great Calm"', 102
  'Aquae Sulis', 47, 55
  'Aristodemus the Messenian', 81
  'At a Fashionable Dinner', 141
  'At a Pause in a Country Dance', 80
  'At Casterbridge Fair', 141
  'At Castle Boterel', 144–5
  'At Mayfair Lodgings', 61
  'At the Entering of the New Year', 94–5, 105
  'At the Piano', 47
  'At the Word "Farewell"', 60
  'The Ballad of Love's Skeleton', 79
  'Beeny Cliff', 149, 155, 162, 164, 167
  'Before and after Summer', 14
  'Before Knowledge', 167
  'The Bird-Catcher's Boy', 79, 83

Hardy, Thomas (*cont.*)
  'The Blinded Bird', 88
  'The Boy's Dream', 87–8
  'By the Barrows', 79
  'Channel Firing', 48
  'The Chosen', 160
  'The Christening', 80
  'A Christmas Ghost Story', 47
  'Christmas in the Elgin Room', 47, 55
  'The Church and the Wedding', 47
  'Circus-Rider to Ringmaster', 169
  'Come Not; Yet Come!', 148
  'A Commonplace Day', 77
  'The Contretemps', 20–1
  'The Convergence of the Twain', 112–26
  'A Conversation at Dawn', 80
  'Cross-Currents', 160
  'The Dance at the Phoenix', 139–40
  'The Darkling Thrush', 49
  'The Dawn after the Dance', 80
  'Days to Recollect', 168
  'The Dead Bastard', 79
  'The Dead Man Walking', 137
  'The Dead Quire', 20
  'A Dream of No', 136–7, 141, 142, 169
  'A Drizzling Easter Morning', 159
  'A Duettist to Her Pianoforte', 156
  'During Wind and Rain', 22, 43, 167
  The Dynasts, 6, 26, 36, 90, 98–9, 109, 111, 122, 123, 127
  'The End of the Episode', 157
  'Epitaph', 165
  'Epitaph on a Pessimist', 80
  'Exeunt Omnes', 12, 15
  'An Experience', 63
  'The Faded Face', 61
  'Family Portraits', 43, 65–72
  The Famous Tragedy of the Queen of Cornwall, 65
  'The Five Students', 43
  'The Flirt's Tragedy', 43, 61, 80, 83, 102, 139
  'For Life I Had Never Cared Greatly', 15–16
  'Fragment', 102–3
  'The Ghost of the Past', 47, 102, 105
  'The Going', 141, 155
  'The Graveyard of Dead Creeds', 47
  'The Haunter', 157, 162–3, 167, 170
  'Haunting Fingers', 108
  'The Head above the Fog', 58
  'He Never Expected Much', 16, 22–3, 87
  'He Prefers Her Earthly', 147, 152
  'He Revisits His First School', 95
  'Her Death and After', 80–1, 141
  'Her Haunting-Ground', 50–1
  'Her Immortality', 158
  'He Wonders about Himself', 10
  'His Heart', 158
  'His Immortality', 55, 102, 141, 158
  'His Visitor', 170
  'The House of Silence', 51
  'A Hurried Meeting', 160
  'I Found Her Out There', 167
  'I Looked up from My Writing', 13
  'I Met a Man', 131
  'In a Former Resort After Many Years', 100, 103
  'In a Whispering Gallery', 48–9
  'In Her Precincts', 159
  'In St Paul's a While Ago', 95
  'The Inscription', 56–7
  'In Tenebris, I', 11
  'In the British Museum', 49
  'In the Mind's Eye', 34
  'In the Moonlight', 141
  'In the Night She Came', 35
  'In the Old Theatre, Fiesole', 101
  'In the Restaurant', 80
  'In the Small Hours', 18
  'In the Vaulted Way', 138
  'In Time of "The Breaking of Nations"', 106, 132

'I Said and Sang Her Excellence', 87
'I Thought, My Heart', 158
'Jezreel', 129–31
'Jubilate', 95
'June Leaves and Autumn', 13
'Lament', 170
'The Last Signal', 141
'Last Words to a Dumb Friend', 15, 160
'The Later Autumn', 13–14
'Lines', 84
'Looking at a Picture on an Anniversary', 61
'Lying Awake', 60
'The Man Who Forgot', 18
'The Master and the Leaves', 14
'The Memorial Brass: 186–', 56–7
Moments of Vision, 27
'Moments of Vision', 60
'The Monument-Maker'
'The Mother Mourns', 47
'The Moth-Signal', 101
'Music in a Snowy Street', 108
'Mute Opinion', 100–1
'Near Lanivet', 160
'Near Tooting Common', 145
'The New Dawn's Business', 13
'A Night of Questionings', 107
'The Noble Lady's Tale', 52
'Nothing matters much', 159
'The Obliterate Tomb', 55
'Old Furniture', 49–50, 140
'On a Discovered Curl of Hair', 60, 152
'On the Esplanade', 22
'Overlooking the River Stour', 141
'The Pair He Saw Pass', 141
'Panthera', 75–7, 80
'The Peasant's Confession', 99
'The Pedigree', 38–43, 67, 76
'The Phantom Horsewoman', 34, 145–6, 168
'A Philosophical Fantasy', 45
'The Photograph', 59–60
'The Place on the Map', 43

'Poems of 1912–13', 4, 17, 134–8, 141–8, 153, 161
'A Poet', 12
'A Procession of Dead Days', 43
'The Prophetess', 18
'Quid Hic Agis?', 17, 127
'Rain on a Grave', 154, 171
'The Recalcitrants', 48
'The Rival', 61
'Royal Sponsors', 79
'The Sailor's Mother', 55
'St Launce's Revisited', 138, 146
'Sapphic Fragment', 90
Satires of Circumstance, 27
'A Self-Glamourer', 14
'Self-Unconscious', 18
'The Shadow on the Stone', 49, 152, 164–5, 170
'The Sick Battle-God', 141
'Signs and Tokens', 15
'Sine Prole', 102
'A Singer Asleep', 141
'The Single Witness', 62
'Snow in the Suburbs', 20
'The Son's Portrait', 61
'So, Time', 19
'The Souls of the Slain', 47, 101
'The Sound of Her', 170
'So Various', 21
'Spectres that Grieve', 90, 95
'The Spell of the Rose', 146, 152, 164, 168, 171
'Starlings on the Roof', 48
'A Sunday Morning Tragedy', 72, 79
'The Superseded', 55
'The Supplanter', 79
'Surview', 17, 61
'In Tenebris, I'
Time's Laughingstocks, 80, 138
'Thoughts from Sophocles', 16
'To a Motherless Child'
'To an Orphan Child', 73
'To an Unborn Pauper Child', 72, 80
'The To-Be-Forgotten', 55
'To My Father's Violin', 50
'Tragedian to Tragedienne', 20
'A Trampwoman's Tragedy', 80

Hardy, Thomas (*cont.*)
  'The Two Houses', 102
  'The Two Rosalinds', 139
  'The Unborn', 80
  'Unrealized', 80
  'An Upbraiding', 171
  'The Voice of Things', 15
  'Waiting Both', 21–2
  'The Wedding Morning', 79
  'The Well-Beloved', 47
  'We Sat at the Window', 161–2
  'Wessex Heights', 8, 55
  'A Wet Night', 101, 110
  'Where the Picnic Was', 146
  'Where Three Roads Joined', 68
  'A Wife and Another', 79
  Winter Words, 13
  'A Wish for Unconsciousness', 67
  'The Wound', 67–8
  'Your Last Drive', 141, 142, 171

  Novels and other prose
  'Apology' to *Late Lyrics and Earlier*, 19, 107
  'The Dorsetshire Labourer', 6
  Far from the Madding Crowd, 78
  'The Fiddler of the Reels', 154
  'General Preface' to Wessex Edition, 27
  The Hand of Ethelberta, 71, 78, 140
  An Indiscretion in the Life of a Heiress, 74
  Introduction to Joshua James Foster, *Wessex Worthies*, 97
  Jude the Obscure, 8, 54, 78, 83, 134
  A Laodicean, 103
  The Mayor of Casterbridge, 135
  A Pair of Blue Eyes, 52, 74, 135, 137–8, 140, 143, 144, 149, 160, 167
  Preface to *Select Poems of William Barnes*, 58, 97
  The Return of the Native, 24, 185n7
  Tess of the D'Urbervilles, 19, 53, 71
  The Well-Beloved, 24
Harrison, Frederic, 46, 52

Hartmann, Eduaard von, 56, 118
haunting, 7, 79
  trans-generational, 63–5; *see also* phantom
  pain as, 71
  history as, 35–6, 91–2, 129–31
Hawthorn, Jeremy, 119
Heard, Gerald Stanley, 69
Hegel, George, 69–70, 92, 103–4, 110, 121, 185n2
Heine, Heinrich, 3, 156–7
Helmholtz, Hermann von, 49
Herbert, Auberon, 36–7
history
  as annal or chronicle, 2, 95, 99, 101, 106
  catastrophe and coincidence in, 108–9, 111, 117, 124–6
  and the dead, 94–104
  entry into, 2, 95, 99, 131–2
  of the excluded, 90, 93–9
  as haunting, 35–6, 91–2, 129–31
  non-dialectical ('the same'), 104–10
  philosophy of, 103–10, 117–26
  teleological, 93, 106, 109–10, 112, 122, 125
Horace, 90
Hume, David, 'Of Miracles', 52
Huxley, T. H., 33, 69
Hynes, Samuel, 186n18

incest, 73, 75
Ingelow, Jean, 166–8
intertextuality, 134, 140, 166–72
Immanent Will, 123–5

James, Henry, 26
James, William, 52
Jeune, Mary, Lady, 84–5
Johnson, Dr Samuel, 96

Kant, Emmanuel, 30, 32, 34, 54
Kincaid, James, 83–4
Knopfelmacher, U. C., 84
Krell, David Farrell, 136

Lacan, Jacques, 66, 159
Lane, Christopher, 179n2

Lange, Frederick, 32
language, 40, 56–8, 99, 159
  dialect, 58, 99
Lankester, Edwin Ray, 52–3
latency, 23–9, 116, 125
Leighton, Angela, 161
Lewes, G. H., 34
Locke, John, 100
Lucas, John, 148
Lyotard, Jean-François, 158

Mach, Ernst, 32–3
Maeterlinck, Maurice, 70
Mandelbaum, Maurice, 32, 174n1
Mansel, H.L., 45, 145
Marcus Aurelius, 90, 143
Martin, John, 101
Marx, Karl, 4, 31, 36, 92, 177n31
Masson, Jeffrey, 85
materialism, 31–8, 117
Maudsley, Henry, 37–8, 40, 52–4, 56
memory, 80, 97, 110, 138, 141, 144–5, 147
  and the dead, 47, 55, 90–1, 99–100, 102
  organic, 35, 39
Meredith, George
Merleau-Ponty, Maurice, 158–9, 162, 181n32
Mignon, Goethe's, 85–6
Mill, John Stuart, 70, 71
Miller, J. Hillis, 191n48
Millgate, Michael, 9, 24, 73
Monleón, José B., 31
Morgan, Rosemarie, 78
Morley, John, 117, 133
mourning, 11–12, 55, 81, 110, 134–71
  see also ashes, the dead
Müller, Max, 57–8
mutism, 67
  as trope for exclusion from history, 100–4, 110
Myers, Frederick, 52

Napoleonic Wars, 108
necromancy, 91
Nietzsche, Friedrich, 35, 104

O'Toole, Tess, 71
Otis, Laura, 35, 176n21

pain, 68–72, 84–6
Paine, Tom, 92
Palestine, British campaigns in, 129–30
parasitism, 16, 23, 28
Phantom (as psychic structure), 63–8, 72–4
phantasmagoria, 96, 100, 107, 139
Phenomenology, 158–9
photography, 58–61, 178–9n64
Pietz, William, 177n31
Pinion, F. B., 118, 188–9n16
Plato, 175n7
politics, 5–6, 35–6, 82, 90–4, 110, 127
Positivism, 44–6, 117
  see also Comte
Pound, Ezra, 56
Proust, Marcel, 10
Psychical Research, 46, 51–8, 172;
  see also séance

Rabaté, Jean-Michel, 8, 34
Rand, Nicholas, 64
Rankin, Esther, 64
Reade, Charles, 106
Reade, W. H. V., 152
religion
  Hardy and, 17–19, 30, 76, 118, 127
  origins of, 44–6, 77
rhetoric, 40, 156, 165–6
  see also chiasmus
Robertson, Morgan, 112
Rossetti, Christina, 161
Royce, Josiah, 41–2
Royle, Nicholas, 77

Sacks, Peter, 149, 155
Said, Edward, 8
Scarry, Elaine, 69, 180n17–18
Schiller, Friedrich von, 54
Schlegel, F., 89, 93
Schopenhauer, Arthur, 34, 69–70, 72, 104, 112
séance, 6, 31, 32, 36, 55, 56

secrets, 81, 137
  family, 2, 62–5, 72–5, 79
  see also phantom; crypt
Serres, Michel, 105–7
Sexton, Melanie, 163
Seymour-Smith, Martin, 73
Shaw, W. David, 45
Shelley, Percy Bysshe, 36, 62, 89, 100, 109, 138, 147
Sherman, G. W., 175n16
Smith, Stan, 95
Somerville, C. J., 82
somnambulism, 33–4, 36
sound, radiation of, 5, 49, 107
Southerington, F. R., 73
Sparks, Tryphena, 72–4
Spencer, Edmund, 140
Spencer, Herbert, 37, 41, 44–51, 69
spirit photography, 59
SPR (Society for Psychical Research), *see* Psychical Research
Stead, W. T., 82, 113
Steedman, Carolyn, 85–6
Stephen, Leslie, 31–2, 78, 118
sublimation, 140
supplement, 9–10, 12, 16–17, 43, 105, 135, 140, 164
  and syntax, 20–3
  see also Derrida
Swinburne, Algernon Charles, 157–9, 166

Taylor, Dennis, 5, 18, 39, 56, 58, 113, 125
Tennyson, Alfred, Lord, 28, 41, 143, 163
Thaxter, Celia, 114–16
time, 22, 104–7, 138
Titanic disaster, 112–26
topicality, 131–2
Torok, Maria, 63–5, 75, 77, 85–6, 160–1, 179n2
trauma, 84–6
Tylor, E. B., 45
typology, 16–19, 126–9

ventriloquism, 37
Verdi, Giuseppe, 25
Vergil, 91, 135, 148–55
  veteris vestigia flammae, 135, 137–8, 149
voice, 49, 103, 143, 151, 156, 163–6
  see also mutism

Wade, Wynne Craig, 112
Wagner, Richard, 25
White, Hayden, 126
Wickens, G. Glen, 185n1
Widdowson, Peter, 6, 89, 110
Windle, Bertram, 27
Wood, J. G., 16
Wordsworth, William, 28, 130, 154, 157, 181n39
Worsley, Arthington, 33

Yeats, William Butler, 56, 172

Zangwill, Israel, 127–8, 187n22
Zeitlow, Paul, 9
Zionism, 127–33, 187n26